THE MATTER OF THE SECRET BRIDE

Darcie Wilde is the author of:

The Secret of the Lady's Maid

The Secret of the Lost Pearls

A Counterfeit Suitor

A Lady Compromised

And Dangerous to Know

A Purely Private Matter

A Useful Woman

DARCIE WILDE

THE MATTER OF THE SECRET BRIDE

KENSINGTON
PUBLISHING CORP.

kensingtonbooks.com

KENSINGTON BOOKS are published by

Kensington Publishing Corp.
900 Third Avenue
New York, NY 10022

Copyright © 2025 by Sarah Zettel

All Kensington titles, imprints, and distributed lines are available at special quantity discounts for bulk purchases for sales promotion, premiums, fund-raising, educational, or institutional use. Special book excerpts or customized printings can also be created to fit specific needs. For details, write or phone the office of the Kensington Special Sales Manager: Attn. Special Sales Department, Kensington Publishing Corp., 900 Third Avenue, New York, NY 10022. Phone: 1-800-221-2647.

Library of Congress Control Number: 2024943022

KENSINGTON and the K with book logo Reg. U.S. Pat. & TM. Off.

ISBN: 978-1-4967-5063-1
First Kensington Hardcover Edition: January 2025

ISBN: 978-1-4967-5065-5 (e-book)

10 9 8 7 6 5 4 3 2 1

Printed in the United States of America

THE MATTER OF THE SECRET BRIDE

PROLOGUE

An Initial Meeting

*"... this fatal, ill-starred connection so unfortu-
nate, probably, for both the parties concerned."*

Langdale, Charles, *Memoirs of Mrs. Fitzherbert*

London
June 1820

"Mr. Poole?"

Josiah Poole turned and found himself facing a
tall, pale man in a black coat.

"Do I know you, sir?" Poole inquired.

The fellow was impeccably turned out, with a tall beaver
hat and stovepipe trousers. Poole thought he had the look of
a clerk, with that black coat and cravat. He was stooped and
ink-stained like one, as well, with the hard, knowing eyes of
a man who spent his life pouring over ledgers, looking for the
smallest mistakes.

It was early June, but summer's warmth had yet to pene-
trate the gritty air of this particular neighborhood. That,
Poole told himself, was why he shivered.

Up until now, Poole had been enjoying a good morning.
He'd just secured a gratifying new client—a young man from

a highly placed family. Being plump in his pocket gave Poole a satisfaction that even London's shadows could not dim.

"We have not previously met," the clerkish man told Poole. "I, however, have heard great things about your reputation as a man of business."

"Indeed?" Poole's chest expanded at the compliment.

Poole was a solicitor. His specialty lay in straightening out the affairs of gentlemen who found themselves in unfortunate financial circumstances, particularly those who had been relegated to the confines of that institution colloquially known as "the sponging house."

English public life had numerous peculiarities. One was the existence of numerous enterprises dedicated to the collecting and transferring of debt and the punishing of debtors. The sponging house was part of this vast mechanism. A bastard cross between a boardinghouse and a private prison, this house lodged debtors on a temporary basis. The idea was to give them a last chance to discharge their obligations before they were escorted to a less comfortable sort of prison, such as Newgate or the Marshalsea.

That the fees charged by the sponging houses tended to increase the amount of debt owed by the prisoners was one of the little contradictions of English law that Poole chose not to bother his head about. His business was to pull his clients free of the machinery and collect his own fee.

His newest client, for example, had been deposited into the house run by Henry Ross. The young man had made a substantial payment to Poole on the understanding that Poole would help bring a speedy resolution to his various difficulties—preferably before his noble father learned of his current whereabouts. Poole would help this bewildered unfortunate raise money to pay his debts or, at the least, find a friend to stand his bail. Poole was always diligent in his efforts and left no avenue unexplored, however crooked and poorly illuminated the path might be.

Poole squinted at the clerkish stranger in front of him now. This man was most definitely not one of Ross's inmates. He noted the quality of the man's black coat. He further noted that while his fingers might be ink-stained, his shirt was unblemished white lawn. His collar points remained crisp, despite the damp morning air.

"I'm sorry," said Poole. "Who did you say you were?"

"A man with a proposal for you," the other answered smoothly. "If you'd care to walk with me? We can have a drink and discuss matters."

"I do not care to walk anywhere with a man who will not give his name." His business, by its nature, attracted quite a few flattering ne'er-do-wells and some genuinely dangerous men.

"A sensible precaution." The man's smile was thin. "My name is Carmichael."

You're lying, thought Poole at once. "Have you a card?"

Instead of bringing out a card case, Mr. Carmichael— whoever he might really be—pulled his pocketbook from his coat and extracted a folded paper. Poole opened this. With his practiced eye, Poole quickly ascertained it was a draft on the private bank of Ames & King. For twenty-five pounds.

"Shall we see about that drink, Mr. Poole?" Carmichael inquired.

Poole folded the draft and tucked it into his own pocket. Mr. Carmichael made no objection.

"Very well. If you would care to lead the way, Mr. Carmichael?"

In short order, Poole found himself seated in the best tavern the neighborhood had to offer—which was, admittedly, not saying much—and being treated to a bottle of the best red wine the landlord had in his cellar. Again, it was not much, but it showed that Mr. Carmichael had more in his pocket than just the one bank draft.

"Your health, sir." Poole raised his glass and drank. "May

I assume you—or some client of yours—have need of a solicitor?"

Carmichael returned his wintry smile. "As it happens, I do
represent another party, and they find themselves in need of a
person with your particular set of skills. They are willing to
pay handsomely for your time. And your discretion."

"Discretion is everything to a man in my business," said
Poole. "What is it your client requires?"

"My client has an interest in a matter that is heading to
trial, Mr. Poole. A difficult and public business. A divorce, in
fact."

"Not my usual line of work, Mr. Carmichael."

"I am aware," replied Carmichael. "You prefer preying upon
debtors. But in this case, there is a marriage certificate, indicating a prior connection with a person yet living."

"Ah." Poole allowed his face to assume a sympathetic expression. He'd had plenty of practice at it.

While it was true that Poole did not normally take on marital cases, it was also true that such work could be quite lu-
crative. Especially when the involved party was anxious for a
result.

Like many other aspects of English law, divorce was a con-
voluted and contradictory affair. For the most part, however,
it was fairly easy for a man to bring suit against a wife who
strayed from the confines of domestic bliss. The church, the
law, and society at large frowned heavily upon female indis-
cretion.

But there existed several impediments to the man seeking
to end an unsatisfactory union. There was, for example, the
matter of "recrimination." If the defendant (say, the wife)
could offer positive proof that the complainant (say, the husband) had behaved at least as badly as she had, the divorce
would be denied.

Proof of a second marriage would serve such a purpose extremely well.

Poole took another drink of wine and considered. Exposing bigamy did mean the second marriage would be declared invalid. It would also, however, mean that damages and support would have to be paid to the second wife, or at least to her male relations. Also, if proved, bigamy brought the very real probability of jail, not to mention the social ignominy that must accompany such a revelation.

A man might be willing to go to unusual lengths to prevent any of these things from happening.

Poole looked at Carmichael again. He looked at his good coat and his spotless cravat. Poole kept abreast of public affairs. He read the papers religiously, because one never knew what one might find in the advertisements or the agony columns. Divorce cases that made it all the way to Parliament were widely reported.

There was, in fact, much talk of a divorce in the works. An extremely public and prominent divorce, one that had already gotten quite ugly. That divorce brought with it rumors of a previous marriage. Rumors that had been circulating for years. Pamphlets had been published. Accusations traded.

No. Poole grabbed the bottle and refilled his own glass. *Couldn't be.*

Except . . . that coat was of excellent quality. The man who wore it was hard, close, and clever, and thought nothing of handing over twenty-five pounds simply to secure Poole's attention.

Poole took another swallow of wine. He noted that Carmichael had not touched his. "May I ask you something, Mr. Carmichael?"

Carmichael hesitated a moment before he nodded. His face remained inscrutable. Poole was impressed. He'd played at cards as well as at the law for many years. A truly unreadable man was a rarity.

"This client of yours," began Poole. Carmichael opened his mouth, but Poole cut him off. "We'll say, rather, this person your client has taken an interest in. Public man, is he? Very highly placed?"

Carmichael did not so much as move, which gave Poole his answer. Poole felt his heart—a normally insensible organ— thud heavily.

It could be. Well, well, well. It could indeed be.

"Wife been living abroad, maybe?" Poole went on. "Suspected of shenanigans with foreigners and all sorts?"

That, it seemed, was quite enough for Mr. Carmichael. "Mr. Poole, do you wish to undertake this job? I can promise you payment of two hundred pounds upon delivery of the document and verification that it is the true and original certificate. However . . ." Carmichael leaned just a little closer. Poole smelled peppermint and stale coffee on his breath. "Whether you accept my offer or not, if I discover you have breathed one word beyond what is strictly necessary for this business, I promise you will vanish from the face of the earth so completely, it will be as if you'd never been born."

CHAPTER ONE

An Unexpected Summons

*"These dinners are peculiarly agreeable—nothing
to impede the flow of soul, whatever there may be
of the feast of reason."*

Bury, Charlotte, *The Diary of a Lady-in-Waiting*

London
August 1820

"They're here!"

Alice Littlefield seized the brown paper parcel from
the startled footman and raised it over her head. All the
friends and family gathered in the front parlor of 9 Orchard
Street hurrahed and raised their punch cups.

Rosalind Thorne smiled indulgently at Alice's open delight
and raised her cup along with her guests. Alice's brother,
George, was here, along with his wife, Hannah. Sanderson
Faulks lounged beside Honoria Aimesworth and Mr. Clements.

And, of course, Adam Harkness stood at Rosalind's side,
smiling his quiet, devastating smile.

"I can't believe it!" Alice darted through the little crowd to
the tea table. "They're really here!"

She unceremoniously dropped the package onto the table

and herself into the nearest chair. Amelia McGowan—a plump, ginger-haired young woman—hurried to Alice's side. The pair clasped hands and laughed with wordless excitement.

Up until a few months ago, Amelia had worked as a maid for Rosalind and Alice. Now she worked to establish a charity school for young women in service who wished to better their situation. That she was also Alice's sweetheart was a fact their friends kept to themselves.

Adam took up the pair of scissors Rosalind had placed on the mantel for exactly this moment. He handed them to Rosalind, who, in turn, handed them to Amelia, who handed them to Alice. Alice slit the package's twine. The paper fell open to reveal three quarto volumes, bound in red morocco and stamped with gold lettering:

EVERSWARD
A NOVEL
BY
A. E. LITTLEFIELD

A second cheer rose from the assembly, except from the dandy Sanderson Faulks, who confined himself to decorous applause. Alice rose to her feet and gave a single dignified nod, as if she were the queen acknowledging the crowd at the opera, and then handed round the books so they could be more readily admired.

"Congratulations, sister dear." George kissed her on the cheek.

"Even though you never wanted me to turn novelist?" Alice inquired cheekily. "And you were sure I should lose all hope of making any sort of living?"

"Don't tease, Alice," Hannah, George's sturdy, black-haired wife, admonished lightly. "He is terribly proud of you. I can barely get him to talk about anything else."

"That is not true," said George indignantly. "I am perfectly able to talk about our brilliant infant, and the madness in Parliament, as well."

"Oh, Lord, we are not bringing that up!" groaned Honoria Aimesworth. A pale woman with the studied grace that came from years of strict training in deportment, Honoria had refashioned her life after scandal and tragedy. Now she was creating something of a stir among the *haut ton* as a woman of independent means and mind.

Rosalind had not expected Honoria to still be in town to join the party. It was August, and normally, everyone who could afford to do so would have abandoned the swelter and stench of London for the country or the Continent.

This summer, however, Parliament was being called to a special session to consider King George's petition for divorce from Queen Caroline, and fashionable society was determined not to miss the spectacle.

George Littlefield sighed. "I don't see as we will be able to help it, Honoria. I hear the king's divorce has even led to arguments among the lady patronesses at Almack's."

The entire gathering turned to Rosalind. Adam raised his brows, assuming an air of polite inquiry.

"I had not heard," she replied coolly. Adam's eyebrows lifted farther. The fact was that Rosalind had heard a great deal, but now was not the time to repeat any of it.

"Well, I wouldn't be surprised if the lady patronesses were at odds," George went on. "Everyone else is. Between the king's endless investigations and the queen making her return to English shores into a royal progress, we'll probably have a paper shortage from all the special editions." George wrote for the *London Chronicle*, a twice-weekly newspaper that relied heavily on politics and gossip for its sales.

"It is impossible to keep up," agreed Mr. Clements. Ernest Clements presided over Rosalind's favorite circulating library. He had been helping with the efforts to advance the cause of Alice's book by introducing her to a number of the most prominent owners of lady's bookshops. Consequently, Rosalind had felt it only right to invite him to the party. "I have had to employ a pair of young men to eject patrons who grow too heated over the news. A fistfight broke out in the reading room this Monday."

"Was the winner for the king or the queen?" asked Alice.

"Oh, the queen, of course," Mr. Clements replied. "Nearly everyone is for the queen. It is her name they are chanting in the streets."

"In the reading rooms and the streets perhaps," drawled Mr. Faulks. "In the clubs it is all for the king."

"Well, king he may be," Amelia sniffed. "But he's a rascal all the same. The man forced the queen to keep one of his mistresses as her maid, *and* he charged the people for her diamonds!"

"My brothers would thrash the man who treated me with so little respect," agreed Hannah Littlefield.

"A warning to you, George," said Honoria. "Personally, I hope the queen's attorneys make him highly uncomfortable with a full exposure of his clandestine marriage to a Roman Catholic."

Mr. Clements, George, and Hannah exchanged wary glances. Mr. Clements had been born Ernesto Javier Garcia Mendoza y Clemente. He had changed his name to suit English fashions, but not his religion, even though the public celebration of mass remained illegal and Catholics were barred from any number of professions, including the majority of public offices. Hannah, for her part, had been born into a large Italian family. She and George were married in a Protestant ceremony, but she quietly kept the faith of her ancestors. Since his marriage, George had written several anonymous pamphlets on the subject of Catholic emancipation.

It was Mr. Clements who spoke first. "Miss Aimesworth, you make the fact that she is a Catholic sound like a greater offense than the secret marriage."

"I beg your pardon, Mr. Clements," said Hannah. "I should have been more careful with my choice of words. It is the breaking of the succession laws and the concealing of his marriage that I meant to decry. Not the lady's religion."

Mr. Clements bowed.

"I'm not going to defend His Majesty," said George. "But he does have some cause for grievance against the queen. There really can't be any excuse for her to be traipsing about the Continent with such a crowd as she has . . ."

This proved to be too much for Alice. "Rosalind, you must forbid any more talk of the king's divorce. I will not have it at my party!"

"I agree, Alice," said Rosalind. "This is a celebration, and we shall have no arguments over controversial subjects. Mr. Faulks, you were hinting earlier that you had some interesting news from your friend at the *Edinburgh Review*. What can you tell us?"

Sanderson, who never failed to enjoy being the center of attention, drew himself up. "As it happens, I am given to understand that the next issue may include mention of a certain new novel."

"Oh!" Alice clapped both hands over her mouth. Amelia squeezed her shoulder. "You don't . . . He didn't say . . ."

"Of course, I could not ask whether such mention was favorable." Sanderson spoke regretfully to his punch cup. "But it is possible I overheard a word or two later, as we were enjoying a friendly drink. I do believe all Littlefields will be quite pleased with the results."

"Oh!" cried Alice again. She ran to hug Amelia, George and Hannah, and then turned to Sanderson—suddenly all decorum and correct deportment—and curtsied. Sanderson placed a hand over his breast, careful not to disturb the folds of his elaborate cravat, and bowed.

The gathering laughed at this display, and talk turned easily to small matters, light gossip, and stories of family and friends.

For Rosalind, it was almost too much to take in.

Up until recently, she had lived on a knife's edge. Rosalind had all but given up on the possibility of finding herself in the situation she now occupied—mistress of a comfortable and independent establishment, living a life that was both useful and absorbing.

Now, surrounded as she was by so many friends, Rosalind felt her heart swell with a pride and gratitude that she seldom allowed herself to acknowledge.

Adam, of course, noticed and moved just an inch closer.

"You are radiant," he murmured.

"You are a flatterer," she replied under her breath.

He raised one brow. She lifted her chin. He grinned the astonishing crooked grin that lit his blue eyes, which reminded her of the times when this room was empty except for the two of them. Rosalind felt her cheeks begin to warm.

"Mercy," she breathed.

"If that is what you wish," he replied.

"For now."

This scandalous remark was rewarded by Adam's abrupt blush. Rosalind attempted to hide her grin behind her punch cup, but found herself in danger of dissolving into a fit of undignified giggles.

Fortunately, she was saved from this eventuality when her newly hired footman, Mortimer, pushed open the pocket doors that led to the dining room and announced, "Dinner is served."

Rosalind's greatest asset when it came to entertaining was her cook, Mrs. Singh. When she lived with her family in India, Mrs. Singh grew up in the hybrid kitchens of English households. There she absorbed the techniques of French and English cuisine, along with the English language. Mrs. Singh had lived in London for some years now and had been glad to leave the rigors of a large establishment for Rosalind's smaller home. The advantage to her was more regular hours and the ability to go home in the evening to her sister and her sister's children.

When Mrs. Singh discovered Rosalind enjoyed piquant flavors, she began to include dishes from her native Punjab in her menus. Her samosas, tikkas, and highly spiced vegetable ragùs added welcome variety to the unyielding English dinner regimen of sauced turbot and roasted beef.

Tonight Mrs. Singh had outdone herself. She liked Alice personally and had exerted all her considerable talents on the author's behalf. There was a fish soup, followed by leg of lamb accompanied by a vegetable biryani and a series of side dishes with early greens, new potatoes, and fresh cheese. All was crowned by a dessert course of sugar-topped cake and sweet dumplings.

The cake had been reduced to crumbs and Rosalind was just about to suggest the party return to the parlor for tea when a great banging arose from the depths of the house.

"What on earth?" exclaimed Alice.

Someone, Rosalind realized, was hammering at the kitchen door. All conversation momentarily fell quiet while Mortimer stepped smartly away to see what might be the matter.

"Have you gotten yourself into trouble again, Rosalind?" remarked Honoria.

"Not that I am aware of," Rosalind answered. But her mind began leafing through her list of current commitments just the same.

The house was small enough and well ventilated enough that voices could sometimes be heard from the cellars. The entire gathering heard those voices now. The words were indistinct, but the tone was loud and insistent.

Adam wiped his hands on his napkin. "Should I . . . ?" he began.

Before he could rise to his feet, Mortimer had returned, a folded note in his hand.

"Apologies, Miss Thorne," Mortimer said. "But the man says it is extremely urgent, and he insists he must have an answer at once."

Rosalind frowned and rose, taking the note from him. "You will all excuse me for a moment," she said to her guests.

Rosalind retreated to the back parlor, which she used as her writing room. She moved to shut the door, but not quickly enough. Both Adam and Alice had already come in.

Adam closed the door. Alice hurried to Rosalind's side.

"What is it?"

Rosalind turned the note over. The paper was heavy, and the ink quite dark, which told her this missive came from a person of means. The sealing wax was scarlet and imprinted with a curling letter *F*. "I don't recognize the hand or the seal."

Rosalind broke the seal and unfolded the missive. As was her habit, she read the signature first. Her eyes widened in shock.

"Rosalind? What is it?" asked Adam.

"It is a . . . request to call." Surprise had made her throat go dry. She swallowed and tried again. "At once."

"At this hour? That seems a bit precipitous," said Alice. "Who is it from?"

Rosalind found she had to swallow again. "Mrs. Maria Fitzherbert."

"*The* Mrs. Fitzherbert . . . ?" began Adam.

"You can't mean . . . ," said Alice at the same time.

"Yes," said Rosalind. "I do mean. This is from *the* Mrs. Fitzherbert." She met their startled gazes. "The king's wife."

CHAPTER TWO

The Most Scandalous Woman in London

"I hear from everybody that her character is irreproachable and her manners most amiable."

Langdale, Charles, *Memoirs of Mrs. Fitzherbert*

The definite facts about Mrs. Maria Fitzherbert and the man who was now King George IV were very few.

While still Prince of Wales and still a bachelor, George Augustus Frederick of Hanover had taken up with Maria Fitzherbert, a twice-widowed Roman Catholic woman. She had acted as his hostess and companion for several years and had been seen daily with him in public. He wore a miniature of her around his neck. Mrs. Fitzherbert was received into the best houses. In fact, having her attend a gathering was considered a coup for any hostess, because where Mrs. Fitzherbert went, the prince followed.

Gradually, however, the relationship declined, and the prince began being seen most frequently with Frances Villiers, who was then Lady Jersey. Mrs. Fitzherbert's name remained a watchword for the prince's notorious profligacy, but she herself faded from the public eye.

All the rest was rumor. Those rumors, however, remained

omnipresent and remarkably persistent. The most persistent of all was that at some point, Mrs. Fitzherbert and the Prince of Wales had secretly married.

Such a marriage, if it happened, would be illegal. The Royal Marriages Act placed strict limits on the circumstances under which the assorted princes and princesses could marry. The act forbade the heir to the throne from marrying an English citizen without the approval of both the monarch and Parliament. In addition, should the heir attempt to marry a Catholic, they would give up their place in the line of succession. They would also lose all their titles and privileges, including their (considerable) income from the civil list.

For a man like the prince regent, whose debts ran to hundreds of thousands of pounds, this last should have been the greatest deterrent.

Despite that, the rumors persisted. They persisted even after Prince George married Princess Caroline of Brunswick and after he fathered a child with her. Even after he openly discarded Mrs. Fitzherbert and then Lady Jersey and then Lady Hertford.

They came positively roaring back after George III died and the prince regent became the king.

While Rosalind had heard all the commonplace remarks on this subject, she had never devoted much thought as to whether this clandestine union actually took place. Speculation about the private lives of royalty was a popular pastime for the press and the people at all levels of society, and if facts were few, fancy routinely filled the gaps. It had even once been rumored that staid, domestic King George III had secretly married a Quaker woman named Hannah Lightfoot.

But no one had ever clapped eyes on Hannah Lightfoot. Everyone had seen Maria Fitzherbert.

And now, it seemed, Rosalind would see her face-to-face.

* * *

Alice agreed to take over the hostess duties so her celebration could continue. Sanderson agreed to loan Rosalind his carriage and driver, so there was no delay around acquiring conveyance.

"In return, I will expect a full description of the lady and her demeanor," Sanderson told Rosalind. "With the queen's return, the world is anxious to know what Mrs. Fitz is up to." Sanderson was a much-sought-after supper guest, in part because London's hostesses knew him to be a font of amusing gossip.

"Can I come?" asked Amelia. "You'll need someone to talk to the staff."

"Will we?" Rosalind raised her brows.

"Well, something's gone wrong, or she wouldn't be sending for you, now would she?" said Amelia. "So you'll need to know what they're saying belowstairs."

"You'd abandon me for a chance to hear some tidbit of gossip?" cried Alice indignantly.

"Never!" Amelia looped her arm around Alice's waist and gave her an affectionate squeeze. "I'm abandoning you for the *king's* gossip."

Rosalind barely managed to keep a straight face. "Amelia, please stay here and help Alice look after our guests. If it turns out I need your help, I promise I will not hesitate to call on you."

All this time, Adam stood with his hands folded behind him, as if awaiting his turn. When Rosalind faced him at last, her smile was apologetic.

"Will you come with me?" she asked. "If the situation is so dire as to require immediate attendance, we may have need of you."

"If you had not asked, I would have followed."

Of this, Rosalind had no doubt. She was confident in her ability to protect herself, and Adam respected her judgment and her skills. But she was not a fool. A woman traveling alone after dark could find herself a target of mischief-makers even in ordinary times, which these were decidedly not. London's streets were restive. Queen Caroline was widely believed to have been cruelly wronged by the king. Londoners of all classes and conditions were taking to the streets in support of her. Not only were fights breaking out in otherwise quiet establishments, like Mr. Clements's library, but also houses were being robbed, carriages halted, and the drivers pulled down if they refused to take their hats off and call, "God save the queen." Adam's presence might stop at least some forms of trouble before they began.

But it was not only the public unrest that gave Rosalind pause. Her work among the ladies of the *ton* had more than once included dealing with the consequences of blackmail, theft, and even murder. She was fully aware that domestic disarray could have a very high price and that those involved could become desperate. Mrs. Fitzherbert was at the heart of the suit for divorce that the king was bringing against the queen. Or if she was not now, she soon would be.

How desperate might that make those involved?

In the end, Rosalind and Adam were able to reach their destination without any untoward incident. Tilney Street was located in a quiet, prosperous neighborhood. Mrs. Fitzherbert's house, number six, was a large residence. Its otherwise simple facade was made striking by the many graceful windows, especially on the curved balcony that overlooked the expansive walled garden.

If the mob was abroad tonight, it had chosen other places to be. Nonetheless, Adam surveyed the darkening street for a long moment before he helped Rosalind down from the carriage. As they walked together to the door, she felt a distinct tension radiating from him.

"What is it?" Rosalind murmured.

"We're being watched," he replied just as quietly. "Or the house is."

Rosalind suppressed a shiver. It was difficult to keep herself from looking around. Adam, however, kept his gaze rigidly ahead, and she followed his silent example.

They reached the door. Both the lantern and the knocker were in place, indicating the owner was currently in occupancy. Adam knocked for them, and the door was instantly opened by a young footman in striking scarlet livery.

This was a surprise. It was tacitly understood that only royalty's servants wore scarlet. Rosalind felt an urge to raise her brows.

"Miss Thorne and Mr. Harkness for Mrs. Fitzherbert," Adam was saying to the footman.

"Good evening, Miss Thorne. Mr. Harkness." The man bowed. "My mistress is expecting you and has instructed me to bring you in at once. This way please."

As they followed the footman up the broad staircase and down the carpeted hallway, Rosalind was aware of an inexcusable attack of butterflies in her stomach. She had met and helped women on many rungs of society's shifting and unsteady ladder. Mrs. Fitzherbert, however, was of a different order. Her name was a watchword in society. Once, it had appeared in the papers on a daily basis. It had been featured on invitation cards that circulated among the highest members of the *haut ton*. It had been printed in thunderous—and near libelous—pamphlets. It had been shouted in Parliament.

Everyone knew who she was, and yet even after all this time, no one could agree exactly *what* she was. Some declared she was a virtuous woman who had refused to surrender herself to a man outside the bounds of marriage—even when that man was the heir to the throne. To others, she was the worst sort of opportunist, wielding her feminine temptations to enrich and empower herself, and perhaps even to claim a crown.

So it was a surprise when the first word that occurred to Rosalind as the footman showed them into the sitting room was *maternal*.

Maria Fitzherbert was short and plump. Silver streaked her dark hair, which was mostly covered by a modest lace cap. Her dress was black silk of the best quality, and it did nothing to hide the fact that her bosom and hips were larger than was considered fashionable. Her face was lined from laughter as well as concern, and her large dark eyes were as intelligent as they were anxious.

At her throat, she wore a painted miniature on a blue velvet ribbon. Rosalind attempted not to notice it displayed the likeness of the former Prince of Wales.

Mrs. Fitzherbert came forward to take Rosalind's hand. "Thank you for coming so quickly, Miss Thorne. I apologize for such a late, and hasty, invitation."

"Mrs. Fitzherbert, I am glad to meet you," Rosalind replied. "If I may introduce Mr. Adam Harkness?"

"Mrs. Fitzherbert." Adam bowed.

"Mr. Harkness?" said Mrs. Fitzherbert. "It seems to me I have heard your name. You are with Bow Street?" Worry deepened the creases on the lady's brow.

"I am here entirely in a private capacity," answered Adam. "Given the urgent nature of your note, Miss Thorne did not want there to be a delay should additional assistance be required."

"Yes, yes. Very correct, I am sure. Thank you for your consideration." Mrs. Fitzherbert's tone was breathless and uncertain. It was plain she was quite upset. But the house seemed quiet. The comfortably appointed room was calm and in good order, with the lamps and fire brightly lit.

"Will you not sit?" Mrs. Fitzherbert gestured to a pair of brocade chairs and took her own place on a striped settee. Like her clothing, all Mrs. Fitzherbert's furnishings were the best quality and thoroughly fashionable.

"I . . . I hardly know where to begin." Mrs. Fitzherbert clasped her hands together. "I thought to have some tea, but"—she gestured helplessly toward the empty table—"it is hardly an ordinary social call, is it?"

"It is not," agreed Rosalind. "And I am sorry it has been made necessary. However, we should perhaps address the matter directly? It is quite clear something alarming has occurred."

"Yes, it has." Mrs. Fitzherbert drew a deep breath. "But the situation is extremely delicate, and I must ask for your complete discretion on the matter." Her eyes flickered toward Adam.

"Anything you say to Mr. Harkness or me will be held in strictest confidence," Rosalind assured her.

A shadow of anger passed across Mrs. Fitzherbert's features. Rosalind wondered how many times this woman had heard that promise, only to have it broken. She twisted her plump hands as her gaze drifted from Rosalind, to Adam, to a painted portrait that hung above the fireplace. The portrait showed two dark-haired girls—one still a child, the other in adolescence. Both were dressed in white ruffled gowns, with white roses in their hands. The sight of the painted faces seemed to harden something inside Mrs. Fitzherbert.

"I have been robbed," she said. "It happened today, while I was away from home."

"What was taken?" asked Adam.

Mrs. Fitzherbert hesitated. She twisted her hands again. When she did speak, her voice was low and hoarse. "My marriage certificate."

Rosalind blinked. "Your . . ."

"My marriage certificate," Mrs. Fitzherbert repeated. "Signed and witnessed, testifying to my marriage to George Augustus Frederick of Hanover, then Prince of Wales."

CHAPTER THREE

A Mere Slip of Paper

"... had she entertained mercenary views, she believed she might have obtained any price she had chosen to ask, for the correspondence ..."

Langdale, Charles, *Memoirs of Mrs. Fitzherbert*

So.

The rumors were correct. A wedding had taken place. George IV had married a Catholic. The law declared that this action rendered him ineligible to occupy the throne. And yet he had already been declared the lawful king and he was said to be as busy planning his coronation as he was with his divorce from Caroline of Brunswick.

But here in this calm, fashionable parlor sat his other wife—a living woman, never divorced but never fully acknowledged.

If proof of their marriage was revealed, his eligibility to hold the throne could be challenged by Parliament or indeed by any or all his brothers. Or by the people themselves.

It felt like an opera or a fairy tale. But it was as real as the woman in front of her. Rosalind forbade her gaze to stray down to the miniature at Mrs. Fitzherbert's throat. Part of her was already backing away, whispering, *This is too much. There are too many consequences. This is beyond me.*

If Adam was as stunned as Rosalind by this revelation and its implications, he was also able to set them aside more quickly.

"When did you discover the certificate missing?" he asked.

"This afternoon," said Mrs. Fitzherbert. "I was out paying my morning calls. When I returned, I went to my room to change my dress. There I found my strongbox had been broken open and all my papers scattered about."

"Was anything else missing?"

Mrs. Fitzherbert shook her head. "Not even the banknotes. I need it back, Miss Thorne, Mr. Harkness," she said abruptly. "It must be returned quietly and without fuss. I know you make it your business to help ladies with deeply private troubles, and I will pay whatever it costs."

"My man of business will be in touch about the details, should it be decided we can be of material assistance," Rosalind told her. "May I ask, however . . . Have you sent word to . . . your husband?"

"No," said Mrs. Fitzherbert flatly. "I have not spoken to him in a number of years. He has made it very"—her voice broke—"very plain that he does not wish to continue our alliance on a footing of domestic intimacy, and I have determined I do not wish to continue under any other circumstance."

The combination of pain and dignity in Mrs. Fitzherbert's declaration went straight to Rosalind's heart.

"I understand this is difficult for you," she said. "However, he would have far more resources at his command than any we can bring to bear upon this matter."

Mrs. Fitzherbert shook her head. "My husband was never a strong or a discreet man, and in the years since our separation, he has become much degraded. If I tell him the marriage certificate has been stolen, it is very likely that he will panic, and in his panic, he will speak to the wrong person. If that happens, neither he nor I will be safe from what comes afterward."

Because she was Catholic. Because King George had no legitimate heir. What he did have, however, was five brothers, none of whom were particularly fond of him. If one of the royal dukes chose to contest the succession, the effects would reverberate throughout the whole kingdom for a generation.

There were already calls for the king to abdicate because of the way he treated the queen. If his previous marriage were proved . . . the king's enemies would come for him. The mob would come for him.

Rosalind knew her silence had stretched on for too long, but she could not seem to muster an answer.

Instead, it was Mrs. Fitzherbert who spoke. "You will now perhaps ask yourself why I did not destroy the paper, for the good of the king and the kingdom. Knowing me only from rumor, you wonder, perhaps, if I intended to profit from it in some way?"

Rosalind felt Adam stiffen ever so slightly at this imputation of her character. But she calmly absorbed the accusation and the anger behind it. It was plain that Mrs. Fitzherbert felt wounded and exhausted. She could not be blamed for her suspicions or a defensive tone.

"This could not come as a surprise," Rosalind said. "We must consider all possibilities, including those which are unpleasant."

Mrs. Fitzherbert wilted slightly. "I apologize. You see, if it was only myself who could be hurt by this, I would simply leave London and exile myself to the Continent. But I have two wards." She gestured toward the portrait of the girls over the fireplace. "They are not the daughters of my body, but I love them as if they were. Mary Ann has been with me since she was a girl, and Minney since she was an infant. Now she's ready to make her debut."

As Mrs. Fitzherbert looked at the portrait, a host of expressions flickered across her features—pride, fear, determination, love, and fear again. "If I'm publicly libeled as a loose and immoral woman, my marriage certificate stands as the only proof of my fitness to be their guardian. Without it, I could lose them both."

A father might participate in numerous dalliances without his rights as a parent being questioned. This was not the case for a mother, let alone a female guardian. It was an old contradiction, and as unfair now as it had ever been.

"I could stand the loss of them." Mrs. Fitzherbert's voice grew hoarse with emotion. "Barely. I think. But if I am imputed, their reputations would be torn to shreds by the press and those who hate me. Even by my husband, if he thought it might help him," she added bitterly. "The girls will lose all chance at a good marriage or acceptance into society. That I will not stand for."

Rosalind's gaze flickered toward Adam. He gave the briefest possible nod. He believed what Mrs. Fitzherbert had told them, at least thus far.

And yet . . .

Rosalind regarded the woman in front of her for a long moment. Something about the situation gave her pause. Something she had glimpsed or remembered.

"You are aware that the certificate may have already been destroyed?" Rosalind asked.

"Yes," said Mrs. Fitzherbert. "But it is also possible the thief feels there is a use for it. Perhaps they mean to sell it to the papers or to give it to some interested parties . . ."

"Such as the men arguing the case of the royal divorce in Parliament?" said Rosalind.

"Just so." Mrs. Fitzherbert tried to suppress her shudder. "You can understand, Miss Thorne, why it is vital that we move quickly."

"A last question, Mrs. Fitzherbert," said Adam. "Do you

have any men guarding your house? To deter curiosity seekers, perhaps?"

She frowned. "I do not, but it is a suggestion I will take seriously. Especially now."

The house is being watched, Adam had said as they entered. He said nothing of it now, only got to his feet.

"I can recommend some good men, if you need the help," he told Mrs. Fitzherbert. "For now, I would suggest that you show Miss Thorne the room the paper was taken from. In the meantime, I will go outside and see if I can find anything useful. I'll start with your garden, if I may."

"Yes, of course." Mrs. Fitzherbert also rose and rang the bell to summon the footman who had showed them inside. "Faller will show you the way. Thank you, Mr. Harkness."

Adam bowed. Rosalind caught his eye as he straightened.

Be careful, she thought toward him, and in his glance, she read his answer.

You also.

CHAPTER FOUR

The Scene of the Crime

"I need not point out . . . what a source of uneasiness it must be to you, to her, and, above all to the nation, to have it a matter of dispute and discussion whether the Prince of Wales is married."

Fox, Charles James, *Private Correspondence to George, Prince of Wales*

Once Adam left them, Mrs. Fitzherbert took up a lamp and led Rosalind out of the sitting room and up a staircase with an elaborately carved railing.

"If I may," asked Rosalind as they climbed, "where are your wards now?"

"They are in the country with my brother and his family. I felt it best that they not be in London at this time."

During the divorce trial.

"A sensible precaution," agreed Rosalind.

The third-floor hallway was as broad and luxuriously carpeted as the second was. She might be out of favor in many circles, but Mrs. Fitzherbert continued to live well and keep her home up to the minute in terms of fashion.

Mrs. Fitzherbert opened the door to what Rosalind assumed must be her private apartments. Like the rest of the house, it was richly decorated, but the furnishings here were older and heavier. There was a wealth of velvet and carved wood, as opposed to the pale silks and painted furniture downstairs. The atmosphere, however, had been lightened by the addition of gold window draperies, a white marble fireplace, and several large mirrors.

A woman—very evidently Mrs. Fitzherbert's lady's maid— rose to her feet from the chair beside the empty hearth.

"It's all right, Burrowes," said Mrs. Fitzherbert. "You can leave us."

"If you are certain, madam." Burrowes looked hard at Rosalind, attempting to size her up with one uncompromising glower. Rosalind returned her steely assessment stoically. Burrowes, she judged, was close to Mrs. Fitzherbert's age. Her hair and eyes were both iron gray, and her expression was as severe and correct as her black dress.

"Yes, I am certain," said Mrs. Fitzherbert. "Thank you."

Mrs. Fitzherbert said nothing more until Burrowes had curtsied and departed. Only then did she turn to Rosalind. "Before you ask, Miss Thorne, Burrowes has been with me for years. She has kept all my secrets, and I would suspect my daughters of robbing me before I would suspect her. If she wanted to profit from my . . . unusual situation, she could have done so years ago."

"I know it is painful to have to contemplate such a possibility," said Rosalind. "But in a case of robbery, it is unavoidable."

Mrs. Fitzherbert's hand strayed to her miniature. "No, it is perfectly all right. I brought you here precisely because this is necessary." She let her hand fall. "There is my box." She pointed to the broad, marble-topped desk and the chaos around it.

Rosalind took the lamp so that she might see better. Papers and letters were heaped in piles on the desktop, with a few scattered on the carpet. One drawer gaped open. The box it-self—a perfectly ordinary black metal strongbox about the size of a loaf of bread—sat on the desk, its lid thrown open. The broken lock lay beside it.

Rosalind moved closer. "Is that where the box was stored?" She indicated the open drawer.

"Yes," said Mrs. Fitzherbert. "I keep it locked, and I have the key."

Rosalind bent closer. She could see no splintering or scratches around the drawer lock.

"Where is the key now?" she asked.

Mrs. Fitzherbert moved to her bedside table, opened the drawer there, and removed a ring of keys. She sorted through these and held one up. Rosalind nodded.

"Are they normally kept there?"

"No. I keep them in my desk in the sitting room down-stairs, where I do the household accounts. But I brought them up so I could go through my drawers and see if any-thing else was missing." Mrs. Fitzherbert frowned. "I sup-pose . . . if someone knew where the keys were, they could have simply taken them from the sitting room."

"What about the key for the strongbox? Is it also on that ring?"

"No, I keep that with me, along with the key to my jewel case."

Rosalind picked up the broken lock from the desktop and held it closer to the lamp. Now she could see the hasp had been cut—the break was too clean for the lock to have been smashed or twisted.

"Oh, Lord. Have I been a fool?" Mrs. Fitzherbert pressed her hand against her cheek. "I did not . . . I refused to believe it could have been one of my servants . . ."

"We cannot come to any conclusion yet," said Rosalind. "Drawer locks are easily defeated. Even a schoolgirl with a let-ter opener could get into such a desk without leaving a trace."

As I have reason to know. She turned back toward the desk.
"Are all the things here as you found them?"

"More or less. I did look through what remained, to see if
anything else had been taken." Mrs. Fitzherbert paused and
swallowed. "I saw immediately that the marriage certificate
was gone."

Odd. Rosalind pondered the disorder. Why take time to
break open the box lock and search for one particular thing?
she asked herself. It would have been faster, and quieter, to
take the whole box.

The answer came a heartbeat later. The whole box would
have been more difficult to conceal.

Rosalind's natural environment was the parlor. She knew
sitting room etiquette intimately. She understood how to create an atmosphere of trust and comfort, and how to use conversation and convention to lull someone into saying more
than they might otherwise. But she had also made her way
into places where she would not have been admitted, to acquire things that she would not have been given. These experiences, along with afternoons spent in conversation with
Adam and other Bow Street officers, had given Rosalind an
unexpected education in the minutia of housebreaking. She
had heard stories of how much professional thieves could
conceal about their persons, especially women, with their
aprons and their voluminous skirts.

But a person who was not a professional, who was acting
because they saw opportunity or was following another person's instructions, might decide that it would be best to steal
only the single piece of paper.

Then, too, there was the matter of the law. Her quick pe-
rusal showed there were indeed banknotes among the stacks
of documents. If the thief was caught and the contents of the
box were worth more than five pounds, the penalty for their
actions could very well be transportation to a penal colony.

Or hanging.

"Is this room's door locked when you are not at home?" she asked Mrs. Fitzherbert.

"It is, as a precaution. There have been attempts at burglary before."

Rosalind turned to the door and bent down to examine the brass plate around the keyhole. There were no scratches there or splinters in the wood. She straightened. The box had been forced. The drawer might have been forced. The door had not. At least not that Rosalind could see. There were, she knew, tools for defeating locks. However, no one but an experienced housebreaker would have them or the knowledge of how to use them. And that was the exact sort of person who would have taken the whole box.

"Where are the household keys kept?" she asked.

Mrs. Fitzherbert opened her mouth and closed it again. "Do you know, I have not the faintest idea. My housekeeper has a set, of course, and Burrowes has the keys to my door and jewel case . . . The butler, of course, keeps the keys to the cellar, but beyond that, I don't know."

"And you have made inquiries of the servants?"

"I have." Her expression told Rosalind she'd found this a distasteful exercise. "I learned nothing, but I suppose I should not be surprised at that."

"Has the staff been with you long?"

"Most of them for years."

"No one has left recently?"

"No. But surely, if one of my servants was the thief, they would leave immediately after taking what they wanted."

"Not if the theft was planned before it was executed."

"Because if they left immediately afterward, they would be the first one suspected," said Mrs. Fitzherbert. "Yes, of course. I should have thought of that."

"There is no reason that you should have."

It was frequently and unfortunately the case that whenever any item went missing in an aristocratic household, the servants were blamed. In Rosalind's experience, the staff was seldom at fault, especially if the item was rare or valuable. However, it was also true that even people who were normally honest—and who understood the risks perfectly well— could falter in the face of unusual temptation.

Or if they believed they were helping a beloved mistress, despite initial appearances. Or, indeed, if they believed they were helping their country.

Rosalind set these thoughts aside for later.

"How many staff do you keep?" she asked.

"Fifteen living in, not counting the coachman and grooms, of course. There are between twenty and twenty-five during the day, with extra help brought in as needed for the laundry and so forth."

That was a large staff for a house this size, but even in her relative retirement, Mrs. Fitzherbert lived and entertained at a rarified level. So many servants meant that a daytime disturbance would be quickly noticed. Any would-be housebreaker would have little time for mistakes. They would need to know where to go and what to look for.

"Were the windows closed at the time?" asked Rosalind, mostly to gain time to think.

Mrs. Fitzherbert considered. "I believe they may have been opened to air the room. It has been so stifling of late."

Rosalind moved to the windows and parted the drapes. She did not truly expect to see anything there, but she wished to be thorough.

Motion in the twilight street below caught her eye. She froze.

"What is it?" asked Mrs. Fitzherbert.

It was an odd, in-between time. Those still at home were quiet in their houses. Those who had gone out—for a supper or a rout or the theater—would not be back for some hours yet. So, the street below remained as empty as when Rosalind and Adam had first knocked on Mrs. Fitzherbert's door.

This made the man on horseback quite visible.

From this angle, Rosalind could see only that he was a large man in a high-crowned hat. He sat the horse uneasily, with his feet in the stirrups sticking out awkwardly on either side. He rode slowly past the house to the end of the street and then turned and rode back.

Mrs. Fitzherbert, noticing Rosalind's stillness, moved to her side. She looked down into the quiet street and saw the rider.

In that moment, Rosalind felt sure the other woman would faint dead away.

"Who is it?" she asked.

But Mrs. Fitzherbert just gripped her shoulder as she stared into the street. It was enough. Rosalind knew who she saw.

"Mrs. Fitzherbert, is that your husband?"

CHAPTER FIVE

On Watch

" 'Tis such nights that unfit us for the days that are to follow."

Bury, Charlotte, *The Diary of a Lady-in-Waiting*

Mrs. Fitzherbert's footman, Faller, led Adam down the servants' stairs and into the warren of workrooms that undergirded even a modest London household. Faller was a youngish man, perhaps in his midtwenties. Tall and White, with only a few pockmarks on his cheeks, a straight back, and good calves to his legs. He walked on ahead of Adam like he was afraid to look behind, and maybe he was. The whole house would be on edge just now, not only from the theft but from wondering what the outcome would be for them. Adam had once seen an entire household staff sacked over the theft of a ring. In that particular case, it was discovered that the master of the house had sold the ring to cover a debt. To keep the secret from his wife, he'd allowed the servants to be blamed.

Faller and Adam passed the kitchen and the servants' hall, the laundry and sewing rooms. A few of the staff were still awake, and they glanced sharply at Adam, an intruder in their domain, but no one said anything. No one would. Not until they knew who he was and where his sympathies lay.

"How long have you been with Mrs. Fitzherbert?" Adam asked Faller.

"Four years, maybe five."

"Good berth?"

Faller shrugged. " 'S all right. Food's good. Pay's regular. Treat you fair. Butler's no more dishonest than some, an' never one to blame you for the silver going missing and what all." Faller's face creased, as if an unpleasant memory had just come to him.

They'd reached the back of the house and a latched door to the outside. Faller hesitated a moment and then turned toward Adam. "You really with Bow Street, then?"

"I was," Adam answered.

"And that lady, that Miss Thorne"—he jerked his chin toward the low ceiling—"she's the genuine article?"

"She is."

Faller glanced over Adam's shoulder, back toward the workrooms, looking to see if anyone was listening. "Cuz everybody's on pins and needles right now. Not sure what the missus is going to do, what with the divorce trial coming up and now this. Nobody knows which way is up."

"Wish I could help you there," said Adam, and he meant it. "I'm not sure even the king knows which way is up right now."

That got a chuckle out of the younger man. "Can't argue that. What's your name, then?"

"Harkness. And you're Faller?"

" 'S right. Tom Faller."

Adam lowered his voice. "Look, Faller, I know how it is. You don't want to be the one to peach. But if anybody knows something, they'd be doing the missus a favor if they were to tip the wink to me—or Miss Thorne. Nobody need know where it came from."

"I'll keep it in mind." Faller shot the bolt on the outside door and pushed it open. A blast of hot August air rolled through the confined entryway. "But you know how it is."

He did. Belowstairs was a small world. Carrying tales to the family or, worse, to outsiders could be punished in any number of ways big and small.

Adam nodded his thanks and walked up the stairs into Mrs. Fitzherbert's walled garden.

The summer darkness was settling in; so was a low canopy of rain clouds. Adam let himself glance back at the house. From here, he couldn't see any light in the upper story. He wondered where Rosalind was. He wondered what she had discovered, and wished he could be there beside her. If there were still signs of the thief's work, that was where they'd be.

At the same time, they needed to know who was watching the place. It was possible they were some harmless curiosity seeker or a newspaperman come to see if anything interesting might be happening in the Fitzherbert household. They might even be a special constable or guardsman, sent by the king to keep watch so that Mrs. Fitzherbert wasn't harassed or talking to the wrong people.

Now that Adam's eyes had adjusted to the deepening twilight, he could see the garden was shaped more like a triangle than a square. The wall of the house made its base. He also spotted a small door set in the right-hand wall. It hadn't been visible from the high street and probably led to a mews or an alleyway.

A raindrop hit the brim of his hat. Another fell against the back of his palm.

Adam avoided the path and crossed the lawn instead. It wasn't likely that the sound of gravel under his boots could be heard beyond the walls, but there was no point in taking chances.

He paused at the arched door and listened. He heard the clatter of traffic. The rhythm of the watchman's call lifted in the distance. Then, closer, he heard the sound of men's voices, low and grumbling.

Adam found the latch. He slipped it back and eased the door open just the barest inch. Fortunately, Mrs. Fitzherbert's staff were diligent. The hinges were well oiled and made no sound. The voices continued to rise and fall, without hitch or hesitation.

Adam pressed his eye to the crack. As he suspected, the garden opened onto a narrow mews. He couldn't see anyone, however. Adam eased the gate open a little farther and ducked through.

On the other side, he held still, taking in his immediate surroundings. To the right, the mews ended at the high street. Their corner made a Y shape—the narrow end of the garden's triangle.

There, perhaps three yards in front of him, stood a cluster of men in low-crowned hats and shirtsleeves. They all had their backs to the garden door (and him) and their faces toward the high street and Mrs. Fitzherbert's front door.

And, clearly, none of them were happy about it.

"Bloody hell, it's raining."

"So button your coat."

"How much longer you planning on keepin' us here?"

"I'm not keepin' you anywhere. You go on if you want."

Not one of the three looked behind them. Adam would have shaken his head at such carelessness, but he didn't want a stray rustle of cloth to alert the men. This was hardly a crowd of experienced lurkers, but inexperience did not mean they might not be dangerous.

Adam held his breath and moved closer. The light patter of fresh rain helped cover any stray noise.

". . . had enough," muttered one of the men in front of him. "Nothing's happening tonight."

"Patience, Langton. The toffs still all have their boots under the table. It's a long night yet. Plenty might happen."

The first man—Langton—grumbled under his breath. His compatriot on the right slapped his back and pulled a flask out of his pocket to pass. Langton took a swig and, sociably, passed it to the man on his left.

The third man took his swallow and wiped his mouth with his sleeve. "Can't believe I let you two talk me into this." He passed the flask back. He also pulled his hat brim lower.

"Liar." The first man took his drink and handed the flask back to Langton. "You begged to be here. You said the *Times* was sure to pay double for anything on the Fitz."

Adam's mouth settled into a tight, hard line. These weren't housebreakers or constables or loyalists of one stripe or another. These were newspapermen, looking for gossip.

Adam had spent some years apprenticed to a gamekeeper. He'd learned the art of silence. Slowly, patiently, he stepped forward. As soon as he was at arm's length, Adam reached out and tapped Langton on the shoulder.

Langton shouted, and the flask flew into the air, spilling liquor in every direction. Adam jumped back as the three of them whirled around.

"Bloody hell!" shouted the right-hand man. "What d'ye think yer doin'?"

"Finding out what you're doing," answered Adam. "It's getting late, gents."

"Aw, clear off," said Langton. "This is none of your business. Whoever you are."

But the third fellow, the one on the left, squinted at Adam. "Harkness?"

Now that he was facing the round, slouching man, Adam recognized him.

"Hello, Ranking," he said amiably. Ronald Ranking was a regular hanger-on at the magistrate's court and in Bow Street's lobby.

"Who is this fellow, Ronnie?" demanded the right-hand man.

"Parke, this is the famous Watchdog Harkness," said Ranking. "Late of the Bow Street Runners."

"Oh, ho!" sneered Parke. "*That* Harkness, is he?" His tone turned blatantly curious. "Story is you pulled Townsend's nose over the Cato Street business."

Adam said nothing.

"And that he shoved you out the door with a boot up your arse," Parke went on.

"Now then," said Adam mildly.

"What are you doing here?" asked Ranking. "You're not working for the Fitz now, are you?" He squinted harder, trying to read Adam's expression. "Are you?"

Adam ignored this. "Tell you what, Ranking. How about you and your friends come with me to the pub around the corner? I'll buy us a jug of beer, and we'll talk the whole thing over."

Langton surveyed the quiet street with an attitude of disappointment. "No pub around any corner near here."

"Then we walk till we find one," said Adam. "Otherwise, you can all just clear off."

"Or what?" snickered Parke. "You'll call your friends in the runners?" He snapped his fingers. "Oh, wait, they ain't your friends anymore! Cuz of that boot to your arse and all."

Adam cocked his head ever so slightly, as if listening for something. The watchman's shout drifted between the houses. "Nine o' the clock, and all's well!"

"The watch is two streets away, by the sound," he remarked. "Much easier to just move along or come with me to find that beer. Unless you all fancy a night in lockup, which means your stories, and your excuses, will be late to your editors."

The three looked at each other. They looked at Adam.

"Watch is a bunch of old men and drunkards," Parke assured the other two. "Nothing to worry about."

"Maybe," agreed Adam. "But I'll be helping them."

All three newspapermen looked at Adam again.

"Ain't worth it, Parke," said Ranking. "We seen enough."

Parke looked ready to argue, but Langton shook his head, indicating either that Parke shouldn't be a fool or that Langton wasn't going to back him up. Perhaps both. Parke's shoulders slumped.

"All right, lads," he muttered. "Let's go."

Langton slapped his friend's back, clearly glad to be on his way.

"Ranking," said Adam quietly.

Ranking hesitated and turned his head.

"I'll be at the Bell and Anchor at noon tomorrow. We might have some things to say to each other."

Ranking's eyes narrowed. Then he nodded once and hurried after his compatriots.

Adam waited until the newspapermen were entirely out of sight. He was about to turn around and head back through the garden door when he heard the slow clop of a horse's hooves.

Habit more than genuine worry made him step back into the shadow of the wall. As he watched, a single dispirited horse came round the corner. It was a fine animal, but the rider was a large man perched awkwardly in the saddle. Instinct or warning stirred in the back of Adam's mind. His eyes narrowed.

The man rode past Mrs. Fitzherbert's door, heading toward the corner where Adam waited. Adam pressed himself closer to the wall. The rider reached the corner. Now he was close enough for Adam to see his face.

Adam froze.

He'd seen the rider exactly once before, but he was not inclined to forget that face. Because the man seated so painfully on that fine horse was George IV, the king of England.

CHAPTER SIX

Only What Was Seen

"She owned she was deeply distressed at this formal abandonment, with all its consequences . . ."

Langdale, Charles, *Memoirs of Mrs. Fitzherbert*

Rosalind stood at Mrs. Fitzherbert's shoulder. The pair of them gazed down into the darkening street at the large man sitting awkwardly on his horse. He rode past the door, turned the reluctant beast, and rode back. Pacing. Waiting.

Or trying to make up his mind.

Mrs. Fitzherbert met Rosalind's eyes. For one heartbreaking moment, Rosalind saw her warring emotions.

Mrs. Fitzherbert knew full well she should let the drapes fall and pretend not to have seen. And yet the man out there was one she had loved. She had believed in his love for years and had depended on it. She had called him her husband. She could have easily protected herself and her adopted daughters by marrying again. She was a rich, charming woman. She could have had her pick of men.

But she had not. She had remained true to herself, as well as to her royal husband. And now he had returned.

Rosalind reached out to touch the other woman's hand, but she was too late.

Mrs. Fitzherbert ran for the door and threw it open. Rosalind ran after, grappling with her hems so that she would not trip and fall.

"Ma'am!" Burrowes shouted from the hallway behind them. Rosalind heard her on the stairs, running to catch up with Rosalind and her mistress.

Neither Rosalind nor Burrowes was fast enough. Mrs. Fitzherbert reached the foyer. She dashed to the front door, threw it open, and ran out into the rain.

But she also was too late. The street was empty. Or it was almost empty. Adam emerged from the shadows by the garden wall and ran to their side.

"Are you all right?"

Rosalind had no time to answer. Burrowes had reached her mistress now and took her gently by the shoulders.

"Ma'am, you must come inside. You must not be exposed to this rain."

Or prying eyes, Rosalind added to herself. But a single glance at Adam told her that he had already taken care of whoever had been watching the house.

"Yes," replied Mrs. Fitzherbert, but her gaze remained fixed on the street. "Yes, of course, you are right."

She let herself be led back to the house, but Rosalind could feel the disappointment trailing in her wake.

They all returned to the parlor. Burrowes rang the bell and told the footman to bring some hot tea. Rosalind did not miss the way the man looked toward Adam or the infinitesimal shake of Adam's head. Nothing was wrong. No tale needed to be carried belowstairs.

"I'm all right, Burrowes," snapped Mrs. Fitzherbert. "You can stop hovering." She pressed her hand against her brow.

"I will not," replied Burrowes with the stubborn firmness

of a longtime servant. "You are not well, and you need rest and dry things." She glowered at Rosalind and Adam.

"I am neither a fainting child nor an invalid yet," Mrs. Fitzherbert answered tartly. "I will not be rushed off to bed because—" She bit down on whatever she meant to say and raised her head. "Mr. Harkness, did you find anything outside that needs to be taken into immediate account?"

"Nothing related to the burglary," answered Adam. "But there were three newspapermen watching the house."

"What!" cried Mrs. Fitzherbert. "Are they still there?"

"I cleared them off. They had no chance to see . . . anything else." Mrs. Fitzherbert practically wilted with relief. "If you do decide you'd like some assistance in keeping such men away in the future, I know of some trustworthy men. I can have them here in the morning."

"Yes, yes, thank you." Mrs. Fitzherbert's voice shook. "I believe that would be . . . prudent under the circumstances."

"Mrs. Fitzherbert—" began Rosalind.

"I know what you are about to say," she said, cutting Rosalind off. "Could my husband be here because he knows the certificate has been stolen? Or—heaven forbid!—could he be coming to offer some apology or explanation for what has been done in his name?" Mrs. Fitzherbert poured the words out as if they were poison. Anger burned in every syllable. It shone in her eyes, as did the tears, which came from a heart broken past repair. "You want to know if perhaps, having drunk too much *again*, he has come to explain why, once more, he must utterly disregard our connection and our promises, along with my feelings, my reputation, and those of my girls. All because he needs . . . *he* needs . . ."

Mrs. Fitzherbert stopped abruptly and pressed her hand to her forehead.

"I am sorry," she whispered. "My nerves are under more strain than I realized." She looked down at her skirts. "And I believe Burrowes is correct. I should get into dry things."

"Of course," said Rosalind. "But it is also the case that we must continue with this matter, if possible. If you could give permission for Mr. Harkness to interview your staff?"

Mrs. Fitzherbert waved her hand wearily. "Yes. That must be done. I see that. May I take it I have your assistance, Miss Thorne?" Her smile was tentative, almost pleading.

"We shall do what we can."

"Thank you." The words came out as a sigh of deep relief.

The footman, Faller, returned with the tray at this moment. Mrs. Fitzherbert gave her man instructions to take Adam belowstairs and introduce him to the butler. She further assured Rosalind that she would return momentarily and that Rosalind should ring if she required anything at all.

Rosalind, alone in the parlor, poured herself a cup of strong tea. She cradled the warming cup in her hands and let herself remember everything she had seen and heard so far this evening. In one way, it was all very simple. An important paper had been stolen. She had dealt with similar matters frequently.

It was the persons involved that made this matter different from any she had yet been concerned with. They took this so far beyond her experience, she felt dizzy.

Could she set that aside? Could she, for example, consider whether the next thing Mrs. Fitzherbert could expect was a letter demanding payment for the document's return?

That seemed unlikely. It seemed more plausible that any such letter would go to Mrs. Fitzherbert's husband or his friends. Those persons would certainly be willing and able to pay a considerable sum to obtain it.

And then what? Would the paper be tossed into the nearest fire? That would be the most prudent action.

Rosalind frowned at her thoughts and took another sip of her tea. As she did so, there came a soft scratching at the door. A moment later, Burrowes entered.

"My mistress sends her apologies," she said. "She will be

down again in a moment. May I ask, miss, if I should have Faller send for your carriage now?"

What she meant was, did Rosalind and Adam plan to stay much longer? Without instructions from her employer, Burrowes could not possibly ask them to leave. She could, however, give them a powerful hint.

"Yes, thank you, Burrowes," said Rosalind.

"And will there be anything further, miss?" Burrowes clearly did not want there to be anything. She wanted to be back upstairs with Mrs. Fitzherbert.

Rosalind set her cup down. "I would very much value your opinion of what happened here today."

"It's not for me to say, miss."

"Certainly not under normal circumstances," agreed Rosalind. "And if this was a normal burglary, I would never suggest you speak out of turn."

Rosalind held her breath. It was possible she had gone too far and had made her future work here more difficult.

But Burrowes glanced over her shoulder, as if she suspected someone was listening.

"Is it possible the king's people looked for help acquiring the certificate?" prompted Rosalind. "It would be no one's fault if they believed they were assisting Crown and country to let . . ."

"No," said Burrowes. "If that was the case, Mr. Holm or the housekeeper, they'd know by now. Or I would. Such a consequential thing could not remain a secret for more than an hour, I promise you."

"Has any representative from the palace been to speak with Mrs. Fitzherbert?"

"Not about this. She still dines with the Duke of York regularly. In fact, he's expected tomorrow night." She paused at the flicker of surprise on Rosalind's face. "I'm sure I don't need to tell you, miss, that royalty has its own ways, and it's good to keep friends with who you can."

If only so you can hear what is being said about you. "Of course."

"But His Royal Highness hasn't brought up the marriage, and there's been no one direct from the king. Not for years. Nor has any written. They've all forgotten her." These last words were laden with bitterness. "Or pretended to, at least."

Rosalind nodded.

"Mrs. Fitzherbert is a good woman, an honest woman," Burrowes told her. "She has seen a great deal of the world, and much of it unpleasant. But despite all, she has a loving heart. *People* take advantage of that."

Burrowes was looking hard at Rosalind, willing Rosalind to understand without her having to speak plainly.

Without having to name names. Which meant she was worried about someone inside the house. But not a member of the staff.

Then who?

Rosalind's gaze drifted to the portrait over the fireplace—the two girls with their white dresses and carefully arranged curls. Minney and Mary Ann. According to Mrs. Fitzherbert, these girls were now grown with the younger of the pair ready to make her debut. But they had also been sent away to the country to keep them from the chaos of the divorce trial and the gossip it might bring.

Burrowes followed Rosalind's gaze.

"It is the case that sometimes those closest to us are the ones who do us the most harm," said Rosalind, keeping her eyes pointed toward the portrait.

"Just so," said Burrowes. "And it can be those who owe us the most that will take the most from us."

"I trust you are speaking in general terms, Burrowes."

Burrowes whisked around. Mrs. Fitzherbert stood in the doorway. She was still pale, but she walked steadily to her chair and sat easily, if a little stiffly.

"Of course, ma'am," Burrowes replied. "One hears stories of these things, in other houses."

"Repeating gossip is not like you," Mrs. Fitzherbert remarked.

"No, ma'am," said Burrowes. "I was just going to send Faller to ready Miss Thorne's carriage, if you will permit?"

Mrs. Fitzherbert nodded. Burrowes made her curtsy and left them. Mrs. Fitzherbert stared at the closed door for a heartbeat too long before she turned to Rosalind.

"I do apologize, Miss Thorne. I find my nerves are rather more affected by the day's events than I thought."

"It would be very strange if they did not affect you," replied Rosalind.

"But now you must tell me, what can be done? You must have some method by which you proceed."

Rosalind had to work to keep from biting her lip. Her head was spinning from what she had heard and seen so far, and from the understanding that speed was essential. The marriage certificate was not a necklace that might be found at a pawnshop, or even a stray letter that might be pulled from a blackmailer's desk. This concerned the Crown.

And it was possible the Crown knew it.

How was it that she came to be sitting here, contemplating such matters? Rosalind swallowed a nervous laugh and forced her mind into motion. She thought about the open box, about the man on horseback, about Burrowes and her insinuations, followed so quickly by the fraught exchange between her and Mrs. Fitzherbert. About the girls sent away for their own protection.

Rosalind drew a deep breath.

"I am afraid I must reconsider my original thesis," said Rosalind. "Appearances tend to suggest that this theft involves someone connected to your household."

Mrs. Fitzherbert's face lost some of its color. "I did . . . I did not want to believe it."

"We have a series of facts that require us to consider this possibility. No door or window appears to have been forced to gain entry to the house. Whoever took your certificate was able to move about a busy house without arousing notice. The strongbox in your desk was opened, and there were signs of a hasty search, but nothing else in the room was disturbed. This seems to indicate that the thief knew where they wanted to look."

Mrs. Fitzherbert stared at the portrait of her daughters, as if begging them for something. Answers? Forgiveness?

Perhaps both. She thought again of Burrowes's hard, meaningful glower at the same painting. She wondered if Mrs. Fitzherbert worried, or even suspected, there was something wrong.

But all Mrs. Fitzherbert said was, "How do we proceed?"

"I would suggest you choose a person among your staff whom you can trust absolutely," Rosalind told her. "You dismiss them for the theft. That person will then be replaced by a young woman in my employ named Amelia McGowan." Privately, Rosalind hoped Amelia meant what she said about being willing to help talk to the staff. "She has experience both as a housemaid and a lady's maid and will be able to join the staff without arousing too much suspicion."

"And spy on them?" inquired Mrs. Fitzherbert lightly.

"Yes," said Rosalind.

"Is it necessary to blame the theft on . . . the person to be dismissed?"

"I am sorry," Rosalind told her. "But as you yourself said, speed is paramount. Creating the appearance that a culprit has been identified will cause the true thief, or accomplice, to relax and possibly to become careless."

Mrs. Fitzherbert absorbed this in silence, but her expression turned wary. For a moment, Rosalind felt sure she would refuse. But at last, she lifted her chin.

"Your Amelia McGowan, can she do hair? I am giving a dinner tomorrow."

"She can do hair, and she can look after a wardrobe." For a time, at least. Amelia was adept with a needle, but her time in Rosalind's employ had not given her much experience with the most luxurious fabrics.

"What a strange interview this is," Mrs. Fitzherbert murmured. Then she turned and rang the bell. A moment later, Burrowes reentered the room.

"Yes, ma'am?"

"Burrowes," said Mrs. Fitzherbert, "I am about to ask you a very great favor. I would not do so if this were not an emergency, and if I did not trust you absolutely."

Burrowes's quick glance toward Rosalind was wary, and Rosalind could not blame her. "If there is any way I can be of assistance, I am, of course, ready to do so."

Mrs. Fitzherbert lowered her voice. "You know what was taken from me, and you know how urgent it is that it be recovered. But . . . there is reason to believe that the theft may have been abetted by one of the staff."

This time Burrowes's glance toward Rosalind burned. She had attempted to tell Rosalind something quite different, and to all appearances, Rosalind had ignored her. Rosalind resisted the urge to look away.

"If you wish me to speak further with the maids—" began Burrowes.

Mrs. Fitzherbert cut her off. "I wish it was that simple, but I'm afraid it must appear that I have dismissed you for the theft. I shall then appear to hire a new maid. She is the one who will make the inquiries among the staff."

"If speed were not so necessary, I would never suggest such a deception as a first course of action," said Rosalind. "I do fully understand what is being asked."

"Do you, miss?" replied Burrowes. "Well. That is some comfort, I suppose."

She did not mean a single word of it.

"You may be certain that when all is resolved, I will welcome you back instantly," said Mrs. Fitzherbert. "You have been my constant friend all these years, Burrowes. There is no one I place so much faith in. When this is over, I will make sure it is known that you were acting solely under my orders, not because there was any true suspicion against you."

Burrowes's silence was long, and it was deep. For a moment, Rosalind was afraid the woman would tender her resignation on the spot. She would have reason to. For an honest woman, one who had stayed at her post through a host of turbulent transitions, the whole situation was grossly insulting.

She is not going to agree, thought Rosalind. *She is going to make Mrs. Fitzherbert order her.*

Burrowes lifted her chin and turned fully toward Mrs. Fitzherbert. "I would not be party to such a thing for any other employer. But I will do what you ask, because it is you who asks."

Mrs. Fitzherbert let out a long whoosh of breath. "Thank you, Burrowes."

"How should we proceed?" Burrowes looked directly at Rosalind as she asked the question.

"Mr. Harkness should be returning from questioning the rest of the staff shortly," said Rosalind. "If you leave after that, it will appear . . . understandable."

Burrowes sniffed audibly. "Very good, miss."

"I'll call you to the bookroom once Miss Thorne and Mr. Harkness are gone," said Mrs. Fitzherbert. "I can pay your wages then and . . ."

"If you please, ma'am," said Burrowes. "Perhaps we should arrange for them to be sent later? It will look more the thing if I am dismissed without wages."

Mrs. Fitzherbert drew back. In her surprise, she looked to Rosalind.

"That is an excellent thought. Thank you," said Rosalind.

"You have somewhere you can go?" Rosalind asked.

"Yes, miss," replied Burrowes. "I can go to my sister." She paused. "Shall I make a scene?"

"Only if that is what you would naturally do upon being accused of theft." It surprised her that both Mrs. Fitzherbert and Burrowes should be so quick to fall into the deception. A moment later, however, it occurred to Rosalind that given Mrs. Fitzherbert's past, these women could both be experienced practitioners of the high social arts of excuses and pretense.

A thing it would be well to remember.

"I may—with your permission, Miss Thorne—blame you for the thing," Burrowes told them.

And probably enjoy doing it. Rosalind smiled. "You may certainly blame me." She had the distinct feeling her reputation belowstairs might never recover after Burrowes was done having her say, but it was a fair exchange for what she was about to put the woman through.

Burrowes brushed down her skirt. "Then I had best get on with it, hadn't I?"

CHAPTER SEVEN

Merest Speculation

*". . . and expressed surprise at so much forbear-
ance with such Documents in her possession and
under pressure of such long and severe trials . . ."*

Langdale, Charles, *Memoirs of Mrs. Fitzherbert*

"Mrs. Fitzherbert seems badly shaken."
Rosalind and Adam sat side by side in the bor-
rowed carriage. Rain thudded on the roof and pattered against
the windowpanes. Sanderson's coachman, Nicholson, drove
them with a light, sure hand. The traffic outside was beginning to thicken as people made their way to the theater or to
a late supper or from one party to the next.

"Far more shaken by the king's appearance than by the
loss of her marriage certificate," Rosalind said. "Was anyone
besides the newspapermen watching the house?"

"Not as far as I could tell," said Adam. "And if they learn
I turned them off just minutes before the king came to play
the lovesick swain, I suspect it will be my safety that we need
to be worried about."

"It seems like a scene from a farce," said Rosalind. "How

could the king wander away from the palace of an evening? Someone must have seen him."

"If it was a servant, they couldn't say anything," said Adam. "And his companions at Carlton House may have been too drunk to notice anything."

Rosalind felt herself staring. Adam smiled without any hint of amusement.

"Townsend's palace gossip was not always entirely complimentary." John Townsend had been Adam's superior at Bow Street. The proudest accomplishment of his life was his relationship with the regent—the man who was now the king. "He could be quite scathing about some of the men who battled for the prince's attention."

Rosalind looked at Adam; Adam looked at Rosalind.

"Should I remark on the irony in that statement?" he inquired.

"If you choose."

"I think we may pass over it for now," said Adam blandly. "Instead, we might focus on the fact that His Majesty chose to make an appearance this evening, immediately after the certificate had been stolen."

"Yes. That cannot be ignored." The carriage jolted over a pothole, causing Rosalind to grab for the squabs. "He may have wanted to apologize or explain his actions. He is said to still care for her. I heard that Queen Caroline herself refers to the king as 'Mrs. Fitzherbert's husband.'"

Adam said nothing.

"Yes, I know," said Rosalind in acknowledgment of that silence. "If he does care, he has an odd way of showing it."

"And Mrs. Fitzherbert seems to be at the end of her patience."

Rosalind nodded, remembering the tears and the anger in Mrs. Fitzherbert's eyes.

Having drunk too much again, *he has come to explain*

*why, once more, he must utterly disregard our connection
and our promises, along with my feelings, my reputation,
and those of my girls. All because he needs . . . he needs . . .*

Which raised a question, and a possibility that Rosalind
found she was not quite ready to acknowledge. So, instead
she asked, "What happened when you found the newspapermen?"

"I cleared them off." Adam glanced out the window. "I
did recognize one of them—a fellow named Ranking. I invited him to have a drink tomorrow. I have a feeling he's been
keeping an eye on Mrs. Fitzherbert for a while now and may
have something useful to tell us."

"He knew you?" said Rosalind, startled.

"Yes. You sound worried."

"I . . . I am. It's not something I stopped to consider. If this
man, Ranking, knows you, does he know you and I are associated?" With one look, she saw that he did. "Then it won't
take them long to realize Mrs. Fitzherbert must have wanted
to consult with me—with us—about . . . something more
than the security of her house."

Adam scrubbed at his face, probably uttering a few soft
curses into his hand. "And that might appear in the papers."

"It might," agreed Rosalind. *It will.*

For much of her career, Rosalind had moved in perfect ob-
scurity. She was, after all, merely a minor aristocrat's daughter forced to supplement a meager income by making herself
useful to her more fortunate friends. But invisibility was a
comfortable state. She had been trained all her life to avoid
attention, especially once her father had abandoned the family and her mother had died. According to the iron dictates of
polite society, an unfortunate woman must do her best to
vanish, lest she become an object of pity or make others uncomfortable.

But word of Rosalind's accomplishments had flown from

house to house and had at last reached the newspapers. Alice and George had assured her this was most beneficial to her livelihood, and it was true she now had far more requests for her services than ever before.

But this new aspect of her reputation made it harder to move efficiently and effectively, because it was also necessary to look over her shoulder more frequently.

And if I am—if we are—connected in the gossip columns to Mrs. Fitzherbert . . .

It would all get worse very quickly.

"You were suggesting Mrs. Fitzherbert have some extra men come watch her house," said Rosalind.

She didn't have to finish. "I'll find some for your door, as well," Adam said. "My brother-in-law will know some reliable fellows that are glad to earn a bit extra."

"Thank you."

Rosalind looked out the window at the passing streets. With an effort, she set aside personal considerations and tried to focus her mind on what she had heard and seen at Mrs. Fitzherbert's house.

"Were you able to learn anything from the staff?" she asked him.

"Nothing useful. No one heard anything. No one saw anything." Adam spoke blandly, as if commenting on the weather. "We could not reasonably expect more than that, especially with the butler and housekeeper glowering over my shoulder the whole time. However, it was as well to get it out of the way." Rosalind looked at him curiously.

"Many people react badly to a first questioning," he said. "But as circumstances change, minds frequently change with them. With luck, I've presented myself as a sympathetic ear for when that happens. What about abovestairs? What was Mrs. Fitzherbert able to show you?"

"She kept her strongbox in her private apartments," Rosalind told him. "She said it was locked in her writing desk, with the drawer keys kept in another desk downstairs. She kept the key to the box itself with her. The door to the apartments was locked as well, or so she said."

"Do you believe her?"

"It all matches with what I saw. The door and the desk showed no signs of tampering, but the strongbox lock had been cut."

"Which would seem to indicate that our burglar had access to the keys that were in the house," said Adam. "Which might very well point toward a servant."

"Perhaps," said Rosalind. "But I was able to speak with Burrowes—Mrs. Fitzherbert's maid. She was not willing to name names, but it was very clear she suspects that the two daughters—Minney and Mary Ann—might be in some way involved in this."

"But Mrs. Fitzherbert said both daughters are in the country."

"Yes," said Rosalind, aware that she sounded distant.

Of course Adam noticed. "There's something else, isn't there?"

Rosalind smiled, just a little. "I admit, I am wondering if everything is as clear as it seems." She shook her head. "No. It's ridiculous."

"What is?"

"Mrs. Fitzherbert is a proud woman, and she has been put through a great deal." Rosalind spoke slowly, trying to set her thoughts in order. "She maintains a brave face, and I believe she was in earnest when she said she wanted to protect her girls. But she also believes that her marriage is morally binding, even if it is not legally so." Rosalind paused. "And she is angry. She's been insulted and cast aside and made to fear for herself and her family, and now she might be denied once again, this time in front of Parliament." Because if the divorce trial went on as far as the stage of recrimination, the king's affairs would be brought up. And the rumors of the king's previous marriage.

"Does she want to be queen?" asked Adam.

Rosalind arched her brows.

Adam's mouth twisted into a wry smile. "I know," he said. "How is it you and I come to be discussing such things?"

Rosalind shook her head. "I don't know the answer to that. As to the other . . ." She paused again. "I wonder if perhaps she did covet the crown when she was younger. She may even have been promised she would have it. The prince—the king—is said to have the capacity to dazzle. But I cannot believe the Mrs. Fitzherbert we spoke to thinks she can take the crown, especially not when there's a living queen, who enjoys the sympathy of so much of the citizenry."

"Then what does Mrs. Fitzherbert want?"

Rosalind considered this. Adam was referring not simply to the return of the marriage certificate, but to the deeper, more personal reasoning that brought Mrs. Fitzherbert to them.

"She wants to maintain her pride and her personal dignity," said Rosalind at last. The lengths to which men would go to preserve their pride were much talked about. What was less acknowledged was that women would go just as far. Perhaps even farther, because sometimes their pride was their only real possession.

"Does she want vengeance?" asked Adam.

"I don't think so. She wants her station to be understood, at least privately. She wants the correctness of her moral conduct recognized."

"Yes," agreed Adam. "She wants that a great deal."

"But she does not wish to be seen as betraying the man she married, for whom, despite all, she still has a regard." She met Adam's gaze in silence while they both acknowledged the contradictions inherent in such a set of desires.

"So," said Adam. "Given all this, she might have decided to arrange for the certificate to . . . come to light."

Rosalind nodded. "If she can say that the certificate was stolen, and if there are people who can verify that this must be the case . . ."

"Such as me and you," put in Adam.

"Then if and when the certificate is unveiled as evidence during the king's divorce trial, or if it is printed in the papers . . ."

"Mrs. Fitzherbert can't possibly be seen as being responsible for whatever judgment may be rendered against the king, because her house was robbed after she took every reasonable precaution."

"Yes," said Rosalind. "And yet it would still be openly acknowledged that she did marry the king, and that she is his victim, rather than simply another grasping mistress. Her reputation remains intact, her position is vindicated, and any immediate reason to ask her to surrender guardianship of her daughters should be erased." Rosalind's mouth tightened. "What have I become? A woman comes to me asking for help, and I immediately wonder if she is attempting to use me as part of a ruse."

"Experience does not always leave us charitable and forgiving souls," said Adam. "The trick is not to let it blind us to the fact that sometimes things are exactly what they seem."

"I suppose," said Rosalind. "And this is, of course, all raw speculation."

"It is," agreed Adam. "So, tomorrow I'll go to the Bell and Anchor to meet Ranking, and I'll also round up a few fellows to put on watch at your door. Then perhaps we can begin to flesh out some of this speculation."

"You might take George or Alice with you—" began Rosalind, but she stopped because Adam was no longer listening. Instead, he had hooked the curtain back with one finger and was looking out the window.

"Damn," he muttered. "There's trouble coming."

CHAPTER EIGHT

Greeted by the London Mob

*"... the throne totters, and the country which has
hitherto supported it is not steady."*

Bury, Charlotte, *The Diary of a Lady-in-Waiting*

As Adam spoke, Rosalind became aware of a rumbling in
the distance. The carriage slowed and stopped. Rain
pounded on the roof, but it was not loud enough to cover
over how the rumble was getting closer.

Rosalind felt the hairs on the back of her neck stand up.

She lifted the window curtain and peered through the
blurry pane to try to see where they were. She recognized
none of the buildings and could hear no church bells.

But that distant rumbling grew louder.

Adam let the window glass down. "What do you see?" he
shouted up at the coachman.

"Torches," Nicholson called back to them. "Coming this
way. I'll try to turn us!"

Adam swore again. Now Rosalind realized that rising swell
of sound was a mix of men's voices and booted feet pounding
the cobblestones.

A *mob*. Fear closed her throat.

All the *haut ton* excoriated "the London mob." It was referred to the same way as a wild beast might be—mad, inexplicable, and likely to leap out of the shadows at any moment. No one spared much thought as to why the people of London (or Manchester or Lancaster or Yorkshire) might become so angry that they would spill into the streets to break windows or accost passersby. In the drawing rooms there was no talk of the right to vote, the right to be governed by men of moral quality, the right to a living wage so that families would not starve. All that was said was that persons who rose up in protest of their lot must be tracked down, arrested, hanged.

Rosalind barely had time to think all this before the mob was upon them.

"God save the queen!" bellowed a dozen voices.

Flickering light engulfed them. The carriage rocked. Rosalind bit her tongue and grabbed at the squabs. Overhead, Nicholson shouted—at the horses to calm them, at the boys to order them up onto the box, at the horses again. His whip cracked. Curses rose, and the carriage rocked again.

"Take your hat off!" bawled somebody. "Take your hat off and give us, 'God save the queen!'"

"Or we'll give you what for!" bellowed someone else.

"Who's in there!" shouted yet another. Fists hammered against the carriage door. "Show your faces!"

Adam stared at Rosalind, and Rosalind stared back. The voices rose; the carriage rocked; the coachman's whip cracked. The horses whickered, the noise high and tinged with panic.

"Get the horses! Hold 'em here! You in there! Come out where we can see ye!" The doors rattled on their hinges. Fists hammered on the window glass. "Come out and show loyalty to the queen!"

An idea, desperate and possibly foolish, flashed through Rosalind's mind. She mouthed silently to Adam, *Queen's business.*

Adam, of course, understood. He tossed his hat aside, shoved back the curtain, and let down the glass.

A wave of heat rolled into the carriage, along with the acrid stench of burning wood and turpentine. Raindrops sizzled where they met the torch fire, making it flicker crazily across a shifting sea of men's faces. The torchlight gave them all masks of orange and black as they pressed forward, shouting and jeering. One of them had leapt onto the boards and looked ready to climb in through the window.

"Good evening," said Adam calmly. "What's the to-do, good man?"

If Rosalind thought Adam suddenly sounded more like Sanderson Faulks than his usual self, she remained silent.

The face that leered back at them was ruddy and unshaven. Broken teeth reflected the torchlight, and dirt-stained hands gripped the carriage door.

"Well, well, look at you! Got us a pretty couple of toffs here, lads!" he hollered over his shoulder. "Now, you listen to us!" The man shook his fist in Adam's face. "We're the people's committee! We won't 'ave no whores in the palace, robbing the country blind! We won't 'ave no drunken, layabout king what takes our taxes and buys diamonds for 'is women and can't follow the law nor treat our queen as 'e should!"

"God save the queen!" roared the mob. "God save the queen!" The carriage rocked hard, pushed by a dozen hands.

It would be easy enough to say the words, but would they be enough? What else might these men demand from Adam? From her?

Rosalind tried not to think of the carriage tipping over,

of the men pulling Adam out, pulling her out, the bite of cobblestones against elbows and knees, the shouts and the hands pinching and bruising. Blood on their hands, blood on Adam's face, blood on her . . .

"If you're the queen's man, you'll let this lady pass," Adam was saying. Rosalind focused on his voice and willed herself to calm. "She's on the queen's business."

"A likely story!" the man growled. One of the horses whickered again, and the carriage lurched. "'Old 'im, Jeffries!"

With an act of will, Rosalind drew on all the deportment she had so carefully practiced across the years. She held her head and shoulders straight. She made sure that her expression was bland, distant, and entirely disinterested.

"It is no story, good sir," she said coldly, as if she could not even think of being afraid. "I am possessed of urgent news and cannot keep Her Majesty waiting."

The man looked her right in the eye. When the carriage was stopped, Rosalind assumed that the men were the worse for drink, but he gave no sign of that. Even in the uncertain torchlight, she could see his eyes were clear and shrewd. Rosalind did not let herself blink as his gaze traveled over her. She did not allow her expression to shift.

I have a right to proceed. I will proceed. Birth and bearing are my passport. The world will step aside.

Outside the crowd rumbled and hands rocked the carriage hard. "Come down! Come out! Hats off for the queen!"

"You hear her," said Adam. "We are asking that you let the lady through, in the queen's name."

The man's jaw worked back and forth.

Rosalind's heart contracted. *It won't be enough. It won't . . .*

He turned back to the mob. "It's all right, lads! She's on the queen's business! Let 'er through. Let 'er through!"

The fear bubbling inside Rosalind said this could not possibly work, and yet it did. The men surrounding them backed away; the shouts grew jubilant.

"God save the queen! God save the queen!" The torches waved. The man on the step jumped down. Nicholson wasted no time. He cracked his whip, and the horses bolted forward. The carriage lurched, and Rosalind slammed back against the seat so hard, her head banged and she bounced. The cheers grew fainter as they rattled pell-mell over the cobbles.

Adam righted her.

"Thank you," she whispered.

"That was well thought and well played," he told her. "Are you all right?"

"Yes, yes." She squeezed his hand where it held her shoulder. "I've seen far worse than those men."

"Have you?" Adam's tone was dubious.

"You've never seen Lady Jersey on one of her crusades," said Rosalind, relieved that her voice was light and steady. Rosalind smiled, even though Adam probably could not see it in the darkness. But she also shivered, which was ridiculous and also made a lie out of her attempt at levity.

Adam said nothing. He just wrapped his arm around her and pulled her close. Rosalind leaned against him. She felt a dozen things at once. She was embarrassed at how much she needed his reassuring touch, and aware there was no need to be ashamed. She was still stunned that her ruse had worked. She was grateful for the skills and daily drilling that gave her a mask to wear when she needed it.

But she was also grateful beyond words to have Adam with her now, so she could put the mask aside to simply be tired, be worried, and be held for a quiet space by the one she loved.

The carriage turned a corner, and Rosalind peered out

from the curtains. They had arrived at Orchard Street. The rain had eased, becoming nothing more than a fitful drizzle. Adam helped Rosalind down and told Nicholson he need not wait. Arm in arm, Rosalind and Adam walked to the door. Through the drawn curtains, Rosalind could see that a light burned in the front parlor.

"Alice is still awake," she remarked.

Alice still officially lived with Rosalind, although she generally spent her nights with Amelia. They shared a small flat above the shop front that Amelia was busily turning into Miss McGowan's School for the Improvement of Working Women. Despite this, Alice spent most of her days writing in Rosalind's back parlor, just as she always had. The arrangement provided a fig leaf of propriety that allowed Rosalind to receive male visitors without eyebrows being raised among her more genteel acquaintance. It also allowed Alice and Amelia to continue their relationship while lessening the chances of starting rumors about its true nature.

"Did you expect anything less?" asked Adam. "Alice would never leave while you were off answering Mrs. Fitzherbert's express invitation."

Rosalind chuckled softly. "Perhaps I hoped this once."

Adam smiled. "I need to go rouse the men to guard Mrs. Fitzherbert's door, and yours, by the by. Should I come back afterward?" he inquired lightly.

A bolt of warmth shot through her, along with a very cold river of regret.

"I would like that," she said. "But I expect things are about to become very busy, and I expect it to start quite early." She frowned. "But will you be all right walking . . . ?"

She did not need to finish. "I'll be fine," said Adam. "It would be good to get a sense of how things stand in the streets, and I might even overhear something useful. I bid you good night, my dear." Adam raised her hand to his lips and kissed it gently. "I will be back tomorrow." He kissed her mouth then, long, warm, and lingering.

At last, they were able to let each other go. Rosalind hesitated on the doorstep, watching Adam walk down their (thankfully) quiet street until he rounded the corner and was gone.

CHAPTER NINE

Events Set in Motion

*"It is certain, that having a man there has as yet
produced but little good . . . and therefore I
should like to try a woman . . ."*

Bury, Charlotte, *The Diary of a Lady-in-Waiting*

"Well, at last!" cried Alice from the parlor. "We were
getting ready to send out a search party!"

"I'll be with you in a moment!" Rosalind took off her
bonnet and coat and hung them beside the door. She laid her
gloves on the hall table. She used the small mirror beside the
door to check that her expression was calm and that the flush
that came over her as a result of Adam's kiss had faded.

Alice and Amelia were in the front parlor, with a pot of tea
and several crumb-covered plates on the table in front of
them.

"I'm sorry to have kept you waiting," said Rosalind as she
took her usual chair. It was only eleven, according to the
clock on the mantel, but the servants would all have gone
home, with the exception of Laurel upstairs.

"We forgive you." Alice poured out a cup of tea and held
it out to her. Rosalind accepted the tea gratefully. Even

though it was not very late by her usual standards, the strain of the evening had left her entirely exhausted.

Alice gave her a moment to drink, but only a moment. "Now, what on earth is happening?" she said. "And how does it involve the most notorious woman in the kingdom?"

Rosalind told them about Mrs. Fitzherbert and the marriage certificate, which appeared to have been stolen. She told them about the king riding back and forth in front of the house, about Burrowes's insinuation that the certificate had been stolen by one of the girls or some other close friend. She told them about the suspicions she and Adam had formed—that this apparent burglary might in truth be a ruse by Mrs. Fitzherbert to provide public confirmation of her marriage. Or, equally, it might be a very private, very personal betrayal.

Rosalind was aware of a certain indecorous satisfaction in watching their eyes widen with astonishment.

"Goodness!" exclaimed Amelia, cheerfully scandalized. "I should've stayed in service. Now I'm going to miss it all!"

But Alice's reaction was quite the opposite. All the humor, and some of the color, drained from the writer's face.

"Rosalind," said Alice. "Please tell me you turned her away."

"I did not."

"Then you must do so now. At once."

Rosalind's brow furrowed. "I have already promised to help. So has Adam."

"What's the matter, Alice?" asked Amelia.

But Alice ignored her. She leaned forward and laid her hand over Rosalind's. "Rosalind, this is not something I say to you lightly, but have you entirely lost your mind?"

"I admit, I wondered that more than once," Rosalind told her.

"Then why on earth did you do it?"

"Because if Mrs. Fitzherbert is telling the truth, I could not leave her to be exposed to blackmail, or worse. She is a woman in need of assistance."

"You do realize that those who took the document might be allies of our king, George IV, long may he reign? *Or*, what's even more likely, they might be partisans for our angry, defamed Queen Caroline?"

"Yes," said Rosalind, a trifle impatiently. "I do."

"And you do realize that one of the people in the queen's camp is your patroness, Lady Jersey?"

"Lady Jersey is not my patroness," said Rosalind, a bit more tartly than she meant to.

"Lady Jersey may not be an official, investing patroness, but what about Mrs. Levitton? Do you know where she and her board—who have loaned you rather a lot of money and expect to make a profit off it—stand on the divorce question? Whether they are for the king or the queen?"

"Alice," said Amelia. "She can't have had time to consider much of anything yet."

"Which is part of the problem," Alice snapped back. "She hasn't *thought*. Which is not at all like you, Rosalind."

Weariness threatened to make her impatient. Rosalind finished her tea and poured another cup, giving herself time to remember that Alice was only concerned and that her concerns were not misplaced. Rosalind did have people other than herself to answer to.

"I have thought enough to know that what you're saying is true," said Rosalind. "This is no ordinary matter. However, I also don't believe Mrs. Fitzherbert and her daughters should be made to suffer simply because it might help gain some sort of spiteful victory over someone else, whether that particular someone wears a crown or not."

"Come along, Alice," said Amelia coaxingly. "You can't say fairer than that."

"I suppose." Alice sighed. "And truth be told, I don't think

I could have walked away from such a problem. But if it all comes back to haunt us, you can't say I didn't warn you!"

"Never," said Rosalind. "Now. If I am to do this thing properly, and quickly, I need help." She turned toward Amelia. "I have a favor to ask of you."

"Me?" Amelia looked startled.

"Yes." Rosalind set her cup down. "I know you are very busy with your school . . ."

Amelia snorted. "Don't I wish! We've got all of four girls, and they can come only twice a week, and that's only if they give up their half day on Sunday. I've spent so much on books and pens and ink, and the chalkboard and all the rest of it . . . I was hoping to hire another teacher so we can give classes at night, but . . ." She stopped. "I'm sorry."

"I might be able to help a little with finances," said Rosalind. "Or, rather, we might. I wanted to ask you if you'd be willing to return to service as a maid for a few days. To Mrs. Fitzherbert."

"Maid?" stammered Amelia. "To the king's wife?"

"Maid," said Rosalind. "As you yourself suggested. And spy."

When she'd had more anonymity, Rosalind would contrive to set herself up in her client's household as a guest or a private secretary. Now that she had become a known entity, she must use a proxy. She wondered if she would ever become reconciled to it.

Amelia's green eyes lit up with sparks of mischief and daring at the prospect of this new task.

Alice looked away.

"Oh, Alice, it will be all right," said Amelia.

"Alice?" said Rosalind softly.

Alice sniffed. "Not that you need my approval, of course. You're perfectly able to take care of yourself."

"You know that I am," Amelia told her. "But I'd rather have your agreement."

"We both would," said Rosalind.

Alice sniffed. "Well, if it's going to be done, there's no point in holding back, is there?"

"Tell the truth, dear." Amelia squeezed Alice's hand. "You just don't want to have to make your own tea of a morning."

Alice lifted her nose. "I made my own tea for any number of years before you came along, young lady. Besides, you know I only drink coffee in the mornings, and of course, I'll be staying here, because Rosalind will not be able to accomplish a single thing without me."

"I certainly could not," agreed Rosalind soberly.

"So, there we are," said Alice. "We shall have no problems at all."

"Well," said Amelia slowly. "As I see it, there is one very real problem."

"Which is?" asked Rosalind.

Amelia looked shocked. "Well, I don't have a thing to wear, do I?"

CHAPTER TEN

The Diligent Men of Bow Street

"He knows many things which, if told, would set London on fire."

Bury, Charlotte, *The Diary of a Lady-in-Waiting*

"What's it looking like out there, Lavender?" John Townsend waved Stephen Lavender into his lavishly appointed private office. The gilded clock on the mantel was just chiming the hour. It was five in the morning, and Townsend had been at his desk a day and a night.

The famed Bow Street Police Station was seldom quiet. The principal officers and the "runners" might be the most well known of the station's functionaries, but they were far from the only persons involved in the station's work. There was also a small army of clerks, who sorted the cases as well as created and curated the mountains of documents needed by the station and the magistrate's court. Then there were the constables and captains of the foot and horse patrols. In times like these, with mobs roaming the streets, accosting the public, and breaching the peace, the night patrols were vitally important. The council and the lord mayor were touchy about calling out the militia to occupy more than a street or two around the houses of the great. That left it to Bow Street and its few sister stations to keep the peace across a broad swath of the city.

This job had been made that much harder because yesterday the queen had returned to London. This ill-advised and indecorous move had sent all London's rowdy, idle cits pouring into the streets to shout their approval. And, of course, by the time night fell, that shouting had been accompanied by heavy drinking.

"We arrested a few dozens," Lavender told Townsend. Lavender was a narrow man. There was a joke going around that he'd gotten his place because he could slip through cracks and catch thieves in their dens. But narrow also described Lavender's thinking. Lavender saw only the job in front of him. That made him tenacious, and his tenacity made him useful. This was a liability. A first-rate officer had to be a creative man. He needed to consider the full scope of his circumstances and how duty and the law could be put to the better service of the Crown. He needed to anticipate where circumstances might lead and work to head them off.

There were still times when he regretted the loss of Adam Harkness. Harkness was a thinking man. Unfortunately, Harkness's thoughts had led him down unsuitable, dangerously democratic pathways. Townsend blamed the Thorne woman.

". . . arrested, charged with disorderly conduct and property damage," Lavender was saying. Townsend cursed himself and forced his attention back to the man. He was woolgathering, and that would never do.

Townsend motioned Lavender to a chair. "Coffee?" he asked as he lifted the pot.

"Thank you, sir." Lavender sat and took the cup Mr. Townsend handed him.

Lavender just had time to take a swallow when a fresh knock sounded on the office door.

"Come!" called Townsend.

The door opened, and Sampson Goutier leaned in.

"Ah, Goutier!" said Townsend, genuinely pleased. "Come in. Lavender was just giving me his report on the conditions we're likely to face today."

Sampson Goutier had recently been promoted to principal officer, filling the spot left vacant when Adam Harkness turned his back on Bow Street and Townsend personally. There had been quite a bit of discussion between Townsend, Stafford, and the other officers about the advisability of the promotion. Goutier and Harkness were close friends. Lavender had been dead set against it, and Stafford had sided with him. But Townsend had overruled them both. Goutier was a good man, was broadly experienced and, unlike Lavender, possessed of an expansive view of the gargantuan snarl that was London.

"You worry too much about Harkness, Stafford," Townsend had told him. "But I agree we need to take some precautionary measures, and this is one."

As long as Goutier remained a friend of Adam Harkness, it was better to keep him close and make quite sure he knew which side his bread was buttered on. This was especially true in case Harkness and that Thorne woman took it into their heads to interfere in any of Bow Street's business.

That, at least, was reasoning Stafford could appreciate. Lavender had shrugged and acquiesced. Or, at least, he had appeared to. Lavender was not a deep man, but he knew how to hold a grudge, and Townsend had the feeling he was simply biding his time.

And from Goutier's closed expression, Townsend suspected he knew it, too.

Physically, Goutier was a direct opposite of thin White Stephen Lavender. Sampson Goutier was a tall, broad Black man. His parents had come to London from Barbados, via

Paris, and Goutier had been with the river police before he'd joined Bow Street and worked his way up through the ranks.

Which, as it happened, was another reason Lavender and some of the others did not like him. They distrusted a man who had come to his rank without breeding and family. Townsend had done both, which gave him some sympathy for Goutier. But—and this was crucial—such men as they must know their place. God made some men to lead and some to serve, and the order had to be preserved. That was the fact that underlaid all the rest of their work.

As Goutier sat down, Townsend poured another cup of coffee and pushed it forward. "Lavender was just giving me a report. Go on, won't you, Lavender?"

Lavender obliged. "The militias are keeping the streets mostly clear, but it's a struggle. Lord Sidmouth's house was attacked, the Duke of Wellington's carriage had its windows broken . . ." He shook his head. "Whenever our men catch up to them, the mob just melts away in front of them and re-forms in the next street. And today it's bound to be worse."

"I agree," said Goutier. "The queen's arrived. Everyone knows where she's staying. I went past the house on my way in, and the crowds are already forming. Talked with a Lieutenant Howard there. He says now that the sun's up, it's far more than just drunkards or agitators. Says all sorts of respectable folks are swarming in, and their wives with them."

Lavender's face twisted at the idea of respectable women displaying themselves in the streets. Townsend understood, but now was not the time for overmuch delicacy.

"Well, we shall let the gentlemen in the scarlet coats deal with the ladies who wish to play at politics," said Townsend with a depreciating smile. Lavender chuckled. Goutier did not. "In the meantime, we will handle the real work." He leaned forward. "This is where we'll want your help, Goutier," said Townsend. "You know London's byways as well as any man.

You'll direct the patrols to the alehouses and gin mills, where the troublemakers are likely to congregate. You know who I'm talking about—radicals and malcontents and such like. They are the kernels around which the mob will form, and we must root them out." He sat back, satisfied with his metaphor.

"Are we waiting for the malcontents to act or just clearing them out on principle?" asked Goutier mildly.

Lavender frowned hard. Townsend didn't like the question, but Goutier's tone was so bland, he couldn't take immediate offense, either.

"I want our people there listening and taking note," said Townsend. "And I want the constables stationed so they can bring in the troublemakers before they have a chance to get started."

"Disturbing the peace should cover most of it," said Goutier, his statement as bland as his question had been. "I'll pass it on to the patrol captains."

"Good," said Townsend. "The militias will try to take the credit for keeping the streets calm, but I want Bow Street in the thick of it. I want to be able to report to His Majesty that we were not found wanting in our duty or our loyalties."

Another knock sounded on the door. Lavender was on his feet and opening it before Townsend had to say a word. This time, it was the stooped figure of John Stafford who stood at the threshold.

Townsend suppressed a sigh. He very much wanted to be on his way home. "Yes, Mr. Stafford?"

"A word, if you please, Mr. Townsend." Stafford slid a glance toward Goutier and Lavender.

"Of course. Lavender, Goutier, keep me abreast. And close the door, if you would."

Both men made their bows, and left smartly.

"Coffee?" Townsend gestured to the pot. "Stone cold by now, I'm afraid, but better than nothing."

Stafford's placid face suggested he did not agree. Reading Stafford was an art. He had spent years recording the statements of prisoners and officers and giving depositions in court, as well as countless hours in the boisterous lobby of the station, helping the junior clerks take statements and complaints from the crowds of Londoners who inevitably congregated on the station's doorstep.

But Stafford had other duties, as well. What made Bow Street effective was its network of informants—the network that Mr. Stafford managed with as much care and attention as Townsend managed the runners.

"What have you to tell us about the current business, Mr. Stafford?"

"It seems the matter is largely what it appears." Stafford sat down carefully, as if he feared the chair might break apart under him. But then, Stafford did everything carefully. "The lower class of cits in the city has determined that the queen has been badly wronged. They don't like the king." Townsend swallowed his anger at this. "And the queen's arrival and the impending divorce trial are excuses to express their displeasure and, of course, to drink and run riot. So far, my contacts have not given any indication of a seditious conspiracy or plot of any kind, although that may yet come."

"It may." Townsend knuckled his eyes. "Now that Parliament's got its teeth in the thing, we can expect it to drag on for weeks. Perhaps months." Townsend's skin curdled at the thought. "What of our other matter?" he asked.

"I have had a note from my man this morning," replied Stafford. "He says the document is in his hands."

"Excellent." Townsend sat up straight, the news sending a jolt of fresh energy through him. "How soon will you have it in yours?"

"I go to him this afternoon."

"What? He cannot bring it here?"

Stafford's expression did not shift. "He does not wish to call extra attention to the matter, and I agree."

Townsend felt his face flush. "The situation is too delicate to leave the document in the hands of such a person. What if he decides to demand a higher price or to sell it outright to some other party? What if he decides to give it to the newspapers?"

Dear God . . . Townsend felt his chest tighten at the very idea.

Stafford remained infuriatingly calm. The man was rumored to have ink rather than blood in his veins. Normally, Townsend considered this a positive attribute. Right now it made him want to wring the clerk's crooked neck.

Steady, steady. He could not be guided by a temper frayed from one sleepless night.

"My man is not known for giving away valuable items," said Stafford. "Neither is he a fool. He knows that if he sells it to anyone besides me, he will find himself in very grave trouble with various aspects of the law." There was a flash in Stafford's dark eyes that was as close as he ever came to a smile. "What does concern me, Mr. Townsend, is reports that Mr. Harkness has visited Mrs. Fitzherbert, and in the company of Miss Thorne."

Townsend did not let himself blink or allow his expression to shift. *Damn it,* he thought. *Damn the man and damn that woman.*

"Miss Thorne's an enterprising female, as well as an interfering one," he said, striving to match Stafford's bland tone. "I'm sure she offered Mrs. Fitzherbert her services for an excellent price."

"And if Mrs. Fitzherbert has asked her and Mr. Harkness to retrieve her property?"

Townsend allowed his brows to arch. "Don't tell me you think they can get to your man before you do? You just told me all was in hand, or as good as."

"It is," replied Stafford. "But if they are able to find out how the document came to be missing . . ."

Townsend spread his hands. "What then? What will they do? Harkness is nothing but a common thief-taker now, and one in a dubious association with an unmarried woman, who is rapidly becoming notorious."

"One with connections to the newspapers, as well as to some powerful Queenites," Stafford pointed out. "They can talk, Townsend. They can spread rumors."

Townsend felt himself smile. Here, they were on his home territory.

"Stafford, you are a man of sense and experience, but you do not understand the way things work among the aristocracy," he said patiently. "That society is dedicated to maintaining its own balance. It is fiercely vigilant of its own interests. The queen has no party there."

"Lady Jersey—"

"Is being politely ignored on the subject," said Townsend. "No one dares contradict her openly because she may rescind their Almack's vouchers, but it goes no further. I have it on the very best—the *very* best—authority that no one of importance thinks her support of the queen is anything more than another show."

"Where one goes, the others will follow," said Stafford stubbornly.

"Not so. The more the mob and the middling classes come out to cheer the queen, the more our first circles will come to regard Lady Jersey as tainted by the association. Those whose support might truly do some good, or who could pose some danger, will avoid her to avoid contagion. The lords, and their ladies, will rally around the king to preserve their reputations among their own kind."

"I am amazed at your confidence."

"I understand our aristocracy, Mr. Stafford. All my long years at the king's right hand gave me a particular insight."

He beamed. "After all, it was one of our most prominent ladies who warned us to act, was it not?"

"She is not our lady," said Stafford sourly.

And there it was. A distrust of the woman because she was foreign born. With no consideration to her place in society, or to how much good she had done them in the past. "If Miss Thorne makes any trouble, our lady will deal with her. Our job, *your* job, is to retrieve the document. After that, a good hot fire puts an end to the matter."

"Well then." Stafford rose. "I suppose I had better go see to my business and let you see to yours."

They nodded to each other, and Stafford left Townsend. Townsend, exhausted as he was, stayed behind his desk for quite some time, trying to see into his own fogged mind and wondering if perhaps this time he had missed something.

CHAPTER ELEVEN

In the Clear Light of Day

*"If no one is to read what one writes, there is no
satisfaction in writing; and if anybody does see it,
mischief ensues."*

Bury, Charlotte, *The Diary of a Lady-in-Waiting*

"Rosalind!"

Rosalind blinked, her mind rising heavily from sleep.
Usually, if someone needed to wake her, it was Laurel, the
upstairs maid and de facto lady's maid. This morning, however, it was Alice standing beside her bed, in threadbare slippers and rumpled blue wrapper, her nightcap still on her
head.

"What is it, Alice?" Rosalind struggled to push herself upright.

"This." Alice dropped a newspaper on Rosalind's quilt.
"You were seen!"

"Yes, I know. I suppose I forgot to tell you." Rosalind
blinked down at the newspaper. In the center column was a
large dark headline:

WHAT'S WORRYING MRS. FITZHERBERT?

*With our beleaguered Queen Caroline returned
to London to defend herself from the petition for
divorce being most cruelly leveled against her, attention once again turns to the woman at the root
of all this strife—the venerable and, so say all her
admirers, amiable Mrs. Maria Fitzherbert.*

Rosalind wondered where Mrs. Fitzherbert was now and
if she had read this description of herself.

*Mrs. Fitzherbert has yet to voice a public opin-
ion over the matter of the man long purported to
be her husband attempting to obtain a divorce for
a second marriage, which may not have been legal
in the eyes of God or Man. But surely, she must
harbor secret hopes, or fears, that there might soon
arise an opportunity to confirm her particular status, at least in the eyes of the public.*

*These days, when the Lady About Ton is faced
with any seemingly insurmountable difficulty—be
it deciding which silver service is the best choice
for an upcoming dinner with Lady Formidable, or
how to obtain a set of possibly indiscreet letters
that have fallen into the hands of Mr. Scoundrele-
son—she increasingly turns to one Miss Rosalind
Thorne.*

*Now it seems Miss Thorne's reputation as a
solver of all problems large and small has carried
her as far as Mrs. Fitzherbert's doorway, which
portal she was seen entering last evening in the
company of Mr. Adam "Watchdog" Harkness, for-
merly of the famous Bow Street Runners . . .*

THE MATTER OF THE SECRET BRIDE   83

Rosalind laid the paper down. Slowly, with as much dignity as she could muster, she folded the bedcovers aside and stood. She walked quite calmly over to the window. The drapes were still closed. Using two fingers, she very, very carefully lifted the edge back.

The street below was a sea of men's bodies. They pressed against the area railing and would have swarmed the steps if Mortimer had not been standing there, arms folded and sleeves rolled up to display the muscled and tattooed forearms, which proclaimed to the world that he had once served in the Royal Navy and therefore was no stranger to a serious brawl.

Slowly, so the movement would not draw any stray glances, Rosalind closed the drapes and stepped back from the window.

"Did Amelia get away all right?"

"She left at first light. The street was still empty."

"Well, thank goodness for that." She rubbed her eyes. She'd gotten only a few hours of sleep. They had all stayed up late last night, working to alter a plain, conservative blue silk dress of Rosalind's for the shorter, rounder Amelia. "Well, I had best get myself dressed. Can you send Laurel to me?"

Alice knew Rosalind better than anyone, even Adam. As Rosalind hoped, her friend understood at once that she was not ready to talk. So, all Alice said was, "Yes, of course. And I meant to tell you, Mrs. Singh has breakfast ready downstairs."

"Thank you."

Alice retreated and closed the door. Once she did, Rosalind uttered a selection of words that would have shocked Mortimer's former shipmates. This gave vent to her immediate anger, at herself and at the world in general, but it did nothing to address the immediate problem. The men Adam promised to send had clearly not yet arrived, while the news-papermen had all proved to be early risers.

Rosalind hurried to her writing table. By the time Laurel appeared, Rosalind had finished her first note. "This needs to be taken down the street to Dr. Kempshead."

If Adam had still been with Bow Street, Rosalind would have written to him at the station and asked for help. He would have dispatched a clutch of constables to clear the scrum outside and to stand guard afterward.

As things stood, however, Rosalind did not have the lux-ury of being able to command a constable whenever it might be convenient. Yes, she and Adam still had friends at the sta-tion, but her reputation with Bow Street's most senior officer, Mr. Townsend, was only that of interfering female. Any re-quest known to be from her was likely to be ignored or to incur an extra charge. Any officer or constable who answered a request without informing Mr. Townsend would put their livelihood in danger.

Dr. Kempshead, however, was a respected physician, and if he made a request that the street be cleared and quieted, that would be paid attention to.

"The butcher's boy is downstairs with the day's delivery," said Laurel. "I'll see if he can go round to the doctor's on his way back."

"Thank you," said Rosalind gratefully.

That initial matter attended to, Rosalind wrote two other notes. The first was to Mrs. Levitton, asking permission to call later that day. The second was to Adam, letting him know that it had now been publicly reported that they were both seen going to Mrs. Fitzherbert's, in case he had not read the paper that morning.

She had the notes sealed by the time Laurel returned. The maid pocketed the missives and promised they would go by hand as soon as Miss Thorne was dressed.

While Laurel helped her into a light day frock of blue patterned muslin, Rosalind's stomach rumbled in a most undignified manner. She was desperately hungry, but at the same time, she was conscious of an urge to be sick. She could not help but remembering Alice's warning from the night before. And the mob that had stopped their carriage. And the king on horseback in front of Mrs. Fitzherbert's door. Not to mention Mrs. Fitzherbert herself.

She also remembered her own misgivings about agreeing to inquire into this matter and wondered if she should have listened to them.

But it was too late for that. She could not call any of yesterday's events back. Amelia would already be at Tilney Street. Adam was surely on his way to talk with Ron Ranking.

Still, Rosalind managed to drag together the appearance of calm so she could enter the dining room without causing immediate exclamations. Alice was already tucking into the breakfast Mrs. Singh had laid out on the sideboard. Normally, by this time, the curtains had been drawn back to allow sunlight into the room. Today the curtains remained closed, and the lamps were lit. The effect was stuffy rather than cozy. But Rosalind did not remark on it. Instead, she helped herself to coddled eggs and a beautifully warm roll from the modest sideboard. She carried her plate to the table and sat down.

And found she could do nothing but stare at the fresh food and listen to the vague rumble of men's shouts and jeers that filtered through the curtained window.

"Eat, Rosalind." Alice filled her teacup. "I'm assuming you've sent for the constables?"

"I've sent for Dr. Kempshead to send for them," Rosalind told her. "And Adam said he would be calling in some men to help."

"Well, that's taken care of, then." Alice spread jam lavishly on her roll. "What's your plan, Rosalind?"

"The first order of business is to call on Mrs. Fitzherbert and make sure all is in order there. Then I must speak with Mrs. Levitton. Now, Alice, I have—"

The crowd noise outside picked up in volume and outrage. Rosalind turned her head toward the closed curtains. Could Dr. Kempshead have summoned help this quickly? Or had Adam's men arrived?

Alice hopped up from her chair and ran to the window. Rosalind followed and peered over Alice's head as she lifted the curtains to see the commotion.

And commotion it was. Mortimer had leapt off the porch steps and waded into the crowd. But he was not alone. Several young men and a pair of boys, all in canary-yellow and sky-blue livery, were setting to with the crowd of newspapermen and seemingly getting the best of them. While Rosalind and Alice watched, the newspapermen, in their dark coats and low-crowned hats, scattered before the determined blows of the men and boys in colorful silks.

Alice laughed out loud at the incongruity of it all. Rosalind's gaze, however, fastened on the carriage with its matched chestnut bay horses and the crest on the door.

She left the window and rang the bell. "We'll need coffee and rolls in the front parlor as soon as possible," she said to Mrs. Napier as soon as she entered the dining room. "And when the lady arrives, show her in immediately."

Rosalind was already on the way to the door when Alice called, "Oh, good heavens! Rosalind, did you see the crest on the carriage?"

Rosalind didn't pause to answer her. She took herself into the parlor and, with a quick sweep of her gaze, ascertained that all was in order and that all traces of Alice's celebration had been cleared away. She moved the three volumes of

Eversward from the table to the bookshelf. Outside, the noise, and presumably the crowd, had dissipated. Rosalind settled into her usual chair and had just time enough to compose herself before the parlor door opened again.

Claire came into the room. "Pardon me, Miss Thorne . . ."

She got no farther. Sarah Villiers, the Countess of Jersey, strode past her.

"Well, Miss Thorne!" Lady Jersey declared. "What on *earth* have you done!"

CHAPTER TWELVE

A New Situation

"If wrong, it should not be done; if right, it should be done openly, and in the face of all her enemies."

Bury, Charlotte, *The Diary of a Lady-in-Waiting*

The first thing Amelia noticed about Number 6 Tilney Street was the unusual number of windows, especially on the second floor, where a conservatory curved out over the garden.

The second thing she noticed was the pair of slouching men in dark coats and stovepipe trousers arguing with a third man, who held a stout staff in the crook of his arm and stood squarely in front of the gate.

Amelia gave the quarrelers a wide berth as she headed toward the area railing that surrounded the stairway to the servants' entrance. Another man touched his wide, battered hat brim to her, all polite.

"Miss McGowan, is it?" he asked.

"That's right. And you are . . . ?"

"Jim Geery, at your service." He bowed. "Mr. Harkness

said we was to keep an eye out for you, and to lend a hand if need be."

"Well, thanks for that," Amelia said, but she didn't linger to talk. She had a job to get on with. Amelia took herself down the area stairs to the servants' door. She tried not to think too much about being stuck in a house where she might need help from a man with a stout stick and a strong right arm.

When she knocked, the door was answered by a harried young woman with a grubby apron and her sleeves rolled up past her elbows. When Amelia gave her name and business, the girl rushed her inside with barely a word.

Something was definitely on. Miss Thorne had said one of the royal dukes was coming to dinner, and Amelia could believe it. The corridors were filled with all manner of persons—upper and lower servants both—all of them hurrying back and forth. An enormous banging and a string of shouts in several different languages emerged from the kitchen.

The girl left Amelia standing at the threshold of the servants' hall and bolted back into the hurly-burly without a word.

There was, however, no time to think much about any of it. The door at the far side of the hall opened, and Amelia found herself face-to-face with a woman who was quite obviously the housekeeper for this establishment.

She did not look happy.

Best not waste her time then. "Amelia McGowan," she said. "I'm here for the place of lady's maid."

"Hmph." The housekeeper's gaze raked her slowly up and down. Amelia stood still and let the other woman have her look, even though holding on to her valise was starting to make her hand ache. Entering into a new household meant putting oneself up for inspection. It might be the lady of the house who would hire her, but if the staff didn't approve, the job would quickly become impossible. It all began with the housekeeper.

Amelia felt fairly confident in her appearance. Miss Thorne had brought out a sober blue silk gown that was exactly the sort of thing an upstanding lady's maid would wear. She and Miss Thorne had spent several hours the night before taking up the hems and letting out the sides so it would fit. With the addition of her straw bonnet with the black ribbon and her best black gloves, she fancied she looked ready for anything. Her only visible jewelry was a silver chain with a small cross on it. Her other ornament, the ribbon with the gold heart that Alice had bought her, she wore beneath her gown, where no one could see it and ask questions.

"Young one, aren't you?" said the housekeeper finally.

"Twenty-five next month," said Amelia, which was stretching the truth only a little. "I hope that will be satisfactory."

"Hmph." The housekeeper was a sturdy woman with a broad face and sandy brown skin. Her dark hair had been ruthlessly tamed into a plait, which she wore as a coronet. Amelia tried not to take the sour face personally. According to Miss Thorne, Amelia was taking the place of someone who any number of the staff might say was fired under false pretenses. This was more than enough to account for the hostile glare. In addition, Amelia's arrival was yet one more complication while there was a dinner party to get ready for.

"I'm Mrs. DeLupe," the housekeeper offered finally. "I been with Mrs. Fitzherbert going on twenty years now."

"Pleased to make your acquaintance, Mrs. DeLupe." Amelia made her best curtsy. She had no intention of leaving anyone with the impression she was one of those standoffish sorts who fancied themselves better than the rest of the staff.

"Madam asked to see you as soon as you arrived. You can leave your things by the door. Faller will take them to your room."

"Thank you."

Amelia hung her cloak and bonnet by the door and put the valise beneath them. Then she followed Mrs. DeLupe down the long central corridor between the workrooms and up the servants' stairs. It was slow progress. Every few feet it seemed someone stopped the housekeeper to ask a question or she stopped them to rap out an order.

They had reached the foot of the stairs when Mrs. DeLupe finally decided to notice Amelia's quizzical look.

"The Duke and Duchess of York are to dine with madam this evening. I trust you will be able to rise to this occasion."

"Of course," Amelia answered. Thank goodness Miss Thorne had tipped her off. Who would believe the king's brother would be friends with his cast-off mistress? *Wife*, Amelia reminded herself. Not that it made things less surprising. "Although, I would have thought—"

Mrs. DeLupe cut her off. "We do not think, McGowan. We serve."

And that tells me what I need to know about you, doesn't it? Amelia kept the thought far away from her expression.

Not that Mrs. DeLupe was looking at her. She was climbing the stairs, and Amelia hurried to keep up.

"You will know that this is a very particular household, and madam has exacting requirements." Mrs. DeLupe's words stabbed through the air like a needle through stiff fabric. "Discretion is required from all of us, above anything. The first hint of gossip means dismissal. Mr. Holm"—that would be the butler, Amelia assumed—"and I have madam's complete confidence. Neither one of us will hesitate when it comes to making that dismissal should there be any talking out of turn. Do you understand?"

"Yes, Mrs. DeLupe." *Because what else would I say?*

"Good." They'd arrived at the door to upstairs. Mrs. DeLupe led her through to the second floor and the family rooms.

She looked Amelia up and down again, in case she'd become unacceptably disheveled during their journey from belowstairs. She then scratched at a door and opened it.

"The new lady's maid is here, madam," Mrs. DeLupe announced. She stepped back to give Amelia room to enter.

Amelia squared her shoulders and breezed past. She'd sort out Mrs. DeLupe later. Just now she needed to meet the king's wife.

Mrs. Fitzherbert was exactly as Miss Thorne had described her. A surprisingly matronly woman who dressed conservatively but well. She definitely didn't look like a temptress scheming to bring down the king. Or like a woman with money troubles. The good black satin that made up her dress had cost a pretty penny, even before you added in the antique lace trimming.

She did, however, look fair tired. But that didn't dampen the sharp suspicion with which she looked Amelia up and down. She may have agreed to this business, but she was not entirely happy about it.

Going to have my work cut out for me.

"Thank you for coming on such short notice," Mrs. Fitzherbert said. "As you will have seen, we are going to be quite busy today. The Duke and Duchess of York are coming to dinner."

"Never fear, madam." Amelia drew herself up. "We'll have you ready."

"Thank you." The relief in Mrs. Fitzherbert's eyes was unmistakable. "Now, Mrs. DeLupe will show you to your room so you can have a little time to settle in."

"Thank you, madam." Amelia gave a small curtsy. "I shall be ready as soon as you have need of me."

"Very good," Mrs. Fitzherbert said. It was acknowledgment and dismissal.

Amelia turned and walked back out into the corridor, past

Mrs. DeLupe. This time the housekeeper's hard glance told her she might just be acceptable.

Amelia let out the breath she'd been holding.

Every other job she'd had, Amelia had slept in the maids' quarters at the top of the house, right below whatever attics there might be. If the house was big enough, there would be a whole corridor of rooms for the various maids and a door at the end of it, which could be locked to deter any males of the species who might consider mischief. Sometimes it even worked.

But a lady's maid didn't sleep with the rest of the girls. She had her own room next to her lady's, which allowed her to be there instantly anytime her employer called—day or night.

So, instead of going up the concealed servants' stairs, Mrs. DeLupe took them up the broad stairway from the entrance and straight down the family corridor. But to Amelia's surprise, the door to her room was already open when they reached it, and the room itself was occupied.

"Faller!" snapped Mrs. DeLupe at the young footman idling inside. "What are you doing there?"

"Just bringing up McGowan's bag." He gestured to Amelia's valise, which was sitting on the trunk at the foot of the narrow bed.

The housekeeper frowned hard and narrowed her eyes. It was a look that said she would not be taken in this time.

"Well, now that you've done that, you can be about your business, before Mr. Holm starts bellowing for you."

"Yes, Mrs. DeLupe," Faller said, all polite and correct.

The housekeeper watched him go, shaking her head. "You look out for that one, McGowan."

"Trouble?"

"Not as such," said Mrs. DeLupe. "But he fancies himself God's gift to women, doesn't he? He's had a look at you now, and you're younger than some and pretty, for all that ginger hair of yours. Means he's more than likely to come sniffing about."

"Well, I'll say thanks for the warning," Amelia told her. "Nothing's worse than backstairs romance when there's a job to be done."

"Quite right." Mrs. DeLupe's expression softened a bit more. "I'll leave you to get settled. I've no doubt madam will have need of you soon enough."

Left to her own devices, Amelia set about unpacking her small valise. Alice had promised to have her trunk sent over later today. This bag had just enough in it to get by for a day or two, in case there was any delay.

The room itself was scarcely bigger than the ones she'd had as a chambermaid, but it was furnished like one of the family rooms, with carpets and a mirror and a clothes press and even a vanity table. There wasn't a window or a fireplace, but otherwise she looked to be more comfortable than she'd been anywhere except Miss Thorne's.

Even as she was thinking this, the hairs on the back of her neck prickled. In the next heartbeat, she was aware of a long, slow creaking. Amelia whirled around to find the door to the corridor hanging open and Faller standing at the threshold, looking entirely too pleased with himself.

"It wasn't shut properly," he said.

"Liar," Amelia shot back.

He ignored her. In fact, he took a step inside. "All right, then?"

Amelia gave him a look guaranteed to freeze a cheeky young man dead at twenty paces. "And what do you want?"

"Just to make sure you've got all you need." He drew himself up, snapped his heels together, and bowed as if she was a visiting duchess. "Thomas Faller, at your service."

Under other circumstances, Amelia would have sent him away with a flea in his ear. But she was here to make friends and hear all the gossip. Thomas Faller already looked to be a bit dodgy. Who better to tell her all the business of the house? Especially business some might want to keep hidden?

Amelia lifted her chin haughtily. "Well, I've no need of your service, thank you very much." She turned away too quickly and picked up the shawl she'd been folding when he came in. "Not just yet, anyway."

From the corner of her eye, Amelia saw that remark had earned her a saucy grin. "Well, you've only to say the word and I shall be right at your side."

"I'll remember that. But you'd best be getting on. That Mr. Holm sounds a right tartar."

Faller shrugged. "Oh, he's all right. I've seen worse."

Amelia laid her folded shawl across the end of her new bed. "Been in service long?"

An expression she couldn't read rippled across his face, but he answered easily. "Not as long as some. Wasn't bred to it like most of the others here. You?"

"All my life."

"Well, you know the way of things, then."

"What do you mean by that?"

Faller shrugged again. "Lots of the quality come through here." He jerked his chin toward the door. "They're particular and confidential, and they sometimes expect a few extras."

Amelia stiffened, and Faller laughed. "Oh, not that! This is a decent house, decent as they come, anyway. Just, sometimes a word here or there, a bit of keeping your eyes open . . ."

"Or keeping your mouth shut?" she put in dryly.

"That's the way." Faller nodded approvingly. "But careful like, you get me?"

Amelia locked eyes with him and let him see she understood. Plainly, he thought he could show her a thing or two about how to get on in the world, and she might as well just let him think that. Let him believe they were two of a kind, or that they could be.

"Is that what happened to the one that was here before me?" she ventured. "She wasn't careful?"

Faller's face fell. "She was turned off for a thief. They're saying she robbed madam's strongbox."

"Did she?"

Faller glanced over his shoulder, for the first time showing a trace of concern. "Wouldn't have believed it of her, but who knows?"

Amelia made a great show of arranging her brushes on the dressing table in a neat line. "There's plenty that pay for all sorts of things," she said. "Letters and such like."

"What makes you say that?" Faller snapped.

Now Amelia shrugged. She nudged the tortoiseshell comb Alice had given her so it lay tidily next to the carved wooden brush she'd bought secondhand. "Lady I used to work for," she said. She had worked out the story on the way here and was quietly pleased to get to use it so soon. "She had an outside gentleman friend. And then somebody got hold of her letters. Caused a huge ruckus, let me tell you." She met Faller's gaze again. "They said it was one of the footmen who stole them."

"More fool him, then," said Faller. "You got to keep in mind where your best interests really lie, that's what I say." His eyes went distant and more than a little worried.

What are you thinking of just now, Mr. Faller? Amelia wondered. But it was too soon to be asking such a question. "Well," she said briskly, "*I* say you'd best get back to your work." As much as she wanted to keep him talking, it wouldn't do for her to be caught having one of the staff idling in her room, especially when it was one of the men.

Faller sighed. "Yeah, probably right. But I'll be seeing you, Miss McGowan." He winked.

She laughed and made a little shooing gesture. "Go on, Thomas Faller, and take your sauce with you."

He bowed again, this time in a showy, mocking style. He also closed the door firmly behind him as he left.

For a time, Amelia stared thoughtfully at the place where he'd stood.

That, McGowan was either a good beginning or the start of some trouble. Amelia shivered. Because it just might be both.

CHAPTER THIRTEEN

Lady Jersey's Opinion

*"Lady Jersey is very active in making proselytes
for the Queen, but very cautious herself."*

Quennell, Peter, ed., *The Private Letters of Princess Lieven*

Not only was the Right Honorable Sarah Villiers, Countess of Jersey, the wife of the Fifth Earl of Jersey—which would have been enough for most women—but she was also the undisputed leader of the board of patronesses for Almack's ballroom. Almack's Wednesday night balls were the heart and soul of the *ton*'s marriage mart, and no one was admitted to the festivities without Lady Jersey's acquiescence. Her slightest disapproval could, and did, crush the hopes of the noble houses for generations.

Because of this, Lady Jersey was regularly named as the most powerful and influential hostess in London society. Her arrival at Rosalind's door would be even more widely reported and speculated about than Rosalind's arrival at Mrs. Fitzherbert's.

The sensation of seasickness Rosalind had felt earlier threatened to return. She suppressed it ruthlessly and rose to greet her guest.

"Good morning, Lady Jersey. I am so glad you have decided to call."

"Decided!" cried Lady Jersey. "What choice did I have!"

Without waiting for an invitation, Lady Jersey plumped herself down in the chair farthest from the fire. For Lady Jersey, strict personal decorum was something to be expected in others. When it came to her own behavior, her standards were noticeably more lax.

"Now, no more delays." She pointed an imperious finger directly at Rosalind. "Explain yourself, Miss Thorne!"

"I would be glad to," Rosalind said placidly. Lady Jersey abominated displays of emotion, in others. "If you could please let me know which point you wish me to clarify?"

Lady Jersey had already sprung out of her chair and begun to pace. "Which point!" she cried. "Miss Thorne, are you joking? *Joking!* When the fate of our queen, our *queen*—who ought to be respected as the very *soul* of the kingdom!—hangs in the balance, and *you*, Miss Thorne! You! Are seen entering the house of *that woman*!"

"I do apologize for any distress you have been caused, Lady Jersey." It did not matter that she had done nothing. Once Lady Jersey perceived an injury, it would be impossible to change the subject until an apology had been delivered.

Rosalind sat down in her own chair, hoping her gesture would encourage Lady Jersey to sit back down, as well. Lady Jersey, however, did not seem to notice she'd moved.

"I have trusted you, Miss Thorne! I have *defended* you. Others challenged your want of taste and *ton*. They have even suggested you were descending to *gross commerce*." She sneered the words. "That you were deliberately turning the most delicate matters of friendship and private understanding into a *profession*. But I, *I*"—she laid her hand over her heart—"said that Miss Thorne maintains an impeccable judgment, taste, and discretion."

"I have always been grateful for your support," murmured Rosalind.

"So, what on earth could you have to do with *that woman?*"

Rosalind did not answer. The parlor door had opened again, and Mortimer entered. The footman's coat was crumpled, and he had the beginnings of a truly impressive black eye. This in no way affected his dignity as he carried in the coffee tray, which contained not only more warm rolls but also ginger biscuits and an apple tart.

"Thank you, Mortimer," said Rosalind. "I will call if anything further is required."

Mortimer bowed and departed. Rosalind hoped that Mrs. Singh would provide a poultice for his eye. It looked truly painful.

"May I pour you some coffee, Lady Jersey?" Lady Jersey had never lost the habit of taking coffee first thing in the morning, even though tea had long been the more fashionable beverage. "And won't you try a slice of this tart? It is a new recipe, and I would be grateful for your opinion."

The deflection worked. Lady Jersey could never resist being asked to pronounce judgment on any matter. She left off her exclamations, took the plate and the coffee cup that Rosalind passed her, and returned to her chair. She sipped, and she nibbled, her face sour with concentration. This gave Rosalind a few crucial moments to breathe and steady her nerves as she fixed her own coffee.

"Quite acceptable," Lady Jersey mumbled. "A bit energetically spiced perhaps, but quite acceptable." Indeed, she'd left behind nothing but crumbs.

"That was my opinion," Rosalind told her. It wasn't. She loved Mrs. Singh's flavorful reinterpretations of the otherwise unvaried English cuisine. Rosalind permitted herself a decorous swallow of coffee before she set the cup down. "Now, if I may, ma'am, I do understand your concern regarding the report in the paper. I read it myself this morning, and I was quite distressed."

"Well, I am relieved to hear *that*. I must say, Miss Thorne, I would be *most* disappointed if you became one of those publicity-seeking sorts of women."

Rosalind bit the tip of her tongue. "Certainly not," she murmured. "I do admit that I received a letter from Mrs. Fitzherbert last night requesting a consultation on a matter of personal business. Given her delicate position in society, I did not feel I could refuse her. I deeply regret that I was not more careful. I should have realized that her house would be watched for any unusual activity."

"Which I could have informed you of, had you seen fit to take me into your confidence." Lady Jersey sniffed.

So. That was it. Lady Jersey was offended not by Rosalind's actions but by the fact that she'd had to learn about them from the papers. Her conversation with Alice from last night flickered through Rosalind's mind.

"Lady Jersey is not my patroness," she'd told Alice. Lady Jersey, it seemed, did not agree.

"I had intended to call this morning," said Rosalind, which was not a complete untruth. "But the possibility that I might be followed by those persons"—she nodded significantly toward the window—"made me hesitate. The last thing I wished was to bring such unpleasantness to your door."

"Hmmph." But Rosalind could tell Lady Jersey was mollified. "Well, what is done cannot be undone. The important thing—no, the vital thing!—now is to prevent the king from being able to wriggle out from under the facts of his relationship with Mrs. Fitzherbert. I am the last, Miss Thorne—the very last—to wish that the personal be made public for anyone, let alone for the king! But he has brought this on himself!" She sighed at the deep tragedy of such misjudgment in one so highly born. "Now, what is it Mrs. Fitzherbert wanted of you?"

This was as gross a breach of etiquette as Rosalind had ever been a party to. Rosalind felt herself immediately grimly offended. How could anyone, even Lady Jersey, think that they simply had to ask and she would break a confidence?

Fortunately, she was saved from having to make any immediate reply by Mortimer entering with the salver in hand. On it lay not one, but two calling cards. Rosalind excused herself to Lady Jersey and took them. *Lady Anne Hamilton*, read the first. The second was for Lord Hamilton.

Rosalind's brows wanted to arch. Her mouth tried to frown. She did not allow either gesture.

"Please make my apologies, Mortimer," she said. "But I am not at home at present."

Mortimer bowed and retreated. Rosalind set the cards face down on the table at her elbow, pretending to ignore the way Lady Jersey craned her neck trying to read them.

"I do apologize for the interruption, ma'am," Rosalind said. "As to the other matter, of course I wish to help you, and Her Majesty, however I can. But as of yet, I have learned nothing beyond speculation and innuendo. It would go entirely against my conscience to say anything until I was in firm possession of the facts. I do not wish to cause alarm over what might turn out to be a trivial matter, especially—as you rightly point out—during such a time."

Condescension filled Lady Jersey's smile. "I have always admired your delicacy of feeling, Miss Thorne. But surely you understand that *because* the times are what they are, we must look to considerations beyond our personal inclinations." She leaned forward. "It is as women we must support the queen, Miss Thorne. If her rights are taken from her—if her husband can set her aside without proof—what is to become of the rest of us?"

It was not an idle question. English law declared that marriage made two persons into one. It did so by erasing the independent identity of the woman. The legal terms told it all.

An unmarried woman was *feme sole*—woman alone. A married woman, however, was *feme covert*. Woman hidden. The only separate right that law and custom recognized as remaining to her was the right to her husband's material support.

If it was declared that the hidden woman had been unfaithful, that last right vanished.

Women at all levels of society were frightened and outraged by the possibility of the king's divorce. If the king could discard his queen based on the mere accusation of infidelity, what chance did the rest of England's wives have?

Lady Jersey, it seemed, shared their fears. Rosalind was not surprised. Despite having been declared the arbiter of all that was correct in society, Lady Jersey was known to have carried on several affairs. And then there was her mother-in-law, Frances Villiers, the previous Lady Jersey. That lady had been one of George IV's many mistresses when he was still Prince of Wales.

The door opened again. Again, it was Mortimer, with the salver and three more cards. Rosalind took them up and laid them on the table without looking at them. "I am not at home to anyone, Mortimer," she said.

The footman was still looking at the cards where they lay, unread. Curiosity dug hard at Rosalind's ribs, but she did not relent. Mortimer bowed and retreated.

"Miss Thorne." Lady Jersey's tone changed, becoming confidential. "I ask you to understand me. I do not criticize His Majesty—of course I do not! But he is not able to see that this attempt to divorce the queen injures not only his reputation but also that of the Crown. Why, it threatens the very kingdom! But he is, in the end, simply a man, is he not?" Her smile turned knowing. "And men are so easily misled by their . . . weaknesses. I tell you in confidence, he has never recovered from the loss of his beloved daughter and her son. This has affected his judgment. It is our duty as his subjects to stand by him, and as Englishwomen to prevent him from injuring himself—just as we would protect our own husbands or brothers. Why, there are already rumors that he is thinking of returning to Mrs. Fitzherbert!"

Rosalind kept her expression mild, but only with difficulty. She needed to end this conversation and to remind Lady Jersey she was not entirely without resources of her own.

"Lady Jersey, I just realized, I forgot to inquire how your mother-in-law does."

Lady Jersey's mother-in-law, the dowager countess Frances Villiers, had had a singularly successful career as the king's mistress. When the then Prince George was forced to marry, it was rumored that Frances Villiers had personally selected Princess Caroline of Brunswick for his bride. It was further said that she had done so on the grounds that the princess would never become her rival for the prince's affections.

It was further rumored that part of the reason Sarah Villiers had begun the highly exclusive Almack's assemblies was to get out from under the long shadow cast by her mother-in-law's outrageous behavior.

Rosalind's question had the desired effect. Lady Jersey's mouth clamped shut. She drew herself up. "My mother-in-law is enjoying excellent health, thank you. She has taken a little cottage in the country for the summer."

"Really?" Rosalind raised her brows the barest fraction of an inch. "I was under the impression she preferred Brighton."

Lady Jersey sniffed. "Brighton is far too crowded for her taste."

"I have heard many people find it so," said Rosalind sympathetically. "Indeed, Mrs. Fitzherbert remarked on it the other day."

Rosalind sipped her coffee and watched Lady Jersey from under lowered lashes. The bolt had hit home. Lady Jersey was powerful, but she was not invulnerable. If gossip about the king and his relationships was to be brought up during the trial, the machinations of the previous Lady Jersey could easily be included. If that happened, the current Lady Jersey—despite all her efforts and influence—might find herself swept up in the tide.

"I am glad to hear that the dowager Lady Jersey has chosen a quiet retreat," said Rosalind conversationally. "No doubt her new home is too far from London for any persons"—again, she delicately nodded toward the window—"to pay unsolicited calls upon her."

The look of horror in the current Lady Jersey's eyes was real. "Surely they would not dare!"

Rosalind sighed. "Unfortunately, we've already had a taste of what the newspapermen would dare just this morning. Whatever can convince the reading public to choose their paper over some other is seen as fair game. Nothing is beyond the bounds of propriety."

"You cannot have heard—"

"Oh, no!" said Rosalind quickly. "I have not heard anything about any newspaper seeking out the dowager countess. However, with such a scrape and scramble to fill the pages, I should not be surprised if the thought occurred to some ambitious person. If you wished for me to make some inquiries among my acquaintance, to see if there are any plans afoot—"

Rosalind met Lady Jersey's calculating gaze with calm sincerity.

I am still useful, she said silently toward the other woman. *I still help to look after your interests.*

And I still keep your secrets.

"That, Miss Thorne, would be very helpful indeed," said Lady Jersey.

"The atmosphere around us is so charged, and temperaments have grown so warm . . . it is important for us to protect each other, do you not agree?" said Rosalind. "We will all be looking to our hostesses to lead us through these troubles with calm and decorum."

"Your understanding does you credit, Miss Thorne." Lady Jersey's tone was warm and slightly relieved.

"You may be sure I will do whatever I can," Rosalind went on. "And if I hear anything that has bearing on our conversation, I will let you know just as soon as I am able."

She had never in her life spoken a more carefully worded promise, or one that skirted so close to the edge of compromise.

"That is all I ask, Miss Thorne," said Lady Jersey regally. "Now, I simply must fly!" She got to her feet. "The queen has said she requires my attendance. I must change, and of course, the lady patronesses must all be marshaled to show their support, although I must say *some* among us are making some *very* ill-considered remarks on the subject. Dorothea Lieven will *not* be persuaded. Stubborn creature. It may be that she has come to regard herself too highly. Indeed, it may be that she is no longer quite *suited* for the board." Lady Jersey's voice curdled with disdain.

Rosalind rose and rang the bell, pretending she had not heard this last remark.

Claire, the parlormaid, arrived with Lady Jersey's shawl and bonnet. Still talking, Lady Jersey allowed herself to be helped into both. Rosalind made appropriate—and entirely meaningless—exclamations at the correct moments. At last, Lady Jersey left, and Rosalind was able to return to her seat. She picked up her cooling cup of coffee and gulped its contents in an entirely undignified fashion.

She was just setting the cup down when Mortimer returned, with the salver in his hand.

"I am still not at home, Mortimer," she said. Any conversation with Lady Jersey left Rosalind a little worse for wear. This one had left her positively exhausted. She needed to collect herself, and then there were the cards that had already been left. Letters of regret and invitation to call again must be dispatched at once.

"Yes, miss," he said, but he hesitated. "I'm afraid there's rather a considerable line in front of the house."

There would be. Rosalind felt the beginnings of a headache clench behind her eyes. She was known to have called on Mrs. Fitzherbert, and now Lady Jersey had called on her, and she had done so in her own carriage, with its crest plainly visible for all to see, including any errant newspaper—

Rosalind froze. The newspapermen. All those writers sent back to their editors with hands and notebooks empty. All their angry editors scheming how to fill their pages and . . .

Alice.

CHAPTER FOURTEEN

A Gentleman of the Press

*". . . she was soon placed by him in difficulties
from the same earnest and almost desperate pur-
suit . . ."*

Langdale, Charles, *Memoirs of Mrs. Fitzherbert*

"I didn't know you knew Ron Ranking, Adam."

Adam Harkness sat with George Littlefield on the
bench by the chimney at the Bell and Anchor public house. It
was nearly noon, and the men coming from their work on
the ships and the docks crammed themselves into the common room. The air was filled with talk and shouts in seamen's rude cant. The door had been propped open to let in
the air and also the women and children with jugs and pails
to be filled with beer to take home.

"I can't say I know Ranking. Not well," Adam told
George. The landlady deposited a jug of her home-brewed
lager on the table, along with two-pint pots. She was a
spindly woman in a plain blue dress and an apron that, like
her, had seen better days. "He's a regular around the station
and has dropped some useful information from time to
time."

"And I thought you were true only to me!" George laughed as he poured out two mugs of the lager. "And Alice, of course."

"Beggars can't be choosers," replied Adam mildly. He raised his mug to George, and they drank.

The Bell and Anchor was, for the most part, a seamen's bar. Adam had started coming here with his brother-in-law, Bill. Bill had been in the navy, but with the defeat of Napoleon and the eventual peace, an enormous number of sailors had been abruptly furloughed. Bill had been luckier than some. When he couldn't find a ship, he found work in the Drury Lane theater. Now he used his skills with knots and ropes to rig and work the scenery, as well as doing the lifting, toting, building, painting, and any other job that required a strong back or a good head for heights.

Adam liked the place well enough. It was clean and airy for a London pub. The landlady and her big sons saw to it the place stayed relatively orderly. The men in it had a rough cheer and ready camaraderie. Bill had seen to it that they welcomed Adam, and Adam was grateful.

Still, Adam missed the Brown Bear and the Staff and Bell. When he'd left Bow Street, he'd also stopped going to either house. Partly because he didn't want to cause any awkwardness for old friends, and partly because he found he did not want all the reminders of what he'd lost.

Adam had walked away from Bow Street of his own volition. He couldn't follow the orders he was given. So, it was either quit or keep on until Townsend had no choice but to sack him. His work for Sir David Royce, the coroner for London and Westminster, was satisfying, if intermittent, and along with the work with Rosalind, it came close to making up for his old pay.

But there were things that he missed. First among them was the depth of the camaraderie. Adam was not a heavy drinker. It got costly, and drunkenness as a pastime held no attractions for him. But he missed going to a public house, where he could gripe and laugh with a group of men who thoroughly understood all the hardships, complications, and blood-boiling frustrations of their shared work. More than anything else, it was that loss that left him feeling cut off from his own life, and it nagged at him.

Rosalind noticed, of course, because Rosalind noticed everything. She did not ask if he regretted his decision. She knew his answer already, and she respected him enough to let it stand.

Thoughts of Rosalind made him touch his coat pocket. He'd been carrying around a possibility of yet more change for days now. The only question was when he'd find the time, not to mention the nerve, to talk properly with Rosalind.

Now, however, was definitely not that time. Adam wrapped his hand back around his tankard.

"Have you heard any rumors about our business?" he asked George.

George shook his head. "And you can be sure if any item regarding . . . that missing paper were in the offing, there would be plenty in the air. As a class, we newspapermen are not noted for being quiet, confidential sorts."

"Is that true of Ranking, as well?"

George shrugged and took another drink. "Ranking's not especially bright, but he is canny. Specializes in the lurid. People do love a story of others' trouble."

Adam nodded, acknowledging the truth of this.

"He's honest enough," George went on. "Got some initiative, as we can tell from the fact that he thought to reconnoiter Mrs. Fitzherbert." George chuckled. "Not that I can throw stones there."

Adam shared George's laugh. He hadn't been entirely sure George would be free to come to meet Ranking. But Adam had said the words "Mrs. Fitzherbert" to George, and George had repeated them to the Major. In return, the Major had immediately granted George the time and leisure to go anywhere he liked.

"And speak of the devil." George jerked his chin toward the door.

Seen in daylight, Ranking was a small, plump, pale man. He wore mended breeches, a blue coat, and a low-crowned hat that made him look perfectly at home among the seamen around them.

"Hullo, Harkness." Ranking dropped onto the bench. "Hullo, Littlefield. Suppose I should have known you'd be here. How's your sister?"

"Very well, thank you," replied George. "And Mrs. Ranking?"

"Bit of croup got her laid up, poor old thing." Ranking poured himself a mug of beer without being invited. "I'm hoping to scrape enough together to take her to the seaside. Your health, gentlemen." He raised his beer and drank deeply. "Now, what is it we can do for each other?"

It was an interesting, and honest, question. Adam appreciated Ranking's brashness, but he did not ignore the cutting edge to his gaze. Ranking was here because he scented an advantage.

"How long have you been watching Mrs. Fitzherbert's house?" Adam asked.

Ranking shrugged and took another pull at his mug. "A few days, on and off. Her name's always good for selling a few papers. Thought we might see something of interest."

"And make it up if you didn't," said George.

"Ah, now, Littlefield, you know I'd never."

"Do I?" George said. "Sorry, I misspoke."

"You keep a civil tongue, young man," said Ranking, but the words were spoken mildly. "No need to spoil the beer with salty words, is there?"

"And while you were watching the house, did you see anything interesting?" asked Adam.

Ranking didn't answer immediately. Instead, he looked Adam over, weighing and judging. Given what he'd said in front of Mrs. Fitzherbert's house last night, Ranking knew something about Adam's leave-taking from Bow Street. Adam suspected Ranking had come to this meeting out of curiosity as well as the hope of learning something he could spin into news.

"I saw a pair of girls packed off to the country," said Ranking. "An' I saw the lady herself coming and going on those delicate errands that are the business of our finer class of females." His tone was dismissive but not mocking. "The Duke and Duchess of York came by, if you can believe it, all respectable in daylight."

Adam wondered if Ranking was fishing. If he'd heard rumors about visits from another royal personage.

"Anyone else?" asked George.

"A few representatives of the high and mighty," said Ranking. "She's got her friends and her supporters, does our Mrs. Fitz. What's your interest? Or should I ask, what's the very busy Miss Thorne's interest?"

"Aw, come on now, Ranking," said George affably. "You've told us less than nothing, and you expect us to give up the goods? Fair's fair."

Ranking shrugged again. "Well, that's the end of that, then." He drained his mug. "Thanks for the drink."

George looked quickly to Adam, who nodded.

"It's a matter of law," George told him. "Bit of a tricky thing, I'd say."

"Oh, is it now?" This time, Ranking seemed genuinely interested. "What law would that be?"

George glanced over at Adam. "If you agree to help," George said, "you'll be the first to hear all about it."

"An' that's worth about as much as a pot of piss," Ranking growled. "Gimme something I can take to my editor, and maybe I'll have something to say."

"Look, Ranking," said George. "It's still playing out. Walk away and you'll join the rest of 'em worrying over the same bits about the crowds and the queen's affairs and the king's affairs. Help us out, and you'll have something fresh and new to hand over to your man."

Ranking's eyes narrowed.

Adam rested his elbows on the table. "Ranking, you're a smart one."

"Flattery now, is it? Not like you, Harkness."

Adam ignored that. "You know that these things take time to unravel. I've got nothing for you now. I admit it. But if you saw something that can point me or Miss Thorne in the right direction, it will be as Littlefield told you—you'll have the whole story well ahead of the others."

Ranking pursed his mouth, considering. "And there is a story?"

"There is," replied Adam.

Ranking said nothing, but he also stayed in his seat.

"Surprised you're going along with this, Littlefield," he remarked, finally. "I'd expect if there was something real, you'd keep it all for yourself."

George shrugged. "Normally, I would, but I can't do the legwork on this one. My wife's not as understanding as Mrs. Ranking about me staying out till all hours."

"Well, we can't all be so lucky."

"And you know that being on good terms with Alice and Miss Thorne never hurts," George added. "Plenty of little items to be learned, if they are able to trust you."

Adam watched Ranking turning over the possibilities. Finally, he leaned forward. "Is the Fitz paying Miss Thorne for her services?" he asked.

George frowned. "What has that to do with anything?"

Ranking grinned, clearly enjoying the fact that he knew more than the men in front of him. "Just that if she is expecting payment, your Miss Thorne better make sure she gets the brass up front."

"Why's that?" asked Adam.

"Well, the Fitz's got money troubles, hasn't she?" said Ranking. "And bad ones."

"There's been rumors she helped the prince with his debts, and lived to regret it," said George. This was news to Adam, but he kept that to himself. "Do you know something more?"

"I know she's had Josiah Poole to the house," replied Ranking.

"Who's Josiah Poole?" asked Adam.

"Attorney. Of a sort. Makes a specialty out of helping those who can't pay what they owe."

"You're sure about this?"

"That I am, Mr. Harkness. Know him quite well." Ranking looked at them both and chuckled at their stoic expressions. "Oh, not in a professional way, at least not his profession. But he's been known to drop a hint or two that's turned into a good story."

George cocked his head skeptically. "You know him, but you didn't talk to him when you saw him?"

"Well, I did try," said Ranking. "But Poole didn't exactly come in what you'd call the front way. It's his habit to drive his gig himself, so I sees him well enough from my spot on the corner. But he come up through the mews, an' it was plain he didn't plan to stay long, cuz he tied up his horses right there. Didn't even bother to take the bits out their mouths, did he? Went in through the garden gate. You know the one." He touched his nose and nodded toward Adam. "Well, I'm thinking, 'That's odd, innit?' So I watches a bit longer, an' sure enough, not a quarter hour's gone before Poole nips out again, and he's pretty pleased with himself, by the look of things.

"So, I steps up and makes myself known, or tries to, but he just touches up the horses and takes off. Almost ran me down."

"When was this?" asked Adam.

Ranking took another pull at his beer. "Just yesterday, as it happens."

"And you'd not seen him at the house before?"

"Not I, but then I can only stand about for so long."

Adam nodded. "And you say Poole deals principally with debtors?"

"You only bring Josiah Poole round when the choices are him or Newgate," Ranking replied. "Says to me the Fitz needs money, and needs it in a hurry."

Adam thought about the conversation he and Rosalind had had the night before, and about how Mrs. Fitzherbert might have her own reasons for wanting the marriage certificate to become public. Money as a motivating force had not been their first suspicion, but a grand lady had grand expenses, especially when she had daughters to be brought out and married up.

"So," said Ranking. "That worth something to you, Mr. Harkness?"

Adam pushed the jug toward Ranking.

"If I wanted to find this Mr. Poole, where would you recommend I start looking?"

CHAPTER FIFTEEN

The Consequences of Notoriety

*". . . being generally grounded upon knowledge of
the world, and experience of its inhabitants, it unfortunately follows, of course, that the information which it conveys must be of a disagreeable
and humiliating complexion."*

Bury, Charlotte, *The Diary of a Lady-in-Waiting*

"Is she gone?"

Rosalind swung around to see that the parlor door was
open again, only this time it was Alice, leaning inside, looking entirely like a naughty child checking to see if the coast
was clear.

When it came to Lady Jersey, Rosalind had a certain
amount of sympathy.

Rosalind could not help but smile. "Yes, Alice, she's gone."

Alice, of course, immediately heard the weariness in Rosalind's voice. "What's wrong? What did she say?"

Rosalind shook her head. "I should have listened to you."

"Always the best course of action." Alice sat down on the
sofa and reached for the coffee. Mrs. Singh, as usual, had included an extra cup. She had been with Rosalind's household

long enough to understand that the number of guests in the parlor could change quickly. "What convinced you of it this time?"

Rosalind sighed. Evasion was pointless, and highly inadvisable. "I'm assuming the Major will have read about me and Adam visiting Mrs. Fitzherbert. Has he written you?"

"I expect word from him at any minute." Alice drank a good half of the cup in a single gulp. Alice had learned her drinking habits among the men of the *Chronicle*. She could still summon all the deportment required by the finest ballrooms, but she had long since discovered she preferred the free and easy manners of the newspaper office. "He won't have missed your name in the *Standard*, and I do expect he will be eager for details about your visit. Do you want to know what I'm going to tell him?"

"I fully expect you'll put him off. It's George I'm worried about. The Major is not above using pressure on him to get a story."

"No, he isn't," agreed Alice. "And yes, that could extend to putting pressure on me and threatening to give George the sack," Alice said. "That's what you're worried about, isn't it?"

"Yes," admitted Rosalind.

"So am I." Alice made a face at her remaining coffee. "But George would quit the *Chronicle* rather than betray your confidence." She paused. "You do know that, don't you?"

"Of course I do, but where does that leave him? And his family?" George had a wife and a young child. He could not afford to lose his job. None of the Littlefields could afford it.

"We shall simply have to cross that bridge when we come to it," said Alice. "I've been managing the Major for years. He cannot resist my winning smile or the possibility of a brilliant story. You've been an excellent source before. I can convince him to give you some time. Plus, A. E. Littlefield will be able to work up some entertaining speculation to fill the column inches."

"I'm sorry to put you through this."

Alice shrugged. "We'll make do, Rosalind. I know you don't like the attention, but honestly, you've managed this sort of thing for other people for years. Is it really so difficult to manage for yourself?"

"It's different," murmured Rosalind.

"Yes, but not that different."

Rosalind looked down at her folded hands. She had spent so many years hiding. Not only because it was expected that a woman like her—unmarried and unmarriageable, without family or fortune—should fade into the background, but because she had secrets that could not be known. Her father's debts had driven him to become a forger and eventually led to his brutal murder. Her sister had for many years been a courtesan, first in Paris and then in London. Achieving a public reputation as a confidential assistant and itinerant problem solver might gain her invitations and income, but her livelihood was predicated on her standing as a gently bred lady. If the darkness in her past were to become known or, worse, to become common gossip, that standing would crumble.

"What is it, Rosalind?" asked Alice. "What are you thinking?"

"I'm thinking about the nature of a woman's reputation," she said. "Mine specifically. And wondering if there will ever come a day when I can stop worrying about it."

"Probably not," said Alice. "But honestly, Rosalind, did you ever expect that?"

"No, not really." She sighed. "So I suppose I should not complain that it's exhausting."

"It is exhausting. It's also monstrously unfair, and it always has been," said Alice. "But I'll say it again—you will manage. You are Rosalind Thorne, and you will always find a way."

"And if this time I fail?" she asked.

Alice didn't even bat an eye. "Well, Amelia needs someone to teach her students diction, and I happen to know where you can find some good translation work. Is your German still up to snuff?"

Rosalind surprised herself by laughing. "Oh, Alice, thank you."

"You're welcome," replied Alice. "Now, have some more of Mrs. Singh's coffee and tart and tell me what Lady Jersey had to say for herself."

It was excellent advice. Rosalind and Alice both devoured healthy slices of tart and poured each other additional cups of coffee with plenty of milk and sugar.

Feeling much more rational, Rosalind wiped her fingers on her napkin. "Alice, I have a question for you. Mrs. Fitzherbert told me she is worried about losing her custody of her daughters if she cannot prove she married the king."

"So you said."

"But I'm not sure that was the whole truth."

Alice's brows arched.

"Do you know if either of the girls has been caught up in any sort of scandal or gossip?"

Alice leaned back on the sofa and stared at nothing for a long time. Rosalind waited patiently while her friend sorted through her mind's deep store of sensational gossip.

"I believe there was something," Alice said slowly. "The older girl."

"Minney," supplied Rosalind.

"Yes, Minney. She'd been seen in unsuitable company of some sort. I'm afraid I don't remember the details."

"Do you know what came of it?"

Alice shook her head. "I don't know that anything did. Mrs. Fitzherbert is very careful with her girls."

With good reason. Rosalind sighed. Perhaps it was nothing. Perhaps she was becoming too suspicious for her own good. Sometimes things, and people, were exactly as they seemed.

The ideal person to ask was Burrowes, if Burrowes would agree to speak with her, and if Mrs. Fitzherbert would agree to give Rosalind the address where she could be found.

Even as she was thinking this, Alice said, "I suppose we could ask Mrs. Dowding."

"Who?"

"Mrs. Dowding," Alice repeated. "You've heard me talk about her, Rosalind. She's the queen of us all. She and her husband all but invented the gossip sheet. It's said she retired on the bribes she used to get from the likes of the Duchess of Devonshire for favorable mentions of her doings and parties."

"And for discreet non-mentions?"

"That too," agreed Alice. "I don't pretend she's a principled person, but she knows absolutely everything society tries to sweep under the bed, and there's some suggestion that she's still making money off of it. If anyone knows anything about Mrs. Fitzherbert's Minney, it's the Dowding."

"Very well. Do we go to her, or does she come to us?"

"I'll write and ask permission to call. She'll love it, now that you're news."

Rosalind looked down at her cup. But she did not miss how Alice rolled her eyes.

"It's *happened*, Rosalind. There's no going back. You're going to have to at least make peace with it. It would be better, however, if you made use of it."

But before Rosalind could reply, the door opened yet again. This time it was Mortimer, with his salver.

"The post has arrived, Miss Thorne."

Rosalind found herself staring. The salver was piled with letters to the point it was nearly overflowing.

"Good heavens," she murmured. "What on earth . . . ?"

But she knew, of course. This was the result of her name being in the newspaper.

"Is there anything from Mrs. Fitzherbert?" she asked.

"Not at this time," answered Mortimer. Then he eyed the unsteady pile. "Although, it's possible I may have missed something."

"Thank you. But where should . . . ?" Rosalind glanced about the parlor.

Alice did not wait for her to finish but began taking up the letters by double handfuls and piling them onto the tea table.

"You'd better ask Mrs. Singh to make some tea," Alice told Mortimer. "And sandwiches. It's going to be a long day."

"Is it?" came a familiar, cheerful voice.

George Littlefield stood on the parlor's threshold.

"George!" Alice leaped to her feet and ran to give her brother a resounding kiss on the cheek. "What are you doing here?"

"I am sent as a messenger from our Mr. Harkness." With a dramatic flourish, he produced a folded note from his pocket, which he handed to Rosalind with an exaggerated bow. "Is that Mrs. Singh's tart?"

"It is, and since you are here on a vital errand, you may have some." Alice set about cutting her brother a generous slice. "How does Ronnie Ranking?"

"As greasy and ingratiating as ever he was." George sat and accepted the wedge of tart his sister held out. "I'm starved."

Rosalind scanned Adam's brief missive. "Adam says Mr. Ranking saw an attorney taking the back way into Mrs. Fitzherbert's house."

"Josiah Poole," said George for Alice's benefit. "A special-ist in debt, debtors, and the problems thereof."

"What would Mrs. Fitzherbert need with—?" began Alice, but then she stopped. "Never mind."

Rosalind nodded. It was very common for members of society to find their expenses outpacing their incomes. If they were heavy gamblers or were addicted to the glamour and gaiety of social life, their debts could run to tens of thousands of pounds. The Littlefields' father and her own had both fallen victim to their own desperate desire to keep up appearances, and both had ended very badly.

"Adam writes he has gone to find this Mr. Poole," finished Rosalind.

"And sent me to tell you all about it," said George. "And enjoy this excellent tart."

"So, begin at the beginning, dear brother." Alice filled George's coffee cup. "And leave nothing out."

Rosalind listened while George told them Ranking's story of Mr. Poole slipping through Mrs. Fitzherbert's garden gate and leaving as quickly as his gig could carry him. She thought about Mrs. Fitzherbert's house—so tastefully furnished and so very well staffed. Surely, when she was entertaining the prince on a regular basis, she had been required to put on even more of a show.

"I've heard Mrs. Fitzherbert actually loaned the prince money on occasion," said Alice. "I don't imagine he ever paid her back."

"No, probably not," agreed Rosalind. The staggering sums that the prince, now the king, owed were the subject of regular debates in Parliament. It was well known that the main reason he decided to marry Caroline of Brunswick was so that his allowance would be increased.

"So, a decision by Mrs. Fitz to sell her marriage certificate might serve more than one end," George said slowly. "It could bring in some income, as well as serving as a tidy bit of revenge."

"How disappointing," said Alice. "I'd always believed that Mrs. Fitz was the one person in the great royal mess who had some principles."

"We don't know anything yet," said Rosalind, as much to herself as to Alice. "It is very possible Mr. Poole has some connection with someone else inside the house."

"You mean he bribed one of the staff?" asked George.

"Or . . . Oh, Rosalind, you don't think . . . one of her girls?" exclaimed Alice.

"What I think," said Rosalind, "is that I had better call on Mrs. Fitzherbert at once."

CHAPTER SIXTEEN

The Sponging House

"I shall die and nothing tell of my existence!"
Bury, Charlotte, *The Diary of a Lady-in-Waiting*

Adam had no need to ask Ranking, or anyone else, the way to Ross's sponging house. He had often visited Ross's, and other houses like it, to fetch out a man under suspicion or to coax information from a desperate soul.

The sponging house had stood on this spot since the days of William and Mary. The original structure had been expanded by each passing generation of Rosses. Now it was a dubious combination of soot-stained brick, dirty timber, and a roof that looked like it might not last out the week if the weather turned stormy. It also stretched back a surprising distance from the street, with crooked gables and puzzling additions jutting out here and there.

The sponging house's servants were turnkeys dressed as shabby footmen. It was their job to check the men out and check them back in again before the doors were locked for the night. Bribes were a matter of routine. Many residents handed over rings or stickpins or watch chains in exchange for a few extra hours out in the fresh air.

Adam asked the man at the door for Ross and was reluctantly told to look in the office.

"I know the way," Adam told the man and started down the long, narrow hall before the other could heave himself up off his stool beside the door.

There had been some effort to turn the inside comfortable. The paint on the walls was fresh, and if the linen and furnishings were not precisely new, neither were they threadbare. There were fireplaces in most of the rooms. Adam happened to know the residents were charged extra for the coals.

The men residing there—and it was all men—defied all attempts to create comfort. They looked haunted. The air around them smelled heavily of the spirits they drank (and were charged for). The writing tables in the parlors were always crowded with fellows sporting crooked collars and loose cravats, penning yet more begging letters as they tried to raise the necessary sums from someone. Anyone.

The costs of pen, paper, and ink were all added to the bill.

It made no sense. It never had. How was a man who could not pay his existing expenses to pay the added bills from the sponging house? And yet it was the system, and it ground on, and that seemed to suit Gareth Ross well enough.

Ross's office was the one genuinely comfortable room in the house. The open window had clean muslin curtains, and the lamps were turned well up. The broad table was piled high with papers and ledgers.

Adam pushed the door open without bothering to knock. "Hello, Mr. Ross."

Ross was a big man with mottled pink skin, a long nose, and a bald head. He wore a good black coat and stovepipe trousers and looked much more like a schoolmaster than a jailer, at least until he looked right at you. Then you felt the cold calculation of a man who saw his fellow human beings in terms of how many shillings might be wrung out of them.

Or, in Adam's case, how much of a danger they posed.

"Well, now, Mr. Harkness," said Ross, his voice low and heavy. "What brings you here?"

"I have a question I was hoping you could answer."

Ross's eyes narrowed shrewdly. "Do you? And why should I bother myself with answering your questions? You ain't Bow Street anymore. In fact, I heard you've made yourself all snug behind some very nice petticoats."

Adam leaned across the desk. He did not shout. In fact, he lowered his voice. "You speak about the lady in question again, and I will see you in the dock."

"For what?" Ross spread his hands. "I'm as honest as the day is long."

"For all the little items that find their way into your hands, whether their owners know it or not," said Adam. "It's all strictly for the benefit of the sterling clientele you keep here, I know, and of course they all are the right owners of whatever they give you to sell on."

"Now, then, Mr. Harkness, it's all by way of business." Ross's attempt at joviality sent a shudder down Adam's spine.

"Naturally," agreed Adam. "And you and I both know the magistrates have the warmest regards for men in your business and will demonstrate their complete faith in your honesty as soon as you explain the matter to them."

"I don't care for your threats."

Adam said nothing. He just held his gaze steady. Ross threw out his chest, and for a moment Adam thought he had misjudged the other's bravado. But as the silence stretched, Ross withered. His brow and bald scalp also took on a noticeably damp sheen.

"Well, I don't see as a few questions can do anyone any harm," Ross muttered.

"Of course not." Adam straightened up. "In fact, all I need from you is to tell me where I can find Mr. Josiah Poole."

"Poole?" exclaimed Ross, both surprised and relieved. "What d'ye want with him?"

Adam didn't answer.

Ross sighed. He also pulled out his heavy silver watch and checked the time.

"Well, you're in luck." Ross tucked his watch away. "He has several clients among my guests, and he generally stops by before lunch. If you care to wait, you should meet with the man before the hour's up." He waved an expansive hand. "An' if for some reason he don't make his appointments today, you can look for him at the White Swan. Will that do?"

"It should."

"The parlor is at your disposal." Ross gestured grandly toward the door.

"Thank you," replied Adam gravely. "But I think I'll wait outside. I've no wish to make any of your guests uncomfortable."

"Suit yourself," said Ross. "Was that all? Don't see why you need to make such a fuss."

"Thank you for your assistance, Mr. Ross." Adam made his bow.

"Always glad to help the law," said Ross.

Adam did not bother to reply.

The street outside the sponging house was relatively quiet, especially for the heart of London. What people there were slunk by quickly. Even the barrow pushers seemed in a hurry to get out of this street in the shadow of Newgate, as if its bad luck might cling to them.

Adam found himself an unobtrusive spot in the shadow of the sponging house and composed himself to patience. It seemed that much of his life had been spent like this—waiting for someone else to make up their mind.

Like Rosalind.

Adam frowned at the stray thought. It was ungenerous, and he didn't like himself for having it. Rosalind loved him, and he would love her until he took his last breath. That was not in doubt. From the day he made his decision not to fight against the dictates of his heart, he had known it would be difficult. The demands of class, and the narrowness of the path that her past had fitted her to, were not going to go away for wishing, or for love, no matter how deep.

They had both been raised to the idea of marriage. Adam had always seen it as the fit state for a man and a woman. It was a pledge of support and the heart's commitment to the work of life and family, as well as the love and respect for the other.

For Rosalind, it was a tangled morass. It was loss and danger and enforced dependence. That was a great deal to ask anyone to see beyond.

And yet her inability to do so left him not angry, not even sore or frustrated, but puzzled. He wanted to do something but didn't know what that something ought to be. Because the fault was not Rosalind's. It lay in her past, and in the world they must try to navigate together. These truths left him uncertain that there was anything that *could* be done, now or ever.

Except there was something. Adam touched his coat pocket. And he knew how to be patient. Their time would come.

While Adam sorted through these thoughts, he also noted the fresh sound of horses' hooves. A closed carriage, somewhat battered, drawn by unmatched and undistinguished chestnuts, rolled up the street. The driver had his hat pulled down and his coat collar turned up. A dirty scarf muffled his face.

Adam resisted the urge to straighten, but his attention fastened on the driver. The day was warm. The man must be stifling.

The carriage stopped in front of the sponging house, and its door opened. It rocked slightly, and a fat, dark bundle dropped onto the cobbles.

Adam sprinted across the street. The bundle unfurled, turning into the unmistakable figure of an unconscious man.

A man with fresh red blood pouring out over the front of his shirt.

Adam dropped to his knees beside the man, aware even as he did that the carriage was already clattering away.

"Stop that carriage!" Adam bellowed to the world in general. "Raise the hue and cry and stop that carriage!"

Passersby shouted. Some ran forward, but it was too late. The carriage driver lashed his horses mercilessly, and those who tried to reach the carriage reeled back to avoid being run down.

The carriage rounded a corner and was gone.

Adam looked down at the fallen man and saw that he was also gone beyond recall. He held his palm to the man's mouth to be sure, but there was no breath to feel.

"Dear God!" shouted a man behind him.

A crowd was already gathering—a mix of bystanders and men from the sponging house. The doorman he'd talked to earlier was first among them.

"Do you know him?" Adam shouted to whoever might be able to answer.

"Know him!" cried the doorman. "I should say! That's Josiah Poole!"

CHAPTER SEVENTEEN

A Few Domestic Matters

*"Surrounded by so many personal advantages . . .
she was very reluctant to enter into engagements
so fraught with so many embarrassments . . ."*

Langdale, Charles, *Memoirs of Mrs. Fitzherbert*

When Rosalind arrived at Mrs. Fitzherbert's house, there were two footmen standing outside the door. A man at the corner of the garden wall held a stout stick in his hand and watched alertly as she climbed down from the hired cab. Another man, similarly armed and attentive, watched from beside the area railing.

Rosalind gave her name to the footmen and was admitted. Inside, a parlormaid took her through from the entrance hall to the walled garden.

There they found Mrs. Fitzherbert in a straw hat, gray smock, and work gloves. She knelt on a cushion and was engaged in gently tying some heavy-headed lilies to a complex arrangement of garden stakes.

"Miss Thorne!" Mrs. Fitzherbert climbed to her feet, only a little stiffly. "Thank you, Belinda. We'll have some tea," she added to the maid, who curtsied and retired.

"Will you sit with me?" The widow led Rosalind to a small stone terrace. Rosalind thanked her and took the indicated chair.

"What have you to tell me?" asked Mrs. Fitzherbert as she removed her gloves and smock. "You cannot have found my paper so quickly!"

"No, I'm afraid not," said Rosalind. "I came to see how you do and whether you might require any additional assistance now that reports have circulated in the papers regarding my visit to you."

"There were some . . . unwelcome idlers this morning," Mrs. Fitzherbert said. "But the men Mr. Harkness recommended were able to deal with them, and I have two of my own staff at the door, as you will have seen."

"A very sensible measure," said Rosalind.

"Well, it is not the first time I have had to deal with unwelcome attention." Mrs. Fitzherbert wasn't looking at Rosalind. She was looking at her flowers and her carefully trained vines. "This is my favorite place," she said absently as she sat down and smoothed her skirts. "This and my conservatory. Do you garden, Miss Thorne?"

"I do not. I have never had the time." Or, indeed, a garden in which to practice. Even the Orchard Street house had only the barest strip of green running from the back of the house. Mrs. Singh had claimed most of that for a pair of cucumber frames.

"Yes, it does require a measure of dedication. But the rewards are more than one might think." She touched the leaves of a blossoming yellow rose near her elbow and smiled.

Rosalind looked at Mrs. Fitzherbert. She was struck again by how perfectly and comfortably the other woman filled the role of a widow living in elegant retirement. She found herself searching for the spark that could have conquered the heart of a king. But all she saw was mild regard, ordinary sincerity, and a deep concern for what was closest to her.

Perhaps that was enough.

Rosalind felt ashamed of her suspicions that Mrs. Fitzherbert might be playing some double game. Still, she could not dismiss them, especially now that they had been told the story of Josiah Poole. The stakes in this matter were far too high for her to allow herself to be blinded by personal inclination.

She needed to know if she and Adam were being used, and she needed to know it before this matter progressed any further.

Belinda and a portly footman emerged from the house. Belinda carried a white cloth. The footman, a tray with tea and delicate slices of bread and butter. When the cloth was laid and the tea things arranged, the servants retired back to flank the door to the house.

Mrs. Fitzherbert poured out a cup and, after inquiring how Rosalind took her tea, added a thin slice of lemon.

"Since you can't say what I most hoped for"—she handed Rosalind her tea—"what brings you here?" She paused. "My new lady's maid arrived this morning, you know. She seems a capable girl and is settling in upstairs."

"I am glad to hear it," said Rosalind. "Mrs. Fitzherbert, we did learn something that might be of use." Rosalind waited until she was certain she had the other woman's full attention. "Do you know the name Josiah Poole?"

If Mrs. Fitzherbert recognized the name, she gave no sign. Indeed, her brow creased in thought. "No, I do not believe so. Who is he?"

"He is an attorney who makes a specialty of helping find debtors relief from their obligations."

Mrs. Fitzherbert set her teacup down carefully. "And this man has spoken to you about me?"

"No. But he was seen coming to your house."

Anger flickered across Mrs. Fitzherbert's face. "May I know who told you this?"

Rosalind did not answer.

"Well, whoever they were, they are mistaken," Mrs. Fitzherbert said flatly. "I will admit that I have had difficulties, but there are no obligations that I could not eventually meet, and even were it the case, my brother and my own man of business have both advised me on my affairs since Mr. Fitzherbert died. I have no need to reference a stranger on private business."

"The witness was quite confident," Rosalind said. "They are well acquainted with Mr. Poole and spoke to him as he was leaving."

"Ridiculous," said Mrs. Fitzherbert. "Unless you believe I am lying to you now?"

Do I? Rosalind considered the woman in front of her, in her plain matron's black, surrounded by her carefully tended garden. Did she truly believe this woman had brought her here only as a means to help humiliate the man she had loved, wisely or not?

But before Rosalind could speak, the sound of voices and laughter erupted from inside the house. The door burst open, and two young women in travel-stained coats and broad straw bonnets skipped onto the terrace.

"And here's a surprise for you!" cried the leader, who was also the taller and more determinedly cheerful of the two.

Mrs. Fitzherbert rose to her feet. "Minney! Mary Ann! What on earth!"

CHAPTER EIGHTEEN

Unexpected Arrivals

*"... but she saw everything through the mist of
her own passions and prejudices; and,
consequently, saw everything falsely."*

Bury, Charlotte, *The Diary of a Lady-in-Waiting*

"I told you she'd be angry, Minney," said the younger of
the two. The hems of her green coat were dusty. Her
silk-lined bonnet had gone crooked somewhere in her travels,
and she had not yet righted it.

"And I told you it didn't matter," said the older girl.
"Mama will forgive us. Won't you, Mama?" Minney Seymore ignored Mrs. Fitzherbert's shocked exclamation as well
as her furrowed brow and pressed her cheek to the older
woman's. Then she straightened up and whisked around to
face Rosalind, who had also risen to her feet. "Now, may I
take it you are the famous Miss Thorne?"

Miss Seymore was a slender, pale young woman with deep
brown eyes. Those eyes carefully evaluated Rosalind's appearance and affect. She might be young, but Minney Seymore had been raised in the labyrinth of the *haut ton*, and

clearly, she had learned that if one did not want to be left floundering, keen observation was required.

Mrs. Fitzherbert had recovered herself enough to make introductions. "Miss Thorne, may I introduce Miss Mary Seymore and Miss Mary Ann Smythe."

The adoption of a child was an entirely private matter. The terms, conditions, and length of the child's residence were determined solely by the families involved. Mrs. Fitzherbert had been given charge of these girls by families who could not, or would not, raise them. One, if Rosalind understood correctly, was her niece; and the other, the daughter of a dear friend. She looked upon them as her own and treated them as such, but there was no legal requirement that they change their names, or observe any other formality. Indeed, Mrs. Fitzherbert could have handed them back to their birth families at a moment's notice.

"You may call me Minney," the older girl told Rosalind. "It saves confusion. We are a household of Marys."

"How do you do?" Rosalind made her curtsy.

"Exhausted." Mary Ann selected a chair and perched on the edge of it. "We've been traveling practically since dawn." Her glower at her sister spoke volumes about whom she held responsible for that.

"My brother might have sent word," said Mrs. Fitzherbert sardonically.

"I expect it will arrive with the afternoon post." Miss Seymore dropped into the remaining chair. She undid her bonnet ribbon and tossed the hat aside. A riot of dark curls sprang up as if eager for the touch of the sun. "We left before he came downstairs. And I'm afraid we've already sent the carriage back. Which means you're stuck with us, Mama." She stripped off her gloves and reached for the teapot. "And as I imagine you must be wondering, the reason we're here is because we read about Miss Thorne's visit in the paper."

She passed a teacup to her sister with the air of one making a peace offering and filled another for herself. "Aunt said something must be seriously wrong, because everyone knows Miss Thorne's business is solving problems, and with the queen back in the city and everything in such a stew . . . well, we simply couldn't leave you alone, could we?"

"You do understand that, don't you, Mama?" asked Miss Mary Ann anxiously.

"I understand that you two have behaved most impulsively and thoughtlessly," said Mrs. Fitzherbert. "And my brother will be out of his wits with worry. You should have at least let the coachman wait long enough for me to write a note saying you had arrived safely. That must be done first thing."

"But, Mama . . . ," began Miss Mary Ann.

Mrs. Fitzherbert did not let her get any further. "You will go to your rooms at once, both of you. I will send for you once I have written, and then you will hear what there is to say."

"No, Mama, I will not," said Miss Seymore. "I am not a child, even though you *persist* in treating me like one." Her tone told Rosalind there was a swarm of old arguments behind her words. This was not surprising. Miss Seymore was on the cusp of adulthood and wanted to test her own powers. Some clashes with her parent were inevitable.

Rosalind remembered Burrowes's warning hints and Alice's mention of the penniless cavalry officer. Possibly the disagreements had been more than the usual clashes between parent and child. Possibly Miss Seymore and her sister had been sent away for more than their protection.

Miss Seymore drew herself up, assuming a mature dignity. "If something has happened that affects you, Mama, it affects us all. Isn't that so, Mary?"

Miss Mary Ann raised her chin in a show of strength and

solidarity. "We really could not stay bottled up in the country if you were in trouble."

"That is very good of you," said Mrs. Fitzherbert. "Truly, girls. But you must realize you make the situation so much more complicated by being here."

"How could we when we don't know what the situation is?" replied Miss Seymore pertly.

Mrs. Fitzherbert threw up her hands. "What am I to do with you? Miss Thorne, do please excuse me. As you can see, I must take care of my girls."

"Of course, Mrs. Fitzherbert. I was about to take my leave." She got to her feet.

But Miss Seymore was not about to let her go so easily. "Now, you will wait a moment, Miss Thorne. I insist on knowing what you have come to Mama about."

Rosalind opened her mouth to make an ambiguous reply, but Mrs. Fitzherbert spoke first. "My room was broken into, and some things were stolen. Miss Thorne was assisting with the inquiry into how this happened."

Miss Seymore's face went dead white. For a moment, Rosalind thought she might actually faint.

"Good Lord!" exclaimed Miss Mary Ann. "What was taken?"

"Some private letters," said Rosalind.

Miss Seymore steeled herself. "And did you find who took them?"

"I'm afraid," said Mrs. Fitzherbert, "it was Burrowes."

"Burrowes?" Miss Mary Ann cried, genuinely shocked. "She'd never!"

"How awful!" exclaimed Miss Seymore. "I can't believe it."

"I'm afraid you have to believe it, and so do I," said Mrs. Fitzherbert. "I have had to dismiss her for the theft."

"On the word of a . . . a stranger?" Miss Mary Ann's shock was quickly dissolving into anger.

Miss Seymore had rallied. She pressed her sister's hand. "Oh, Mary, Mama would not do such a thing unless she was sure." Her tone was reassuring, but Rosalind noted how the other hand had curled itself into a tight fist.

"I am not going to discuss this now," said Mrs. Fitzherbert flatly. "It has been done, and my new maid is in place. Now, *please*, both of you. Let me have a moment's peace. I promise I will come speak with you as soon as I have dispatched the letter to my brother."

Miss Seymore stood, very much on her dignity, but Rosalind got the distinct feeling she was glad to get away. Miss Mary Ann, however, hesitated. It seemed that she wanted to add more protests, but at the sight of her mother's weary expression, she closed her mouth around whatever she meant to say. The young woman now looked genuinely uneasy. This pricked at Rosalind's awareness.

It could, of course, have simply been a young woman's genuine concern for a beloved parent in distress. Rosalind, however, could not help wondering if there was something more. At last, however, Miss Mary Ann rose to follow her older sister as she retreated into the house.

"You must forgive my girls, Miss Thorne," said Mrs. Fitzherbert as the door to the house closed. "They are young and apt to be impetuous and . . . well, they are young."

"They are worried about you."

Mrs. Fitzherbert continued to stare at the place where her daughters had been. "Yes," she said absently. "I believe they are." Then she shook herself. "Now I must write to my brother and think of *something* to tell the girls."

"If I may ask . . . Miss Smythe and Miss Seymore clearly know something of your marriage . . . ?"

"They do, and they do not," Mrs. Fitzherbert said. "One cannot bring girls out into society and keep them from hearing rumors. Have I sat them down and told them the full story? No. That is my fault, I suppose. But they were so young, and the matter is so complex, I could not find the words." Her fingers strayed to her miniature. "My husband was very fond of Minney when she was a child," she finished softly. "People even wondered if, well . . ."

If she was the king's daughter. Rosalind nodded.

Mrs. Fitzherbert sighed sharply, shaking off whatever unwelcome memories were crowding in on her thoughts. "Now, Miss Thorne, regarding our conversation before my daughters' abrupt arrival—this Mr. Poole you spoke of is a stranger to me. He has never been admitted to this house by me and has no part in any business of mine. Does that satisfy you?"

Did it? Rosalind let the question hang between them for a moment.

"I apologize," she said at last. "You understand that all considerations must be entertained at the beginning of a complex inquiry, and since speed is of the essence . . ."

Mrs. Fitzherbert bowed her head. "Yes, I do understand, and you are hardly the first to question my integrity." Rosalind suppressed a wince. "Do you believe this Mr. Poole is associated with the theft?"

"Mr. Harkness has gone to find him," said Rosalind. "I hope we will know more soon."

"Well. That at least is good news. Please let me know as soon as there is word."

Mrs. Fitzherbert rang the bell on the table. Their interview was at an end.

The maid Belinda reappeared to take Rosalind to the foyer and help her on with coat and bonnet. Rosalind noted the stout young woman's face was pale and her eyes darted suspiciously toward Rosalind's. The footmen were frowning at her, at each other, at the maid.

All of this told Rosalind that her involvement in Burrowes's dismissal had become known. It was even now being talked over, and either believed or doubted. Amelia had been dropped into the middle of a beehive.

But there was no help for it. The arrival of Mrs. Fitzherbert's daughters only made it more urgent that there be someone in the house who could ask questions and look for answers.

Rosalind thought back to the young ladies' arrival and how Miss Seymore so blithely said they'd come because they read in the paper about Rosalind visiting their mother. It struck her that if that were true, the young ladies must have risen very early indeed or their coachman had covered the distance back to London at breakneck speed.

She found herself wondering if they had already been on the road when they read the newspapers, and if the report of her visit to Mrs. Fitzherbert proved to be a better excuse for their return than the one they'd already formulated.

Rosalind remembered what Alice had said about Miss Seymore's "unsuitable company." She would not be the first girl to invent a way to escape exile.

And to see someone her mother very much wishes to keep away from her.

Rosalind found herself wondering where this cavalry captain was now.

CHAPTER NINETEEN

A Series of Abrupt Departures

*"In all circumstances your enemies might take
such advantage as I shudder to think of . . ."*

Langdale, Charles, *Memoirs of Mrs. Fitzherbert*

"Get back!" roared Adam to the crowd pressing around him and the dead man at his feet. "This is—" He stopped before he could say it was Bow Street business. "You!" he hollered at the sponging house's doorman. "Clear the way!"

Startled, the man turned to face the crowd and waved his arms. "All right, all right, you seen it! On your way now!"

But the ones in front could not move, because of the press of the ones behind. Oaths sounded, along with shouted questions.

"Give way!" bellowed a fresh voice. It was Ross. The sponger made his way through the crowd by the simple expedient of grabbing men by the shoulders and shoving them ruthlessly aside.

"My God!" he cried when he saw the dead man. "Poole! Who done this?"

Adam didn't bother answering. "Have someone bring a sheet. Is there a cellar to your house? We need to get him off the street and clear these people."

Ross, thankfully, was a man hard to paralyze. He shouted, and a pair of men came running. He barked his orders. Shortly, a tarp was produced, and the men hoisted Poole's corpse with surprising efficiency.

"Not the first we've had someone go on us sudden like," said Ross in response to Adam's inquiring glance. "Though not like this. Good God!" Ross wiped at his face. "What was it did for him? Knifed, was it? Looks like 'e was knifed."

As it happened, Adam agreed with him, but he wasn't going to say so while the crowd was trying to press close enough to hear every word. He just led the morbid procession inside, leaving the remaining bystanders to the tender mercies of Ross's doorman.

Not that inside was much better. The entire household seemed to be trying to cram itself into the hall, with more crowding into the parlor's threshold and filling up the stairs.

"All right, all right!" called Ross. "I don't know, and neither do any of you. Just calm down! You'll hear what there is soon enough. Go on! Get!" Ross shooed at them like they were a pack of dogs, and took Adam to the office while his men carried the corpse down into the cellar.

"We'll need the coroner," Adam said as soon as Ross shut the door. "Have you someone you can send?"

A boy was summarily dispatched to the address Adam gave. With luck, Sir David could be quickly found. The coroner was responsible for all cases of violent death in London and Westminster, and before any other measures could be taken, he needed to be on the spot.

"I imagine you'll be wanting a better look at the man?" Even as he said this, Ross was pulling a ring of keys out of his pocket.

Ross took Adam through the busy kitchen. He unlocked the door to the cellar and ushered Adam down gloomy stairs to a cool earthen room filled with casks of wine and bottles of spirits.

Someone had lit a lamp on a shelf, so Adam could see the shrouded remains of Josiah Poole lying on a crude table made from two boards and three barrels. Adam peeled back the canvas.

The wound in Poole's belly was clear and deep, right beneath the rib cage. Blood was still oozing from the dark slash. The thing must have been done mere moments before he was so unceremoniously dumped from the carriage.

"Poor bugger," Ross muttered. "Slippery as an eel, and I'd not be surprised to learn 'e brought it on himself, but still . . . poor bugger." He paused. "What do I say? I'll have to tell upstairs something, otherwise I'll have a riot on my hands."

"Tell them the truth," said Adam. "Tell them it looks like Josiah Poole died in a brawl, and the coroner is on the way. Be sure to keep the cellar locked until Sir David gets here." He paused. "Do you know where he lived? Does he have a family?"

"I know aught about the man," said Ross. "He'd come, do 'is business among such gents as he reckoned were worth 'is time, and be off. If anyone asked to get hold of 'im, we sent word to the White Swan."

"All right. Thank you. Best get upstairs. I'll be a while longer."

Ross shuddered. "Better you than me."

Ross retreated up the stairs. When he heard the door close, Adam reached out and closed Poole's unseeing eyes. Then he began the grim business of going through the dead man's pockets.

There was a surprising amount to find. Poole's watch still hung on its chain, and he had two rings on his fingers. His handkerchief was still in his pocket, as were several loose sovereigns and some coppers, as well. But the buttons on his coat and pockets had been torn.

Someone's already searched him. And yet they'd left tens of pounds of valuables behind. So, it was no ordinary thief.

It was what was missing that told the tale. Poole had no keys in his torn pockets. Likewise, there was no notebook or any other papers. Adam had never met an attorney about his business who did not carry a full printer's shop worth of paper with him.

Adam found a piece of sacking and wiped his hands.

Poole had been robbed, but not by someone looking for such stuff that could be readily converted into cash. Maybe the robber had found what they were looking for in one of Poole's pockets, but Adam didn't think so. Because if they had, they wouldn't have bothered to take the keys. Most likely, the person was now on his way to Poole's place of business.

Or his house.

Adam tossed the sacking aside and went back up the stairs and into Ross's office. Ross looked up as he entered, mouth open to ask a question.

Adam cut him off. "Which way to the White Swan?"

CHAPTER TWENTY

Mrs. Levitton

*". . . she had a bold and independent mind, which
is the principal ingredient in the formation of a
great queen, or an illustrious woman."*

Bury, Charlotte, *The Diary of a Lady-in-Waiting*

"And here you are at last, Miss Thorne." Mrs. Levitton rapped out this sharp greeting as Rosalind was ushered into her library.

"I do apologize," said Rosalind. "I came as quickly as I could."

Rosalind had begun her association with Mrs. Levitton only a few months ago. Since then, however, the formidable woman had become one of the principal figures in Rosalind's life.

Mrs. Levitton was a wealthy widow who ran a number of flourishing business concerns. Rosalind had assisted her, and her family, during a particularly delicate crisis. Her efforts had impressed the entrepreneuse enough that she offered to invest a sum with Rosalind, to put her on a stable footing.

It was Mrs. Levitton's money that had hired Rosalind's new household staff and paid a number of her daily expenses while her clientele expanded. In return, Rosalind, and her man of business, Etienne Prescott, met once a month with Mrs. Levitton, and the ladies with whom she had formed an unofficial consortium, to show her the accounts. It was agreed that once Rosalind's monthly income was above a certain level, she would begin to repay the investments, with interest.

As matters stood, they would reach that threshold far sooner than Rosalind had anticipated.

Mrs. Levitton was a tall, thin White woman with snow-white hair. She dressed in widow's black not, she said, from any overwhelming attachment to her late husband, but because it was simpler. "I have no interest in keeping up with fashion," she'd told Rosalind. She was difficult, mercurial, and kept her mental accounts as accurately as she did her monetary ones. She was also acerbic and cynical, and even with all Rosalind's practice at reading the intent of those around her, it was sometimes difficult to tell when or if Mrs. Levitton might be joking.

"When we entered into our arrangement, it was absolutely my intention to remain a silent and distant partner," Mrs. Levitton said as she waved Rosalind to a chair. "But I find myself compelled to ask, what on earth have you gotten yourself into?"

Which seemed to be very much the question of the day. Rosalind took her seat. "I'm afraid that remains to be seen."

The library was Mrs. Levitton's favorite room, and she conducted most of her business here. She was an avid reader not only of classics but also of new books. She spent her mornings with the papers and periodicals. To continue to make sound investments, she said, one needed to keep abreast of the news of the world, in large things and small.

"Well, you can at least say what took you to Mrs. Fitzherbert's door?" said Mrs. Levitton.

Rosalind had—rather pitifully, perhaps—hoped this question might not arise. Mrs. Levitton seldom asked her for details about the matters she worked on. If she knew the people involved, she might offer Rosalind some information or observation, but Mrs. Levitton did not press Rosalind to share confidential details.

As soon as royalty was involved, all manner of rules and suppositions changed.

"No, I'm afraid I cannot," said Rosalind.

Mrs. Levitton arched one pale brow. "And if I insist?"

"I must hope that you will not," replied Rosalind. "This is a confidence I cannot break." *Not any more than I already have done*, she added to herself guiltily. She met Mrs. Levitton's cynical gaze and felt sure the woman had understood that thought as clearly as if she'd spoken it aloud. "If you do insist, then we must turn this discussion to how I may best repay the money you have been so kind as to loan me."

Rosalind spoke calmly, but her mind was already frantically flipping through her ledgers as she tried to ascertain if she had enough money to cover her expenses until the quarter day.

Mrs. Levitton simply nodded. "Very good. Never let anyone dictate your principles, especially not the person who pays your rent. Now, what *can* you tell me?"

Relief flooded through her. When Rosalind's family fell apart, she had been taken in by her godmother, Lady Blanchard. Lady Blanchard had provided Rosalind a safe harbor—and had brought to her life a steady, experienced presence. If Lady Blanchard had not been loving, she had wanted the best for Rosalind, and she'd been there when Rosalind needed someone to turn to in moments of perplexity.

Since she had lost Lady Blanchard, Rosalind had missed such a presence badly. Mrs. Levitton had come to fill that void, at least a little.

"I can tell you that I have accepted a commission from Mrs. Fitzherbert, and the repercussions may be quite serious."

"Really?" Mrs. Levitton sounded surprised but hardly shocked. "Well, that tells me a great deal right there."

There was no possible way she did not guess what the matter was regarding. There was only one reason that the public in general knew Mrs. Fitzherbert's name.

"And may we assume that this matter is also why Lady Jersey has landed on your doorstep?"

There was not a racehorse at any track that ran faster than London gossip. "That would be a reasonable and natural assumption."

Mrs. Levitton nodded her approval at Rosalind's careful answer. "I should think so, especially as she's been lobbying the whole of London society on behalf of the queen." Mrs. Levitton saw Rosalind's momentary frown and smiled at it. "Oh, not me. She does not deign to acknowledge that women such as me exist."

Quite beyond the fact that Mrs. Levitton engaged in what Lady Jersey called "gross commerce," she came from a family entirely deficient in fortune, name, or title and did not aspire to gain them.

"However, like you, Miss Thorne, I have friends in odd places," Mrs. Levitton went on. "I believe you know the Countess Lieven?"

"Somewhat."

"Ha! I think that's all any of us can say about knowing her grace. Well, she was here this morning."

"Was she?" Now it was Rosalind who was genuinely surprised.

"Yes, indeed. Right at the stroke of eleven, with a footman to convey her gilt-edged calling card, so she should not have to descend from her carriage unnecessarily," Mrs. Levitton said. "She was so filled with compliments that at first I thought she'd come to ask for a loan." Her mouth curved into a thin smile at this idea. "However, in the midst of a rather breathtaking range of conversation, she inquired about you. It seemed to me she was hoping you might turn up during her visit. When you did not, she mentioned that she had not seen you in an age, and sighed that she would be so grateful for a visit. 'Life is so dull,' she said. 'I am starved for intelligent conversation.'"

But she could not send an invitation directly? Rosalind blinked in surprise.

She had become acquainted with the Countess Dorothea Lieven at about the same time as she first crossed paths with Lady Jersey. The countess was married to the Russian ambassador to the Court of St. James's. She had enough rumors swirling about her for a member of the royal family. They said she had conducted multiple affairs, including with the current king. They said she controlled her husband's policy. They said she spied for the tsar.

What Rosalind knew for certain was that Countess Lieven had helped her on several occasions. Furthermore, she was a powerful and influential figure in London society and was the person who had introduced the waltz to the *haut ton*. She also had a seat on the powerful board of patronesses of Almack's ballroom.

"Lady Jersey did indicate there was some disagreement between herself and the countess," said Rosalind.

Dorothea Lieven will not be persuaded, Lady Jersey had said. *Stubborn creature. Indeed, it may be that she is no longer quite suited for the board.*

"I should not be surprised," said Mrs. Levitton. "It's quite well known the countess favors the king's side when it comes to his marital difficulties. She faults the queen for not behaving as a woman ought."

And there, of course, was the reason the countess could not invite Rosalind directly. If the countess sent Rosalind an invitation or called herself, word might get back to Lady Jersey. This circuitous method of communication was an attempt to avoid notice.

That left Rosalind distinctly uneasy. If there was one thing that could be more tangled than the lives and scandals of royalty, it would be the machinations of the Almack's patronesses.

"Well," murmured Rosalind, "if her grace was so kind as to take the trouble to mention me to you, I had best take the time to call as soon as possible."

She and Mrs. Levitton talked a little more—of Mrs. Levitton's family, of Alice's novel and Amelia's school. Mrs. Levitton evidenced an interest in the project and promised Rosalind she would investigate it. Rosalind concealed her satisfaction. Such an investigation might well end with a donation from Mrs. Levitton or one of her friends.

The polite fifteen minutes over, and the question of whether Mrs. Levitton might be concerned about Rosalind's newest venture settled, Rosalind rose to leave.

As she did, Mrs. Levitton stopped her. "Miss Thorne?"

"Yes?"

An odd expression Rosalind could not entirely read passed over the older woman's face. "Should you find yourself in need of a solicitor at any point, I will send my man to you. And he may apply to me for his expenses."

"Thank you, Mrs. Levitton," replied Rosalind. "I do not think it will come to that."

But the truth was, she could not be sure.

CHAPTER TWENTY-ONE

The White Swan

*". . . had those letters been published . . . they
might have produced a revolution; for they not
only told all that is true, but a great deal that is
not true."*

Bury, Charlotte, *The Diary of a Lady-in-Waiting*

The White Swan wasn't the worst public house Adam had
ever been in, but it was far from the best. The place
slouched gloomily on its corner, and in this it was a match for
its patrons. The common room was filled with down-at-the-
heels men, who crowded over their pots of beer as if they
fully expected them to be taken away. The burly serving
woman looked as if she'd been chosen for her ability to haul
these men out by their ears, should they dare to breach the
moody peace. Still, she was ready enough to shout for the
landlord when Adam asked.

The Swan's landlord was a big, beefy man. He stomped up
from his cellar, a crockery jug in either hand. Looking at him,
Adam guessed the serving woman might well be his sister.

The landlord sized Adam up with a glittering eye that be-
lied the numb, dark nature of the place around him.

"An' what can I do for you, sir?" he drawled, indicating that it better not be much.

"I'm looking for Josiah Poole."

The landlord looked Adam up and down, judging him and not bothering to hide it. "Ain't seen 'im today," he said finally. "Ye can leave a message. I'll see 'e gets it."

"Do you know where he lives?"

The landlord shook his head. "But I'll let him know ye was—"

"He's dead," said Adam.

The man's mouth clapped shut. "'S truth?"

"I've just left his corpse," said Adam. "And there's reason to believe he was killed for something he might have left in his rooms or his house, so I need to know where both of those are."

The man's paralysis broke quickly. "And who might you be?" he demanded.

"Adam Harkness, assistant to the coroner."

It took another long moment, but the landlord eventually decided to believe him. "Couldn't tell you aught about where Poole lived, but he kept a room upstairs . . ."

"Show me."

But by this time the landlord had recovered from his shock. "Now you just see here—"

Adam cut him off. "It's possible we can still catch up with whoever murdered your tenant, but I must move quickly. Show me his room."

The words had the intended effect. The landlord shoved both jugs into the serving woman's hands. He grabbed a ring of keys out from under the bar and led Adam up a flight of rickety stairs.

The corridor above was as dark and as grimy. One door hung open, allowing a dim yellow beam of sunlight to shine feebly on the warped floorboards.

Adam shoved his way past the landlord, not even bothering to ask if that door led to Poole's room.

It did, and it looked as if Adam was already too late.

Beyond the doorway waited a small room, and the whole place was adrift in papers. Every drawer of the writing desk had been yanked open. The doors on the wardrobe gaped, and its contents had been heaped on the narrow bed. More papers were scattered around and over the table by the narrow window.

Adam swept his gaze across the disaster. Did they find what they were looking for?

There was no way to know.

The landlord stood in the doorway behind him. He uttered several oaths that would have blistered the paint on the walls, had there been any.

"Did you see anyone come up here?" asked Adam.

The man shook his head. "Been in the cellar past hour and more. Sara!" This last was a furious bellow directed down the hallway. A moment later the serving woman came puffing up the stairs.

"What 'cher . . . ?" Sara saw the ruin made of the room and swore with the same impressive intensity as her brother.

"Who'd you let up?" demanded the landlord.

"Nobody, I swear!"

"When was the last time you saw Poole?" asked Adam.

The pair exchanged a glance, and Adam watched them try to decide whether to tell him the truth.

"'Twas this morning," said Sara finally. "''E came round for a pot of bitters and a roast bird. 'Twas his habit."

Which was not what the landlord had told him, but Adam set that aside. "Did he say anything?" asked Adam. "Seem any different in way?"

Sara rested a fist on her hip. She looked at the ruined room, doubtlessly considering how long it would take her to clean it out. "He was in a good mood," she said. "I reckoned 'e'd come into some money or got himself a good fish on the hook, as 'e sometimes did."

"And he met with no one?"

"Not this morning," said Sara. "Not that I'd be able to swear to that," she added hastily. "People 'as always comin' in after him, weren't they? Sometimes they'd ask was he in. Sometimes they'd just go straight up. Couldn't keep track of everyone, could I? I got my own work to do."

"And you heard nothing unusual this morning?"

"Not a sound," said Sara.

"Thank you," Adam said to them both. "I need a message sent. Have you someone who can go at once?"

"I'll rouse the boy," said Sara. " 'E's a good lad, and quick."

Again, Adam thanked her. He pulled out the notebook and pencil he kept in his pocket. He scribbled a note, folded it, and wrote *R. Thorne* on the outside. He handed it to Sara with a couple of coins. "It needs to be there at once," he said.

"I'll see it done," she answered. Her gaze flicked to the mess. "You find who brought this on my house, you understand me?"

Adam nodded. "I'll do all I can."

That seemed to satisfy her. Sara stumped quickly away, hollering for someone named Toby—presumably the fast and reliable boy.

"I'll be a minute here," Adam told the landlord. "If anybody comes looking for me, or for Poole, let them up, would you?"

"As you like," said the landlord. He hesitated a moment. "An' if you do find the covey, you bring 'im round and I'll save you the price of the hangman. Poole was a good bloke. Ambitious, maybe, too full of 'imself sometimes, but a good tenant. Generous when 'e was in funds, liked to share what 'e had. You understand me?"

"I do. Thank you."

The landlord grunted and stumped off after Sara.

Left alone, Adam faced the chaos. He did not have much time. He needed to get back to the sponging house and speak with Sir David. Adam silently cursed whoever had turned this room into such a disaster. If the papers were in some sort of order, he might be able to quickly lay his hands on some personal correspondence or other document that had Poole's home direction on it. As it was, he might be here for hours before he hit on such a thing.

But he could not leave without making some kind of search.

Adam looked carefully at the lock on the door. There was no sign it had been forced. The door closed smoothly, with no more than an ordinary creaking of the hinges. Those hinges were rusted and caked with old grease but had no fresh marks to show they'd been meddled with.

The lid of the desk and what drawers had keyholes were likewise undamaged.

Adam glared sourly at the spilled mass of papers and belongings, the tipped chair, and the overturned drawers. He thought about the murderer with Poole's keys in his pockets. He thought about him trotting up the stairs, if not unobserved, at least unremarked on and quickly forgotten.

Something was wrong. That thought itched in the back of his mind and would not be quieted.

To all appearances, someone had met with Poole, had stabbed him, and had robbed him. They'd come here immediately afterward with the stolen keys and tossed this room, carelessly and frantically.

Looking for the certificate? Adam wondered. *Or something else?*

He thought about how neither Sara nor the landlord had heard anything odd. He looked again at the overturned chair and drawers.

And he knew.

The scene was staged. This apparent chaos was part of the murderer's plan.

CHAPTER TWENTY-TWO

The Gentle Art of Discovery

*"I have stated this danger upon the supposition
that the Marriage be a real one . . ."*

Langdale, Charles, *Memoirs of Mrs. Fitzherbert*

Adam's note was waiting for Rosalind on the front hall table when she walked into the house.

She let Claire help her out of her bonnet and coat and then took the missive into her private parlor. She closed the door. Her heart was hammering. She knew Adam's hand and could see at once that he had written her name quickly. She seemed to feel the uneasy brush of his agitation rising from the penciled script.

Rosalind unfolded the note and read the contents and sat down heavily in her desk chair.

She was still staring at the hastily written scrap when Alice knocked on the door and leaned inside.

"Hullo. I heard you come in, and . . . What's happened?"

Rosalind did not bother to ask how Alice knew something was very wrong. "Josiah Poole's been murdered."

"The lawyer?" Alice came inside and closed the door. "The one Ranking said was at Mrs. Fitzherbert's?"

"Yes." Rosalind held up Adam's note.

"Good Lord! Why? Was it because of the certificate?"

"There's no way to know yet," said Rosalind. "Adam says that he was thrown from a carriage in front of a sponging house and that he'd been stabbed."

"Lord!" Alice pressed a hand to her stomach, but Rosalind could see the wheels of her newswoman's mind already turning. "That might mean anything. He dealt in debtors, you said, and was not always honest."

Rosalind nodded. "Adam says he's found the public house room Poole used as an office, but it's been ransacked. He cannot tell if the certificate—or even the man's home address—is there."

"What can you do?"

"I don't—" Rosalind began, but even as she spoke, an idea dropped into her mind. She crossed the room and pulled one of her books off the shelf.

All gently bred ladies kept books of various sorts—household lists, accounts, records of visits paid and visits owed, records of dinners planned and given—in addition to files of correspondence from all manner of friends and acquaintances. Alongside all these usual books, Rosalind also kept volumes of newspaper clippings that detailed dinners, balls, marriages, deaths, and even items of planted gossip, many of them annotated with her own careful hand.

She opened a volume from the previous season and leafed through it until she found the page she wanted.

"What is it?" asked Alice.

"Miss Margaret Huntingdon," replied Rosalind. "Do you remember her?"

"Yesss . . . ," said Alice slowly. "No, wait. Wasn't she a drawing mistress?" For a short time, Rosalind and Alice had attended the same boarding school.

"Yes," replied Rosalind. "She married a Mr. Cotes some years back. He's a solicitor." She tapped the page. "It is late for calling, but if I leave at once, I can still be there before the dinner hour."

Alice's brow furrowed. "You think Mr. Cotes might know Mr. Poole?"

"Possibly. There are a great many attorneys in London, of course, but we already know this Mr. Poole has something of a reputation. Mr. Cotes might be able to give us a direction or point us to those who might. It could be quicker than sifting through a mountain of papers."

"It's certainly worth a try," agreed Alice. "Should I come with you?"

"Could you stay here? Adam may come looking for me or send another note, and I'll need it forwarded. If I don't find anything out from the Coteses, I'll send word and you can meet me at the White Swan."

Alice stepped back and gave a fair imitation of a military salute. Rosalind smiled but also began gathering up her reticule and notebook and gloves. She had fully intended to ask Alice if she'd had time to write to her professional gossip, Mrs. Dowding. With Minney Seymore so suddenly returned to Mrs. Fitzherbert's house, it was important to know everything she could about her and her sister. But that would have to wait until later.

Murder must come first.

Rosalind presented her card for Mrs. Cotes's gray-haired maid to take through to her employer. A moment later, the woman returned to usher Rosalind into a small but comfortable sitting room.

"Rosalind Thorne!"

"Mrs. Cotes. How good it is to see you again." Rosalind had maintained a casual level of correspondence with Margaret Cotes after her marriage but had not seen her in several years. Rosalind remembered a sturdy young woman with

long hands who had made a specialty of painting miniatures
and landscapes, which sold at respectable prices. This had
helped keep the household comfortable while Mr. Cotes finished his clerkship and was taken up as a junior partner at his
firm.

Now Mrs. Cotes had grown stout, as she herself had once
predicted would happen. Her hands were still strong and capable, and she bustled forward to grasp Rosalind's.

"How good to see you, Miss Thorne! You are looking very
well, I must say. But do sit down! Tea is here, as you see, and
you must try this walnut cake. I begged my sister's cook to
make it for me. She's German, and you know how they excel
at cakes."

The cake was excellent, as was the tea. Rosalind heard
about Mrs. Cotes's sons, away now at school, and her
daughter, still in the nursery, and about the cares and delights
of housekeeping for a busy husband and a variety of children.

"But you, Miss Thorne!" Mrs. Cotes cried. "We hear all
about your doings in the papers! I know old Mrs. Wallis
would tell me I should be appalled that you have come to any
such notice."

"I'm sure she hopes I never think to mention her school,"
agreed Rosalind.

Mrs. Cotes waved this away. "I say it is a tribute to our
teaching that one of our students should become so useful
and original. Now, I am going to press you shamelessly for
gossip. Have you truly met Lady Jersey? What is she like?"

Rosalind offered a few small anecdotes about the lady patronesses and a description of Almack's rooms and one of the
balls. A voice in the back of her mind urged her to hurry, reminded her that a man was dead, and that even now the papers might be printing news of Mrs. Fitzherbert's stolen
marriage certificate, but she silenced it firmly. It was neces-

sary to observe the formalities when renewing an acquaintance. A few moments' conversation must be had before she set her cup down.

"Mrs. Cotes, you must forgive me, but I had a particular reason for calling today."

"Did you?" said Mrs. Cotes happily. "You may believe I am all ears. Is it for one of your . . . clients?" Even as she spoke, her eyes grew rounder, because she had already as good as informed Rosalind that she, too, had seen the papers. "Is it—"

Rosalind did not permit her to go any further. "I'm afraid I cannot say, Mrs. Cotes. It is a matter of some delicacy."

"Oh!" Mrs. Cotes's cheeks colored. "Oh, of course you cannot say, my dear. I am quite ashamed of myself for asking. As an attorney's wife, one might think I would know better! But I am delighted to help, if I can."

"I am looking for information about an attorney, a man named Josiah Poole."

Mrs. Cotes considered this. "Poole? No, I do not know the name. He is no one I have met, I am sure, and I have met many of Cotes's colleagues. Shall I summon him? He came home for his luncheon today, and he's still in his bookroom. He might be able to tell you something or know who might."

Which was exactly what Rosalind had been hoping for. "Thank you. That would be most helpful."

Mrs. Cotes rang the bell for the maid. A few moments later, Mr. Emmet Cotes joined them. Mr. Cotes was an energetic aging White man with keen dark eyes, an arched nose, and a deeply receding hairline. He had come late to his profession and was ten years older than his wife, but that fact did not seem to discommode either of them. He wore a brightly patterned waistcoat with a heavy gold watch chain. He greeted Rosalind with breezy respect and looked on Mrs. Cotes with open affection as she fixed him a cup of tea.

"Miss Thorne has a question for you, my dear," said Mrs. Cotes as her husband settled into his chair. "About a man, an attorney. Josiah Poole, I think you said it was, Miss Thorne?"

All the good humor drained from Mr. Cotes's expression. "I do hope, Miss Thorne, that you have not been forced into dealings with Josiah Poole."

"I have not," said Rosalind. "I am inquiring on behalf of an acquaintance."

"Well, you may tell your acquaintance that they should have nothing to do with that man." Cotes leaned forward and stabbed the air with his blunt finger. "He's crooked as a rusty pin and thinks only of lining his pockets. Debt's a dirty business, Miss Thorne, but there are respectable men who practice honorably in that area. I can give your acquaintance a list if they are in need. Poole's name, needless to say, will not be on it."

Just the sort of man to slip into a house through the garden gate. And slip out again the same way.

"May I take it, then, he is not too particular of the sort of work he takes on?" asked Rosalind.

Mr. Cotes snorted. Mrs. Cotes frowned, and the lawyer instantly blushed. It was rather charming.

"If Josiah Poole scents profit, he will go after it, by fair means or foul," Mr. Cotes told her. "He will lie, cheat, or steal to gain his fee."

"Do you mean that literally, Mr. Cotes?" asked Rosalind.

Cotes's eyes narrowed, which turned his jovial face shrewd. Rosalind felt certain that it was a look honed by his experience in the courts.

"I do. When Poole is on the case, vital papers—receipts, ledgers, letters, the lot—have an excellent chance of going missing."

Rosalind's heart thumped once.

"I see. And this is widely known?"

"Within the profession. Obviously, nobody's actually accused him of outright housebreaking, but there's been one too many persons caught flat-footed in court by a demand to produce a vital document that is found to be missing."

"I see," said Rosalind again. She took a sip of tea to help calm the whirlwind of her thoughts.

"I would never pry into a lady's confidence," said Mr. Cotes. "But if you know anything that can help us hound that rascal out of the practice of law, I should be gratified to hear it."

"You will not be called on for such an effort," replied Rosalind. "Mr. Poole is dead."

The Coteses stared at her, frozen in absolute surprise. Mr. Cotes recovered first.

"Is he b'ghad?" he exclaimed. "What did for him? A client or his heart, if he had one?"

"Cotes!" cried Mrs. Cotes. "In front of a guest!"

"I apologize, Mrs. Cotes, Miss Thorne." Cotes bowed his head but this time did not look at all contrite. "That was more than I should have said."

"No apology necessary, Mr. Cotes," Rosalind told him. "I expect it will be in the papers quite soon—he died by violence. The coroner's office is conducting an inquiry into the matter." Surely by now Adam was speaking of the matter with Sir David Royce.

"Did Mr. Poole have a partner of any sort?" Rosalind asked. "Anyone who would have known his business or his plans?"

"None that I know of, but then I kept as far from him as I was able."

Rosalind paused and arranged her expression to show that she understood she was asking about a matter of some delicacy. "Would you happen to know his personal address?"

"Lord, what do . . . No, no." Cotes held up his hand. "I

withdraw the question. Give me a moment . . ." He heaved himself out of his seat and left the room.

"I'm so glad we were able to help, Rosalind." Mrs. Cotes refilled her teacup. "I know you cannot say why you need to know, but you must believe me, this is most exciting for us."

Rosalind's expression must have shifted, because Mrs. Cotes's eyes flew open wide. "Oh, no, you mustn't think I'm going to gossip! You would be amazed at what's been said in this house, and I promise you, none of it goes any further."

"I didn't mean to imply . . ."

"Of course not, of course not. But you do look a little tired. How horrid to have the death of even a bad man land at your doorstep. I am sure your nerves must be close to breaking."

Rosalind let herself smile a little weakly and drank her tea. This allowed her to avoid formulating a reply.

Thankfully, Cotes returned a moment later. He handed Rosalind a visiting card.

"Poole and I had dealings a year or two ago," he said. "The man actually called here rather than going to chambers." He snorted again. "And well he might. He meant to sound me out to see if I'd take a bribe." He tucked his fingers into his waistcoat pocket. "So, you can see, I'm not exactly startled to hear he's come to a bad end."

Rosalind read the address and felt her eyebrows rise. Mr. Poole had a terrible reputation, but he lived in a fashionable, and expensive, neighborhood.

"Thank you for your assistance, Mr. Cotes." She tucked the card into her reticule. "I'm afraid I have to ask another favor."

"Of course, dear," said Mrs. Cotes. "What is it?"

"I need to send a message, and after that, I need to send for a cab."

CHAPTER TWENTY-THREE

In Service

"I avoided all questions, and endeavored neither to deceive nor be deceived; but sometimes it was next to impossible not to ask a question or make an observation, which the next moment was repented of."

Bury, Charlotte, *The Diary of a Lady-in-Waiting*

Amelia was ready when the bell rang in the adjoining room. About half an hour before, she had heard the unmistakable sounds of young women coming along the corridor—the rustle of skirts, high, urgent voices bantering back and forth. Since Mrs. Fitzherbert's daughters were meant to be in the country, she knew something must have changed.

"Yes, madam?" Amelia said as she entered Mrs. Fitzherbert's private sitting room. She did not look pleased. Indeed, she appeared both tired and put out.

"I'm afraid you'll be rather busier than we initially believed, McGowan. My daughters have arrived quite unexpectedly."

"Yes, madam."

"They are young enough that I have not yet engaged them their own maids, so I'm afraid you will have to do for the three of us for dinner this evening. Will you be able to manage?"

"Yes, madam. " Which would have been her answer even if she wasn't sure. It was her job to manage. "I have experience with young ladies."

"Well, that gives you an advantage over me. Good heavens, what can she be *thinking*—" Mrs. Fitzherbert broke off. "But then I gave my own mother more than one opportunity to wonder what I could be thinking, and that after I was a woman grown."

"I'm sure all mothers must say it once in a while, no matter what age their daughters." Her own, for instance, had had plenty to say. So much so that Amelia had not spoken to her in years.

"Yes, I'm sure you're right." Mrs. Fitzherbert straightened her spine and shoulders. "Well, let's go introduce you to my girls."

Amelia bobbed a curtsy in acknowledgment and stepped aside to allow Mrs. Fitzherbert to take the lead.

The young ladies' rooms proved to be just down the corridor from Mrs. Fitzherbert's. The door might be closed, but there was no question as to which was theirs. The sounds of an argument became clearly audible as they approached.

Mrs. Fitzherbert's face creased with frustration and embarrassment.

"Minney!" she called as she knocked. "Mary Ann!"

The voices ceased immediately. A moment later the door was opened by a dark-haired young woman.

"Yes, Mama?" Her innocence was as forced as her smile.

One look at the sitting room, and Amelia knew she was in for a time. These girls had only just arrived, and already it looked as if a storm wind had swept through the place. There were no trunks in view, but half the drawers had been pulled open, and their contents spread across the tops of the bureaus and dressing tables. The doors hung open on the two elegant wardrobes, and all the dresses hanging there had been rifled through.

Minney—Miss Seymore, Amelia recalled—the taller of the pair, clutched a thin pink fichu, while Miss Mary Ann had a green silk ribbon dangling from her fingers, looking like a startled doe.

Sensing an opportunity, Amelia stepped forward briskly and helped herself to the ribbon. With practiced motions, she looped the ribbon around the crown of Miss Mary Ann's head and tied it in a pretty bow by her ear, then adjusted things so that the ends draped fetchingly over her shoulder.

"There." She turned the young woman toward the nearest mirror. "A perfect picture."

Miss Seymore sniffed.

"McGowan is my new maid, Minney," said Mrs. Fitzherbert. "She'll be helping both of you, as well."

"Oh, no," said Miss Seymore quickly. "There's no need to bother with us . . ."

"I'm afraid there is," said Mrs. Fitzherbert. "You forget, the Duke of York is coming to dinner."

"Oh, well, yes, for that, I suppose, but we're settling in quite nicely, aren't we, Mary?"

Amelia very carefully did not look at the disorder that had blossomed all around them.

"Oh, yes," said Miss Mary Ann, with all a younger sister's aggrieved feeling. "When you've been hunting for your coral brooch for the past half hour, and all the time wailing about how we're going to be late . . ."

"We're supposed to meet Dulcie Walsford," said Miss Seymore to Mrs. Fitzherbert, and far too quickly. "She sent around a note inviting us."

"But you've only just arrived." Mrs. Fitzherbert frowned, and both the girls tensed. But the moment passed. "Well, be sure you're back in plenty of time. Since you insist on being here, I expect you at the table."

"Oh. No. I can't, Mama!" cried Miss Seymore. "I've nothing here to wear."

"Your silver gown will do quite well. McGowan can see to it. And, Mary Ann, you can wear your pink."

"Must I? It makes me look such a child."

"Unless you've brought something better, then yes, you must," said Mrs. Fitzherbert. "Or do you both wish to spend the rest of the day at the modiste's, while she tries to make you up something vaguely acceptable from whatever she may have on hand?"

From the look on Miss Seymore's face, you would have thought Mrs. Fitzherbert had just suggested they be confined to the cellars.

Vanity, is it? Or something else?

"No, Mama," said Miss Mary Ann. "My pink will be just fine."

"I'd forgotten about the silver," said Miss Seymore meekly. "Of course, that will do very well."

She looked helplessly at the crumpled fichu she held. Amelia took it from her and folded and tucked the scarf about her shoulders. A perfectly lovely little turquoise brooch lay to hand on the dressing table.

"This will look very well," she remarked as she pinned it in place. "It matches your sash."

Miss Seymore did not look ready to concede any such point, but she also plainly did not have time to argue. Instead, she simply let out a long-suffering huff.

"Now, where have I put my gloves?" Miss Seymore pulled open one of the few drawers in the room that had not already been left gaping and retrieved a pair of kid gloves. She slammed the drawer shut immediately. "Yes. I'm quite ready now, Mary Ann." She paused. "Thank you . . . McGowan, is it?"

"Yes, miss," replied Amelia calmly.

"We'd best be on our way," said Miss Mary Ann with forced brightness. "Mama? Are there any errands we can run for you while we're out?"

Mrs. Fitzherbert's expression was meant to let her girls know she was not being fooled. "Oh, go along, both of you."

Miss Seymore's relief was obvious, at least to Amelia. The girls both kissed Mrs. Fitzherbert's cheeks as they filed past her. Amelia watched them retreat through narrowed eyes.

If they're going to meet any Miss Dulcie, she thought, *I'll eat my bonnet.*

She had to work to keep her gaze from shifting toward the drawer Miss Seymore had closed so firmly and so swiftly. *So, my girl, if not Miss Dulcie, then who?*

Once Mrs. Fitzherbert had left Amelia with instructions to make sure her girls' gowns were ready for dinner, she began tidying the room. She folded scarves and handkerchiefs that Miss Seymore had scattered and put them away. She closed drawers. She laid the straw bonnet tossed onto one of the two narrow beds on its shelf in the wardrobe.

If one wanted to be fussy, one could say this was all the business of the chambermaid. Amelia, however, thought it would be best to show herself a willing worker and not above helping out.

In the wardrobe she found the lovely silver and white dinner gown and the much-derided pink silk. Both would need brushing and pressing. The silver had a tear in the hem, and a ruffle on the pink's left sleeve threatened to come loose. Suitable gloves would have to be unearthed, and hair arrangements planned.

While she worked, Amelia kept one ear on the hallway.

She heard no movement. A glance at the crack under the door showed no shadows.

Patiently and methodically, she tidied her way around the room until she reached Miss Seymore's dressing table and the one drawer the young lady had been very careful to close.

She picked up the gloves that had been tossed aside among the brushes and bottles and opened the drawer.

Inside, she found several other pairs of gloves and hand-kerchiefs, a silver card case, a beaded reticule, and a hastily crumpled scrap of paper.

She was just about to reach for this when she felt a breeze brush the back of her neck. Carefully, and without any sign of startle or panic, she laid the gloves in the drawer, closed it, and turned around.

Faller stood in the doorway. "Well, that was unexpected, wasn't it?"

"You have nothing better to do but hang around in my doorway?" demanded Amelia, unable to decide whether she should be worried or simply miffed.

"I can help with the lifting if you like." He nodded toward several hat boxes, which had probably been taken out of the wardrobe and should be replaced.

"What? And have your mucky hands all over their good things?" Amelia snorted. "I don't think so!"

He looked genuinely affronted. "Just offering. You only just got here, and they've already put you to work."

Amelia swallowed a sigh. Probably she should keep on en-couraging him. Get him used to the idea she was always ready to hear from him. But she kept thinking about that crumpled bit of paper in the drawer, and how careful Miss Seymore was to shut that same drawer when she was per-fectly willing to leave every other one hanging wide open. What was in there she didn't want seen? Amelia couldn't know until she got Faller out of here.

"Work's what I came for," she reminded him.

"Well now." He sauntered into the room. Amelia resisted the urge to stamp her foot. "There's work, and there's work. Now—"

"Faller!" A portly man in the scarlet house livery sailed into view in the doorway. "What are you doing in there?" The new man cast a quick, sharp glance toward Amelia. She stiffened. "Oh. hello," he said to her, but there was no warmth in the greeting. "McGowan, is it?"

"That's right."

The fat man grunted, gave her another scathing glance, and turned back to Faller. "You're wanted downstairs at once. Mr. Holm's about to burst looking for you."

"All right, all right," grumbled Faller. "I'm coming."

"You better, or you'll be out on your ear." The fat man gave Amelia a look, as if to include her in the warning. Amelia remembered what Mrs. DeLupe had said about her and the butler having madam's confidence, and their willingness to use it to sack those they didn't think were up to scratch.

Reluctantly, Faller let himself be herded off. The fat man followed close, like he thought Faller might make a run for it. But he still managed to spare Amelia one more sharp glower.

Amelia closed the door and stared at it.

Faller's idling had just made her look bad to whoever that fat man turned out to be—head footman most likely. Did he think she was encouraging Faller? That would set her off on the wrong foot in ways she couldn't afford.

Or was it just that Faller was the sort that would stop working as soon as someone stopped watching? She'd met plenty of those.

But that didn't sit quite right. Having Faller come sniffing about once was understandable. He was curious about the new addition to the staff.

But twice? That started to feel like he was looking for something.

Well, I'll sort out Mr. Faller later.

Amelia hurried over to the dressing table. She pulled open the drawer and snatched out the crumpled paper.

She glanced toward the door. It remained shut. Nothing she could see or hear moved outside.

Amelia opened the paper. It was a note—very brief and to the point.

Tonight. Ten o'clock.

Well, well. No wonder Miss Seymore was so upset about having to be at dinner. Miss Thorne had told her Burrowes suspected one or the other of the girls was up to something. It seemed she was right.

Now, I wonder who wrote this? And what's our Miss Seymore going to do about it?

If she really was in service here, the correct thing to do would be to show this to Mrs. DeLupe or to madam at once. It might even be the right thing to do now, considering she was supposed to be snooping around.

But it was no good telling tales until she knew what she was talking about. Amelia crumpled the paper up and put it back right where she'd found it. Besides, just now it would be far too obvious that she was the one who blabbed.

Much better to wait and watch.

One eye on Miss Seymore and one on Mr. Faller.

Amelia sighed. And more likely than not she'd need another eye or two before this business was finished.

CHAPTER TWENTY-FOUR

The Dead Man

*"If this is true, it is a pity, and I have other
reasons for thinking there may be some truth in
the story."*

Bury, Charlotte, *The Diary of a Lady-in-Waiting*

Adam delayed longer at the White Swan than he had originally intended, but even so, he made little progress sorting through the swamp of papers, and what he did find yielded nothing useful.

In the end, Adam instructed the landlord to lock the room and see it was left undisturbed, and set out again for Ross's.

He was in luck, and in time. Sir David was still in the cellar with Poole's corpse when Adam arrived.

"Well, Harkness," Sir David greeted Adam as he descended the stairs. "What's this you've landed in?"

Sir David Royce was the coroner for London and Westminster. All, or at least most, cases of violent or suspicious death within those precincts were his purview. It was his duty to inspect the corpse and to question any witnesses, or at least see that they were questioned. He was also tasked with arranging further inquiries he felt might be needed to deter-mine if the matter was an accident, a fault of nature, or if the king's peace had been breached.

The coroner was in the act of washing his hands in a battered tin basin. Poole's form was visible under the makeshift canvas shroud.

Adam glanced again toward the cellar door to make sure it was closed. Sir David noticed.

"Ross told me our fellow here was found in the street," Sir David remarked as he dried his hands on a strip of gray toweling that had seen better days.

"I saw him thrown from a carriage."

Sir David pursed his lips in a silent whistle. "That's deeply cold-blooded."

While Adam was still a principal officer at Bow Street, he had worked with Sir David several times. When he walked away from that post, Sir David had offered him work as one of his assistants. Adam had accepted readily. He liked Sir David. The coroner was a careful, scrupulous man whose interest in discovering the truth was greater than his interest in politics or social advancement. Like Adam, Sir David had more than once found himself at cross-purposes with those who did not appreciate that view of the world.

Sir David busied himself with rinsing his scalpels in the basin. Unlike most coroners, Sir David had trained as a physician and had a good understanding of human anatomy. He'd been appointed to the post after a tenure as the head of a teaching hospital.

"It looked like he was stabbed," said Adam. "Is that what did for him?"

"It is, and it was done with a good sharp blade. A kitchen knife, perhaps, or a hunting knife. The assailant got him in the guts, and it was the loss of blood that killed him."

Adam nodded. Stomach wounds were almost always fatal. If the blood loss did not finish the victim off, the infections that invariably set in afterward did. It was frequently a more reliable target than the heart, although most people did not know that.

Which made the assailant lucky, or experienced.

"Would it have taken much strength to deliver the blow?"

Sir David considered. "It was very clean, a single thrust. There were no marks that would indicate the assailant hesitated at all, so we can suppose Poole was taken by surprise. A small man could have done it." He looked again at Adam. "I see what you're thinking. Yes, a determined woman could have done it, as well." He paused. "I gather Poole did a lot of business with the guests of this particular house?" Sir David gestured toward the ceiling with a scalpel before he laid it in his case.

"So I'm given to understand," said Adam.

"A man could make enemies in that line of business. How did you happen to be here to find him?"

Adam stepped closer and lowered his voice. "I was looking for him. There's a possibility he was involved in a robbery at another house, where the lady called on Miss Thorne to help retrieve her property."

"What was missing?"

Adam leaned closer. Sir David's brows rose. Softly, Adam told him about Mrs. Fitzherbert and about Ranking's story of seeing Josiah Poole slip into her garden and out again.

"Good God!" Sir David breathed. "You don't mean to say this fellow got his hands on the Prince of Wales's marriage certificate?"

"I don't know," said Adam. "The certificate has been stolen. He was seen. I didn't find the thing on his body when I searched him, but Ross pointed me to the pub Poole used as an office, and when I got there, the room had been thoroughly tossed."

"So there's no saying what the assailant was looking for." Sir David squinted at Adam. "What's wrong?"

"Aside from the obvious?" said Adam sardonically. "When

I searched Poole, I didn't find any keys on him. When I got to his rooms, the door was open, but not forced."

"So, it's likely the person who killed him, or at least a person with him when he was killed, took his keys and went to his rooms, looking for something."

"And knew where to go," said Adam. "And what room it was. The house has several guest rooms in its upper story, and neither the landlord nor the serving woman remembers any person asking for Poole that morning."

"Any chance they found what they were looking for?"

"I think they did, and I think they found it on him either before or after they killed him."

Sir David paused in packing his knives away. "Why's that?"

"When I got to the pub, it was still fairly early in the morning, and the place wasn't that crowded. The mess I saw would have created a commotion. The serving woman at least would have heard it. But she says she did not, and I'm inclined to believe her. I think that mess was staged."

"To what end?"

"Someone might want to make us think that Poole's death was related to something other than the certificate. They may be trying to make it all look like a crime of opportunity rather than something premeditated."

Sir David nodded. "Or perhaps Poole had been paid to get hold of the certificate, and that someone decided that Poole should not be left alive to speak about what he'd done. Perhaps Poole didn't bring the document to the scheduled meeting, because he intended to ask for more money."

"It could even have been both," said Adam. "The client planned the murder, and Poole was intending to extort more money from them."

"Well, regardless, there will have to be an inquest, and it will have to be soon," said Sir David. "Given the nature of the . . . situation surrounding the man, I'll rely on you to take care of the questioning of potential witnesses. What has Miss Thorne to say?"

Not only did Sir David respect Rosalind's particular gifts, but he also had called on her to help with cases of violent death that touched the lives of the aristocracy. It was another reason why Adam felt comfortable working for the man.

"I haven't spoken to her about Poole's death. I only had time to send a note."

Sir David puffed out his cheeks. "Well. You'd better talk to Ross, and anyone else in the house who had doings with Poole, just in case we're wrong about the killer's motives. I'll have the body taken to the morgue. Do we know if the man had any family?"

"I asked Ross, but he didn't know. Neither did the folk at the White Swan."

"Hmph. Well, I can see where a man like him would have reason to keep his business and his family life separated." He glowered at the canvas-covered figure. "No chance of finding the carriage he was pushed from, I suppose?"

"Not much," said Adam. "It was plain black, and the horses were chestnuts, but not matched or blooded that I could see. The driver was muffled to his eyebrows."

"On such a warm day?"

Adam nodded. "Which is another reason to believe the crime was planned. Poole was still bleeding freely when he hit the cobbles, so the thing practically had to be done inside the carriage, and done quickly. There'd be no need to hide the driver if the owner of the carriage had simply intended to pay Poole for the certificate."

"Yes, I'd have to agree there." Sir David sighed. "Well, I'll have to inform Bow Street. We may need their help. But first—"

The sound of the cellar door opening cut off whatever Sir David had been about to add. A moment later, Ross thumped down the stairs, his air filled with restrained impatience.

"Now, Sir David, you've had your look at him," said Ross. "When can you get him out of here? Knowing he's down here, it's upsetting my guests."

"Guests?" remarked Sir David.

Ross shrugged. "Gentlemen expect to be treated like gentlemen, no matter where they happen to be lodged."

Sir David did not say what he thought of this, but his expression suggested it was not much. "Well, I'm afraid you'll have to make do with one more guest for a few hours longer."

"What for?" demanded Ross. "There's a porter with a cart on the corner, and this one"—Ross stabbed a finger at Adam—"he can vouchsafe that Poole's getting stuck in his guts has nothing to do with this house."

"That would seem to be true," said Sir David calmly. "But there's questions that will have to be asked. I trust you can help make sure your guests are ready to answer?"

Ross looked mulish, but in the end he sighed. "Well, I suppose there's no help for it. But, listen, this won't interfere with my warrant to keep this house, will it? Because even if one of the guests did some'at, it's aught to do with me."

"We'll see about that," replied Sir David. A bolt of fear flickered behind Ross's eyes. Sir David did not trouble himself to reassure Ross there was no danger.

"All right, Mr. Harkness—" began Sir David.

"Oh, Harkness." Ross snapped his fingers. "Boy came looking for you. Had a message." He produced a note from his pocket and handed it across. Adam took it, saw that it was addressed in Rosalind's hand.

"I'll finish here and find you in your office," said Sir David to Ross.

Ross looked at Adam and at the dead man and the coroner. Seeming to find no help for his situation, he turned and climbed heavily up the stairs.

The door shut. Adam unfolded the note, read, and smiled.

"What is it?" asked Sir David.

"A message from Miss Thorne," Adam told him. "She's discovered Poole's residence and asks to meet me there."

"You are not in the least surprised."

"I'm not. Are you?"

"I find I am not," said Sir David. "Go on, then. I'll arrange matters here and see what can be done to stop Ross from talking or panicking." He paused. "Take care, Harkness. Once word of this mess gets out, there will be very powerful people scrambling to find out what is known or what might be told."

CHAPTER TWENTY-FIVE

Hearth and Home

*"... but it is all glitter and glare, and trick; every-
thing is tinsel and trumpery about it; it is
altogether a bad dream."*

Bury, Charlotte, *The Diary of a Lady-in-Waiting*

Josiah Poole lived on Great Cumberland Street, near Port-
man Square. It was a neighborhood where the well estab-
lished lived alongside the still ambitious. The houses here
were a little older and a little smaller than those in the most
fashionable areas, but they were still well appointed. The carriages pulling up to the doors were new and neatly kept,
though they lacked coats of arms on their doors. Servants
here were not in livery, but they were plentiful.

Adam arrived less than a quarter hour after Rosalind.
Rosalind let the driver help her down and hurried to meet
him, even though the only greeting they could exchange in
the public street was a polite nod.

"I've just come from Sir David," Adam told her. "Unfortunately, he did not discover much beyond the obvious. Poole
died of a stab wound recently delivered."

"And you have found nothing to indicate whether the at-

tack came because of the certificate or Mrs. Fitzherbert?"
They fell into easy step together, making their way up the
street.

"Nothing," said Adam. "We'll have to hope his family can
enlighten us, or at least that they'll give us permission to go
through his papers." He paused. "That was well done, by the
way," Adam remarked. "Sir David was impressed with how
quickly you were able to find his private residence. How did
you manage?"

"One of the drawing mistresses from my old school left to
marry an attorney. We kept in touch. I admit I was not at all
sure my inquiry would bear fruit so quickly. There are a famously large number of men at law in London."

"You have a way of defying the odds."

"Thank you, sir." Rosalind took a moment to enjoy his
compliment before they both began the serious business of
crossing the street in the midst of the evening traffic. They'd
arrived at a busy time. The men who had been out at their
places of business, and the women who had been out making calls and running their own errands, were all returning
home.

The address on Mr. Poole's visiting card was Number 23.
This proved to be a respectably sized house in the middle of
the block. Although it was barely twilight, the lamp was lit.
The clean windows, tidy stoop, and polished brass announced
it as an efficiently run establishment.

"This is not going to be easy," said Adam. "Will you be all
right?"

"We will find out." Rosalind smoothed her sleeves and
straightened her bonnet. "I have delivered unpleasant news
before, certainly, but seldom to complete strangers."

Adam's fingers brushed hers. Then he took hold of the
knocker and rapped firmly.

A few moments later, a maid in tidy black and white
opened the door. Adam presented her with his card.

"We wish to speak with Mrs. Poole," said Adam. "I'm afraid the matter is urgent."

The maid looked at the card. She also looked at Adam and Rosalind, but much more skeptically. Rosalind could see her trying to work out what sort of urgent business brought a well-dressed woman to the door after polite visiting hours.

Nonetheless, she did ask them to step in and took the card through.

Adam looked about the foyer and cocked one eyebrow at Rosalind. She nodded. This was not a home that fit with the character of unprincipled Josiah Poole, who kept his office in a public house. From what they could see, all was in excellent taste and arranged with the elegant moderation favored by the most skilled hostesses.

The maid returned. "If you will follow me, please? Mrs. Poole will be down in a moment."

The maid took them to a small library. As they entered, the man seated by the hearth rose. He ducked his head, hunched his shoulders, leaned heavily on a walking stick, and held Adam's card.

"Mr. . . ." The man glanced at the card. "Mr. Harkness? My name is Considen. Mrs. Poole is my sister."

Mr. Considen was a tall, broad man. He was also no longer in health. His white skin sagged against his bones. His color was not merely pale but tinged with gray. His eyes were clouded, as if he suffered prematurely from cataracts, but she could still see the grim determination in them.

"How do you do, sir?" Adam made his bow. "May I introduce Miss Rosalind Thorne?"

Rosalind made her curtsy.

"May I ask what your business is with my sister?" said Mr. Considen, mostly to Adam. "If it is anything to do with money, you will need to wait until her husband returns home." His whole body spasmed once, as if he were trying to hold in a hard cough. "We do not expect him for at least another hour."

"Unfortunately, it is regarding her husband that we've come," said Adam.

"What is this about my husband?"

Mrs. Poole entered the room, then closed the door carefully behind her. She was approaching her middle years but seemed to have accepted them with equanimity. Her hair was a fading auburn, swept into a simple twist and pinned underneath a lace cap edged with silver. She wore a dignified blue silk tea gown with only a single row of ruffles at the hem and simple lace cuffs and collars. Like the household around them, she was tasteful and absolutely correct.

Like the house, nothing about her fit with what they knew of Mr. Poole. Except possibly the old, haunted look in her blue eyes.

"Melora," said Mr. Considen. "This is Mr. . . ." He glanced at the card again. "Adam Harkness and, erm, Miss Rosalind Thorne."

"How do you do?" Mrs. Poole said uncertainly.

"Thank you for seeing us, Mrs. Poole," said Rosalind. "I believe we have an acquaintance in common. Mrs. Cotes?"

Mrs. Poole's face went blank for a minute but then brightened. "Oh, yes. I knew her much better as Miss Huntingdon. How is she?" She gestured for them to sit. Her brother also returned to his seat, slowly and cautiously, as if he could not fully trust his body to obey his commands. He kept tight hold of his stick, as if he expected to need to rise again at any moment.

Once her hostess had been seated, Rosalind said, "Mrs. Cotes is very well. I called on her specifically to find your address. I am afraid we are here with very bad news."

Mrs. Poole's face lost a bit of its color. Mr. Considen's fingers curled more tightly around his stick.

"I am sorry we must tell you that Mr. Josiah Poole is dead," said Adam quietly.

Mrs. Poole's expression froze. She trembled slightly where she sat. Mr. Considen heaved himself to his feet, abandoning his stick, then stumped quickly to his sister's side. His pale hand closed around her shoulder.

"I'm all right, William." Mrs. Poole's reassurance was harsh and breathless. She swallowed hard and pressed her hand against her stomach, as if she feared she was about to be sick. Indeed, her face had turned a pasty gray.

Not seeing a bell, Rosalind hurried to the sitting room door. She opened it to find the maid standing there, and judging from the stricken look on her face, she'd overheard the entire conversation.

"Some tea and brandy quickly," Rosalind said and closed the door again.

Mr. Considen gave her a reproving glower for presuming to give orders when she'd only just set foot in the house, but he did not contradict her.

"What happened?" Mr. Considen asked instead. "What"— again, his body spasmed—"what did he do?"

Once again, here the assumption was that Mr. Poole was to blame for his own death. Rosalind and Adam exchanged a glance.

"Please," Mrs. Poole said, and her voice shook only a little. "Tell me what happened."

"We do not yet know the reason behind his death," said Adam. "I am here as an assistant to Sir David Royce, the coroner. He will be conducting the inquiry." Such circumnavigation was very different from Adam's usual plain speaking. There was, of course, no truly gentle way to tell such a tale, but he was doing what could be done to put some distance between the events and the family. "It is known that Mr. Poole was found in Newgate Street, and there were marks of violence on him."

Mrs. Poole looked ill but not surprised. Indeed, if anything, she looked angry.

The door opened, and the maid reentered, carrying a tray of tea things and a decanter of brandy. A young woman in a pink and white dress entered with her.

"Letitia!" cried Mrs. Poole. "You were meant to be resting."

Rosalind was instantly struck by the young woman's appearance. Rosalind was used to being the tallest woman in any gathering, but the new arrival was at least her equal. Most young people, when they suffered sudden growth, became painfully awkward and hunched over to try to hide this strange new self. This girl moved with confidence, even poise. Her face was as strong as the rest of her. She had an air of maturity, even though she could not have been much more than seventeen.

"What is going on? Judith says . . ." Letitia paused, her oval face twisted with anger and confusion. "Judith says Papa is *murdered*. Is this true?"

"Judith!" cried Mrs. Poole to the maid. Judith stood with her eyes lowered and her hands folded, but her face was stubborn.

"Is it true?" demanded Letitia.

"Yes," said Mrs. Poole. "Yes, it is."

A spasm of anger crossed the girl's face. She seemed to notice Rosalind and Adam for the first time. "Who are these? *What's happened?*" The question threatened to become a shout.

No one answered her. Mr. Considen spoke to the maid instead. "That will be enough, Judith."

The maid made her curtsy and left, but with visible reluctance. Only then did Mr. Considen turn to Letitia.

"Letitia, go back upstairs. Melora . . ."

"I'll be there in a minute," said Mrs. Poole. "Then I'll tell you everything."

Letitia did not move. "Just tell me why this has happened," she demanded. "What did he do?"

Again, that question. Letitia stared into Mrs. Poole's eyes for a long moment. Rosalind could not read what was passing between them, but Letitia's eyes grew bright and hard as glass.

"Go upstairs, Letty," Mr. Considen ordered. "Make sure the boys are all right. Tell Nanny, if you must, but don't frighten them. Melora will be there as soon as she may be."

"Melora?" said Letitia.

Mrs. Poole nodded. Letitia's face hardened, but she made no further protest. She simply turned and swept from the room.

"Letitia is my husband's daughter by his first wife," said Mrs. Poole, sinking back into her chair. "She will take this very hard."

"Where . . . how may we . . . Arrangements will need to be made," stammered Mr. Considen.

"You will be sent word about when and how you may retrieve the body," said Adam. "It will be tomorrow at the latest."

"And you can say nothing about his death?" asked Mrs. Poole plaintively. "Nothing at all?"

"It was our hope you might have something to tell us."

A laugh escaped Mrs. Poole, a short, sharp sound. She immediately pressed her hand over her mouth. "I do beg your pardon," she murmured and cleared her throat. "My husband—" She stopped and began again. "My husband was not one to confide in me about his business. He kept his domestic life as far away from his practice as possible."

"Did he have a bookroom or an office in the house?" asked Adam.

Mrs. Poole blinked. "Well, yes, of course. There is not much of his work in it."

"May we see it?"

"Really, you cannot ask that." Mr. Considen's words grated harsh and painful against his throat. "You come here, you tell my sister she's a widow, and now you want to run riot through the house!"

"We have a very short time to try to find who did this thing before they disappear," replied Adam patiently. "Mr. Poole's papers may tell us if someone harbored enough of a grudge to wish him harm. Unless you can?"

Considen snorted, and the sound dissolved into a brutal cough that doubled him over. His sister moved toward him, but he threw up his hand in a curt gesture, and she stopped.

"My brother knows nothing of my husband's business," said Mrs. Poole.

Mr. Considen straightened. "Less even than Melly," he gasped.

"And Josiah kept no papers here," said Mrs. Poole. "No important ones, at any rate."

The brandy and tea things had sat forgotten on the table. Now Mr. Considen lurched to the tray and lifted the decanter. His blue-veined hand shook.

"William, you must sit down, before you collapse." Mrs. Poole quickly took the decanter from him. He glared at her but quickly dropped back into his chair. Melora poured him a glass of the brandy, which he drank at a single gulp.

"I am so sorry," Mrs. Poole whispered to the room in general. "I should have offered you tea."

"Thank you," said Rosalind.

Adam declined.

Mrs. Poole quickly poured Rosalind a cup and passed it to her. Mrs. Poole filled her own cup, as well, and Rosalind caught her glance at the brandy decanter. She felt that if there had not been guests present, Mrs. Poole would have added a healthy splash to her tea.

But then she had the feeling that if guests had not been present, a great many things would have happened.

"Mrs. Poole," said Rosalind, "was there any trouble you, or your husband, might have been particularly concerned about?"

Mrs. Poole's face twisted. Her expression was mirrored by Mr. Considen. Rosalind had the distinct feeling they were both trying not to laugh.

"No," said Mrs. Poole at last. "But then, as I have told you repeatedly now, he did not take me into his confidence regarding business matters." Her gaze drifted to Rosalind. "You understand how some men are regarding their wives, I'm sure."

"Yes, of course," said Rosalind. "As you understand the question had to be asked."

"Yes, of course. What I do not understand is why *you* are here, Miss Thorne," said Mrs. Poole to her. "What can you have to do with . . . my husband or the coroner?" She gestured toward Adam.

"I am engaged to look into a private matter on behalf of an acquaintance, and there were some questions we believed your husband could answer."

"This is preposterous," rasped Mr. Considen. "My sister has just learned that she has been widowed! I must ask you both to leave at once, for decency's sake."

"It's all right, William," said Mrs. Poole. "I'm fine. It is important . . . We must know what happened."

"You have nothing to tell!" shouted Mr. Considen.

"We do not know that!" Mrs. Poole answered. "You will remember, we do not know *anything*!"

"Mrs. Poole, Mr. Considen," said Adam quickly. "I have only one other question, and then I hope we will be able to leave you in peace, once we've seen the bookroom. Do you know if Poole took on any new clients recently?"

Mrs. Poole began to shake her head but paused. "Yes," she whispered.

"Melora . . . !" Mr. Considen choked.

"William, what good is it holding back what little information we do have?" replied his sister. She turned fully toward Adam and Rosalind. "Yes, he had a new client. He would not say who it was, but he was . . . very full of himself. He said that there was a great deal of money to be made." She swallowed, apparently attempting to gain hold of her rising distress. "If I knew who they were, I would tell you at once. I am afraid now all I can do is beg of you not to cause us additional scandal. I do not care for myself, but Letitia is vulnerable. We hope she will be married soon, but the family is already uneasy . . ."

This, Rosalind noted, was very close to the plea Mrs. Fitzherbert had made—that the theft be kept quiet for the sake of the daughters.

There were so many questions she wanted to ask, so many things about this scene that did not quite fit. But Mrs. Poole had started toward the door.

"If you wish to see Josiah's bookroom, I can show you." This left Rosalind and Adam with no choice but to follow.

CHAPTER TWENTY-SIX

The Chambermaid's View

*". . . there is an expression in her features of
something very like deceit . . ."*

Bury, Charlotte, *The Diary of a Lady-in-Waiting*

M r. Poole's bookroom was at the back of the house. Much of the space was taken up by a mahogany desk situated facing the door. Rosalind's shoes sank into the rich Turkey carpet. The shelves were filled with heavy volumes, which did not look as if they'd been touched since they were purchased. There was an almost equal number of ledgers and notebooks, all of which were well thumbed, broken spined, and battered.

Mrs. Poole glanced about her, as if she wanted to make sure everything was in order.

"If you will be all right on your own?" she asked them. "I need to go see my stepdaughter."

"Yes, of course," said Rosalind.

"You may ring for Judith if you need anything."

Mrs. Poole left them there. Rosalind closed the door.

Adam gave a low whistle.

"Yes," agreed Rosalind. "They are a conundrum."

He looked thoughtfully at the door. "What do you think of Mrs. Poole particularly?"

Rosalind also found herself watching the door. She wondered if Adam noticed the shifting shadows just visible in the narrow space between the door and the floorboards. Someone was there, listening.

Mrs. Poole? Not likely. She was genuinely worried about Letitia and wanted to speak with her.

"Mrs. Poole confuses me," said Rosalind out loud. "I wonder how she came to be married to Mr. Poole. I suspect money will be behind it, and the need to care for her brother."

Adam nodded and turned from the door. "I'll begin with the desk. And you?"

Rosalind stepped closer to him. "I'll begin with the maid," she murmured.

Adam cocked his brow. Rosalind nodded once. Adam stepped back, gesturing that she should proceed.

Rosalind lifted her voice. "I will go now and find Miss Poole." The shadows shifted and vanished. Rosalind waited for a single heartbeat and then opened the door. She was just in time to see Judith vanish into another doorway at the end of the hall.

Rosalind did not rush. She did not need to. Judith very obviously wanted to know exactly what was happening with the family. She would not have gone far. She also probably did not think Rosalind might breach the invisible barrier between abovestairs and below.

In a house of this quality, the doors to servants' stairs would be discreetly placed and generally fitted to look as much as possible like a portion of the wall. When she reached the door, Rosalind paused to listen. Her eyebrows rose. From the other side came the faint but unmistakable sound of weeping.

Rosalind pulled her handkerchief from her sleeve and opened the door.

Judith stood on the bare landing. The maid looked up, startled. Tears streaked the young woman's pale face, and her eyes were bright red.

Wordlessly, Rosalind handed Judith the kerchief. She also stepped onto the landing and closed the door behind them, shutting off most of the light, leaving them in the dim and dust of the servants' stairs.

"Thank you, miss." Judith wiped her eyes and nose. "I just . . . I didn't . . ."

Rosalind did not make her finish. "You must have been quite devoted to your employer."

"Yes, miss," whispered Judith. "He was a good man, a kind man. No matter what *she* says." She glared at the door over Rosalind's shoulder, but clearly, she was seeing Mrs. Poole. "What *they* say," she amended.

"It seems to me that Mrs. Poole is in a difficult place."

"Huh!" Judith sniffed and wiped her nose again. "Don't waste your sympathy on that one. She got what she wanted."

Rosalind let her brows rise. "It was not a good marriage?"

Judith hesitated. Rosalind's eyes had adjusted to the dim light, and she could see that the maid was torn between trusting someone from the world of upstairs and wanting to discomfort a woman she disliked.

"That depends what you consider good. As I say, she got what she wanted."

"Was the marriage for money?" asked Rosalind. "Mrs. Poole appears to be a woman with elevated tastes."

"Oh, she looks the part, all right," said Judith. "That's how she drew him in, isn't it? He wanted someone who could give him polish. Get him in with the quality. Find the girl a husband with a title and all that." She waved the handkerchief, indicating what she thought of "all that."

"Men in Mr. Poole's position often choose wives who can help them socially."

Judith shrugged. "Well, he could have chosen better."

"They did not agree, then?"

"Agree?" Judith snorted. "She barely spoke to him. Was pleased enough to take his money but thought he was beneath her. Her kind, beg your pardon, can't see past their own noses. She thinks all about her place and her family but doesn't spare a minute's sympathy for anyone else."

"But Mr. Poole did?"

Judith touched the place just beneath her collar but let her hand quickly fall. "He got a man I know out of Newgate. He'd been put in for stealing." Anger glittered in her eyes. "He didn't do it," Judith added quickly. "He never. The master of the house slipped him some extra to keep his mouth shut while there was a house party, and he was . . . well, not where he should be. Then his wife found the money and said T . . . the man I know must have stolen it, and the mister wouldn't speak up."

Rosalind nodded. "It is a shame that such things happen."

The glower Judith gave her said that *shame* was not the word she'd use. "Well, even once he'd finished his sentence, he couldn't afford to pay the fees for his keep in prison, so he had to stay there, didn't he? Mr. Poole paid for him and got him a new place."

"That is very generous of him," said Rosalind. "Did he help many in such positions?"

"He always said that the law was made by the rich to use against the poor, and he wanted to help right the balance."

Positively revolutionary, Rosalind thought. "What will you do now?"

"I'll get along, miss." Judith sniffed again. "Never you fear."

"I can recommend the name of a good registry office if you want to find a new place."

"Thank you, miss, but you needn't bother," said Judith. "I can go to Mrs. Percivale's as soon as . . . well, as soon as I have need." Judith took a deep breath. "I mustn't stand about any longer. Thank you for the loan, miss. I'll have this washed," she indicated the handkerchief.

"You're very welcome, Judith."

Rosalind slipped back into the main corridor and stood still for a moment, thinking about all she had seen and heard since she entered the house. She thought particularly about the moment where Judith touched her collar. She knew that gesture. She'd seen Amelia make it, and Alice.

Alice, a month or so ago, had bought herself and Amelia matching charms—gold hearts that they wore tucked away beneath their dresses.

Rosalind wondered what Judith kept hidden close to her heart, and exactly who the man Mr. Poole had saved from Newgate might be.

She turned and began to make her way back to the book-room. She walked slowly, hoping she might encounter Mrs. Poole or Letitia on the way.

Luck was not with her this time. She met no one. When she opened the door to the bookroom, she found Adam seated behind Poole's desk, patiently leafing through stacks of correspondence. Two folios of documents had been set aside. Rosalind closed the door.

"It appears Mrs. Poole was right," Adam said. "There is not much here. Household bills primarily. Some requests for consultation. A few begging letters from various charities."

"Given Mr. Poole's *penchant* for privacy, I'm surprised he did not keep his desk locked," remarked Rosalind.

"Perhaps he did," replied Adam.

"You shock me, sir!"

"Still?" Adam murmured.

Rosalind turned away before she could begin to blush in earnest. She felt, rather than saw, Adam's warm smile.

But the warmth quickly faded. "What there is not is any strongbox or safe or hidden space," he said. "Or anywhere else that a man might secure especially valuable documents."

Rosalind moved to the shelves of ledgers. From the notations on the spines, they looked like they might be household accounts. She pulled a notebook at random and felt her brows inch up.

These were not accounts. These books were collections of newspaper clippings—articles from the social columns mixed with records from the courts, all of them heavily underlined and annotated. In fact, they reminded her very much of her books at home.

Something tapped at the back of her mind.

"Did you catch up with Judith?" Adam asked her.

"I did—"

But before Rosalind could get any further, the door opened. It was Mrs. Poole.

"Were you able to find anything useful?" she asked.

Adam did not look at Rosalind as she reshelved the book of clippings. "I'm afraid not," he said. "However, we do know that Mr. Poole kept a room at the White Swan public house."

"Yes," said Mrs. Poole. "He conducted a great deal of his business there."

"With your permission, I'd like to search his papers to see if we can find any hint as to who might have wanted to harm him."

"Yes, yes, of course." Mrs. Poole looked at the room around them, her expression angry, as if the room itself was to blame for not yielding answers.

"How is Miss Poole?" asked Rosalind.

"Distraught, angry, confused," said Mrs. Poole wearily. "As are we all. Will you be much longer? The servants . . ." Mrs. Poole's voice faltered. "We must settle the house, and, as my brother pointed out, arrangements must be made."

"Of course, Mrs. Poole," said Rosalind. "We will not keep you any longer."

Adam climbed to his feet. "I am very sorry for your loss. Mr. Considen has my card. You may send for me at any time should you have any questions or think of anything that might assist with the inquiry. You will be contacted when the date of the inquest is settled. It will be soon."

"Thank you." Mrs. Poole's reply was flat and reflexive.

Rosalind paused. Anger burned in Mrs. Poole's eyes, but there was fear in her glance, as well.

"Mrs. Poole, your tragedy has come at a sensitive time for your family. If there's any help I can offer, you may call on me at any time."

Some part of Rosalind cringed even as she spoke. She was too forward. She would be seen as grubbing after this woman's money, seeking to advance herself through the pain of others.

"Thank you," said Mrs. Poole, and Rosalind heard both relief and genuine consideration in the words. "I may do so, especially—" She stopped. "Thank you," she repeated.

Rosalind and Adam murmured their sympathies again and allowed themselves to be led downstairs and ushered out the door into the pale summer evening.

Judith did not reappear.

The bustle in the streets had ebbed. In the distance, church bells chimed the hour of seven. Soon it would be time for those who were going out for the evening to make their departures, but now was the lull.

"Shall we walk a little?" asked Adam. "We should be able to find a cabstand closer to the high street."

"Yes, thank you." Rosalind let herself glance backward toward the house. In one upstairs window, the drapes had been pulled back far enough for her to glimpse a silhouette watching them. Adam noticed, of course, and Adam looked, as well.

"Who is it?" he asked.

"Difficult to say," she replied. "But we have caused a stir."

Adam nodded. "I very much suspect that the members of that family know more about Mr. Poole's business than they have said."

"I agree. Even if he did not directly share confidences, men of Poole's description do like to brag, and when they cannot brag to their friends, they will brag to their families."

"Do you think Mrs. Poole will take you up on your offer to call?"

"She might," said Rosalind. "If Letitia Poole is engaged to be married, and the potential groom's family was uneasy before this, they may now try to cry off. She'll want to be able to reassure them, and she may hope I can help her do that."

"Do you have any suspicion as to what might be bothering the groom's family?"

Rosalind frowned. "There will be the general fear of scandal, of course, and there might be money troubles. All of which would be exacerbated by Mr. Poole's death."

"Indeed," said Adam. "Given the lack of grief displayed by his family, I'd very much like to know the provisions of Mr. Poole's last will and testament."

"You think this might be a domestic matter?" asked Rosalind.

"It happens more often than people care to believe."

They reached a street corner and became absorbed in the business of finding their way across between the carriages and carts. Safely on the other side, Adam took up the thread of their conversation again.

"What did you learn from Judith?"

"That Mr. Poole made a practice of freeing persons trapped in debtors' prison and helping them find new positions. Given his careful clipping of newspaper articles, I suspect he gave a great deal of consideration as to which houses he placed his people in." The something that had tapped at her thoughts before returned—a sense that she was overlooking something—but the idea would not form itself into anything definite.

Adam halted in his tracks. "Do you think Poole had someone placed with Mrs. Fitzherbert?"

"It is possible." When Adam didn't reply to this, Rosalind turned so she could see past the edge of her bonnet. His eyes were fixed straight ahead.

"Have you thought of something?" asked Rosalind.

"Not as such," he answered slowly. "A feeling only. As word of Poole's death gets out, I can't help but wonder if others might try their luck searching his office for useful documents."

"And if you might catch them in the act?"

Adam nodded. "Such persons may have useful information."

Rosalind felt her breath constrict. Her mind showed her Adam alone in the dark and a desperate person beyond the door, perhaps one who had already killed a man—

She carefully set these thoughts aside before she spoke. "Then all I can say is take care."

"I will," said Adam softly. "What of you?"

"I will go home. I have an ocean of correspondence that must be dealt with, and I will need to let Amelia know what we've learned as soon as may be. Then there's still the matter of how to find Mrs. Fitzherbert's marriage certificate."

"And what else?"

She did not ask him how he knew she'd left something out of her recitation. He understood her as well as she understood him. "I have been invited, most circuitously, to call on the Countess Lieven."

"Lieven?" Adam's voice held surprise and concern. "Have you any idea why?"

"No. But she did take particular care that Lady Jersey not find out she was inviting me."

"What do you suspect?"

"That it has to do with Mrs. Fitzherbert, of course," said Rosalind. "Beyond that . . ." She gestured helplessly.

"You do know that the countess is a spy?" said Adam.

"I know it's rumored."

"Her name is in Stafford's files."

"You have seen Mr. Stafford's files?" said Rosalind. "I was under the impression those were kept very close."

"They are, but I wanted to see what he was recording about you," said Adam. "So, I didn't exactly ask permission."

Now Rosalind truly was surprised. "Is there anything in these files that I should know?"

"He pays attention to you," said Adam. "But no more than that. He pays closer attention to the countess. So, I suppose I should ask you to take care, as well."

"When dealing with Dorothea Lieven, that is something one must always do," said Rosalind blandly.

Especially when there was something her grace wanted, and especially when what her grace wanted was secrets.

CHAPTER TWENTY-SEVEN

The Principal Officer

"Why do they shrink from straight-forward deal-
ings and rather have recourse to crooked policy?"

Bury, Charlotte, *The Diary of a Lady-in-Waiting*

"If you please, Mr. Townsend," said the page boy. "Sir
David's here."

"Send him in at once," Townsend told the page. He
pushed himself heavily to his feet. He flattered himself he
was still a strong and active man, but after so many years,
London's unforgiving stones played havoc on a man's knees.
He swept his glance around the office, making sure all was in
order. He ran a rueful hand across his chin. He'd had no time
to shave or indeed to go home. His stubble was at risk of
growing into a beard, and Mrs. Townsend had begun sending him meals and strengthening cordials.

Someone had hung out a sign within sight of the Houses of
Parliament declaring THE QUEEN FOREVER, THE KING IN THE
RIVER! He had Lavender out trying to discover where it had
come from, but he did not have much hope, and that
weighed on him.

"Sir David." Despite his exhaustion, Townsend greeted

the coroner heartily. "How can I help you?" He gestured that the other man should sit and asked if he would care for coffee or brandy. Sir David declined both.

"I've got an ugly death on my hands, Townsend," he said as he took one of the armchairs in front of Townsend's desk. "Sensational too. The papers will be all over it by tomorrow." His face turned sour. "I'm sorry to be bringing this to your door. I know that you're stretched thin with the commotion around the queen's return."

Townsend sighed and settled himself back down behind his broad desk. "A man should not criticize his betters lightly, but I would have thought Her Majesty would have some decency of feeling—" He stopped himself. "Well, that is neither here nor there. Of course Bow Street is at your disposal, sir. What's happened?"

"An attorney has been killed. One Josiah Poole."

"Poole?" The name sent a jolt through Townsend, and he could tell that Sir David noticed immediately.

"You've heard of him?" Sir David asked.

"It's possible . . ." Townsend steepled his fingers, as if thinking deeply. After a decent interval, he shook his head. "No, I cannot recall exactly. He may have had some business in the magistrate's court recently."

"Perhaps I'll ask Sam Tauton," said Sir David. "His memory ought to be considered a national treasure."

"Yes, well, if he's in. He's been very busy with several matters. The queen's arrival has brought out the mob, as you remarked just now, and there've been vandalizations and thefts. And several threats." *And banners and graffiti.* "Our resources are being tested."

Sir David nodded in sympathy.

"What happened to this Mr. Poole?"

"He was stabbed, thrown from a carriage, and left to die in the street."

Townsend reached for his coffee and downed a gulp as if it

were neat brandy. His stomach rebelled briefly. "Ugly, as you say."

Sir David was watching him. Sir David was a careful man, and a perceptive one. He and Lady David had been to dine with Townsend and his wife several times, and, of course, Townsend made it his business to be on good terms with all the officers of the Crown who crossed his path. Bow Street was an important cog in the machinery of public order, but it was only one cog. It was vital that it mesh smoothly with all the others.

At the same time, he'd never quite been able to cultivate the friendship he would have liked with the coroner. Ordinarily, he shrugged this off. Some men were naturally diffident. Now, though, it worried him.

"It was Adam Harkness that found him," Sir David said.

Townsend frowned before he could stop himself. "What was Harkness doing there?"

"He had business at the sponging house nearby. Been hired to deal with a matter of stolen property."

"For that woman, I've no doubt," Townsend said lightly. "Miss Thorne."

"I believe Miss Thorne is connected with the matter." Sir David's expression, like his voice, remained studiously bland.

Townsend was, of course, aware that Sir David had engaged Miss Thorne and her infinite capacity for gossip to help tease out details for certain of his cases. He had no quarrel with this. The king held Sir David in esteem, and the magistrates relied on his professional acumen. However, with Harkness as his assistant, Sir David might easily become bamboozled by the woman and her clever banter. He should have taken precautions the moment he heard that Harkness was working directly for Sir David, but other matters had arisen, and he'd put it off.

That might now prove to be a mistake.

However, it was Townsend's policy not to waste time on

regrets. The problem was before him. He must work with what he had.

"It's a shame, Sir David, to see such a man as Harkness . . . such a mind, and an officer second to none . . . I looked to him as my protégé. I even thought he might take over this office." Townsend gestured to the space around them, which was filled with tokens of appreciation from the highest in the land, given to him personally. "But instead, he's allowed himself to be put in leading strings by an eccentric spinster."

"Miss Thorne has been very helpful to my office," Sir David remarked.

Townsend smiled. "To be sure, to be sure. Eccentrics have their uses for us, as well. And she is admitted into the drawing rooms of some of our finest hostesses. The gossip of ladies can be very enlightening. And I must say, she has done Bow Street a considerable favor by keeping the more . . . susceptible sort of woman from writing to us to find their lost lapdog or missing earbobs. I should remember to thank her for that.

"But we must be careful." Townsend leaned back in his chair. "She's being encouraged by some radical and mischievous persons. They have given her the idea that she can do our work, the work of solid professional men. I'm afraid that sooner or later, this must run her into serious trouble. Even danger." It was seldom a mistake, Townsend found, to appeal to a gentleman's sense of chivalry.

Sir David's own smile was sharp, and his eyes sparkled. "You do not, I hope, include me among your radical and mischievous persons?"

Townsend laughed. "No, no, of course not, Sir David. In fact, His Majesty spoke of you the other day, when I was with him to discuss arrangements for Caroline of Brunswick's arrival and, of course, the upcoming trial. He said that he was fortunate in being so well served by his officers, beginning with the coroner."

The king had said no such thing. Indeed, Townsend had barely exchanged three words with His Majesty in recent months. Not that it signified, of course. He could not expect to enjoy as much of the king's time and confidence as he did the prince regent's. He must wait and be patient and serve humbly.

"If opportunity arises, you may tell His Majesty I am deeply sensible of his trust in me," Sir David was saying.

"As are we all," replied Townsend, hauling himself out of his own thoughts with a certain difficulty.

"I suppose I should tell you, Townsend, that I've put Harkness to work on this matter of Poole's murder. Is that going to cause any problem?"

Townsend spread his hands. "I will not say I am comfortable with the man doing any sensitive work these days. I know you have taken him under your wing, Sir David, but I still worry about his radical tendencies. Who knows where they will lead him?"

"Well, today I hope it will lead him to finding out who killed our man." Sir David gave Townsend a small flicker of a smile as he got to his feet. "Willful murder by person or persons unknown is not a verdict I care to hand down. For now, if you can spare me a runner, I'd be grateful. My clerk will forward you a draft for the fees. I'll write you as soon as we schedule the inquest. Hopefully, it will be in two or three days."

"Very good, Sir David." Townsend also rose. "I'll have a man for you as soon as you send word." He paused with his hand on the doorknob. "Where is Harkness now?"

"He's gone to speak with Poole's family and search the house for possible reasons behind his murder. After that, I expect he'll return to the White Swan public house in Carter Street. Poole kept a room there, along with a large number of his papers. Harkness said it had been tossed, possibly by the murderer."

This news caused Townsend's jaw to clench.

"Then perhaps what you need is one of Stafford's clerks," said Townsend as soon as he could trust himself to speak normally. "He can sift the papers while Harkness is out interviewing this man Poole's associates and neighbors."

"A good thought. Let's put it into action. Thank you, Townsend."

Townsend shook Sir David's hand and opened the door for him. He stood back and watched as the coroner walked briskly through the wardroom.

Once Sir David was out of sight, Townsend turned to the page boy on his stool beside the door.

"Find Stafford," he growled. "Now."

CHAPTER TWENTY-EIGHT

The Consolations of Friendship

*"... she is frank and kind-hearted and has much
aquirement, with a thirst for more, which it is
pleasing to see."*

Bury, Charlotte, *The Diary of a Lady-in-Waiting*

"Rosalind, if I am going to continue to act as your private secretary, I'm afraid I must insist on my wages."

Rosalind had just entered her front parlor to discover Alice on the sofa, wearing her old blue wrapper and threadbare cap. The tea table was filled with tidy stacks of paper. Alice herself—bent double in a way that would have caused her fastidious mother to turn faint—scribbled her eccentric shorthand into a battered notebook. A tray of coffee things had been relegated to the nearby chair.

"What—" began Rosalind.

"We'll discuss that later." Alice cut her off. "In the meantime, the notice for your at-home days has been placed with the principal newspapers. It's Tuesdays and Thursdays, by the way, which gives us a full day to prepare, as tomorrow is Wednesday. Mrs. Napier has two reliable girls she can bring in to help Claire with the ladies' wraps and serving tea and so forth."

Rosalind tried again. "Alice—" She got no further this time.

"Adam's men arrived, and Mortimer has had a good look at them and pronounced them more or less sound, and at least one is able to wear one of his spare coats and meet the carriages."

"I had hoped—"

"I've spoken with Mrs. Singh about the need to have plenty of biscuits and sandwiches on hand, and she has already sent to Twinings for some of that special tea blend you like."

"But . . . ," suggested Rosalind.

"Now, as to the correspondence," Alice went on, "I've got that sorted." She indicated the left-hand pile of letters. "These are the ones you need to answer personally." She tapped a middle pile. "These I've penned a polite reply to, and you'll just need to sign." She held up the right-hand stack. "These can safely be ignored for the time being. And those over there . . ." She pointed at a smaller pile, which had been exiled to the embroidered footstool. "Those are the current bills. The letters from people I know that you know personally are on the mantel."

Rosalind was aware she should have been affronted. To open a person's correspondence without permission was a near criminal violation of privacy. As it was, the sensation that poured over her was a profound sense of relief. She had been dreading the necessity of plowing through the mountain of correspondence that had arrived that morning. A mountain that had surely grown with the arrival of the afternoon post.

"Oh, and I've arranged for George to come first thing tomorrow morning with all the dailies. We can read through them to see if there are any hints about the certificate being noised about . . ."

Alice looked up, and this time she seemed to truly see Rosalind.

"Good Lord, Rosalind. Sit down. You look terrible."

"I am tired," Rosalind admitted as she sank into her chair. "And you've reminded me of something that I had entirely overlooked."

"I'll add it to your account," said Alice. She then hurried from the parlor and returned with a cup of tea.

"Thank you, Alice." Rosalind drank thirstily.

"Now, what's happened?" asked Alice. "Has something gone wrong? What is it you overlooked?"

Rosalind took another swallow of tea. "Ronald Ranking."

"Ranking?" cried Alice. "He shouldn't frighten you that much. He can't really make that much—"

"He saw Mr. Poole going into Mrs. Fitzherbert's garden," said Rosalind. "He knows Adam and I are involved with Mrs. Fitzherbert and are asking about Mr. Poole," said Rosalind. "And by tomorrow, he will know that Mr. Poole has been found murdered."

"Oh, Lord," breathed Alice. "Have you warned Mrs. Fitzherbert yet?"

Rosalind shook her head. "I must write to her at once." She paused. "Is there any chance Mr. Ranking is the sort who could be persuaded to delay publication . . . ?"

"Of the fact that a murdered man was seen at Mrs. Fitzherbert's? I'm afraid there's very little chance of that."

"Is there any way to get a message to him tonight? Perhaps with some inducement?"

Alice glanced at the clock. "With all the extra editions being printed about the queen, there should be someone at the *Standard* until quite late. And even if there isn't, I could leave something with the night porter."

Rosalind smiled weakly. "I really should be paying you wages."

"What you should be doing right now is eating supper,"

said Alice. "Mrs. Singh left a cold collation in the dining room."

This was quite possibly the best news she'd had all day.

Mrs. Singh had risen to the occasion. There was ham, pigeon pie, bread, and a cake with cream and strawberries, and a wedge of blue-veined cheese to finish.

Rosalind's stomach made a deeply unladylike noise. She wasted no time in helping herself from the array of dishes, once again blessing Mrs. Levitton and her investments, which made employing Mrs. Singh possible.

She was at least as grateful that Alice seemed to understand that she really did need time to eat and to compose herself. But before long, Rosalind could tell her friend's patience was being sorely tested.

"Thank you for all your help, Alice," she said sincerely. "I really have felt at my wits' end."

"You? Never," said Alice, but her eyes sparkled. "Now, tell me what happened today. I am on pins and needles. You discover a man has been murdered and rush out of the house, and here I am left to twiddle my thumbs!"

"You have done everything except twiddle your thumbs," said Rosalind. "Still. We were fortunate, at least at first. Mrs. Cotes, or her husband, I should say, was able to direct us to Mr. Poole's family." Rosalind described Mrs. Poole and her brother. "But both of them denied any knowledge of Mr. Poole's business matters, and on the whole, they were far less sorry to hear of his death than they might have been."

Rosalind took a sip of her wine, another addition to her table now that she had grown more prosperous. "There is a grown daughter, as well, Mr. Poole's from a previous marriage, and two boys, both still in the nursery." She paused, remembering Letitia's poise and Mrs. Poole's anger. "There's a maid in the house, Judith, who says that Mrs. Poole is, or was, a fortune hunter, but I am not sure that can be entirely correct."

"What does Adam say?"

"Adam wants to find Poole's will. He's returned to the White Swan to see if he can discover anything, and to be there in case someone else tries to burgle the rooms. But . . ."

"But the certificate's still out there."

Rosalind nodded. "How are we to find one slip of paper in the whole of London? Has it already been put into the hands of someone who plans to bring it out at the king's divorce trial? Or print it in the papers? Has it already been destroyed? How would we even know?" She drained her teacup. "And until we can be sure what's happened to it, Mrs. Fitzherbert and her daughters will remain vulnerable to every story, every lie, every threat."

"In other words, Ron Ranking," said Alice. "And all the rest of us."

"If it was just the newspapers, that would be one thing, but it's the lords temporal, and their ladies, who will be playing at tug-of-war over this. There's mobs in the street, and Parliament is at odds with the palace. All of it." With each word, Rosalind felt her spirits depress a little further.

"Oh, Rosalind, it's not like you to borrow so much trouble."

"I know, I know. I . . . Mr. Poole's death has upset me more than I realized. The fact that someone might have been killed over this scrap of paper . . ." She paused, searching for words, but none came.

"And if Mrs. Fitzherbert organized the disappearance of the certificate?" asked Alice.

"Then there's yet more reason to worry." Rosalind sighed. "And that's not all."

Rosalind told Alice about Countess Lieven and her indirect invitation.

"Good Lord! On top of everything, we've got the rivalries of the lady patronesses to contend with? Perhaps you should take a second glass." Alice moved the wine a little closer.

Rosalind smiled, but only a little. "If I'm to deal with the machinations of Lady Jersey and the countess, I will need to keep a very clear head."

"What will you do?"

"Besides pray?" Rosalind pushed the remains of her pigeon pie around on her plate. "Look to Amelia to find out if there was an accomplice inside Mrs. Fitzherbert's house. Look to Adam to find what ended Mr. Poole's life."

"And to yourself?"

"I seem to have some correspondence to attend to," she said. "And then I believe I may write some letters of my own. After that"—now she did reach for the wine—"I seem to have a great many people who want to talk to me. I suppose I had better hear what they have to say."

"Well." Alice drained her glass. "I shall take up your cause. I'll take a note and an inducement to the *Standard* tonight and put them in Ron Ranking's hands, if he's there."

"I feel I should not send you alone," said Rosalind. "The streets—"

"Rosalind," Alice said, stopping her. "I managed for some years under far worse conditions. I will be fine, and back well before bedtime."

Alice would not be dissuaded, and in the end, Rosalind had very little choice but to let her go. If they were to have any chance at all of saving Mrs. Fitzherbert from unnecessary scandal, they must stay one step ahead of the *Standard* and its competitors.

Laurel looked in to see if anything was needed. Rosalind asked her for tea to be taken to her private parlor and that the lamps be lit, as the evening was wearing on. Then she went and gathered up all the correspondence Alice had so thoughtfully sorted through and took it to her work desk.

"I will not despair," she told herself and the sheafs of paper. "We will find a way through this."

Adam would take no hurt tonight. Alice would come home in good time, entirely unscathed, with a fresh load of gossip and possibilities. These things would happen because they must. Because if she imagined otherwise, both her body and her mind would become entirely paralyzed from the fear.

It is not like you to borrow so much trouble, Alice had said. She was right, and yet imagined trouble seemed to appear no matter which way Rosalind tried to steer her thoughts.

Why? Rosalind demanded of herself.

But she knew. It was because she was in no way certain she could bring this business to a successful conclusion. Because no matter what happened, the world would take notice, and it might not like what it saw. Because if she failed in any respect, she had so much to lose—security, comfort, reputation.

Love. Rosalind closed her eyes. *Love, most of all.*

She could picture Adam perfectly as he methodically searched through Poole's room. She saw him patiently righting furniture and sorting papers. He would pause here and there to take note of something that might be significant. No matter what else he was doing, he would keep his face to the door, keep one part of his mind on watch, because that was his habit.

And as Rosalind thought of him at the White Swan, she could not help but think of him with her—beside her on the street, conversing across the table, lying in her arms. Her heart swelled so painfully, she was sure it must break open.

She loved him. She had never loved so surely and completely, not even as a girl, before her father's ruin and her mother's madness. She trusted him to the depths of her soul. He was saving Alice, her best friend. And she desired him with every fiber of her being. Yearned for him like a heroine in an opera.

She had thought that this would be enough. Their relationship—this way in which they were together but not answerable to any convention but their own—was complete as it was, and she needed nothing more.

But some part of her had become greedy.

Every time she sent him away in the dark, so he could be seen coming back at a respectable hour, and every time she met him on the street and could only make her curtsy to him and call him "Mr. Harkness," she felt false. Every day she resented a little more the work of the pretense she herself had insisted on.

Marriage as a whole held no temptations for her. Marriage to Adam—that was a wholly different matter.

The contradiction was agonizing. Rosalind had lost count of the hours she spent berating herself for her foolishness. It was not her heart holding her back, or her mind—at least not her rational mind. But there was some small terrified part of her that looked out at the possibility of marriage and rooted her to the spot. She could not take those steps toward the altar, toward the vow to love and obey, not even in her imagination. Not even when it was Adam waiting for her.

Marriage meant she ceased to exist. Rosalind Thorne was no more. She could not dismiss a servant, could not hold the lease on her house, could not travel, could not earn, could not hold such money as she had without permission. Anyone who wished to withhold any material thing, to deny her entry to a place, or ignore her least request could do so on the grounds that they must speak with her husband first. All she had built would mean nothing. She would be wiped away.

Adam was not her father. He would not leave her. He would not rob her. She knew that.

But the husband's right existed. Absolute right to her money, her body, everything. The children she bore would be his children. The money she had so painfully accumulated would be his money. Her body became his body.

In taking him fully to her, she risked losing herself.

It was all this that made the small part inside her scream with fear and at the same time robbed her of the ability to speak. She knew her silence hurt Adam. But the one thing she would not do was make any promise to him until she was certain she could keep it.

Absently, she opened her desk drawer and took out the folded letter she kept there. She had drafted it months ago. She was just waiting until the time was right to show it to Adam.

And if the time is never right? What then?

Slowly, Rosalind became aware of the tears trickling down her cheeks. She blinked and dashed them angrily away. She turned her mind and gaze firmly toward the letters in front of her and set to work.

CHAPTER TWENTY-NINE

Questions at the White Swan

*"Our friends do more harm than our enemies,
sometimes . . ."*

Bury, Charlotte, *The Diary of a Lady-in-Waiting*

The White Swan's landlord was none too pleased to see
Adam walk back through his doors.

"If you're planning on keeping those rooms locked up,
you'd best be planning on paying for them."

"What's your fee for a night, then?" asked Adam.

"The night, is it?" the man replied sourly. He also named
his price. "An' extra if you'll be wanting your supper."

"Naturally," said Adam.

It was the busiest hour—early evening, with dark just beginning to settle in—and the pub was filled to overflowing.
Sara waded through the crowd, plying her jug and wielding
her powerful elbows to clear a path between inattentive cus-
tomers.

Adam took himself up the stairs. There were neither
lamps nor candles to light the way, so the windowless corridor was pitch black. Even so, Adam saw the shapes of two

men push themselves away from the wall where they'd been lounging.

He froze, his legs flexing and weight shifting, getting himself ready to fight or to flee.

The immediate reaction from the shadows was a burst of laughter. Adam relaxed instantly.

"What are you two doing here?"

Sampson Goutier and Sam Tauton looked at each other. These two men were Adam's closest colleagues when he was still at Bow Street. Tauton had been an officer for donkey's years and knew half the ne'er-do-wells of London on sight. Sampson Goutier had been christened Percival by his mother and rechristened by his mates on the river patrol for his size and strength before he came to Bow Street. As canny a patrolman as Adam had ever met, Goutier worked his way swiftly up the ranks, becoming a principal officer in even less time than it had taken Adam.

"This isn't a conversation to have in the hall." Tauton pushed Poole's door open.

Adam swore. "I left that locked."

"It may be the landlord here is less than trustworthy," remarked Goutier.

Adam swore again, but he followed them both into the room. He kicked the door shut and shot home the bolt.

Tauton tucked his thumbs into his belt and surveyed the chaos. "I was saying to Goutier someone took a disliking to this place."

"I wish that's all it was," muttered Adam.

"Right, Harkness." Goutier folded his arms and assumed an air of getting down to business. "What's going on?"

"What makes you ask?" replied Adam.

Tauton lifted his brows. "Ooh, he's gotten cagey these days." He shoved a heap of papers aside and sat on the bed, which creaked dangerously. "Sir David came to see Townsend. Closed the door to the office and all. Less than half an hour later, Sir David leaves, without a word to anyone."

"Looking like he's drunk an entire vat of vinegar," put in Goutier.

"Next thing we know, Townsend's sent poor little Archie running after Stafford, and then the two of them's behind closed doors, with Townsend hollering at the top of his lungs."

"So loud that if you got too near the door, you'd hear every word," Goutier remarked.

"He went on about Stafford's assurances and his plans and promises and what's he going to do now, and what in God's name is Townsend going to tell the palace—" Tauton broke off when he realized Adam was staring.

"You're sure?" said Adam. "You're certain that's what he said?"

"Half the station is certain that's what he said," said Goutier.

Adam scrubbed at his face, several cold possibilities settling into his mind.

"What was Stafford's reply?"

Goutier shook his head. "Stafford wouldn't raise his voice to say he'd heard the last trump sound."

"And none of the clerks have been particularly forthcoming, even after a couple of pints," added Tauton.

"As they value their jobs," said Goutier.

"And their skins," said Tauton.

"So, we came to find you," Goutier concluded.

"How'd you know where to look?" asked Adam.

"The clerks were not *entirely* silent," said Goutier, a little impatiently. "Now, what's happened, man? Why's Townsend yelling about the palace in one breath and you in the next?"

"And." Tauton leaned forward. "You might want to know,

Townsend's convinced Sir David that they should send one of Stafford's clerks round to help you out. I'm supposing it has to do with this mess." He nudged the nearest drift of papers with the toe of his boot.

"Of course, it might also be to spy on you," suggested Goutier.

Adam pressed his hand against his mouth. When he lowered it, it was to curse, roundly and soundly and with a few phrases that raised even Goutier's eyebrows.

Adam looked from one man to the other, aware of an uncomfortable ambivalence. He trusted both Goutier and Tauton with his life. But he wasn't Bow Street anymore, and this business he was in wasn't entirely his business.

On the other hand, this half-heard conversation between Townsend and Stafford raised some immediate questions. Stafford and Townsend surely knew by now that Rosalind was involved in this matter with Mrs. Fitzherbert. And, of course, they knew Adam helped her in her work, just as he helped Sir David.

"If one of Stafford's men is on the way, you'd best be off, sharpish," he said to Tauton and Goutier. "Townsend won't be happy to find out you're here."

"Oh, no, me lad," said Tauton. "You're not getting off that easy."

"It's already dinnertime. Clerk won't be here until tomorrow," said Goutier. "So, talk, Harkness. Or I'll have to tell Sal who made me late getting home."

Sal was Goutier's wife. She kept a secondhand clothing shop and had a tongue and a right arm that would have done credit to the Royal Navy. She and Adam actually got on quite well, but she was possessive of her husband and his time. Even more so since the birth of their first son.

Adam set aside his concerns and started talking.

There was no question that he was outnumbered—three to one if you counted Sal—but the truth was, he needed to talk. Tauton had been his mentor when he first got to Bow Street, and he and Goutier had worked side by side for some years. They'd mince no words if they thought he was imagining things. More importantly, he could trust them to keep his secrets and Rosalind's.

So, he told them about the summons from Mrs. Fitzherbert, about her marriage certificate going missing, about talking to Ranking the next day. About Ranking's story of Josiah Poole being seen at Mrs. Fitzherbert's house. About tracking Poole to the sponging house.

About seeing Poole's corpse tossed into the street and then finding his rooms in this state. About how Rosalind had found his home and family, and how their first question was not about what had been done to Poole but what Poole had done.

When he finished, he was grimly pleased to note that both men were staring at him in unvarnished shock.

" 'S truth," murmured Goutier.

Tauton whistled. "Well, well, Harkness. You have stepped in it up to your neck, haven't you?"

"Don't think I don't know it." Adam kicked at the papers surrounding his feet. "And now you tell me Townsend and Stafford are in on it, too."

"Do they know about the certificate?" asked Tauton. "Would Sir David have told Townsend?"

"I doubt it," said Adam. "He knows Townsend and how Townsend works. One hint that the marriage certificate had gone missing, and Townsend would be off straight to the palace."

Townsend had been in charge of the king's personal security for years when he was still Prince of Wales. He still boasted of how he had held the prince's watch for him when he'd been at the gaming tables, and he wore the white hat His Highness had given him in all weathers.

There was no question that if he heard about the missing certificate, Townsend would tell the king.

Unless Townsend and the king already know.

"Poole's wife said he'd picked up a new client recently, and a well-heeled one," Adam told them. "Stafford employs all sorts. It could have been him."

"Stafford doesn't stab his informants, as a rule," said Tauton blandly. "Waste of resources. If he needs to keep them quiet, he blackmails them or jails them."

"But he also doesn't act on his own," said Adam. "If Stafford's trying to get his hands on the certificate, it's because someone's asked him to do it."

"Do you really think the proof is in here?" Goutier swept a hand out, indicating the stew of papers.

"I hope something is," said Adam irritably. "Either way, I need to sort this lot before Stafford's clerk shows up. And you need to get out of here," he added. "They'll notice you missing at the station."

"Not me," said Goutier promptly. "I've gone home to supper."

"And I've got croup." Tauton cleared his throat. "Who knows when I'll be fit again?" He picked up a heap of papers from the bed. "So, let's get started." He held up the first document and squinted at it. "Harkness, you'd better roust out the landlord and see about some candles. And a supper."

Goutier must have realized Adam was about to argue, because he smiled easily. "You're not getting rid of us, Harkness. So, you may as well get along, as Tauton says. There's a good lad."

Adam threw up his hands in surrender and went to the door. He shot back the bolt and threw the door open.

And reeled backward.

Tauton shoved himself to his feet, and Goutier straightened up to his full height.

All three of them stared at the thin, crook-necked man who stood quietly in the doorway.

"I thought I might find you here." Mr. Stafford stepped across the threshold. "I believe we need to talk."

CHAPTER THIRTY

The Chief Clerk

*"I am half inclined to like him, yet I feel afraid
of him . . ."*

Bury, Charlotte, *The Diary of a Lady-in-Waiting*

Tauton recovered first. "Mr. Stafford," he said, with a fair imitation of jocularity. "We were just talking about you."

"Were you?" Stafford's voice was bland. "I can only imagine what you might have been saying."

It was an invitation to confess or lie. Neither the officers nor Adam took him up on it. Stafford's dagger-sharp gaze swept across the heaps of paper and then, more slowly, each of the three men.

"What brings you here, sir?" asked Adam finally.

"You do, Mr. Harkness," replied Stafford. "Sir David came to Bow Street to speak with Mr. Townsend regarding Mr. Poole's murder. As I expect you have already been informed." He nodded to Goutier and Tauton.

"Sir David told me he was planning to go to Bow Street when we parted ways earlier," said Adam. "I'm here with his permission, and the permission of Poole's widow," he added.

"I had no question about your right to be here," said Stafford. "It is the logical step."

Adam felt like he'd just been caught wrong-footed, but for the life of him, he was not sure why. Stafford had that effect on a man.

"Then what can we do for you, Mr. Stafford?" asked Goutier. "As you can see, Adam's only just started his search." He nodded toward the nearest heap of papers. "Was there something in particular you thought he should be looking for?"

Stafford's face barely shifted, but Adam got the feeling he was impressed by the men's refusal to be afraid. Stafford was a legend at Bow Street. The younger runners and constables made him something of an all-seeing boogeyman, and the clerks were happy to feed them exaggerated tales to stoke their imaginations.

At the same time, the man really was dangerous. He had made ferreting out secrets his life's work. "There is something we should all be looking for," said Stafford. "And you know what that is, too."

Silence filled the room. All of them were waiting for someone else to say the words out loud. After a moment, Stafford shrugged, as if saying he was perfectly willing to concede the point.

"Was it the missing certificate or Poole's murder that brought you here?" he asked. "Or both?"

Adam allowed his brows to arch ever so slightly.

"Yes, of course, you are no longer under any obligation to answer me," said Stafford. "Although your associates here do not have that luxury."

"Now, then, Mr. Stafford," said Tauton. "It's early in the game to be turning to threats, don't you think?"

"Normally, I would agree, Mr. Tauton, but I'm afraid we are rather short of time," said Stafford. "Therefore, I am forced to be more direct than otherwise. Witness the fact that I am here at all."

"I had thought you might be here because Mr. Townsend is angry about current events," said Adam.

Stafford shook his head heavily. "I'm afraid Mr. Townsend is making a series of mistakes."

"You surprise me," said Goutier. "What's behind it, do you think?"

It was as much a challenge as a question. Goutier meant to see how far Stafford was willing to go.

As it happened, much further than Adam would have expected.

"Mr. Townsend's old friend the prince is now the king," Stafford said. "Despite how he talks, the truth is that His Majesty has rather less use and time for Townsend than His Highness did, and Townsend is feeling the lack, you might say." Stafford's voice filled with a soft, wintry disapproval. "He is anxious to prove he is still useful. Those who know that might find it easier than usual to put ideas into his head, especially during such stressful times."

Adam had difficulty keeping the surprise out of his features. This was not in the least like Stafford. He'd never spoken this way in Adam's hearing, not even about an accused criminal, let alone about the man who headed Bow Street.

So, the question now became, was this Stafford's true assessment? Or was he only trying to convince Adam and Tauton and Goutier that he could be on their side?

That would be very like Stafford.

"You're wondering how far you can trust me," said Stafford.

"You'll forgive us," said Tauton.

"Being an officer makes one naturally suspicious," added Goutier.

"And you have an excellent reputation for getting what's needed from witnesses," said Adam.

"Thank you," replied Stafford, all modesty. "Unfortunately, I have very little with which to placate such *natural* suspicions." He nodded toward Goutier. "But we are in a serious quandary, gentlemen. There has been a murder. There is a missing document that might very well affect the stability of the kingdom, and there are men and women who will not hesitate to use these facts to their own ends, and damn the consequences."

Adam thought of the mob that had stopped his and Rosalind's carriage the night before.

"What do you want?" asked Adam.

"Information," said Stafford promptly. "If I can convince Townsend that I am working in the way that he wishes, that will keep him off your backs while you find the answers we all need."

They were staring again.

"Yes, I am saying I wish you to push forward," said Stafford. "And *quickly*, gentlemen. We must find the certificate, as well as how Poole met his demise. I am also saying that if you keep me informed, I will see that you are not unduly bothered by Mr. Townsend, and yes, I give you my word that the clerk I send will be reporting only to me and that I will not say anything unnecessary to Townsend about what, or who, has been seen in this room."

Adam and the others remained silent for a long moment. Warning bells sounded low and strong in the back of his mind. There was one thing that hung unsaid, but he could not leave it to speculation.

"Did you meet Poole?"

Stafford narrowed his eyes. "We had an appointment for the afternoon of the day he died. Obviously, Poole never arrived."

It was an interesting answer, and a very careful and compact one. "What else can you tell us?" Adam asked. *What else* will *you tell us?*

Stafford looked at him steadily. This time, he appeared

more than ready to meet and match Adam's silence. But Stafford also surely understood he was being dared to speak. How would he answer that dare? Despite all his years of experience, Adam found Stafford unreadable.

At last, Stafford spoke, deliberately and clearly.

"I did not kill Poole," he said. "Nor did I suggest he should be killed. But I am not prepared to say the same of Mr. Townsend."

CHAPTER THIRTY-ONE

The Small Secrets of Delicate Young Ladies

*"The great are not sufficiently attentive to the
wants of their dependents . . ."*

Bury, Charlotte, *The Diary of a Lady-in-Waiting*

Once she finally watched Mrs. Fitzherbert and her girls descend the stairs to meet their royal dinner guests, Amelia went into her own room and collapsed.

The past several hours had been a whirlwind. Miss Mary Ann had torn out the ruffle Amelia had just mended this afternoon, necessitating a last-minute repair. Rather than accepting the simple hairstyle Amelia had planned, Miss Seymore insisted on a confection with dozens of curls and pearl pins, which took well over an hour and had to be accomplished while Miss Mary Ann fretted about her dress and tugged at the neckline in a vain attempt to make it sit just a touch lower. At last, Amelia had to beg her to stop lest she tear something new.

Mrs. Fitzherbert was in a dour mood. She seemed grimly

determined to see this dinner through, but was so distracted, she changed her mind half a dozen times about the jewels she wanted and the gloves and the way she wanted her hair pinned.

Everyone had ignored the occasional shouts from outside as Jim Geery and the other men on watch cleared away yet another group of idlers or newspapermen or both.

But now it was done, and Amelia could take a moment to breathe and consider what she should do next.

The pendulum clock on the wall told her it was half eight. She had no window in her room, so she could not peek outside, but she'd left her door open a crack. From the sounds drifting up from the stairwell, it seemed as if the Duke and Duchess of York, and their party, had indeed arrived.

Amelia considered sneaking down the stairs. There might be something useful to be learned by eavesdropping on the dinner conversation. But she did not, because her mind kept returning to the scrap of paper she'd found in Miss Seymore's dressing table.

Tonight. Ten o'clock.

A real dinner, especially with royalty—which the Duke of York was, after all—would go on for hours. Whatever was meant to happen at ten . . . if it was still in the offing, Minney Seymore would have to make some excuse to get away from the table.

Amelia had served in more than one house with a dramatic young lady. Not to mention a dramatic matron. She had seen many of the tried-and-true methods of escaping from unwanted company.

She strongly suspected that well before ten o'clock chimed, Miss Seymore would develop a sick headache.

As soon as the clock chimed half nine, Amelia heard the patter of slippers and the swish of skirts that signaled a lady coming up the stairs. She set aside the mending she'd been using to keep busy and moved to the door. She smiled. There was Miss Seymore, looking over her shoulder and hurrying along the corridor.

Amelia pushed open the door. Miss Seymore jumped like a scared rabbit.

"Oh! McGowan."

"Miss Seymore. Is something wrong?"

"No, no, that is, yes." She rubbed her temple. "I'm having one of my sick headaches. I need to lie down."

And I'm the Archbishop of Canterbury. "Oh dear!" Amelia came forward. "We must get you out of this gown, and then I shall make you a cool compress."

Miss Seymore very clearly wanted to tell her not to bother, that she didn't need any help. Then, evidently remembering the number of buttons, tapes, and hooks on her dress, she smiled weakly.

"Thank you, McGowan."

Once they were in the young ladies' dressing room, Miss Seymore remembered to wince and sigh every so often as Amelia helped her out of her dress and into her nightgown, but mainly her attention was divided between the gilt clock on the mantel and the green velvet drapes drawn across the window.

Amelia, of course, pretended not to notice.

At last, she got the girl under the counterpane, with a violet water compress on her forehead.

"Thank you, McGowan," Miss Seymore breathed, closing her eyes in a great show of exhaustion. "That's much better. You can go now."

"Oh, I thought I would sit with you awhile," said Amelia. "Just until you're asleep."

"No, no! I shall rest much better if I am left alone."

"Just as you like, miss," said Amelia. "Is there anything else I can do?"

"No, nothing. Well." She cracked open one eye. "If Mama comes up to ask, you'll say you stayed until I fell asleep? And that I'm sleeping still? It's only that she worries so, and I fear if she comes in, she'll get us both into a fret."

"Of course, miss," agreed Amelia. "I'll do just as you say. There is no need to worry her or you any further."

"Thank you, McGowan." The sigh Miss Seymore breathed as she lay back sounded a lot like relief.

Amelia made her curtsy, even though Miss Seymore had her eyes closed. Then she left the room and softly closed the door behind her.

She should have returned to her own room then, to await the sound of the bell or any other summons. But her room was the last place Amelia intended to be right now.

Instead, she assumed a businesslike air and walked to the far end of the corridor, where there stood a pair of pocket doors. She'd done a bit of exploring earlier, and on the far side of these doors, she'd found the dramatic conservatory she'd glimpsed when she arrived. It was even more amazing from the inside—a curving, glassed-in balcony filled with all sorts of exotic plants and flowers in enough colors to rival the painted glass windows in a church. It also happened to overlook Mrs. Fitzherbert's beautiful walled garden.

And if that's not where Miss Seymore plans to be next, I'll eat my bonnet.

Some might think that a supper party was the last time anyone would want to go sneaking about the house, but the truth was there were few better times. The staff was all busy, but all in one part of the house. The rest of the place would be dark and empty for hours yet. You could drive a herd of cows through the upper floors, and no one would notice.

Amelia slid back the doors just far enough to allow her to duck through and closed them at once.

The conservatory was filled with the dull silver moonlight

of a London summer night. It turned the exotic plants into strange silhouettes with long fingers drooping down to clutch at the unwary.

Now's not the time for silly fancies, McGowan. You leave that to Alice.

The thought of Alice rallied her spirits, as it always did. Amelia made her way across the tiled floor to the curving wall of windows and looked down. The terrace and garden spread out below, still and empty.

So far. Amelia moved behind a potted palm to disguise her silhouette, just in case anyone should look up through the windows, and got ready to wait.

As it turned out, she didn't have to wait long.

There was no mistaking Miss Seymore as she crept from the door below onto the terrace with exaggerated care. When the young lady was satisfied that she was not observed, she hurried into the garden and looked all around her. She put her hands on her hips.

Amelia grinned.

But in the next heartbeat, Miss Seymore whirled around, hands to her mouth. There was a blur of motion, and a shape—a man—dropped down from the top of the wall and spread his hands.

Ta-da!

Whoever he was, Miss Seymore ran forward and leapt into his arms. He caught her and spun her around. The next few minutes were spent in a kiss so passionate that Amelia felt her cheeks heating.

It also confirmed every last one of her suspicions. Not only that Minney Seymore had a gentleman, but that she'd also schemed to come back to London to see him. It was so exactly what she had expected that Amelia was conscious of a certain disappointment. Some absurd part of her had hoped the young lady would be up to something more original.

Oh, won't Alice laugh when I tell her that! Amelia smiled to herself.

Still, now we know Miss Seymore has a gentleman, who can manage to sneak into a house even when it's being watched. That's a little something. Amelia tut-tutted as she watched the pair of shadows down below. They were still in each other's arms, but they'd pulled back from their kiss. It was too dark to tell if they were talking or just gazing into each other's eyes.

So, now what, you two? wondered Amelia.

In that same moment, she heard the unmistakable rumble of the pocket doors being pushed back. She faded back further behind the palm, heart in her throat, waiting for the glare of a lamp to give her away and cursing herself for not having thought up a story to explain her presence.

But no light cut through the darkness. Instead, a man's shadow calmly closed the doors behind him.

"Come out, come out, wherever you are!" he murmured.

Faller.

Amelia's first instinct was to shrink back, but that was ridiculous. No matter how he'd known where she was, she was pinched. Trying to hide would only compound the problem by making her look foolish.

She squared her shoulders and stepped out from behind the palm.

"Well, well," breathed Faller. "Look who's here."

"Yes, look," said Amelia as coolly as she could manage. "Aren't you supposed to be waiting at table?"

She heard his grin more than she saw it. "Aren't you supposed to be making sure madam's room is all ready for her when the dinner's over?"

"I needed a bit of air," she said.

"And I believe you," he replied solemnly. "Although thousands wouldn't."

"What should I believe about you?" she shot back.

Faller shrugged easily. "Whatever you like."

"What if I believe you came to spy on Miss Seymore and her beau down there?"

That one stung. He stiffened, if only for a moment, and then relaxed, but it took some doing. "Aw, now, McGowan, there's no need to make a fuss, is there?" he said in his charming, coaxing fashion. "Running to tittle-tattle . . . It just makes for bad feelings all round, doesn't it?"

Amelia folded her arms. "And just why should I listen to you?"

"Because we're friends, aren't we?" He took a step closer.

Amelia didn't move, and she didn't answer.

"And what do we really care what any of them"—he jerked his chin toward the doors—"get up to? It's not as if they care about any of us. So, we need to look out for ourselves and make sure they pays up for what they gets."

Amelia met Faller's gaze. Even in the darkness, she could see something had happened to him, and she knew he saw the same about her. Householders liked to talk about their staff being treated just like family, but when it came down to it, that was just talk. Anyone and everyone in service could find themselves out on the street for any reason, or no reason, just as soon as something went wrong.

That made it all too easy to decide to take what you could get.

Amelia had done it. Faller, of course, was doing it right now, by keeping an eye on her, in case Miss Seymore should get asked about the new maid.

The fact that he was here at all said to her that Faller had known about Miss Seymore's rendezvous. Maybe he'd helped distract the men on watch to help the sweethearts keep their appointment.

Amelia held her tongue and let Faller come to his own conclusions about what she might be thinking just now.

As it happened, his conclusions were dead wrong but absolutely unsurprising. "And if you're worried I might not put in a word for you, McGowan, of course I will."

"Why should you?"

"Well, like I said, because we're friends, aren't we?"

Because you want me to keep my mouth shut. "We could be."

"And Miss Seymore's going to need a friend, and she's the generous type."

"What do you mean by that? She's going to need a friend?"

"Never you mind," said Faller. "You just make sure you're ready when opportunity knocks, is all."

Amelia opened her mouth, but movement caught her eye, and she turned back to the windows.

"Uh-oh."

"What?" Faller looked, as well.

The sweethearts were standing at the edge of the wall's shadow. The young man, had his hands out, pleading. Miss Seymore, though, had both hands clapped over her mouth.

"Love's Young Dream down there said something she didn't like," muttered Amelia.

They both watched as Miss Seymore turned and fled across the lawn.

"Oh, that stupid girl!" groaned Amelia. "I've got to get back."

Faller bolted for the pocket doors and opened one a bare inch. "Coast's clear," he said. "Remember what I told you."

Oh, I'll remember, thought Amelia as she ducked through the doors and hurried down the hall.

She meant to return to her own room, but at the last minute she swerved and darted through to Miss Seymore's sitting room. So, once she was inside, she was able to whirl around and look extremely startled when Miss Seymore burst through the door behind her.

"Miss!" she cried. "I was just coming to check on you!"

Miss Seymore—tear stained, rumpled, her wrapper coming loose and the sash trailing on the floor—stared at her, speechless.

They both heard the sound of footsteps on the stairs.

Amelia moved first. She shut the door to the hallway, grabbed the girl by the shoulders, and shoved her through to the bedroom. Thankfully, Miss Seymore's paralysis broke, and she scrambled into bed and yanked up the covers. Amelia slapped the discarded compress over her eyes.

She heard the sitting room door open. Miss Seymore screwed her eyes shut.

Amelia turned and walked out into the sitting room, perfectly composed.

Miss Mary Ann stood there, her expression shifting from uncertain to suspicious.

"McGowan? Is Minney all right? Mama sent me up to check on her."

"She's sound asleep," said Amelia.

"You're sure?" Mary Ann was looking past her at the closed door.

Amelia moved to the door, putting one finger to her lips. She pushed the door open a little, so Mary Ann could see her sister, eyes closed, under the bedcovers.

Amelia pulled the door closed. Mary Ann looked both surprised and relieved.

"Well, I shall tell Mama. Thank you, McGowan."

"Very good, miss."

Miss Mary Ann was watching her intently. Amelia kept her eyes lowered and her demeanor composed. At last, the girl left her, presumably to go inform anyone who was interested that things upstairs were just as they should be.

If, that is, she hadn't been trying to catch her sister out. Amelia didn't for a minute believe that the existence of the sweetheart was a secret from Miss Mary Ann.

Once she was reasonably sure that the sitting room door would remain closed, Amelia returned to the boudoir.

"All right, miss," she whispered.

Miss Seymore's eyes snapped open. "Oh, McGowan. Thank you! You don't know . . . Well, thank you."

"You should go to sleep, miss," replied Amelia. "Your mother's guests will be gone soon, and she'll be up to check on you herself."

"Oh, yes. Yes, you're right. You won't tell her anything, will you?"

Amelia made a show of hesitation. "Well, I dare say there's been no harm done."

"Thank you!" Miss Seymore caught her hand and squeezed it. "I knew I could trust you."

What happened out there? What did he say to you? Amelia bit her lip. To ask those questions now would be to admit she'd been spying. She'd have to take this carefully.

"Go to sleep, miss." Amelia extricated her hand from Miss Seymore's grip. She also took the dried-out compress. "You'll have rings under your eyes in the morning if you don't."

This appeal to vanity did the trick. Miss Seymore rolled over and burrowed under her covers.

Amelia went back out into the sitting room and closed the door behind her.

Well, well, she thought. *I may not be telling madam much, but won't I have a whole lot to say to Miss Thorne!*

CHAPTER THIRTY-TWO

Company for Breakfast

*"All these projects in their turns are sifted,
and supported and contradicted, and laid down
again . . ."*

Bury, Charlotte, *The Diary of a Lady-in-Waiting*

That night, Rosalind undressed. She braided her hair and pinned it beneath her cap as usual, but when she lay down, sleep would not come. Unwelcome thoughts and worries chased each other through her mind, keeping away rest and gentler dreams.

Alice had come home around ten o'clock. Neither Mr. Ranking nor his editor had been at the *Standard*. She had left her little packet with the night porter as she promised and had lingered a bit afterward to try to pick up any gossip there might be.

"Nothing to the purpose," she'd told Rosalind. "Which is something, I suppose."

Something. But what? Rosalind blinked up at the ceiling. She wished selfishly that there had been something. Not because the answers would be comforting, but because they would keep her thoughts occupied, and away from Adam.

She knew that Adam was in no danger. At least she told herself that. There was no reason for any person to come to Mr. Poole's room in the dark. There was no reason to believe Adam could be caught unawares. She knew his abilities. She had complete confidence in them, and him.

And yet this business was deeper and wider than any she'd been in before. It involved worldly power and privilege, and at the same time it was intensely personal. She could not set aside the crawling sense of danger that worked its way through her.

She thought about the folded letter in her desk drawer and squeezed her eyes shut around the tears that threatened to spill down her cheeks.

She wished she did not have to wait on others to bring her news. She hoped Amelia had been able to find out something, *anything*, that would help them locate the lost certificate and Mr. Poole's killer. Before Amelia left to enter Mrs. Fitzherbert's service, they had arranged that Rosalind would be at the post office nearest to Mrs. Fitzherbert's at ten o'clock tomorrow morning. Amelia would meet her there if she could. If not, she would post a letter at the office, to be held for Rosalind to claim.

But morning felt an unusually long way off, and her ability to trust the plans she had laid was worn shamefully thin.

So, it was a relief when daylight finally showed between the curtains, even though the rain drummed insistently against the windows. Rosalind dressed herself in her plain muslin morning gown. Later she would change and have Laurel do her hair. Her plan was to go to call on Countess Lieven after she had (hopefully) seen Amelia, and she could not appear at the countess's door looking less than her best. Appearances were a form of armor, and she'd need all she had to deal with Dorothea Lieven.

Down in the kitchen, the smell of warm cinnamon filled

the air. Mrs. Singh was already busy with the breakfast. Mrs. Napier, Claire, Laurel, and Mortimer all sat at the table with their mugs of tea. As soon as Rosalind appeared, they all began to get to their feet, but she gestured for them to stay seated.

"Good morning, miss," said Mrs. Singh cheerfully. "Have you any notion how many we will be for breakfast?"

"I am sure of myself and Mr. and Miss Littlefield," Rosalind said. "Perhaps Mr. Harkness, although I cannot be sure."

Mrs. Singh and Mrs. Napier exchanged a knowing glance, which Rosalind decided not to notice.

"Very good, miss," said Mrs. Singh. "We'll have both tea and coffee ready in just a minute."

Back upstairs, Rosalind met Alice coming downstairs at a run.

"Good morning, Rosalind!" said Alice as she breezed past and threw the front door open. George stepped triumphantly inside. He carried a bundle of limp newspapers in his arms. Rain ran in thick rivulets from his coat and hat.

"Good morning, Alice! Good morning, Rosalind!" he cried. "Awful out there! I'm half-drowned."

Alice took charge of the papers, while Rosalind helped George out of his coat and hat, which she promptly hung on the pegs by the door. They all repaired to the front parlor and were followed quickly by Mortimer and Claire, carrying two trays—one for the tea things and one for coffee. When Rosalind thanked them and said there was nothing further, Mortimer left at once, but Claire lingered just long enough to open the drapes and take away the lamps to be cleaned and refilled.

Alice poured a cup of coffee and handed it to her brother. "For your heroics."

"Bless you, sister dear." George cupped his hands around the cup and sipped gratefully.

"Have you heard anything new?" Alice asked.

George shook his head. "If anyone's heard anything, they're not talking. There still might be something in there." He gestured toward the papers.

"Well, I'll take the *Times* and the *Standard*," said Alice, leafing through the stack. "Rosalind, what can I help you to?"

But Rosalind was not listening. From the window, she had already seen Adam turning the corner of Orchard Street, dodging the puddles, with his hat pulled low. Without a word, she left the Littlefields to go meet him at the door.

Like George, Adam came in dripping rain from his hat brim and coat hems.

"I gather I'm expected," he said as he swept his hat off.

She went to him, ignoring his damp coat, and let his arms close around her. They kissed slowly, appreciating this moment, this breath, this touch, this heat, and the depth of this need.

When they finally parted, Rosalind smoothed her hair back into its place and grimaced at her damp bodice. Adam grinned, saying plainly it was her own fault. She turned up her nose, pretending to ignore him.

"Have you had breakfast?" she asked.

He shook his head. "There's been no time. Besides, I'd already had a sample of what the White Swan had to offer last night." His woebegone face told Rosalind all she needed to know about the tavern's bill of fare.

"Well, we should have something shortly. Come in. George is already here."

The Littlefields greeted Adam cheerfully as he entered. Rosalind poured him a cup of tea, and he drank half of it in a single gulp.

"Did you find anything out?" Rosalind asked.

"Well, we burned three candles down to the nubs," Adam said as he sat beside her on the sofa. "But we did manage to find Poole's will."

"We?" asked Rosalind.

"Sam Tauton and I. He and Sampson Goutier came and found me. It seems Townsend and Stafford had a shouting match, and my name got raised, along with Poole's."

Rosalind felt her brows arch. "Why were Mr. Stafford and Mr. Townsend shouting about Josiah Poole?"

"Stafford is the new client Mrs. Poole told us about."

"*Stafford* asked Poole to steal the certificate?" cried George.

"Or Poole let Stafford know he could get it," said Alice. "If he was as canny as we've heard."

"And Mr. Poole might have had someone attached to Mrs. Fitzherbert's household who was in debt to him," added Rosalind. "The Pooles' parlormaid, Judith, gave me to believe that he was in the habit of placing people who owed him favors with prominent families." She remembered Judith standing on the dim landing, and how her hand had strayed to touch the place near her heart.

She wondered again what, or whom, Judith had been thinking of in that moment.

"I think it's more likely that Townsend put Stafford up to the job," Adam was saying. "Stafford said he thought Townsend was making a series of mistakes. Then he admitted—or made it sound as if he was admitting—that it might be Townsend who stabbed Poole."

All three of them stared, open-mouthed, at Adam.

Rosalind recovered first. "Can that possibly be true?"

"I don't know," Adam admitted. "I asked Stafford if he had met Poole, and he said they had had an appointment for the afternoon, but that Poole had never arrived."

"Which could be a lie," said Alice. "About the timing of the appointment, that is."

Adam nodded in agreement.

"What does Stafford gain from such a lie?" asked George.

"He gains Adam," said Rosalind promptly. "His trust and his help. And Mr. Tauton and Mr. Goutier with him."

"Ah. Yes," said Alice. "There is that."

"But if he's there trying to win Adam over, that must mean he doesn't have the certificate," said George. "And he doesn't know where it is."

"Which probably means the king's people don't have it yet," said Adam. "Or the queen's. I'd be very surprised if Stafford didn't have an ear to the ground there."

"I suppose we should be relieved about that," said Rosalind. "But the possibility that Mr. Townsend would go as far as murder . . . It defies belief."

"I only wish it did," said Adam. "But something else Stafford said makes me wonder. He said the king is leaving Townsend behind now that he's ascended the throne. Townsend is eager to prove he's still the king's man, the way he was the prince regent's."

"By getting him the certificate?" asked Rosalind quietly. "So it cannot be used against the king during the divorce proceedings?"

"Yes," said Adam. "But Stafford suggested that the idea didn't come from Townsend. He said that someone who knew he was worried about his standing with the king might be putting ideas into his head."

They all sat for a moment, absorbing this new, unwelcome layer to their problem. Rosalind was forced to admit it made a tidy line. Mr. Townsend was a vain man, and his relationship with the former Prince of Wales was the crowning glory of his life. If he believed his position was in jeopardy, and that the Fitzherbert certificate would help restore him to the king's affection, he would act. Going to Mr. Stafford for assistance was a logical choice. Townsend could present the issue as one of stability and loyalty to the Crown. If the marriage to Mrs. Fitzherbert was proved, the succession could be questioned. The kingdom would be thrown into turmoil, and the Crown itself put into jeopardy.

But Mr. Stafford would not wish to risk being seen as con-

nected to such a dubious enterprise. So he might well go to
Mr. Poole, who would have no such scruples. Mr. Poole gained
entry to Mrs. Fitzherbert's house.

But what then? Rosalind looked at Adam and at the Littlefields and knew they were all asking themselves the same
question. But none of them had any answers.

"Adam, you said you found Poole's will," said Rosalind.
"What does it say?"

"Mostly that if Mrs. Poole knew of its contents, she had
no monetary reason to wish her husband dead. The lease on
the house and all the other monies are bound up in a trust for
Poole's sons. Letitia is to be supported until her marriage,
and there's provision for her dowry. Mrs. Poole has a small
income and the use of the house, but only as long as she is
guardian of the children or until she marries again."

"Singularly ungenerous of him," remarked Alice.

"And hardly a legacy that would drive a woman to take
drastic measures," said George. "Unless there is something
more we do not know."

Adam sighed. "Unfortunately, the amount we do not know
about this business is still greater than what we do."

Their uneasy silence was broken by the sound of someone
plying the knocker on the front door—loudly and repeatedly.
Everyone in the parlor sat up a little straighter, all of them
wondering who else could be at the door this early.

A moment later came the sound of men's heated voices,
Mortimer's first, followed by one Rosalind couldn't recognize.

But George did. "That's Ron Ranking," he said.

Rosalind's throat went dry. She'd hoped for at least another few hours before she would need to address this issue.

Adam, of course, noticed her discomfort. "Do you want
me to speak with him?"

"I'll go with you."

George was already halfway to his feet.

"No," said Rosalind. "I'll see him."

"But, Rosalind—" began Alice.

Whatever Alice had been about to say was cut off when Mortimer entered the room, looking sour and disappointed in himself.

"There's a Mr. Ranking, miss," said Mortimer. "He's insisting that he see you. He says he was invited to call."

Which was blatantly untrue, but Rosalind set that aside. "Thank you, Mortimer. I will see him in my writing room."

Mortimer looked like he wanted to argue. "Very well, miss."

Alice was also on her feet. "Let's—"

"No, thank you," said Rosalind. "I will see him alone."

"Are you sure?" Alice asked. "He'll know you've got company already. He'll think you're hiding something."

"That," said Rosalind, "is exactly what I'm counting on."

CHAPTER THIRTY-THREE

A Few Pointed Questions

*". . . there is something uncertain and wayward
about him, which just as one is going to like him,
prevents one's doing so . . ."*

Bury, Charlotte, *The Diary of a Lady-in-Waiting*

"Well, this is all very nice, isn't it?"

Mr. Ranking looked about Rosalind's writing room with evident interest. Rosalind left the door open a full inch, for appearances' sake. Also for appearances, she wrung her hands together as she lowered herself into the chair by her desk.

"Won't you sit down . . . Mr. Ranking, is it?" She clasped her hands in her lap too tightly. Mr. Ranking noticed this open display of nerves, and a gleam sparked in his sharp dark eyes.

"That's right, miss. Ronald Ranking, at your service." He gave a flourishing bow, very much in the manner of a man who thought himself charming. He also lifted his coattails and settled himself on the chair Rosalind indicated. "Will Miss Littlefield be joining us?" he asked. "Or Mr. Harkness?"

He clearly meant to disconcert her by revealing that he knew who was in her house. Rosalind twisted her hands and dropped her gaze to help him conclude that he had succeeded. She even managed to raise a bit of a blush.

"I had thought we might speak in private," she murmured. "Under the circumstances."

"Oh, yes?" She could hear the grin in his voice. "Well, always glad to oblige a lady."

"Thank you. May I take it you received my . . . message of last night?"

"I did, I did," said Mr. Ranking. "And a most genteel and considerate message it was." His grin widened. "But I do wonder why a lady such as you are would be so condescending to an entirely negligible Grub Street ruffian such as myself?"

"Oh, but surely . . ." Rosalind made her voice breathless. "I thought that would be understood." She widened her eyes and made herself think, *That is why I'm so surprised to see you here.*

A positive fog of smug satisfaction rolled off Mr. Ranking. "In my profession, we learn pretty quick that it's best not to count on mere understanding. Much better to have it all out in the open. Don't you agree?"

Rosalind looked away.

"Now, Miss Thorne." Mr. Ranking was trying to sound both stern and kind, like a schoolmaster. Rosalind bit the inside of her cheek to keep from rolling her eyes. "I've a sister at home. You remind me very much of her. I know if she'd got herself in over her head, I'd hope someone would help steer her right."

Is one word of that statement true? wondered Rosalind. She tightened her hands together.

"This business with Poole," Mr. Ranking went on. "It must be quite the shock for you, eh? And for Mrs. Fitz, I suppose."

"I can't say anything about that," murmured Rosalind.

"No, no, a' course not." From the look in his eyes, Mr. Ranking had already traded *can't* for *won't*.

"Mr. Ranking," said Rosalind earnestly, "you must understand I am sworn to secrecy, and already . . . with my name in the papers and so many people clamoring for answers . . ." She blinked rapidly.

She could also hear Alice's voice warning her that she risked laying it on a bit thick. Mr. Ranking, however, swelled with pride and not a little condescension.

"Just so, just so. It must be a real hardship for you."

He's going to pat my hand, thought Rosalind.

Mr. Ranking reached out and gave her hand three gentle pats. "Now, see, the cat's already out of the bag, isn't it? So, what we have to do next is make sure the thing is put in the correct light."

Rosalind closed her eyes briefly, an indication that she was resigning herself to the inevitable. Then she nodded.

"There." Mr. Ranking beamed. "I can help you through this, and if you'll trust me, we can make sure everybody understands the awful fix Mrs. Fitzherbert's in, and that Poole was nowhere near her house the day he died."

And there it was—the suspicion and the threat, neatly laid out together.

"Surely there's no reason to mention Mr. Poole's connection to Mrs. Fitzherbert or . . . or . . . to me." Rosalind dropped her voice to a whisper.

"To you?" This time, Mr. Ranking's surprise was genuine. "You personally?"

Rosalind looked away again.

"Was it you who introduced Poole to Mrs. Fitz?" asked Ranking. "Was that the help she was asking you for?"

"Mr. Ranking, you must understand everything is so very unsettled," said Rosalind. "If I had a few days to . . . arrange

matters, to gain permission . . . then I could tell you everything."

"What? Me, and not George Littlefield?"

"George is a very dear friend." Rosalind spoke to her tightly
clasped hands. "But there are some things he does not understand."

She peeked at Ranking. He was nodding vigorously. "I
know how it is. There are fellows—best fellows in the world,
some of 'em—but they can't see the thing from someone
else's point of view."

"Yes, that's it," said Rosalind eagerly. "Exactly. He's become so *rigid* in his thinking. I don't dare confide in him."

And I will apologize to him later.

"Yes, yes." Ranking's voice was laden with sympathy.
"Now, you just tell me what's happened and how you came
to put Poole in touch with Mrs. Fitz. I'll help you sort
through it, and we can decide together what should be said."

"That's truly what I was hoping for," said Rosalind. "If I
could just have a day, perhaps two . . . Yes, two days
would—"

"Two days is a long time in this business, Miss Thorne. We
must strike while the iron is hot."

"Yes, of course, I do understand that, but I cannot risk . . .
if I should be wrong in my suspicions—" She bit her lip. "It
all hinges on a letter," she said. "One that I am expecting
hourly. Once I have it in hand . . . well, then I will know for
certain, and then I can consult with you without fear that any
subsequent events will contradict and, well, perhaps embar-
rass . . ." She let the sentence trail away.

"A letter?" Ranking's brows arched. His nostrils quivered,
as if he could scent the story. "From whom?"

"A . . . a particular friend," said Rosalind. "One with connections to some persons involved in the matter."

Rosalind had been raised among the polite nothings of society's drawing rooms. There the native language was hints and innuendo, promises that were not quite made but could sound as if they were, and she had a great deal of practice at it.

The danger now was that Mr. Ranking might recognize her hedging as a set of entirely empty words.

But Ranking's mind was busy elsewhere. She'd seen that look from Alice and George any number of times. He was already imagining the headlines, the column inches, and the bonus from his editor, not to mention extra editions. When his focus returned to her, it was as if he were measuring her up to see how many pieces she could be sliced into to feed a crowd.

Rosalind suppressed a wave of anger and hoped that the flush of color in her cheeks would be taken for shame or worry.

"And I have your word that you'll be in touch as soon as the letter arrives?" he said. "And it will be soon?"

"Quite soon. Certainly no later than the day after tomorrow."

"That's good. That's excellent. Because I would not want to take this business any further without being sure . . ." He let the sentence trail away, leaving Rosalind to imagine the last words.

I would not want to, but I will.

CHAPTER THIRTY-FOUR

A Straightforward Plan

"Surely, sir, this is not a matter to be trifled with . . ."
Langdale, Charles, *Memoirs of Mrs. Fitzherbert*

"Mr. Harkness," Sir David greeted Adam as he walked into his bookroom. "I was beginning to think you weren't coming."

Sir David's bookroom was an untidy place. His broad desk overflowed with stacks of papers and books. More books lined the shelves, mostly medical texts, some of them with cracked and flaking bindings. These, Sir David said, were handed down from his father and grandfather, both of whom were physicians and had served members of the royal family in their day. An oil painting of a group of women in togas scrubbing a pale, weak man in a marble bath hung on one wall. The brass plaque on the frame read HYGEIA DIRECTING HER HANDMAIDENS.

Like many men of his rank, Sir David conducted a portion of his official business from his home. When he was working on a case, Adam reported to the coroner most mornings to inform him of his progress or the lack of it. Most cases were ruled on within a few days of the death. Only a very few lingered on for a longer period.

"My apologies, Sir David," replied Adam. "I was delayed this morning."

"By what?"

"A newspaperman named Ron Ranking. May I?" Adam put his hand on the round-backed chair in front of Sir David's desk.

"Sit, sit." Sir David waved his hand. "Help yourself to coffee, if you will." A tray of coffee things sat on the corner of Sir David's desk. Adam declined the offer, and the coroner leaned back in his own chair. "Have you found anything? I want to move this business along, if that's possible. I've already had some members of the press coming around to find out why I haven't scheduled the inquest yet." He waved at the stack of newspapers on his desk.

Adam grimaced. During breakfast with Rosalind, they and the Littlefields had combed through the papers. It surprised none of them that Josiah Poole's murder had been given a prominent space in all of them, with plenty of grisly detail, much of which was entirely made up.

The only good news was that Ranking had accepted Rosalind's "consideration," and her assurance that an even more sensational story was waiting in the wings. No mention of Poole's connection to the Fitzherbert household had appeared in print so far.

"Unfortunately, there's been a new development there," said Adam.

"Unfortunately?" Sir David echoed him. "What happened?"

Adam told him about Stafford's arrival at the White Swan and his confession of his and Townsend's involvement with the disappearance of Mrs. Fitzherbert's marriage certificate.

As Adam talked, the furrows on Sir David's brow deepened. "You're telling me that John Townsend purposed the theft of one of the most sought-after pieces of paper in the kingdom?"

"That is what Stafford implied," Adam told him. "He said nothing directly, but it was very clearly what he wanted us to believe."

"And do you?"

"In this case, I find I do. What I don't understand is why he'd tell us, especially knowing that I would tell you."

"What would happen if I called Townsend as a witness at the inquest and questioned him about Mrs. Fitzherbert and the certificate?"

"His name would be in the papers, and it would cause a sensation, even if it were ruled he had nothing to do with the matter," Adam said flatly. "The reputation he has worked so hard to create would be badly bruised, perhaps ruined. The king might well cut him off entirely."

"Which would at the very least seriously jeopardize his position as head of the Bow Street officers," added Sir David. "Is there any reason Stafford would want Townsend removed?"

"Yes," said Adam. "He might because he thinks Townsend has lost his way over this business with the king." He paused. "It's also possible that Stafford truly does believe Townsend could have killed the man," he said. "But he does not want to make the accusation directly."

"Because that would jeopardize Stafford's own reputation and position." Sir David sighed and pinched the high bridge of his Roman nose. "God save us from internal politics. Does Miss Thorne offer us any help in this matter?"

"She has placed a young woman inside Mrs. Fitzherbert's household to see if she can learn anything from the staff." He paused. "She is also visiting the Countess Lieven."

"Good God, please don't say the countess is involved in this mess."

"I wish I could."

Sir David gave a wordless groan. "Very well. Our job, Mr. Harkness, is still to discover who killed Josiah Poole. The rest of it . . . that is not our purview." He glowered at the newspapers on his desk. "Unfortunately, that doesn't remove the fact that we have to consider Mr. Townsend as a possible witness."

"Sir . . . may I make a suggestion?"

"Of course."

"Let me go and ask Townsend directly."

Sir David raised his eyebrows. "To what end?"

"First, because it is the simplest thing to do," said Adam. "A question has been raised, and an answer is required. Second, because it may tend to play both ends against the middle," Adam said. "Stafford has made it clear he does not trust Townsend. If Townsend does not trust Stafford . . ."

"Yes, I see. Besides, Townsend may trust what you tell him because he knows that there's no love lost between you and Stafford."

Adam nodded. "It's not my favorite game, but it could give us something more to work with." And if he went, Sir David would be spared the possible harm of having raised what was, on the face of it, an outrageous possibility.

"Well, it could almost certainly help delay whatever either of them is planning and give us some time to sort this out," agreed Sir David. "Very well. Go to Bow Street, but I will expect you to also go to the sponging house and finish with the statements of the guests. We'll need the Pooles' statements, as well. Especially Mrs. Poole. I've written letters detailing her and Mr. Considen's responsibilities in this matter." He lifted a portfolio off the top of one stack and handed it to Adam.

"Thank you, Sir David." Adam got to his feet. "I should have those for you by the end of the day."

"Very good. But be careful, Harkness. If either Stafford or Townsend decides you are making too much trouble for them . . . well, there's only so much I will be able to do to protect you."

CHAPTER THIRTY-FIVE

Comings and Goings

"How little do all these people know of the mat-
ter they are fighting about!"

Bury, Charlotte, *The Diary of a Lady-in-Waiting*

"She's late," said Alice.

Rosalind and Alice lingered in front of the draper's shop next to the post office. Thankfully, the rain had stopped, leaving behind only scudding clouds and puddles in the street.

Alice had insisted on coming with Rosalind to her planned meeting with Amelia, and Rosalind had had no reason to refuse. Even had such a reason existed, she wouldn't have had the heart. Of course Alice would want to see Amelia and know that all was well.

"She may have had difficulty getting away," replied Rosalind calmly. "Do you see Mr. Ranking?" Mr. Ranking had left the house, but that was no guarantee that he had left the vicinity or that he had not managed to follow their hired cab. Newspapermen could be frustratingly resourceful.

Alice turned her head casually this way and that, as if examining the bolt of woolen cloth displayed in the shop window. "I don't see him," she said. "That doesn't mean he's not here." She sighed and shifted her weight. "Where on earth is Amelia?"

Rosalind gave her hand a squeeze. "What was it you were saying to me about borrowing trouble?"

"Oh, I'm not worried, not really. I'm . . ." Alice rolled her eyes. "Good Lord, listen to me. I sound like I expect her to be snatched off the street."

"Do you?"

Alice considered this. "I don't think so. But this situation . . ."

"It's different," said Rosalind.

Alice nodded.

"For what it might be worth, I spent half the night worrying that Adam could be attacked in the dark," Rosalind confessed.

"Oh, poor Rosalind! I wish you'd come to find me. We could have been sleepless together."

Rosalind smiled. She had no time to make a reply, however. At that exact moment, Amelia came bustling around the corner. Alice saw her in the same instant Rosalind did. Alice shot her arm up and began to wave vigorously, all the while jumping up and down on her toes. Rosalind turned away to hide her smile at her friend's exuberance.

"I'm so sorry I'm late!" cried Amelia as she reached them. She and Alice hugged warmly, and if they held on a little too long and looked into each other's eyes a little too deeply, it was a busy street and young women's gentle displays of affection were an entirely unremarkable sight.

"Now!" Alice looped her arm through Amelia's. "Have you something to tell us?"

"I should say so! But I'll have to be quick. The housekeeper's a strict one, and I don't want her to think I'm lazing about somewhere."

"There's a park around the corner," said Rosalind. "We can walk there while you tell us all your news."

The park was little more than a small lawn with bright flower beds surrounding an Italian marble fountain. The break in the rain had brought out the neighborhood. Nurses watched their charges playing with balls and hoops on the cramped lawn. Matrons and young women in maids' uniforms walked together, enjoying the summer sun. It was a perfect place for their rendezvous. Rosalind, Alice, and Amelia fit in smoothly with the general company. However, any man lingering in the same square would be quite easy to spot.

Rosalind walked up to the fountain and stood there, as if contemplating the lively cascade. "Now," she said softly, "what have you learned?"

Amelia leaned close. Quickly, she told them about the footman, Thomas Faller, and how he'd begun watching her almost from the moment she'd entered the house. She described how she'd found a hidden note in Minney Seymore's dressing table; how Miss Seymore had feigned a headache to get away from her mother and her dinner guests; how she, Amelia, had been discovered by Faller in the conservatory; and how they'd watched Miss Seymore meet her beau and witnessed the apparent argument that followed.

"So," said Alice, "Miss Seymore did have a reason for coming back to town, beyond being worried about her mother."

"Yes," agreed Rosalind. "She and her beau must have had the meeting arranged before she left her father's house."

"Faller could have carried the message," said Amelia. "He as much as said she's paying him extra on the side to keep her secrets."

"But you don't know what that argument you saw between Miss Seymore and her beau was about?" asked Rosalind.

Amelia shook her head. "I'd no way to ask. I'm hoping to find out more today."

"Did you see her this morning at all?"

"I checked on her before I left," Amelia said. "She and Miss Mary Ann were both still sound asleep. But there was something else."

"What is it?" Rosalind began walking again, angling her path to follow the street. Alice and Amelia fell into step beside her.

"Well," said Amelia, "last night Faller said something odd. He said Miss Seymore would be needing a new friend soon. Then this morning, as I was leaving the house, I all but banged right into him on the area stairs. He was coming back from somewhere, only he's out of uniform and he's got a box on his shoulder, like a man might use to pack his belongings in if he had planned on leaving his place."

"Did you ask him about it?" asked Alice. "What did he say?"

"First, he told me to mind my own business," said Amelia. "Then he apologized and said he'd gotten some bad news, but he wouldn't say what, but I swear it looked like he might have been crying." She paused, clearly seeing the sharp glance that passed between Rosalind and Alice. "What?"

"We've learned that there was an attorney, Josiah Poole, who may have been involved in the robbery," said Rosalind. "His specialty was debt, and he was in the habit of forging connections inside important houses and prominent families to gain information and also to get hold of compromising papers."

" 'Was?' " Amelia's eyes narrowed. "You said 'was.' "

"He was murdered," Alice said.

"Never!"

Alice nodded and pressed Amelia's hand. The other woman had gone a little green around the gills.

"I'm afraid it gets worse," said Rosalind. "Mr. Poole was seen going into Mrs. Fitzherbert's garden and coming out again quickly about the time the certificate was stolen. We think somebody in the house passed him the certificate to carry away."

"Do you think this Tom Faller could have done it?" asked Alice. "Could he have stolen the certificate?"

Amelia considered. "I don't know," she said slowly. "He's got plenty of nerve and cheek. He's taking extra from Miss Seymore, and from any houseguest who wants something special, but that's a different thing from out-and-out thieving."

Rosalind nodded. Just because one was willing to commit one sort of transgression, that did not mean one was willing to commit all of them. In fact, when it came to accepting such tips and sweeteners for additional tasks—licit or not— many in service would not consider that they had done anything wrong.

"Could Faller have taken money from someone to just leave a door or a gate open?" she asked.

Amelia nodded. "Now, that he might have done. There's plenty who don't plan to spend their lives in service, but once they're in, they find that it's hard to get out. They start taking their extra to try to get a store together so they can afford to get away."

"So, Faller could be the connection to Mr. Poole," said Alice.

"It is certainly possible," Rosalind agreed. "Unless . . ." She paused. "Unless the person who asked for the door to be left open was Miss Seymore."

"There's a thought," murmured Alice. "And she had Faller running messages to Poole and to her beau . . ."

"That's possible," said Amelia. "Carrying messages would be all in a day's work for him."

"But he'd have to know that Poole is dead. It's in all the—"

But Alice caught sight of Amelia rolling her eyes and stopped. "Oh, yes, of course."

Not only was there no time belowstairs for sitting about reading the papers, but Faller might not be able to read.

They came to the edge of the park and continued on up the street, strolling at a leisurely pace, as if simply enjoying the summer morning. Rosalind considered what should happen next. Her first instinct was to go directly to Mrs. Fitzherbert. But the truth of the matter was, Tom Faller might be guilty of nothing more than taking money to turn a blind eye to Miss Seymore's romantic machinations, or what he thought were romantic machinations. If he was called forward, he would very likely be dismissed without a reference, which could sentence a person to destitution.

Her second thought was to speak with Tom Faller directly. Amelia could arrange the meeting, or she could ask Mrs. Fitzherbert to allow her to speak with him. But once that was done, there was no going back. Even if he was not involved in the theft, Faller would know Amelia was there to assist with inquiries among the staff, and he might or might not be inclined to keep the secret.

Rosalind resisted the urge to grind her teeth.

"We haven't much time," she murmured. "Amelia, what do you think we ought to do?"

Amelia looked startled at being so consulted. Alice grinned and gave her hand an encouraging squeeze.

"Well," drawled Amelia. "If I wanted to find out what was what, I'd say I should go back and get Faller talking. He's had bad news of some kind, so he's going to want sympathy. And I can be his pal about Miss Seymore."

Which was important. Because Tom Faller was not the only person in Mrs. Fitzherbert's house who might be in need of money.

"I agree. Thank you, Amelia. This is all extremely helpful."

"Good. I'm glad. And now I've got to dash—"

"Wait," said Alice abruptly. "Ladies, we've got a visitor."

Rosalind turned carefully so she could follow Alice's gaze past the edge of her bonnet. A man in a battered low-crowned hat sat on the edge of the fountain, reading a newspaper. He lowered it just a little to turn the page, and Rosalind caught a glimpse of Mr. Ranking's sharply angled profile.

"Who's that?" murmured Amelia.

"Ron Ranking," Alice told her. "He's a newspaperman, one of the ones who's been watching Mrs. Fitzherbert. Now he's watching Rosalind."

"You stay here, Amelia," said Rosalind. "We'll go away first and see if he follows us."

"All right," said Amelia. "But don't worry if he doesn't. It wouldn't be the first time I maanged to lose a follower." She grinned and hugged Alice again. "I'll see you day after to-morrow!"

Alice gazed at her for a moment, misty eyed and clearly bursting with pride. Then she and Rosalind turned and hurried together up the street, dodging their fellow pedestrians and the occasional wheelbarrow.

At the first street corner, Rosalind turned to the right, caring less about where they were heading than about having a chance to glance behind them. Mr. Ranking strolled up the street casually and at a distance, but there could be no question that he was following them.

Rosalind murmured a rude word and strode ahead, leaving Alice to hurry to catch up.

"Where are we going?" asked Alice.

"I am thinking that we are going to need to pay a call on your Mrs. Dowding as soon as possible, Alice," she said. "We need to know more about Minney Seymore's dalliance with her unsuitable beau. Have you heard from her?"

"Heard from her?" cried Alice. "She all but shouted from the rooftops that I was to bring you around just as soon as ever you like. And she means it," she said before Rosalind could ask. "But I thought you were going to call on Countess Lieven this morning."

"I will go to the countess from Mrs. Dowding's," she said. "This is more important."

"And you said you were to meet Adam at the Pooles' at four o'clock," said Alice. "Dowdy can talk until the sun goes down, but I think I can get you out of there in time."

Rosalind smiled. "And when are we going to discuss your wages as my assistant?"

"Once I have proved fully satisfactory at the job, and you've agreed not to let your demands interfere with my brilliant future as one of England's leading literary ladies."

"So ten shillings the week, would you say?"

Alice made her eyes go wide in mock surprise. "Rosalind Thorne, did I just hear you mention *money* to another gently bred young lady?"

Rosalind sighed. "How far I have fallen. What shall we say?"

"Ten shillings the week and meals," said Alice. "I'd do anything for Mrs. Singh's cooking. Come along. I think I saw a cabstand up the way. What shall we do about Ranking?"

"At the moment, nothing," said Rosalind. "If he's following us, he's not watching Amelia go back to Mrs. Fitzherbert's."

It was vital that Mr. Ranking not know that Rosalind had been talking to a member of Mrs. Fitzherbert's household. If he began making inquiries there, Amelia's disguise might fail, and that would be disastrous.

Because it was entirely possible that Tom Faller was not responsible for the theft of the marriage certificate, but Minney Seymore was.

And if Miss Seymore, or her beau, was involved in the theft, it meant they might also be involved in the murder.

CHAPTER THIRTY-SIX

A Formidable Woman

*". . . and if being indiscreet contributed to her
amusement . . . why (situated as she was) should
she not be so?"*

Bury, Charlotte, *The Diary of a Lady-in-Waiting*

"Alice! Dear Alice! Come give me a kiss and sit by me!"
Mrs. Dowding's rooms were filled with the heavy
scents of musk perfume and hair powder. The lady herself sat
in the center of the silk-covered sofa, her vast acreage of
damask silk skirts spread around her. Her face was painted
much more heavily than was the current fashion, and her
eyebrows had been drawn so as to give her a constant air of
arch surprise. One foot, wrapped in heavy bandages, rested
on a padded stool. Apparently, Mrs. Dowding suffered from
at least one side effect of a life of excess—gout.

"Dowdy!" Alice pressed her cheek against Mrs. Dowding's, heedless of the coating of powder she came away with.
She sat down next to the older woman and squeezed both her
hands. "Dowdy, I want you to meet my best friend in the
whole world, Rosalind Thorne."

Rosalind was just old enough to remember such ladies visiting her mother. Her father had always laughed behind their backs, calling them many uncomplimentary names. As a little girl, she had laughed with him, but the truth was these grand ladies with their broad skirts and elaborate wigs had frightened her a little. She and her sister would whisper stories about those wigs—about how they had almost caught fire or had been found to be full of spiders.

Even now, Rosalind had to swallow hard before she made her curtsy.

"The famous Miss Rosalind Thorne!" Mrs. Dowding gave a girlish shimmy of excitement. "How wonderful to meet you at last!"

"How do you do, Mrs. Dowding?" said Rosalind. "It is very kind of you to see us without—"

"Oh, no, no, no." Mrs. Dowding waved the silk scarf, which she apparently used as a handkerchief. "I have been asking Alice to bring you to meet me for *ages* now. But she, naughty girl, has kept you all to herself. Now, sit there, sit there. You will have some wine? I cannot *abide* tea at midday. Oakley, pour my guests some of the sherry."

The maid complied. Alice and Rosalind took the required polite sips, while Mrs. Dowding downed half her glass.

Alice set her glass down. "Now, Dowdy, I'm afraid we must come straight to the point. Rosalind has something very important she wishes to ask about."

"I'd be delighted to tell you anything at all, my dear. But it won't come for free." She winked one heavy eyelid.

"Then I'm sorry to have troubled you, Mrs. Dowding." Rosalind set her glass down and stood up. "I do thank you—"

"Oh, heavens!" cried Mrs. Dowding. "Alice warned me you were one of our righteous sort. Dear me, dear me, you young things do take such a *serious* view of the world! You would not have lasted a single moment back in my day." She shook her head. "Such larks we used to have! Such *grand* affairs. None of this small, sordid stuff. I blame Georgie Porgie," she sniffed. "All that passion and not an ounce of true *romance* or, dare I say, imagination. Do sit down, Miss Thorne. I certainly shall not ask you to break any confidence you do not choose to."

Given what Alice had said about Mrs. Dowding and her willingness to be bribed to spread rumors or suppress them, Rosalind was not entirely sure that was true. Nonetheless, she sat back down and let herself be eyed by Mrs. Dowding.

"Well, Alice, I will say your friend seems to at least have a bit of nerve about her."

"More than you'll know, Dowdy," replied Alice. "She once put a highwayman's eye out with her mending scissors."

"She never!"

"He was not a highwayman," said Rosalind calmly.

"My word!" Mrs. Dowding pressed her scarf dramatically to her cheek, but at the same time, her eyes narrowed. "Remind me not to anger your friend, Alice! It is always the quiet ones, is it not? Well, well!"

"Now, Dowdy, do stop teasing." Alice patted the older woman's hand. "We're here on serious business."

"How utterly tedious! And I was already bored to death."

"Ignore her, Rosalind. Dowdy, we need to know about Minney Seymore, Mrs. Fitzherbert's oldest girl."

"Oh ho! It's *Minney* you've caught hold of, is it? What's happened to the girl?" she asked eagerly. "Has she been caught gadding about with her dashing cavalry officer again?"

Alice shot Rosalind a glance that said *I told you.*

"Do you know the name of this officer?" asked Rosalind.

"Oh, of course! He's Captain George Dawson. *Quite* the romantic hero, you know. Had his horse shot out from under him at Waterloo and heaven knows what else!" Dowdy waved the scarf energetically. "Excellent family, as well. Very well placed—that is, as well placed as an Irishman can be, you know. Son of an earl—but alas, the third son, so lamentably far down the pecking order in terms of inheritance."

"Not wealthy, then, I gather?" prompted Alice.

"Not a bean," said Mrs. Dowding. "Worse, he's got debts. Also something of a drinker. Not a combination to swell the hopes of a mother, or indeed a father, whether acknowledged or not." She gave another heavy, knowing wink.

Mrs. Dowding clearly wanted her to ask, so Rosalind did. "I gather there have been rumors about Miss Seymore's parentage?"

"How could there not be?" Mrs. Dowding cried. "It's all nonsense, of course. The child's history is a dull, everyday tragedy. Her father is Mrs. Fitzherbert's older brother, and she was an infant still when her mother died. Once the mother was in the ground, the children were parceled out to their relations, as so frequently happens. Mrs. Fitzherbert got handed Minney, and she positively clasped the girl to her bosom. I personally don't see the attraction in the maternal bonds. Shackles more like! When I see what my own nieces have put their families through!" She threw her expressive scarf up in an expansive gesture of despair. "I am thankful I was spared. Not that Mr. Dowding wouldn't have liked a son, but I always told him if he could get himself one, he was welcome to do so." She paused. "And now I've shocked you again, Miss Thorne," she added happily.

"Alice assured me you and Mr. Dowding have had a long and prosperous marriage. I am always interested to hear how that may be managed."

Again, Mrs. Dowding gave her that shrewd, narrow glance. "I think I like this girl of yours, Alice. Possibly despite myself. She's sharp, in more ways than one, if your little stories are to be believed."

Alice blanched. "I promise, Rosalind. I never—"

"Of course you did not, Alice," said Rosalind calmly. "It is very plain that Mrs. Dowding enjoys a tease."

"Yes, I do. It's the problem with gout. It's undignified, and it's dull. So I must take whatever little amusements I can get, and I'm afraid my sense of humor has never been domesticated."

Rosalind smiled and sipped her sherry and changed the subject. "Do you know what became of Miss Seymore's relationship with Captain Dawson?"

"Nothing became of it," said Mrs. Dowding. "The girl is still hooked, to Mrs. Fitz's utter despair. Her father is not best pleased, either. There has been talk that when he returns to Berlin, Minney is to go with him. They mean to see if an ocean's worth of distance can drown the girl's attraction. *And*," she added, "if that weren't enough, Captain Dawson's to leave for the West Indies to seek his own fortune. Now, what do you say to that?"

"I should not like to say anything until I am certain," Rosalind said.

"Hmph! Infuriating girl! No respect for your elders, I see. Well, well." She patted her forehead and cheeks vigorously with her scarf. "I shall have to pine and sigh for my news . . . ah, me!"

"Dowdy, dear," said Alice, "you're laying it on a little thick."

"Yes, I am rather, aren't I? I'm out of practice, you know. Well, well." She reached up under her wig and scratched vigorously, threatening to dislodge the entire construction. "What *would* you like to say, Miss Thorne? Come now, fair's fair! And trust me, my dear, you do not want to be under obligation to me. I always collect."

An entirely involuntary and irrational shiver ran up Rosalind's spine.

"I should like to say thank you, Mrs. Dowding," she replied. "And I should be glad to call again in the near future, when we may have a longer chat."

"Excellent. You shall come to dinner. Just write whenever you are ready, my dear. You shall be the highlight of my party!"

Rosalind was not entirely sure about this, but she smiled and agreed.

"But there's one thing, Dowdy," said Alice. "We may have been followed here."

"Followed! How terribly thrilling!"

"Yes, by a gentleman of the press. Ron Ranking."

"Ranking?" Mrs. Dowding laughed. "My dear, I thought you said it was a *gentleman*."

Alice grinned. "He may try to speak with you."

"He may try all he likes, my dear," said Dowdy. "But we shall have to see if he succeeds, shan't we?"

When Rosalind and Alice emerged from Mrs. Dowding's house, Rosalind took a deep, relieved breath of fresh air—well, what passed for fresh air in London. She started down the steps and up the busy high street, feeling absurdly as if she had just made a lucky escape.

If Ron Ranking was anywhere nearby, he had made himself scarce.

"What are you thinking, Rosalind?" asked Alice. "You look a thousand miles away."

"I'm afraid I am, rather," said Rosalind. "Alice, Mrs. Dowding would not repeat our conversation to Mr. Ranking, would she?"

"To Ranking? Never! Oh, she'll talk to him. It will amuse her, especially if she can get him to believe something truly outrageous. But she'd never throw you away to such a person, not now that she's finally got you in her visiting book."

Rosalind nodded, accepting this reassurance.

"What else?" said Alice. "I know there's more going on up there." She reached over and tapped Rosalind's temple just once.

Rosalind smiled and brushed her friend's hand away. "I'm thinking that Mrs. Fitzherbert trusts her daughters," said Rosalind. *I would sooner believe my daughters had robbed me.* "And I am thinking that one of those daughters is in love with a man who has debts. And that she has recently run away from her father's house, where she was possibly going to be sent packing to the Continent to get her away from that man."

"Oh, Rosalind, you don't really think Minney Seymore and her beau are involved in the theft?"

"I think it is unfortunately very possible," said Rosalind. "What if Captain Dawson came to her with a scheme to allow them to get the money to elope? What if she engaged Faller to steal the certificate and pass it to Poole, who promised to pay them for it?"

"A cavalry officer wouldn't stick at violence," murmured Alice. "But what reason would he have had to kill Poole?"

"Perhaps Mr. Poole tried to cheat him of the money he promised. Or . . ." Rosalind's stride hitched. "Perhaps Mr. Poole blackmailed Dawson into agreeing to help steal the certificate. Perhaps Dawson decided to end the matter and keep the certificate for his own benefit."

"But Poole's keys were stolen, and his rooms searched. If Dawson had the certificate, why would he bother with any of that?"

"There may have been papers that he wanted from Poole, promissory notes or dunning letters. Or"—she paused, remembering Adam's assessment of the rooms—"he may have done it simply as a way to distract attention from the certificate."

"There's another possibility," said Alice slowly. "Minney herself could have planned the theft from the beginning."

"And what Amelia saw between them might not have been an argument," said Rosalind. "It might have been Dawson telling her that their plans had gone very badly awry." Rosalind felt her jaw tighten. "Alice, I need you to take a note to Adam at the White Swan. We need to know if the name Captain Dawson appears in any of Mr. Poole's papers."

CHAPTER THIRTY-SEVEN

Household Business

". . . she was about to meet with a species of attack so unprecedented and alarming, as to shake her resolution . . ."

Langdale, Charles, *Memoirs of Mrs. Fitzherbert*

Thankfully, Mrs. DeLupe was busy elsewhere when Amelia returned to 6 Tilney Street, so Amelia was able to hurry through the servants' hall and back upstairs without stopping for a quizzing about why she'd been out for so long. On the stroke of ten, she was there to open the curtains in Mrs. Fitzherbert's room and set about getting her ready for the day.

"Were you able to make your appointment this morning?" Mrs. Fitzherbert asked as she sat at her dressing table so Amelia could arrange her hair.

"Yes, madam."

"Have you any news?"

"No, madam, I'm sorry."

Mrs. Fitzherbert's hands tightened. "Perhaps it is over already," she said. "Perhaps it has been destroyed and I should simply leave England, as I originally planned."

She sounded so tired, Amelia could not help but feel a twist of sympathy.

"Have you ever been in love with someone who turned against you, McGowan?"

It was an outrageous question, but the role of lady's maid was also one of intimate. It was expected that Amelia would hear and be asked a great deal that she would never repeat, even if she and Mrs. Fitzherbert were only playacting.

"Yes, madam," she said.

"Were you able to forget them? To remove them from your heart?"

"After a while," she said. "And once I found someone else."

"Ah," she murmured. "There, you see, is my problem. I am unable to take that last step."

"But surely . . . That is, you're still a lovely woman, and you've plenty of life about you and m—" Amelia stopped.

"Money?" Mrs. Fitzherbert finished for her. "Yes, and that never fails to make a woman attractive, does it? But you see, there is the nature of my particular attachment. The gentleman in question makes others rather shy. Then there is the fact that should I form a new attachment, I am guilty of the very thing I have so long protested against. So, here I sit." She looked at herself in the glass, and after a moment, she smiled. "Well, never mind me. It is only that I am tired of waiting for my answers, and that makes me melancholy. Go and see to the girls, McGowan. I am quite capable of finishing myself."

The girls, however, were in no mood to be seen to. When Amelia threw back the curtains, both Miss Seymore and Miss Mary Ann burrowed farther under their covers.

"Leave us alone, McGowan," wailed Mary Ann. "It's too early."

"Yes, do." Miss Seymore yanked her pink counterpane up

so only the ends of her curls showed on her bolster. "We'll do each other up. You can just . . ." Her fingertips made a little shooing motion.

Amelia hesitated, the words *I have my instructions from madam* poised on the tip of her tongue. But then she changed her mind.

"I can give you another half an hour," she said. "After that, you need to be on your feet and getting ready. All right?"

A flurry of muffled thank-yous rose from under the counterpanes. Amelia closed the boudoir door and hurried to the servants' stairs. From there, she took herself down into the foyer.

"I'm looking for Faller," she told Peters, the footman on duty at the front door.

"Ain't we all?" he growled. "Says he's too sick to move. My arse he is. Like we didn't all see him coming in this morning with his box and all."

"I heard about that," she said. "What do you reckon he was up to?"

Peters looked like he wanted to spit. "Maybe I should ask, 'What're you up to?'" he said suspiciously. "Not your business, is it? Faller's Mr. Holm's worry."

"All right, all right," said Amelia. "There's no need to get yourself in a twist over it. Just making conversation."

"Well, make it elsewhere, if you please. I'm not giving you any rumors to feed to upstairs."

Amelia turned up her nose and headed away as if she didn't care, but those parting words sent a shiver through her. Maybe she hadn't been as careful as she thought.

Well, that's a worry for later. Amelia took herself down to the servants' hall.

"Cook, can I have a pot of tea, if you please? And maybe some bread and butter?"

"Miss Seymore refusing to get out of bed, then?" asked Cook as she began to assemble the things.

"Thought I'd take them to Tom Faller," she said. "He's saying he's sick."

Cook stopped, knife in one hand, slice of bread in the other. "Ain't no one warned you about Faller yet? He's always using those pretty eyes of his to scrounge a favor or three."

"Oh, I know," she said breezily. "I've seen the type. But I thought I'd give him the benefit of the doubt this once."

Cook gave her a sharp sideways glance, and Amelia thought the woman was going to refuse to give her anything, after all. But she just shook her head and finished making up the tidy plate and filling the pot.

"Thank you," said Amelia. "And don't worry. He's not putting anything over on me."

"We'll see, won't we?" muttered Cook.

Thankfully, this was one of the houses where the male servants slept on the lower floor, on a hallway of their own, past the butler's pantry and the laundry room. Amelia did not fancy toting her tray all the way up to the top of the house.

Cook had told Amelia that Faller had the third room on the right. She kicked at it once to warn him someone was coming and then shouldered her way inside.

Faller was sitting hunched over on the bed, like he'd had his head in his hands just a heartbeat before. "What are you doing here?" he demanded.

Amelia ignored his tone and deposited the tray on the little scarred table by the chimney.

"I came to see if you're all right." She poured a cup and held it out for him. "Thought you might want some tea."

"I don't need you watching out for me," Faller growled. But he did take the tea.

"Well, I think you might. You've got everybody talking, you know." She nodded toward the door, which she now pointedly nudged shut with the heel of her shoe. "What's happened?"

"What do you mean?" he muttered, more to his tea than to her.

"You weren't planning on being back here today."

Faller's head jerked up. "You been spying on me?"

Amelia snorted and held out the plate of bread and butter. Faller just glared at it. Amelia shrugged and took a slice for herself.

"Last night you get all sly, hinting that Miss Seymore might need a new friend," she said between bites. "This morning you're out early, in your civvies, with your box on your shoulder, and I catch you coming back with a face like a wet Monday, and I'm supposed to just say, 'Lawks! What do you suppose happened to him!'" Amelia threw up her hands, scattering crumbs as she did. "*Then* you tell everybody you're sick and vanish into your room, and you think nobody's noticed? They're all talking. I'm just surprised his nibs Mr. Holm hasn't been in here already."

Faller's sour look told her he had been. She rolled her eyes and finished off her bread.

"So, what's gone wrong, then?" she asked as she dusted the remaining crumbs from her hands.

Faller glowered at her but gloomily drained his teacup. Amelia waited in silence until he was done, and then held out the bread and butter plate again. This time, Faller took a slice.

"Thanks," he mumbled around his mouthful.

"Well, don't get used to it," she told him briskly. "I'm no one's nanny, and you can get that back to the kitchen yourself." She nodded to the tea tray. "Now, I've got my own work to do, and if you take my advice, you'll get over this sudden illness of yours, and you'll go apologize to everybody who's been picking up your slack before they really start looking at you even funnier than they are now."

Faller took a deep breath. "You're right. I know you are. I just . . . Well, it was bad this morning, that's all." He stopped. "You . . . you won't say anything? About . . . you know."

"What do you take me for? We got to—"

She was interrupted by the slow creak of the door. Amelia whirled around, and Faller shot to his feet. Both of them stared as Minney Seymore stepped tentatively across the threshold.

"I . . . oh . . . I'm sorry," she stammered.

"Miss Seymore." Amelia drew herself up and arranged her features into the appropriate servant's mask. "What can I do for you?"

"I'm so sorry, I didn't mean to disturb . . . you." Miss Seymore's eyes flicked from her to Faller.

"Not at all, miss," said Faller.

"It's just that . . . Well, I noticed you weren't in the breakfast room, and Mr. Holm said you weren't feeling well . . ."

"Nothing serious, miss," said Faller quickly. "I'm much better now."

"Well, good, then. I expect we'll see you at lunch." She turned to go.

"Miss Seymore?" said Faller.

She stopped and hesitantly turned to face them again. "Yes?"

"Was there anything else?" asked Faller.

Her gaze flickered to Amelia again. "No, no, nothing."

"You can trust McGowan, miss," Faller told her. "I promise, she's a friend."

Miss Seymore bit her lip. Amelia drew herself up and tried to radiate an air of general trustworthiness.

And failed.

"I'm sure she is," Miss Seymore murmured. "Get your rest, Faller." She hurried away down the corridor.

Damn.

Leaving Faller where he was, Amelia trotted after the

young lady. Not that she could say a word down in the bustling warren belowstairs. But Amelia caught up with her just as Miss Seymore emerged into the front hall.

"Miss," began Amelia, but she got no further.

"Minney!" Mrs. Fitzherbert came out of the breakfast room. She carried a folded newspaper in one hand.

That cannot be good.

"What on earth is going on?" said Mrs. Fitzherbert. "Mary Ann said you were still upstairs."

Miss Seymore tried to affect a casual air, but she succeeded only in looking awkward. "I, no, I . . ."

"She had a tear in her . . . blue," tried Amelia. "She came to find me to mend it."

"Yes, my blue pelisse, Mama," said Miss Seymore quickly. "I caught it on the door, and I can't possibly wear it now."

Mrs. Fitzherbert clearly did not believe a single word, but she also clearly did not want to argue the details just then.

"Well, you should know that your father has written me," said Mrs. Fitzherbert.

"Oh," said Miss Seymore.

"Yes, oh," agreed Mrs. Fitzherbert. "And he is grateful to know that you and Mary Ann are safe, and he will be sending the carriage for you the day after tomorrow."

"What!" cried Miss Seymore. "No! I will not leave you alone while . . ."

"Stop it, Minney," said Mrs. Fitzherbert firmly. "I am out of patience with this pretense. You are here because of Captain Dawson, as we are both fully aware."

"No, Mama! Who told you that? Was it Mary Ann? Or—" She turned to Amelia, her dark eyes alight with the sort of rage only a young lady could muster.

"No one told me, Minney," Mrs. Fitzherbert snapped. "Do you think that I could be fooled with a schoolgirl's tricks? You met Captain Dawson last night, when you were supposed to be lying down."

"No, Mama, I promise I did not."

Mrs. Fitzherbert did not bother to acknowledge this statement. "You know how dangerous things are for me at this time, and you used that as an excuse to come and meet with him, when I had *expressly* forbidden such a thing."

"If you had not—"

"And yet you look at me as if my sending you away again was the betrayal."

Miss Seymore closed her mouth.

"Now, I had hoped to send you both back to your father today. Unfortunately, it is now known you are in town." She handed the newspaper to her daughter. Amelia glimpsed the tiny paragraph among the social notices.

> *Their Highnesses the Duke and Duchess of York dined yesterday with Mrs. Fitzherbert. Also in the company Miss Seymore and Miss Smythe.*

Miss Seymore lowered the paper. "Mama," she tried again. "I don't see what the fuss is. Last night I had a headache, that's all. McGowan will tell you—"

"Do not attempt to drag McGowan into this," said her mother sternly. "As I say, I thought you would both be on your way back to your father today, but as your presence has been announced, it would look very odd to have you leave again so suddenly."

Amelia watched the flicker of . . . something in Miss Seymore's eyes, and she found herself wondering just how that little notice had got planted in the papers.

But if Miss Seymore thought she'd scored a victory, Mrs. Fitzherbert did not let her enjoy it for long.

"Now, today I am at home. You and Mary Ann will stay with me and receive our callers. We will let it be known that you came to town to do some shopping and to make your farewells ahead of your departure with your father to Berlin."

Miss Seymore's face went dead white.

"Thursday you will accompany me as I make my calls, and you will make those farewells. You will make them smiling, and you will talk about how excited you are to travel to the Continent. Your father will send his carriage down to us so that Friday you may return to the country, and that, Minney, is my last word on the subject."

CHAPTER THIRTY-EIGHT

A Purely Social Visit

"... she is so witty and so very brilliant, so full of repartee, that her society dazzles my duller senses, and instead of being exhilarated by it, I become lowered."

Bury, Charlotte, *The Diary of a Lady-in-Waiting*

"Miss Thorne, how delightful!" Countess Lieven rose as Rosalind entered her lavishly appointed sitting room. "I was just the other day saying how very much I longed to see you again!"

"I do apologize for arriving without writing first, your grace." Rosalind took the gilded chair that the countess gestured her toward and accepted the cup of tea the liveried footman had brought.

"Oh, do not think on it!" Countess Lieven dropped onto her divan. Rosalind was always impressed by the countess. It took hours of training and much diligent practice to lounge so gracefully. "Surely, such good friends as we are can dispense with tiresome formalities. Burton, you must bring Miss Thorne some of the seedcake, as well. That is your favorite, is it not?"

Dorothea, Countess Lieven, had lost none of her sparkle. The wife of the Russian ambassador to the Court of St. James's, she was widely regarded as a fascinating individual. Certainly numerous aristocratic gentlemen and powerful politicians were said to have found her so. For the most part, the countess spoke French, which was also the language of the Russian court. Her English, however, was quite good, but Rosalind suspected she liked people to forget just how good.

"Now, Miss Thorne, do tell me all the news. How does the delightful Miss Littlefield? I have received a copy of her book, you know. It is most amusing! I shall surely be recommending it to all my friends."

"I shall make sure to tell her, your grace. I'm sure she will be most pleased." Indeed, Alice would be beside herself, and her publisher, Mr. Colburn, would probably faint from sheer joy.

Rosalind ate her cake and made polite small talk. This primarily consisted of Rosalind offering up bits of slight gossip that gave the countess an opportunity to expound on people and circumstances she knew, which she did at dramatic length.

Rosalind tried to keep her mind on what was said, but she could not help imagining what a meeting between Mrs. Dowding and Countess Lieven would look like.

If it was a play, it would sell out its season.

Once a polite interval had passed, Rosalind handed her plate to the waiting footman.

"I am surprised to find you still in town, your grace," she said. "I had understood you were planning to summer on the Continent."

The countess sighed deeply. "Ah, well, that was our hope. But all plans are overturned by the queen's trial. My husband must stay in town in order to observe how matters progress, you understand. Therefore, I am trapped here to swelter and

repine." These depressed words were delivered with a sardonic smile meant to erase any seriousness from them. "But
at least I am not alone. I understand Lady Jersey has recently
visited you, Miss Thorne."

"She was so kind as to call," Rosalind acknowledged. It
was possible this was the reason for the countess's surrepti-
tious invitation—she simply wanted to hear what the famously talkative Lady Jersey was saying behind her back.

And yet Rosalind could not bring herself to believe that
was the only thing her grace wanted.

"Did she mention the current royal affairs?" the countess
asked. "I am sure she positively poured out her bosom to you."
There it is.

"We may have spoken about the matter," said Rosalind
cautiously. "It is, after all, very much on everyone's mind."

"It is certainly on Lady Jersey's." A hint of exasperation
crept into the countess's voice. "She speaks of nothing else
these days. And when she speaks, she cries." Her mouth
formed a moue of disapproval. "I believe she needs to stand
awhile in the English rain to cool off."

Rosalind dropped her gaze.

The countess laughed. "Come, Miss Thorne, I am sorry.
Lift your eyes and do not mind me. It is only I am so discon-
certed. You see, I cannot understand how my good friend
Lady Jersey, who so prides herself on her taste and *ton*, can
press the case of such a coarse and ill-bred creature as Caroline of Brunswick." She shuddered delicately. "I can't tell you
what horrible faces one sees nowadays in the streets and the
main roads, and how insolently they come up and bawl in
one's ears."

It was an invitation to recount her own experiences, but
Rosalind said nothing. She had been acquainted with the
countess for some years and was obliged to her for her help
on more than one occasion. But at the same time, she knew
that Dorothea Lieven was not to be trusted. She was an intel-

ligent and sophisticated woman who danced through society's politics as lightly as she waltzed through its ballrooms. Countess Lieven made no secret of the fact that her goal was to further her husband's career, and that meant her loyalty and her actions were to herself—and to the tsar, the countess would have added—but not to anyone else.

Rosalind could not permit herself to forget that for one moment.

"I am surprised, your grace," she said. "You seem so well informed on Lady Jersey's opinions, I should not think you'd care to hear any more about them."

The countess raised her hand to hide her smile. "You see straight through me, as always, Miss Thorne. Yes, I admit, I am consumed with nothing more than vulgar curiosity."

Rosalind permitted one brow to rise a fraction of an inch and waited.

"Poor Lady Jersey." The countess tsk-tsked. "She cannot comprehend that anyone might see the world differently than she does. And who can blame her? Her view has benefited her so greatly for so many years. But it does leave her with some notable blind spots." The countess smiled at some memory. "Including how fear of her influence might compel others to rash actions."

Rosalind remained silent, her thoughts working furiously. The influence of women like Lady Jersey was routinely laughed at. And yet it was also a very real thing. The hostesses of London brought men together or forced them apart. In social gatherings, they set the subjects of conversation and so piled ideas upon ideas. They could sit alone with the powerful and talk and talk until minds were changed and purses were opened. They started rumors. They ended careers.

Lady Jersey and her drama and her tears brought the strength of the queen's side into society's drawing rooms. From there it would travel into Parliament. And the palace.

The words she and the countess spoke next would travel,

as well, and along some of the same paths, because the countess would make sure it happened.

Countess Lieven leaned forward. "Well, perhaps if we engage in some of that plain speaking that is so popular among you English? You have gone to see Mrs. Fitzherbert. This we have from the newspapers. Lady Jersey, and all her various tear-filled sentiments, have come to see you. One does not need to do much work to infer that these activities have something to do with the particular rumors surrounding King George and Mrs. Fitzherbert."

"What rumors are those, your grace?" inquired Rosalind.

The flicker of annoyance in the countess's dark eyes might have been genuine.

"It is only because there are so many," Rosalind went on. "If I began to work through them all, we would be here past suppertime."

"Which would never do," replied the countess with mock seriousness. "The one in particular I speak of is that Mrs. Fitzherbert intends to appear at the trial."

Rosalind started; she could not help it. Countess Lieven settled back, with an air of someone who had taken a necessary trick at the card table.

"Lady Jersey has made it her work to remain at the center of influence," said Rosalind carefully. "And naturally, Mrs. Fitzherbert's name must come up during such circumstances as the palace finds itself in. But I assure your grace that, to the best of my knowledge, Mrs. Fitzherbert has no plans to insert herself into matters between the king and the queen, either publicly or privately. She is entirely devoted to her daughters, and she wishes only for a quiet, private life."

She watched the countess's dark eyes glitter as she absorbed Rosalind's words and how they were spoken.

But are they what she wanted to hear? Rosalind could not tell.

At last, Countess Lieven leaned forward. "Miss Thorne, will you be advised by me?" Rosalind felt her spine stiffen. The countess's tone was entirely serious, without her usual sparkling mixture of irony and levity.

"I will certainly hear whatever it is your grace cares to say."

"When you speak with the queen . . . Oh, do not look so modest. You will be speaking with her or one of her people quite soon, if you have not already . . . Advise her as strongly as you can to take the settlement she is offered and go quietly to her exile."

Rosalind said nothing.

"This is not a fight she can win, though all the English laws and the hearts of the people stand with her. She must understand that the men surrounding the king are very like him. They have large ambitions but paltry imaginations. It is a dangerous pairing, because it leads them to very obvious and uncivilized solutions."

Rosalind wanted to protest. She wanted to laugh. The countess could not possibly mean to be hinting . . .

And yet. Countess Lieven's face was no longer a cynical blank. She was quite serious.

A chill ran down Rosalind's arms. At the same time she was conscious of a spark of anger. What drove it or where it came from, she could not say. She knew full well that the countess saw her unease. The corner of the other woman's mouth curled in satisfaction.

Rosalind rallied. She had to, even though it might be difficult. The anger was there, and the feeling of slowly sinking beneath an icy surface.

"I am flattered that you think I might come to the attention of Queen Caroline," Rosalind said, because it was easiest and gave her time to choose her next words. "And were that to happen, I should certainly deliver any message your grace might care to impart, although I do think you might be

wise to pick someone with a better chance at being heard."
She paused and let the countess drink that much down. "I
will admit, however, it does make me wonder how you might
advise Mrs. Fitzherbert, were you given the opportunity."

The countess arched her perfect brows, considering this.
Rosalind fully expected another cool, sparkling laugh and
some witticism.

And yet . . . and yet . . .

"Are you fond of the theater, Miss Thorne?"

The question was meant to catch her off guard, and it
would have if Rosalind had less experience with the woman
in front of her. "Very," she said.

"It is so difficult to be a truly great performer. There are so
many different skills required, most of which we mere citizens do not stop to consider. For example, there is knowing
how to leave the stage when the applause is still with one.
That is a mark of true greatness." The countess gestured, indicating the world outside her perfectly appointed room. "I
had heard Mrs. Fitzherbert planned to go to the Continent
for a while. It seems to me this is an excellent plan, for her
and her daughters. Especially if she does not wish anyone to
think she was in the throes of planning a return engagement." Countess Lieven paused. "Or that you were a part of
any such plan. I believe the papers are beginning to speculate
on the subject already, are they not?"

Rosalind felt herself go very cold. The countess smiled and
nodded just once.

Rosalind had been consumed by what felt like an over-
whelming mountain of problems—the theft of the certificate,
Josiah Poole's murder, the publicity and papers, Ronald
Ranking, Lady Jersey, and now the countess herself.

She had not until this moment thought how her involvement with Mrs. Fitzherbert might look to the world outside—especially when the world outside did not know
about the missing marriage certificate. All they knew was

that Rosalind had helped a number of ladies plagued by scandal and disgrace return to their places in society or to good marriages or to families that had previously disapproved of them.

She had not thought that it might look like Mrs. Fitzherbert was planning to step into the queen's shoes as soon as the queen was removed from them, and that she had called on Rosalind to help her do it.

A number of very unpleasant and urgent thoughts flashed through Rosalind's mind, but foremost among them all was the memory of the king riding slowly back and forth in front of Mrs. Fitzherbert's door.

Had he truly left the palace without being seen? Had no one among the staff there, among his aides, counselors, and friends, spoken of where he had gone?

The strength of feeling, realization, and suspicion put her in danger of losing her countenance. She must take her leave, and she must do it at once.

Rosalind steeled her quaking knees and made herself stand smoothly. "Thank you for your welcome, your grace," she said. "It was very kind of you to see me on such short notice."

"But not at all." The countess rose with her. "You are welcome here at any moment. My staff know that I am always at home to Miss Thorne."

Rosalind thanked her and allowed the footman to show her out to the entrance hall, where the maid met her with her bonnet and pelisse.

Rosalind let herself be helped into her things, her heart hammering against her ribs from all that she had heard. The maid curtsied; Rosalind walked to the doors, which were promptly opened for her. She walked down the steps and down the path and out through the gate to the street.

She did not let herself look back, not once. Not even to see if Ron Ranking was loitering at the countess's area railing.

She did not truly believe the countess might be watching her leave, but she would not take even the smallest risk that her face could be seen.

Not when the countess had so carefully suggested the queen might be murdered by the king's associates if she did not cease protesting the divorce.

Not when the countess had so calmly threatened to spread the rumor that Rosalind was helping to topple the queen and set Mrs. Fitzherbert in her place.

CHAPTER THIRTY-NINE

A Return To Old Haunts

*". . . I am, however, not inclined to argue the
question of justice or injustice . . ."*

Langdale, Charles, *Memoirs of Mrs. Fitzherbert*

It felt strange to be walking back into Bow Street.
Adam followed Goutier past the clerks who kept the crowd
at bay in the main lobby. Only the junior clerks glanced up as
he and Goutier worked their way through the crowd, but
none of them moved to acknowledge or stop them. They just
turned back to the press of London citizens, each demanding
their full attention at the top of their lungs.

Stafford was usually to be found on the highest stool, helping his subordinates sort through the sea of shouted claims
and anxious stories. Today, however, he was nowhere in sight.

Adam wondered about Stafford's absence and what he
might be doing. He wondered if he had already heard that
Adam would be talking with Townsend today.

Probably.

It had been agreed that Goutier would go to Townsend on
Adam's behalf and arrange the appointment. In the mean-

time, Tauton would remain at the White Swan, aiding and keeping an eye on Stafford's clerk as he sorted through Poole's papers. Adam himself had spent the morning at Ross's sponging house, interviewing the "guests" and dodging their questions about Poole's murder and whether anyone was going to take over his business. He'd also had to pretend not to notice the coins and signet rings and even a pocket watch pushed so casually across the table as their owners talked about how their cases were coming due soon and asserted that nothing that had happened to them was in fact their fault.

The consistency of the refrain coming from each man left Adam feeling slightly sad and more than a bit angry. But now he must set all that aside.

He had not been away from the station that long, and yet he felt like a stranger here. There were at least a dozen new faces in the patrol room, and even the men he knew started and stared before they leapt to their feet to shake his hand and ask how he did, as if he'd returned from overseas.

"I'm well, I'm well," Adam assured them all, which was true. At the same time, he was conscious of missing his place at the station. His awareness of the questions he needed to ask, and what they might reveal, did not change his feelings.

The wardroom was the haunt of Bow Street's principal officers. A long worktable took up most of the space. It was surrounded by racks of newspapers and cabinets filled with documents. Maps of London and Westminster had been pinned to the whitewashed walls.

The only officer at the table when Adam and Goutier entered was Stephen Lavender. The thin, hatchet-faced man was writing busily away at a report, extra quills and bottles of ink ready to hand. Adam had always appreciated Lavender's comprehensive reports, but he wrote like it was heavy labor. Even now, Adam could see the sweat beading on his brow.

290 Darcie Wilde

Lavender glanced up at Goutier, and then he saw Adam in the larger man's wake.

"What are you doing here?" Lavender climbed to his feet.

"I'm here to see Mr. Townsend," Adam told him.

Lavender smirked. "Come to ask for your job back? More fool you. Mr. Townsend's got no use for radicals and reformers."

Goutier rolled his eyes. "How's he feel about men that don't know what they're talking about, Lavender?" Goutier didn't wait for an answer. He simply strode across the room to knock on the door to Townsend's private office. There was a bark of assent from inside. Goutier stood aside.

"Good luck," Goutier whispered as Adam passed him.

Little had changed in Townsend's office. It was still overly warm, still crowded with knickknacks given as tokens of esteem by various highly placed individuals. The white hat that had been a gift of the prince regent hung in its place of honor.

It was Townsend himself who had changed. He looked more tired than Adam had ever seen him before. His stubbled cheeks were sunken, and his color was poor. He leaned across his desk, planting his weight on both hands, so he could pour over a sprawling map of London. He glanced up as Adam entered, and the look in his red-rimmed eyes was one of pure, simple irritation.

He looked down at the map again.

"Well, Mr. Harkness," he said to Adam and to the map, "Mr. Goutier has made the case that I should listen to you. What do you have to say to me?"

Adam folded his hands behind his back. As he had not been invited to sit, he remained standing. "Sir David sent me to make some inquiries regarding the attorney Josiah Poole."

"Sent you?" Townsend scowled and ran his finger along one of the streets inked on the map. "He could not come himself?"

"He is very much occupied this morning."

"Very well, very well. What can I do for Sir David?"

"It's been implied that you might know some details about Josiah Poole's death."

Now Townsend's head jerked up, and he stared at Adam, frozen in momentary shock. Then, much to Adam's surprise, he burst out laughing.

"Implied, is it? Implied by whom?"

Adam waited until Townsend's guffaw subsided.

"Well?" Townsend dropped into his chair and made a come-hither gesture with two hands. "Let's have it, man. Who was it? Your Miss Thorne, perhaps?" He cocked his head. "Did her woman's intuition tell her I am somehow to blame for what happened?"

Adam held his tongue for long enough to set his anger aside. He waited one more heartbeat, offering doubt and instinct that much time to change the uncertain course he had planned.

At last, he spoke. "No, sir. It was Mr. Stafford who said so."

"*What?*"

Adam took a deep breath and hoped. "The reason Miss Thorne went to Mrs. Fitzherbert's house was that there had been a robbery. Her strongbox had been broken open, and her personal papers stolen."

One muscle at a time, Townsend's face fell into an expression of confusion.

"Josiah Poole was seen entering her garden and leaving in a hurry," said Adam. "It has been determined that Poole most likely had some confederate inside the house, or perhaps someone who has a close connection with the family. His purpose in his illicit entry was to obtain these private papers, possibly to sell or to use to extort some form of payment."

Townsend's pale face had begun to lose the last of its color.

"It is believed that Poole met his death while keeping an appointment with the client who had asked him to acquire Mrs. Fitzherbert's papers. They were not found on his person, and so far, they have not been found either at his house or his place of business."

Adam waited and watched. Townsend re-collected himself and remembered who was standing in front of him now. The cold confusion in his expression turned rapidly to heated anger, but this time, he was able to keep his emotions under strict control. He brought his hands together and steepled his fingers, watching Adam through half-lidded eyes, as if he were a magistrate considering some exceptional case brought before him.

"And Stafford told you I was a client to Josiah Poole?" asked Townsend.

Adam nodded once.

"What else did he tell you?"

"That you feared for the loss of your relationship with the king," said Adam. "That this was what led you to try to retrieve the paper proving his previous marriage to Mrs. Fitzherbert."

"And you believed this?" asked Townsend.

"Because there's now been a violent death, it is my duty to make the necessary inquiries for the coroner's office," he said. "Even if it brings me back here."

Townsend rose slowly to his feet. He paced to the far side of his office and paced to the other. His face was so tightly contorted that Adam could not tell whether he was about to shout at the top of his lungs or break down in sobs.

"Very well," Townsend said. "Very well. You are sent here by Sir David. You have no choice in the matter."

"No, sir," agreed Harkness. *Neither do you.*

In this one area, the coroner's office held a power that Bow

Street's officers did not. Because he acted in the king's name, Sir David could compel testimony from a man who did not wish to speak.

"The king's justice cannot lower its gaze." Townsend faced the wall as he spoke. It seemed to Adam he was testing the words, the way a man might try on a coat to make sure of the fit.

Adam felt the hairs on the back of his neck prickle.

"Remind me," said Townsend. "When was Poole killed?"

"Yesterday, midafternoon."

"Very well. I can and will take my oath that I was here, in this office, at that time. I have been overseeing the assignment of our patrols to control the crowds and the mobs that have come out in response to the queen's arrival. You may ask whomever you please, and they will all confirm to you what I have said."

"If I may speak frankly, I had hoped you would say something of the kind. But there is also the allegation that you orchestrated the theft of the marriage certificate."

"Merest slander," said Townsend. "*Someone* has lied." Now he met Adam's gaze fully. "Tell me, is Stafford prepared to swear to his allegations?"

"I have not yet asked him," replied Adam.

"I think when you do, you will find Mr. Stafford has no desire to take his oath, much less stand up in court," said Townsend. "Further, if you ask him, as you asked me, to give an account for his whereabouts for the time Poole met his end, he will not be ready with an answer."

But I did not ask you, thought Adam. *You offered.*

"Now, unless you have something else, I am extremely busy." Townsend bent over his map again. "You know your way out, I believe?"

Dismissed, Adam made a curt bow and returned to the wardroom, closing the door firmly behind him. Goutier was sitting alone at the table, looking over a copy of the Bow Street paper, *Hue and Cry.*

"Where's Lavender?"

"Went off to find someplace quieter to write," said Goutier. "Any joy?" He nodded toward the closed door.

"I can't tell yet," said Adam. "I need to find Stafford."

"Do you want me along?"

Adam shook his head. "You're in enough hot water on my account as it is. If anybody's going to pull Stafford's nose, it should be someone he can't sack."

"I wouldn't count on that if I was you," said Goutier. "But, as you're determined, I wish you Godspeed."

Adam and Goutier clapped hands. Goutier took himself into the patrol room, and Adam went through to the lobby.

He was in luck. Stafford had returned to his usual perch on his high stool and was busy checking off points in his ledger book, while still managing to keep some sliver of attention turned toward the junior clerks and their activities.

"Mr. Stafford."

"Ah, Mr. Harkness." Stafford finished his notation and laid down his quill. "I was wondering when you would appear. Have you spoken to Mr. Townsend yet?"

"I have."

"And now you wish to speak to me?" Stafford nodded in answer to his own question. "Very good. Dalton!" Stafford did not raise his voice. Adam would not have thought he could be heard over the babble of voices around them. But one of the junior clerks jumped off his stool and ran over, his coattails flapping behind him.

"Take over here." Stafford climbed down from his stool. "Mr. Harkness, if you would accompany me?"

Mr. Stafford's private office was attached to the magistrate's courtroom. Despite the dampening effects of the bookcases full of folios and the tall cabinets of documents, during particularly fraught trials, the rumble of voices could be heard through the walls.

Stafford opened a drawer, rifled the files inside, and inserted the documents he carried. Only when the cabinet was closed and locked did he turn to face Adam.

"What did Townsend tell you?"

Adam looked at him. Stafford returned his gaze stoically. "Ah, yes," he said, his voice as expressionless as his face. "You cannot tell me, because I also might be a witness." He paused. "Or the perpetrator," he added, with just the barest touch of humor seeping into his tone. "Can you at least tell me if you believe him?"

Adam considered this. "In the years I've known Mr. Townsend, I've known him to be many things."

Vain, arrogant, and even self-deceiving, possessed of a certainty in himself and those he considers his superiors, which can lead him to grave mistakes.

"He is, however, experienced and intelligent, and committed to order and the king's peace," Adam went on. "When it comes down to it, he is also a terrible liar."

"And I, on the other hand, am a skilled and considerable liar," said Stafford.

Adam did not bother to disagree. "Which leads me to wonder why you would tell a lie about Townsend's potential involvement in this business that could be so easily disproved?"

Stafford's mouth bent into a thin, wintry smile. "To save us all time," he said. "Sooner or later, you would have discovered Mr. Townsend's role in the theft of the certificate. From there, you would have discovered mine. You would not have believed a direct declaration of innocence on my part or his. Therefore, I had to arrange for you to question Mr. Townsend as soon as possible. This is now done, and you may remove him from your inquiries, at least as far as the murder is concerned. If Mrs. Fitzherbert wishes to make a complaint against him as far as the matter of the theft of her property, that can be dealt with in due course."

Given Mrs. Fitzherbert's desire to avoid publicity, Adam very much doubted it would come to that. This was something else he felt sure Mr. Stafford knew.

It did, however, leave one urgent question.

"And what of you, Mr. Stafford?"

"Mr. Harkness, I am not in the habit of stabbing my sources."

"You are not the first person to say that to me."

"I am delighted to find my reputation precedes me."

"A man's reputation is not proof," Adam said.

Stafford sighed. "There are those who would disagree, but I see you are not going to leave until I give you some better answer. Very well. The death, as I understand it, happened at about one of the clock?"

Adam nodded.

Mr. Stafford reached across his desk and pulled a journal toward him. "At that time, I was taking a deposition from one Mr. Matthew Ashdown on a matter of grand theft, with Mr. Bernie and young Dalton in attendance. Does that answer you?"

"Thank you," said Adam.

Mr. Stafford closed his book. "Now that this is settled, Mr. Harkness, I will tell you this. I resent having to use these circumlocutions in this matter. I want very much to know who did this thing, and more importantly, I want to know why they did it. If it was a simple criminal act, very well. The magistrates and the hangman know their duty. But if it is a matter of the king's enemies seeking to destabilize the Crown, then that, sir, is my business, and I take it very seriously."

"Even though this thing would not have happened without your instigation?" asked Adam.

Townsend would have shouted. Stafford's face betrayed nothing. "It was not at my instigation," said Stafford. "But my mistaken judgment did contribute to this outcome. And so here I am, relying on you to supply my deficiencies. You may take that to your friends and brag on it if you will."

But Stafford, of course, knew he would not. So, Adam simply bowed and walked away.

There was still too much to do.

CHAPTER FORTY

A Life in Letters

*"A man concerning whom great expectations are
formed, and various parties look at him as a card
which . . . they might like to play . . ."*

Bury, Charlotte, *The Diary of a Lady-in-Waiting*

One of the genuine problems with turning novelist, reflected Alice as she entered the White Swan, was that
one developed a tendency to narrate one's own life.

> *Our heroine stood poised on the threshold of
> the iniquitous tavern. Inside, every sort of rough
> and rowdy man might be found. Thankfully, they
> were too engaged with their strong drink and
> merry bragging to notice the slender girl in dark
> coat and wide bonnet slip past them and run—
> heart and slippers pattering—up the dismal stair-
> case. . . .*

It was dark upstairs and smelled of damp and of old dinners. Alice felt her nose wrinkling, both at the odors and the

possibility that she should have taken George up on his offer
to accompany her.

> *Unused as she was to such dim and dangerous*
> *surroundings, she nonetheless summoned her*
> *courage. She reminded herself of the urgency of*
> *her errand, that lives hung in the balance. . . .*

Light seeped out from under the fourth door on the left, il-
luminating a section of stained and splintered flooring. Alice
knocked and waited and knocked again.

She heard the sounds of shuffled papers and rustling cloth.
A moment later the door opened, just a fraction of an inch,
and a bespectacled eye in a pinched White man's face glared
at her.

> *Faced with this penetrating and entirely hostile*
> *glare, she felt herself grow faint. . . .*

Which would do very well for fiction, where heroines were
expected to be close to fainting the majority of the time. The
truth of the matter was that this particular eye most likely be-
longed to a belligerent boy.

"I'm looking for Mr. Tauton," Alice announced.

"What business—" began Young Belligerence. But there
was movement behind him, and a thick hand reached over
his shoulder to pull the door open.

Now Alice could see the dingy, paper-filled room. It was
not a large space, and the presence of Samuel Tauton made it
feel positively cramped.

Still, someone had evidently made a great effort to get things
into order. Three lamps burned their brightest to banish even
the possibility of shadow. Every flat surface was covered with
tidy stacks of paper, most of them bound in black, red, or

blue ribbon and labeled with slips of paper on which were written cryptic notations—*A-1, D-3, 2-L.*

Young Belligerence turned and glowered up at Mr. Tauton. "I am under orders to admit no one." He turned to Alice, taking hold of his spectacles, as if they might fly away. "You'll have to leave at once, miss."

"But I'm not no one." Alice slipped over the threshold. "As Mr. Tauton can tell you." She beamed at the officer and was rewarded with a tolerant chuckle.

"She's right, Bingham," Mr. Tauton said. "This is definitely not no one. This is the legendary scribe and literary light Miss Alice Littlefield."

Alice made her curtsy. "Why, thank you, Mr. Tauton. How do you do?"

"As you see." He swept out his hand to indicate the whole of the room. "Awash in papers and babysitting this young pup." He nodded toward Mr. Bingham, who frowned and resettled his spectacles farther up his nose. "What brings you to these sorry chambers?"

"I'm on an errand for Miss Thorne and Mr. Harkness. I need to know if you have found the name of Captain George Dawson among these papers."

"Mr. Stafford left instructions I am not to speak to anyone," groused Mr. Bingham.

She turned, her heart beating like that of a captive bird, and gazed into the eyes of this brutal man who had set the whole of his will against her. . . .

"Mr. Bingham," she said. "I fully understand you have your duty. Now, I could bat my eyes and cry and so forth to try to gain your sympathies. But you and I both know you are too experienced and too professional for that to have any effect."

Mr. Bingham's chest swelled at this flattery, just a little. Be-

hind him, Sam Tauton's eyes twinkled. Alice made herself ignore that.

"I promise I am not asking out of idle curiosity," she went
on. "Captain George Dawson may be tied to the murder of
Mr. Poole, and the coroner needs to know if they were in
business together or if they had any other ties."

Bingham scowled at her, very much on his dignity. He
glanced at Tauton, but there was no help there.

"Oh, very well." He began flipping back through his
ledger. "Correspondence to one George Dawson, three letters, filed under 4-D."

"This is an impressive system you've created."

Mr. Bingham thawed a little further. "I take pride in my
work." He undid the black ribbon, leafed through the papers, and extracted three pages. "Here we are." He held them
out to her. "They cannot leave here," he warned.

"But may I make notes? I would not want to give Sir
David an inaccurate account."

"You may use the table," said Bingham in a manner that
was surely meant to be gracious.

Alice exchanged a small smile with Mr. Tauton as she
squeezed past him to perch on the edge of the crooked chair.
She opened her own modest, battered notebook.

Mr. Tauton settled himself on the bed, which creaked in
loud complaint.

With trembling hand, she reached for the letter.
At first, her eyes refused to read, and then her
mind rebelled at understanding what she saw. . . .

She spread out the three letters Mr. Bingham had unearthed.
She scanned them rapidly, absorbing the main points, and
then read them again more slowly, noting the language and
the tone, the handwriting and the underlines and exclamations.

Then she read them a final time, this time adding notes to her book in her rapid, irregular shorthand:

> *Item: Geo. D. in debt for 2000 pounds, interest accumulating weekly, three separate moneylenders. Chief expenses: clothes and spiritous liquors . . .*
>
> *Item: Geo. D. applied JP for assistance managing affairs, putting off creditors . . . Father threatens to cut off son. . . . Lenders likewise threatening . . .*

Then came the final letter, dated just three days before.

> *Item: JP delivered good news to Geo. D. that creditors had been satisfied. Terms heavy?*

Alice underlined the last words.

"Have we found something?" inquired Mr. Tauton.

"I believe that we have," Alice said. "In fact, we may have found what everybody's been looking for."

> *Item: Geo. D. writes: "Regarding our arrangement, I know you hold promise, but circumstance changed . . ."*
>
> *Suggests meeting to explain.*

CHAPTER FORTY-ONE

A House of Mourning

"I conclude, therefore, she knows more than is wished."

Bury, Charlotte, *The Diary of a Lady-in-Waiting*

For the second time in as many days, Rosalind found herself sitting in a hired cab outside the Pooles' residence, waiting for Adam. She tried to suppress her reflexive calculations of how much the cab and the extra tip for making the driver wait would come to. But years of habit were proving difficult to shift.

If she was honest with herself, it was a relief to have her mind distracted by thoughts of shillings and pence. It offered a respite from turning over the countess's threats and warnings.

A fact that would no doubt amuse her grace no end.

Rosalind shook her head at herself and raised her hand to push the window curtain back just a little farther. As she did, the front door to the Pooles' house flew open and a dark-haired man in a scarlet coat came bounding down the area stairs. He pushed roughly between a pair of maids walking with their baskets, and she heard their outraged exclamations as he disappeared around the corner.

What on earth . . . ?

Her thought got no further. Adam strode around the opposite corner and started up the street. Rosalind rapped on the cab's roof to signal the driver, who climbed down to open the door, help her out, and take his fee.

Adam, of course, spotted her at once and made his way across the busy cobbles to join her. He bowed, and she curtsied. She wanted badly to kiss him and feel his arms around her, but that was, of course, impossible. A look and a smile would have to do.

Adam's answering smile was understanding and a little sardonic. He shifted the leather portfolio he carried, so he could offer her his right arm. Rosalind accepted gladly. "Were you able to meet Amelia this morning?" he asked.

"We were, and she told us that Minney Seymore is secretly meeting a young man, most likely one Captain George Dawson, a cavalry officer and hero of Waterloo, who has unfortunate tendencies to drink and debt."

Adam sucked in a soft breath.

Rosalind nodded. "He was seen meeting her in Mrs. Fitzherbert's garden last night."

"I shall have to have a talk with my men, I think," Adam muttered.

"I think you might," said Rosalind. "It seems that there's a footman who is aiding and abetting Miss Seymore's affairs, and they may have let themselves get distracted."

"Which footman?" asked Adam.

"Thomas Faller."

"Have you said anything about this to Mrs. Fitzherbert yet?"

"No," said Rosalind. "Nor do I wish to without more facts in hand. I don't believe it does us any good to expose Amelia or Faller just yet."

Adam nodded, but she felt his arm stiffen just a little beneath her hand.

"You do not agree?" she asked.

"I don't know. A great deal will depend on what we hear from the Pooles."

Rosalind nodded in acknowledgment. "I did dispatch Alice to the White Swan to see if Captain Dawson's name has been discovered in any of Mr. Poole's papers. But there is something more," she said. "When I was waiting for you, I saw a man in a scarlet coat coming out of the Pooles' house in an enormous hurry."

"The cavalry uniform is a scarlet coat."

"So is Mrs. Fitzherbert's household livery."

Adam blew out a soundless whistle. "And what of your appointment with Countess Lieven? What did she have to say?"

Rosalind squeezed his arm and gently steered them both away from the curb, and the possibility of being splashed by the passing traffic, and, not incidentally, out of sight of the Pooles' front windows. "She said a great deal, but as this is the countess, I am not certain how much of it is strictly true. She implied the queen's life might be in danger from the king's men."

Adam's brows shot up.

Rosalind nodded. "It seems outrageous, I know, but she was most sincere. She also threatened me, and you, incidentally."

"I would have thought I am beneath her notice." Adam's tone was studiously bland, but Rosalind was fully aware of the anger deep beneath that calm. Not for himself as much as for her. "What was the threat?"

"That a rumor might begin spreading which says our visit to Mrs. Fitzherbert was part of a wider plan to bring herself back into the king's life once he is divorced."

"Or a widower?" inquired Adam with that same studied calm.

Rosalind nodded.

Adam was silent for a long moment, but in his distant gaze, Rosalind saw him remembering the attack on their carriage, and the king at Mrs. Fitzherbert's door. He knew as well as she did the power that someone like the countess wielded. If she picked whom she whispered to carefully, and if her words were repeated . . .

Mrs. Fitzherbert's reputation would be destroyed, and so would her daughters'. They would all have to leave London.

So would Rosalind.

She took a deep breath and pushed that fear aside. She would deal with it later.

"What of Mr. Townsend and Mr. Stafford?" Rosalind asked Adam. "What did you learn from them?"

"Somewhat to my surprise, it seems that Mr. Stafford was telling the truth," said Adam. "Mr. Townsend appears to have been instrumental in organizing the certificate's theft. But Mr. Townsend had no opportunity to kill Poole. Neither, it appears, did Mr. Stafford. We must look elsewhere."

"That, I think, should come as a relief."

"It does." There was a note of mild surprise in Adam's voice. "I don't like Townsend, but I would not have wanted to see him fall so far."

"And Mr. Stafford?" she asked.

"Has stated openly he wants my goodwill."

"That seems like it could be a double-edged sword."

"Very much so."

"And it has led us nowhere."

"Yes and no," said Adam. "We can now be certain why the certificate was taken and what the plan was for it. That is something." He looked at the Pooles' house. "Shall we go in? I still need to gather the statements from Poole's family about the morning of his death." He gestured with the portfolio he carried. "Particularly from Mrs. Poole."

"While we are talking with the family, we would do well to talk with the maid, Judith, also."

"I agree. So." Adam squared his shoulders. "Shall we see what kind of reception waits for us?"

"I cannot believe it will be a warm one," said Rosalind.

"Neither can I."

The Pooles' home had been dressed for mourning. Yards of black crepe had been hung about the rooms. The servants wore black armbands. The mirrors had been covered or taken away, and all the curtains closed. In the front parlor wax candles flickered at the head and feet of Josiah Poole's black casket.

Rosalind did not recognize the silent maid who ushered them inside. Still, she assumed they would find Mrs. Poole waiting for them in the library. Their hostess, however, was nowhere to be seen. Instead, William Considen, drawn and pale, sat beside the empty hearth. He had his walking stick laid across his knees. His thin hands rolled it restlessly back and forth as he stared into the flames.

"Mr. Harkness to see you, sir," whispered the maid. "And Miss Thorne."

At first, he did not seem to hear her. But slowly, Mr. Considen turned his head. Even more slowly, he planted his stick on the floor and leaned on it heavily so he could rise.

"Mr. Harkness." Mr. Considen bowed to Adam. Then his gaze slid reluctantly toward Rosalind. "Miss Thorne."

"Mr. Considen . . ." Adam made his bow. "I was hoping we might speak with Mrs. Poole. I have a letter for her from Sir David Royce."

"My sister is indisposed. You may give the letter to me. I'll see she gets it." Mr. Considen extended his thin hand.

Adam didn't move. "I need to take her statement for the inquest, and yours, as well," he added. "Sir David requires an account of Mr. Poole's movements on the morning of his death."

The hand holding Mr. Considen's stick shook, and the knuckles turned white. But it was not from weakness. It was fury. The heat of it rolled off him like a fever.

"Well, then, Mr. Harkness, you will have to come back later," Mr. Considen said through gritted teeth. "Melora is indisposed and in no condition to give any statement to anyone."

"Mr. Considen, I appreciate your desire to protect your sister," said Adam. "However, the inquest will be scheduled shortly, and we must have all statements in hand before the jury sits."

"Surely Mrs. Poole wishes to do everything in her power to resolve the question of her husband's death," added Rosalind.

Mr. Considen glowered at her. He might be laboring under an illness, but his gaze remained sharp and piercing. "Do you have any understanding in you, Miss Thorne?"

"I understand that your sister has lost her husband and that you wish to protect her from any further suffering," she replied. "I understand the marriage was troubled, and that Mr. Poole's death may have brought fresh difficulties upon the remaining family. I understand that you have reason to doubt that you will have the strength to help your sister through her distress, so you must do what you can now."

Considen stared at her; then, slowly and carefully, he bent his knees and sank back into his chair.

"Do you know how my sister came to be married to Josiah Poole?" he asked as he laid his stick back across his knees. "Poole purchased her. Lock, stock, and barrel. And she let him. Because of me." He rested both hands on the stick. They were scarred, Rosalind noted. Pale lines crisscrossed the mottled skin and shadows of blue veins. "She married him because of my damned endless illness. Because she would not permit me to die in the poorhouse." He cocked a bright eye toward them. Now that she was searching for them, she saw another scar had turned his right brow into a dotted line and another had wrinkled the skin on his throat. *An accident?* she wondered. Or had Mr. Considen led a more active and dangerous life before illness sapped his strength?

"She had no money to support me, you see," he went on. "Her first marriage disappointed our parents, and they cut her off entirely."

"Did she disappoint you?" Adam inquired.

He coughed hard, his pale face flushing a dangerous shade of red. "No. I tried to defend her, and to talk our parents into forgiving her. But . . . well, as it turned out, she would not have been much better off had she remained in the bosom of the family. My father let himself be talked into a stock-jobbing scheme, and when it collapsed, he was finished. We'd no title or land or any such to fall back on. Nothing to do but keep up appearances as long as possible. I was already ill, and Melora . . . well, Melora was determined not to leave us—me—in distress while there was something she could do."

"And what she could do was marry Mr. Poole?" asked Rosalind.

Mr. Considen nodded. "He offered to support the family in exchange for her coming to be his hostess and elevate him in the eyes of society. So, yes, Mr. Harkness, Miss Thorne, I am trying to do what I can to protect her, because I am painfully aware how she sacrificed herself to try to protect me." He spoke these last words softly, almost as if he could not bear to hear them himself.

"What of your parents?" asked Rosalind.

"Dead, both of 'em." Anger sparked in his sharp eyes. "Father first, mother a few months after that. Mother's last words were to berate Melly for all the trouble she had caused."

Rosalind dropped her gaze. This was an all-too-common tale. Families frequently regarded their daughters solely as a means for generating income and enhancing connections. It was why the myriad events of the social season were collectively referred to as "the marriage mart."

"What of Miss Poole?" asked Rosalind. "How is she doing?"

"Eh? Letitia?" Mr. Considen tried to push himself up but failed. "Don't tell me your superior's planning on dragging the poor girl into court?"

"I don't believe so," said Adam. "But if Miss Poole was at home on the morning her father died, she will need to give a statement."

"She was home. We all were," said Mr. Considen. "But, you see, Poole wasn't."

This was unexpected. No one had told them. Rosalind found herself wondering why it had not been mentioned on their previous visit.

"Do you know where he was?" Adam asked.

"Not with certainty," said Mr. Considen. "But I assumed he was sleeping at the White Swan. It was his habit when he had particular business or clients that he didn't want coming round the house, which was most of the time." He attempted a wry grin, but his face did not fully obey, and the expression became a grimace. "So you see, there is nothing Melly can tell you about what Poole might have been up to that morning."

"Even so, it will be important for the coroner to hear as much," replied Adam. "And I must have her, and you, swear to it."

Silent, stubbornly angry, Mr. Considen glowered at them. But he also seemed to realize that they would not be warned away. With a muttered curse, he pulled the bell rope. A scant heartbeat later, the door opened, and the silent maid entered the room.

"Go fetch Mrs. Poole," ordered Mr. Considen. The maid curtsied and left them.

"Is Judith still with you?" asked Rosalind.

"Eh?" He squinted at her. "Judith? No. The girl's stubbornness and stupidity finally got to be too much even for Melly. She was let go today. Why?" he said bitterly. "Did Mr. Harkness want her to swear to something, as well?"

"I wanted the return of some property," said Rosalind. "I loaned her a handkerchief, and I was hoping to have it back."

Mr. Considen shrugged but said nothing.

"Is she by chance still in the house?" asked Rosalind.

"How the devil should I know?" snapped Mr. Considen. "The servants are Melly's business."

"William!"

Mrs. Poole strode into the room. Letitia trailed behind her, her expression openly mutinous. The new maid followed them both, a silent, timid shadow. But at the moment at least, Mrs. Poole ignored them both equally. All her attention was on her brother.

"You should be resting!" She plucked the walking stick off his knees. "Lizzie! Help Mr. Considen upstairs!"

"I can walk perfectly well!" he snapped. "And I'll not leave while these . . . persons are here harassing you!"

"I am as capable of taking care of myself as you are of walking," she retorted.

"No."

"Mr. Considen—" began Adam.

"I said no!" he barked. "This is my house." He thumped his cane against the floor. "Now that my sister's widowed, I am her nearest relative, and I say you and this . . . person"— he waved a trembling hand at Rosalind—"have no right to harangue my sister, her stepdaughter, *or* our servants! Your master, Sir David, may have the right to compel testimony at his inquest, but you, sir, do not have the right to demand it in my house! You can take your . . . this . . . You can both leave us and not return."

Rosalind turned to Mrs. Poole. As she did, she could not help but see how Letitia had faded into the corner, as if deliberately letting herself be forgotten.

"Do not look to her!" snapped Mr. Considen. "I am master here!"

But he was not, and they all knew it.

Mrs. Poole lifted her chin. "William, you are overtired."

"You mean to say I am useless to you!" Mr. Considen's voice broke beneath the strain of his emotions. "Even now, I am a burden!"

Mrs. Poole gripped her brother's arm. "I would never say that," she told him. "But please, William. Do not make this any worse."

Rosalind could tell he wanted to do exactly that. He wanted to heave himself to his feet and stand face-to-face with his sister, with all of them. He wanted to rail at them all, to lash out with his scarred hands. As it was, his fist curled around nothing but air.

"Yes, yes," he croaked. "All right."

With an air of long practice, Mrs. Poole helped him get to his feet. Rosalind once again noted that although he moved like an old man, Mr. Considen was still young. Indeed, she would guess he was not that much older than his sister.

Mrs. Poole handed her brother his walking stick, and he let the maid, Lizzie, support him out of the room.

Only once they had vanished into the hallway did Mrs. Poole turn to Adam. "What is it you need?"

"May we speak privately, Mrs. Poole?"

Mrs. Poole glanced at Letitia, who took a step forward, returning to the conversation as if materializing like a restless spirit. Rosalind wondered how much practice the young woman had had at making herself unseen, and how much that allowed her to overhear.

"Go and do what you must, Melora," Letitia said. "I will . . . entertain Miss Thorne."

Uncertainty creased Mrs. Poole's countenance, but she clearly could not find any reasonable objection. It would not do to leave Rosalind sitting alone.

"We can use my husband's bookroom," Mrs. Poole said to Adam.

Adam bowed and stood back so she could leave the room first. He gave Rosalind a quick, reassuring glance and then followed their hostess out. Letitia moved quickly to close the door behind them both. She turned around to face Rosalind.

"Now, you must tell me, Miss Thorne. Does Mr. Harkness believe Melora killed my father?"

CHAPTER FORTY-TWO

A Daughter's Troubles

*"And now admire, my dear, the strange change of
opinion that takes place in families . . ."*

Bury, Charlotte, *The Diary of a Lady-in-Waiting*

It was a blatant attempt to startle the truth from her.
Fortunately, Rosalind had some experience with this particular tactic.

"Do you believe it?" she asked calmly.

Anger flushed Letitia's cheeks, but it faded just as swiftly
as it bloomed. She sank onto the sofa. "I suppose I deserved
that."

"I very much doubt you deserve any of this."

"Well, thank you for saying so." Letitia clearly wanted to
wilt under the weight of her feelings, to wring her hands, perhaps even to cry, but she had been trained against any of
those things. Was that her father's doing? Rosalind wondered. Her mother's? Or had her education in deportment
and appearances begun after Melora married Mr. Poole?

It was equally clear to Rosalind that Letitia wanted to talk
but had no idea what to say. Rosalind was not surprised.
Letitia did not know Rosalind and had no reason to trust her.

Well-bred young ladies did not advance any but the most trivial topics of conversation with strangers. A loyal daughter certainly did not speak of her father's failings or the family's troubles.

Usually, when she needed someone's trust, Rosalind would work to build a rapport over several visits, especially when the person still struggled with fresh grief.

But there was no time. The inquest and the need to find the stolen certificate pressed far too close, and the threats from Countess Lieven, and perhaps even from Bow Street, were too real.

This left Rosalind with no option but to tell Letitia a truth and hope the young woman would decide to reciprocate.

Although she had not been invited, Rosalind sat in the chair opposite Letitia.

"When I was your age, I had a very good life," Rosalind said. "My family was received in the best houses, I had made my debut at Almack's, and I was in love. My father was a charming and fascinating man. Everyone said so. Everyone was glad to welcome him to their table and their parties. Then one night he abandoned us."

Rosalind seldom told this story. The pain and humiliation were not something she cared to relive. "I remember feeling there had been some mistake. It was as if I had turned down the wrong corridor in a strange house. I was certain that there must be some way to retrace my steps back to a place where things made sense again."

"But there isn't, is there?" murmured Letitia.

"A way back? No. But there is always a way forward."

For a moment, Rosalind thought Letitia was going to laugh. "I'm sure that's true, Miss Thorne, but sometimes the way forward is even worse."

"Is that how it seems to you?"

Letitia looked at her for a long time. Rosalind held her gaze steady and let the silence blossom around them.

"My father arranged my impending marriage," Letitia said at last.

"Not your stepmother?"

"No. He had become disappointed in my stepmother." Letitia smoothed her skirt briefly. "He married her in the hopes that she would help him gain the respect in society that money would not. When Melora failed to do so, he blamed her for not exerting herself sufficiently. They quarreled about it. Frequently."

"What of your mother?"

It took a moment for Letitia to answer. Rosalind watched her arrange her features—carefully angle her head and place her hands—so that she maintained the appearance of complete composure. "Like your father, she abandoned me. Us."

"I'm sorry."

"I don't blame her," said Letitia quietly. "Not really. I've thought of running away any number of times, but . . . well, where would I go?" She looked up at Rosalind, as if to see if she had any opinion on the matter. As if they spoke of dresses or accepting invitations.

"Where did she go?" Rosalind asked.

Letitia shook her head. "I've not heard from her since she left. And she'd been gone for only a few months when Papa had me brought to him and said, 'Well, she's gone, and we needn't ever mention her again.' He then told me I was not to worry, that he would find me another Mama, one just as good. Perhaps better. I was ten years old."

Rosalind could not speak. Anger closed off her breath and threatened to blind her. She forced it down. She could not permit herself to lose control, not when it would disconcert Letitia.

"That, you see, is, was, Papa's attitude toward marriage," Letitia was saying. "It is simply for what one can get. Money. Land. Status. 'If this attitude is good enough for the highest in the realm,' he said, 'then surely it is good enough for the Pooles.'

"So, he arranged my engagement himself, the idea being that my marriage would bring the advancement and acceptance his marriage had not. And the family consented because they owed money, and my father could help them."

This, it seemed, was Josiah Poole's general approach to life—save those in debt and then extract favors for the work. Rosalind found herself wondering idly if he had ever known her father. Or Alice's.

"I will say, objectively, it's quite a good match." Sarcasm dripped heavily from Letitia's words. "My prospective groom is the heir to a baronetcy. The only drawback is that none of the family want anything to do with me."

"I'm sorry," said Rosalind, and she hoped Letitia understood how very much she meant it.

But if she did, Letitia gave no sign. "My fiancé's parents called this morning. They hadn't even finished laying Father out in the parlor." Her gaze drifted toward the door, as if she could see through to that other room, with its lit candles and garlands of crepe. "They told Melora in no uncertain terms they meant to break off the engagement. They'd wait for a decent interval, they said, and then it would be announced that I had changed my mind and they had graciously decided to release me from my promise."

"And what was your stepmother's response?"

"She said those terms were not acceptable." Letitia's voice turned flat and cold. "She said she had reviewed the marriage contract, and that if they broke it off, she would see that the family paid every penny of the settlement they agreed to. She also said she would cause certain letters in her keeping to be sent to persons to whom the baronet owed money."

Rosalind let out a long, slow breath.

"Did she say this in your presence?"

Letitia looked away, which told Rosalind what she needed to know. Letitia had been eavesdropping.

"I confronted Melora about it afterward," Letitia went on. "I told her, in no uncertain terms, that I did not want the marriage, that I never had, especially not under the circumstances by which it was being forced on us all. I said I should be glad for the excuse to break it off. She said that's not possible."

"Do you know why?"

"She said it was money. She said Papa left us less than he might have. But I think she wants me out of the house." Letitia's voice caught in her throat. "Now that Father's . . . gone. She has to manage things for little Josiah and Henry, of course, but that still gives her a great deal of freedom, especially once the boys go to school."

Rosalind nodded. A wife was constrained by her husband's orders, and a daughter by her father's. But society granted a widow a level of freedom it denied other women. Poole's will might have been intended to punish and constrain Melora, but with her sons in school and her stepdaughter safely married off, she would still be her own woman in a way she had never been before.

Such freedom could pose a grave temptation, especially in a disastrous marriage, with responsibility for an invalid brother. Rosalind met Letitia's gaze and saw that the young woman knew exactly what she had implied.

"You tell me there's a way forward, Miss Thorne," she said. "I would be grateful if you would tell me what it is."

Rosalind reached out and touched Letitia's hand. "Consider this. You must remain in mourning for at least a year, and while you are, nothing can be done about your marriage. That is a long time. Let yourself grieve your father. Yes," she said in response to the disbelieving look on Letitia's face. "You can grieve and be angry at the same time. It happens more often than people realize."

THE MATTER OF THE SECRET BRIDE 319

The young woman looked away quickly, but Rosalind was sure she saw something like relief in her exhausted eyes. "Then what?"

"Then more time will have passed," said Rosalind. "There will be more answers."

"Is that a promise, Miss Thorne?"

"Yes, Miss Poole. It is." She paused. "Especially if you agree to help us."

Letitia's fingers curled just the tiniest bit. "How can I help?"

"Can you tell me anything about that morning before your father left the house?"

Letitia was silent for a long moment. Then she said, "Papa was not home that morning. We all assume he was sleeping at the White Swan. He did that sometimes."

Rosalind waited, but Letitia said nothing else. Nor did she look at Rosalind. Instead, she stared into the blazing fire. The room had grown quite close. Rosalind felt her brow growing damp, and she saw beads of perspiration stand out on Letitia's forehead.

"Then, can you tell me what your stepmother was doing that morning?"

Letitia frowned at the fire. One bead of perspiration trickled slowly down her temple. Her hand flew up, wiped the errant droplet quickly away.

"Melora was up early," Letitia said. "Her brother had had a bad night. It has been a bad sennight for him. He was in a collapse, and they thought him in a dangerous state."

"But he clearly recovered." On that day, he had been sitting up to meet them in the library, just as he had been today.

"Yes," said Letitia. "That also happens sometimes. He can be at death's door in the morning and then be sitting up to eat supper in the evening. Melora says the doctors tell her it is a seizure that takes him so."

"So, the doctors were sent for?"

She shook her head. "He recovered quickly enough that there was no need."

Rosalind considered this. "So, your stepmother was in attendance on him all morning?"

"I believe so. I had my breakfast on a tray. I did not feel as if I could . . . Well, I wanted to stay out of the way."

Rosalind nodded. "A last thing. There was a young man who visited here today, a cavalry officer perhaps. Was that your fiancé?"

"No. We've had no visitors this morning." Her eyes flickered to the door. Rosalind wondered if she was thinking of the silent parlor, where people should have been coming to pay their respects to her father.

But Rosalind would have to wait to ask anything further. Adam had returned to the room, and Letitia closed her mouth like she never meant to open it again.

Rosalind saw at a glance that his interview with Mrs. Poole had not been satisfactory.

"Miss Poole," said Adam, "Mrs. Poole is asking for you."

Letitia looked from him to Rosalind. "Am I not required to give a statement?"

"Not at this time," Adam told her.

"Oh." Her relief was only thinly disguised. She rose with that mature, graceful calm Rosalind had noticed when she first saw the young woman, and rang the bell.

"Lizzie can show you out," Letitia said. "Unless there's something else you need from us?"

"There may be more later," said Adam. "But not immediately."

"Thank you, Miss Poole," said Rosalind. "I am sorry for your loss, and your trouble."

The mute look Letitia returned was filled with doubt and anger. But her only reply was the required modest curtsy.

Lizzie appeared on the threshold. She led Adam and Rosalind to the foyer and turned immediately to go retrieve Rosalind's bonnet and pelisse.

Rosalind gave Adam an urgent glance and spoke to the maid's retreating back.

"Lizzie, can you tell me if Judith has left yet? I need to speak with her."

The girl blinked, two spots of color appearing in her cheeks. Rosalind wondered if she'd been especially instructed to hold her tongue around any visitors. And yet she could not refuse to answer a direct question from a guest.

"I believe she is still here, miss," whispered Lizzie. "She was packing her things when I came down."

"Can you take me to her?"

"I . . . that is . . ."

"She has a handkerchief of mine that she offered to launder, and I do not wish to lose it." Rosalind watched Lizzie make the assumption that what she meant was that she did not wish her property to be stolen.

Rosalind did not correct her. She felt a sharp dig of guilt from working on the young woman's vulnerabilities in this way, but she had no time for a kinder plan.

"I'll go see about the cab," said Adam to Rosalind. "Lizzie, if you can take care of Miss Thorne?"

He showed himself out the door, leaving Lizzie and Rosalind. Rosalind smiled and willed the girl to make up her mind what to do. Mrs. Poole might appear at any moment, or Letitia or even Mr. Considen.

At last, Lizzie bobbed a quick curtsy. "Very well, miss. This way."

Rosalind suppressed a sigh of relief and followed the girl up the back stairs. Thankfully, no one was about, and they climbed to the attic without being noticed.

Rosalind found herself wondering where Mrs. Poole and Letitia were and what they were doing.

The maids' quarters were four rooms set directly beneath the eaves. Lizzie knocked on the second door on the left.

"What now!" came a voice from the other side. In the next instant, Judith threw open the door and saw Rosalind.

"Oh," she said. "It's you."

Judith's face was flushed; her eyes were red. She'd been crying from sorrow or anger. Rosalind couldn't tell which. A pair of boxes waited on the narrow iron-framed bed. The things had been stuffed in them haphazardly, not at all how someone trained as a parlormaid would be expected to pack.

Her apron and cap had been hung on a peg beside the door, leaving her wearing a plain gray dress. The black mourning band that would have decorated her sleeve had been tossed onto the trunk at the foot of the bed.

"Thank you, Lizzie," said Rosalind. "You need not wait."

"I . . . yes, miss." Lizzie glanced to Judith, who jerked her chin, indicating the other maid should leave.

Lizzie hurried away, and Rosalind felt sure she was glad to go. Hopefully, she was not going straight to Mrs. Poole.

"What do you want?" demanded Judith.

Rosalind stepped over the threshold. The room was low and whitewashed. The floorboards were dark with age but scrubbed clean. "I was sorry to hear you were dismissed."

"Huh." Judith turned her back and grabbed a pair of stockings off the bed, which she began rolling into a tight ball. "Good riddance, I say. Wouldn't stay in this house another minute. Not if they doubled my wages." She stuffed the roll of stockings into the nearest box.

"Why?"

Judith's thin shoulders stiffened. "You'll forgive me, miss, but I think I'm done answering questions."

"Of course. However, I was hoping I might have my handkerchief back."

"Oh. Right."

There was one dressing table in the room. Aside from the

beds and a footstool, it was the only furniture. Judith opened the right-hand drawer and brought out the neatly folded square. "I'm afraid there was no time to launder it."

"That's quite all right," said Rosalind. "Judith, I do have one question."

The young woman rolled her eyes. "I knew it."

Rosalind ignored this. "A young man was visiting here this morning. Do you know who he was?"

Judith's hand touched her chest, right above her heart. Rosalind remembered the gesture from their previous conversation.

"I'm sure I couldn't—" she began, but she got no further. There came the sound of a footstep making the stairs creak and the swish of skirts.

Lizzie apparently had decided the mistress of the house should know what was happening.

"Judith?" Mrs. Poole appeared in the doorway. "Why are you still here? Miss Thorne? What is your business with my maid?"

"I beg your pardon," Rosalind said. "I had loaned Judith my handkerchief when we were here the other day"—she held up the item in question—"and I did not wish to disturb you to reclaim it."

"Yes, well." Mrs. Poole appeared to accept the explanation, but reluctantly. "You have achieved your aim, I see. Thank you, Judith." The words held far more warning than gratitude. "I will show you downstairs, Miss Thorne."

Mrs. Poole stood back, plainly signaling it was time for Rosalind to leave.

"Thank you, Judith," Rosalind said, and she let Mrs. Poole lead her the long way back down to the foyer. Rosalind's bonnet and pelisse waited on the central table, beside the card salver and the visiting book.

Mrs. Poole picked up her pelisse and handed it to Rosalind.

"Miss Thorne, you will do me a favor and not harass my

staff or my stepdaughter any further," she said bluntly as Rosalind buttoned herself into the pelisse. "They can have nothing to do with this particular matter of yours, this other woman's property that has gone missing." Her smile was tight and dismissive as she handed Rosalind her bonnet. "Unless she has also lost her handkerchief?"

"I wish it were that simple, Mrs. Poole. I am very much afraid a violent death changes the questions that must be asked." She settled her bonnet carefully into place.

Mrs. Poole made a sharp gesture, at once dismissing her husband's murder and whatever questions it might raise. "What did you really want Judith for?"

Rosalind finished tying her ribbon. "A young man visited your house this morning. I watched him leave."

"What is that to you?"

"I do not know," said Rosalind. "Miss Poole could not say who he was, and Judith would not."

Mrs. Poole glanced away. An expression Rosalind could not read rippled across her face. When she faced Rosalind again, there was a gleam of satisfaction in her eye, and that satisfaction echoed in her voice.

"Very well, Miss Thorne. Let me satisfy your curiosity. That young man had business at one time with my husband. He came to pay his respects. I'm sure Mr. Harkness will want his name for his statements and report. Therefore, you may tell him it was Captain George Dawson."

CHAPTER FORTY-THREE

A Quiet Stroll and Many Questions

*"... there is an expression in her features of
something very like deceit ..."*

Bury, Charlotte, *The Diary of a Lady-in-Waiting*

"Dawson?" said Adam when Rosalind told him what had transpired between her and Mrs. Poole. "What was he doing here?"

Although Adam had said he was going to see about a cab for them, Rosalind found him waiting patiently on the street. When she reached him, they fell into step with each other, silently agreeing that they should walk a ways before they found some conveyance, if they did need one.

This had become their custom, Rosalind realized with a jolt. Somewhere amidst all the other flurry of activities, they had each learned how the other worked, and this now was simply their way.

"Mrs. Poole said he'd come to pay his respects," she told him. "But I doubt that."

Adam said nothing. Rosalind turned so she could see his face past her bonnet's brim. She really, she thought, must get herself one of the smaller, modern ladies' hats, at least for good weather. It was too difficult to see Adam around her older, broader straw bonnet.

Another jolt went through her. Her thoughts darted ahead of her—to home, to her desk, and to the letter she was keeping. She forced her attention back to the present.

"It seems to me that Mrs. Poole is very good at misdirection," Adam was saying.

"I take it she was not very forthcoming in her statements for Sir David."

"In fact, she said as little as she possibly could. She told me that Poole was not home yesterday and that she assumed he had slept at the White Swan, as he frequently did when he was deep in some new business."

"Do you believe her?"

"No," he said flatly. "When I talked to the serving woman at the Swan, she told me that she saw Poole come in that morning and that he called for his breakfast."

"Letitia also told me Poole was away from home that morning."

"So, they have all said the same and are willing to swear to it."

"But why that particular point?" asked Rosalind. "What was Poole really doing?"

"What were the family doing?" countered Adam. "Mrs. Poole said that her brother had a collapse that morning and that she was too busy nursing him to take notice of anything else."

"Yes, Letitia also said as much. Indeed, she said he was much taken by seizures this week."

"Did she say why Judith was dismissed?"

"I had no chance to ask," Rosalind told him. "But I now wonder if it was because they could not be sure Judith would lie for them."

"I was wondering the same thing," said Adam. "Do you

think you could find where she's going now that she's dismissed? I'd very much like to hear what she has to say."

"I think so. She mentioned she makes use of a registry office run by Mrs. Percivale. If they do not have an address for her, I can at the least leave a message. I take it Mrs. Poole said nothing about the dismissal?"

Adam shook his head. "She was holding back a great deal, and it was not simply grief or bad memories."

"That doesn't surprise me. When she was showing me out, she very firmly warned me away from the house." There was something else, as well, something in her face and her eyes. Rosalind felt understanding stir in the depths of her mind, but it was too far down for her to reach.

"Did she say anything of her relationship with Mr. Poole?" she asked. "Or the will?"

"Nothing she hadn't said before—that Poole had kept the bargain they made when she married him and that she had asked for nothing else. She did say she had spoken with Poole's attorney about the will, and it was exactly as she expected and that she knew nothing of his business. That he never took her into his confidence about professional matters." Adam glanced at her. "Were you able to learn anything from Miss Poole?"

Rosalind told him Letitia's story—how her fiancé's family had come that morning to break off the engagement and been met with threats of law and blackmail.

Rosalind paused in mid-step.

The world flowed around them—pedestrians, carriages and vans, porters and men with barrows and women with baskets, all the noise and bustle—and she attended to none of it.

When a husband died, a wife frequently took over their business, especially when there was no male relative to do so or there were young children to be supported and cared for.

Mr. Poole's business was laced with blackmail and theft.

Rosalind remembered Letitia sitting by the fire, trying not to twist her hands or betray the depth of her emotions.

"Letters," said Rosalind abruptly.

"Which ones?" asked Adam.

"Letitia told me Mrs. Poole threatened to blackmail her fiancé's family if they tried to break off the engagement. She said she had certain letters in her possession that could cause them embarrassment."

Adam drew in a deep breath and let it out slowly. "So she did know how to lay her hands on some of her husband's papers."

"I thought she must," said Rosalind. "In the bookroom there were those bound collections of clippings and notes. I keep similar books in my writing room. He would not have them unless they were useful to his business, and he would not keep them in a room where he did no business . . ."

"And if he does business there, where are the papers?" said Adam.

"Did Mrs. Poole move them before we arrived?" said Rosalind.

"That," said Adam, "would mean that Mrs. Poole already knew her husband was dead."

CHAPTER FORTY-FOUR

A Disruption at the Dinner Hour

"It is unwise for the old to forget they were once young."

Bury, Charlotte, *The Diary of a Lady-in-Waiting*

"Have you heard anything from Miss Thorne, McGowan?"

"Not yet, madam," mumbled Amelia around her mouthful of hairpins.

Mrs. Fitzherbert sat at her dressing table, staring into her mirror. Amelia stood behind her, brushing her silvered hair.

Mrs. Fitzherbert had lovely hair—thick and lustrous, illuminated by its streaks of silver. Amelia found herself grateful for her experience dressing Miss Thorne's unruly, voluminous mane. By comparison, Mrs. Fitzherbert's hair was easy as pie.

It was evening and nearing six o'clock. Mrs. Fitzherbert had declared that dinner would be at half seven, which meant— owing to the peculiarities of etiquette around even family dinners—that Amelia should have all three ladies dressed and fit to be seen by seven at the latest.

"Perhaps it is over," Mrs. Fitzherbert was saying. There

was no need to wonder what "it" was. "Perhaps it truly has been destroyed, or, better, it was found to be worthless, and I am an old fool, who imagines herself to be of more importance than she is." She paused, waiting for Amelia to say something reassuring. Amelia found herself stymied by a particularly stubborn lock that refused to remain in place.

"You have heard nothing among the staff?" Mrs. Fitzherbert prompted. "Seen nothing?"

"Nothing useful, madam." Amelia pulled the pin out and replaced it, more carefully this time.

It was not for lack of trying. While Mrs. Fitzherbert and her daughters had been occupied with receiving her callers, Amelia had taken a heap of mending and ironing downstairs to the sewing room. She had spent the midday and much of the afternoon alternating between genuine work and talking with the rest of the staff.

She quickly found that the Fitzherbert household was as much a hive of gossip as any other house where she'd ever been employed. Despite recent events, many of the occupants enjoyed having a new ear to listen to old stories.

She had learned all about Mr. Holm's no-good brother and Mrs. DeLupe's worries about what would happen to them all if madam left for the Continent permanently. She'd learned that the youngest chambermaid, Catie, was sweet on Tom Faller, and that her older counterpart, Belinda, was trying in vain to reason her out of her daydream. The head footman, Peters, drank too much on payday; and the undergroom, Wilson, sold extra feed on the sly. Cook had a follower who came by early Sunday mornings. Molly in the scullery was rumored to have a baby, whom she kept with her sister in Camden.

Faller, of course, took his sweeteners from the young ladies and anyone else who needed a favor. Belinda hinted that she thought he might be doing more with them than just passing love notes. Catie gave her a pinch and told her she had gone too far.

All of them agreed it was just too bad that Burrowes had to be dismissed. The debates about whether she'd actually committed the theft were fierce and—at least at the time Amelia was there to witness this—ended in Mrs. DeLupe declaring the subject off limits.

But no one had so far suggested an alternate possibility among the staff. Mr. Holm had apparently taken the theft very personally and patrolled the house every hour on the hour to make sure all was as it should be.

"What about Faller?" Amelia asked. "He seems . . . Well, I wouldn't trust him to mind the henhouse, if you see what I mean."

"I should think not!" Belinda bit off her thread. "That one's out for whatever he can get. You know the kind."

"I most certainly do," murmured Amelia.

"He's got a bit on the side, too. Thinks nobody knows, but he's always running off to see her."

"Stuff and nonsense," said Catie stoutly. "He goes to visit his sister. He told me so. She's poorly."

"Poorly sister, is it?" Belinda's tone told Amelia exactly what she thought of that. "How kind of him. Probably where he is now, I shouldn't wonder." She glanced at the doorway. "Mr. Holm sent him out on an errand an hour or more ago, and he ain't back yet."

And he still wasn't back when the big wall clock in the servants' hall ticked over to four, signaling the end of visiting hours. Nor was he back at half past, when Amelia gathered her mending and climbed back up to be ready should Mrs. Fitzherbert need her before it was time to begin getting changed for dinner.

Now here it was, with the clocks chiming six and the church bells outside beginning their ragged chorus over the rooftops, and as far as Amelia knew, Faller was still gone.

"If you like," said Amelia to Mrs. Fitzherbert as she settled the lace cap in place, "I can make an excuse to go out and see if Miss Thorne's learned anything new."

"No, it's getting late, and it would look odd for you to be running an errand for me at this hour," said Mrs. Fitzherbert. "Besides, I need you to help keep an eye on my girls. I hardly like to ask a member of my staff to spy." She gave a small laugh. "But then, that is the point of your being here, isn't it?"

Amelia shared her smile, but it did not last.

"Has Minney said anything in your hearing?" asked Mrs. Fitzherbert anxiously. "About her plans? About Captain Dawson?"

"No, madam." Amelia carefully set aside the memory of two silhouettes in the garden. She knew what it was to love someone when the world disapproved. She would not give away Minney Seymore's secrets unless she absolutely had to.

Mrs. Fitzherbert's face grew pensive. Amelia took a deep breath.

"Madam, I've been with Miss Thorne for a little bit now, and I've seen the way things work. Sometimes, it's necessary to let events unspool, if you see what I mean, in order to find out what's really going on, and sometimes that's very hard."

"Yes, I believe I see what you mean. But in the case of an impetuous young woman, too long a leash can only lead to disaster. Even when there are no . . . additional complications." Mrs. Fitzherbert gazed into her mirror for a long moment. Her hand strayed to the miniature she wore at her throat. Then she turned abruptly, angrily, away. "You may go and see to the girls now, McGowan. I have some additional letters that must be written before the evening post leaves."

"Very good—" began Amelia, but she was interrupted by a scratching at the door. When the door opened, it was Mr. Holm at the threshold, looking unusually hesitant.

Mrs. Fitzherbert frowned. "What is it, Holm?"

The butler was a tall, stern man, perfectly capable of looming over most of the footmen and underbutlers. But now he looked as if he were trying to shrink down inside his own coat. "I beg your pardon, madam, but it seems . . . Faller has gone missing."

Amelia's shoulders stiffened.

"Faller?" Mrs. Fitzherbert frowned. "The footman? How has he gone missing?"

"I sent him out this morning with an order for more of Fontane's silver polish. It should not have taken him more than an hour. He has not returned."

Amelia remembered just that morning, when she'd met Faller on the stairs, his box on his shoulder and his face tight with disappointment. She remembered him sitting slumped in his room. She'd thought he was done with . . . whatever it had been.

Now it seemed she'd been wrong.

Mrs. Fitzherbert's hand was trembling where it lay on her dressing table, but her voice remained clear.

"What a disappointment," she said coolly. "If he does return, bring him to me. I will listen to his explanation. It may be he has met with some mischance."

"Yes, madam." Mr. Holm bowed and showed himself out, his manner much more assured than when he had entered.

Amelia resisted an urge to sniff. *Worried she'd scold him, I shouldn't wonder, and glad she didn't.*

But Amelia set this aside, too. She had more urgent matters to consider.

"Madam?" she said. "We should let Miss Thorne know about this."

But Mrs. Fitzherbert hesitated. "Yes. I'm afraid you're right. It is possible Faller has met with some accident, or he may have gone somewhere to get drunk, although he's never shown any tendency to that before." Her hand trembled again. "He has never done anything . . . He has always done his work well, never been subject to discipline . . ." Clearly, she was trying to remember what she knew of the young man—when he'd been hired, how he'd come to her and why—and was finding she could not.

Which was the way of it, even in a good household. Most of the servants were unknowns, until they became difficulties.

Amelia took a deep breath. The ironclad rule against carrying tales from belowstairs to abovestairs was difficult to break. "There is talk that he's been taking extra money on the side where maybe he shouldn't."

"Do you think Faller is the thief?" asked Mrs. Fitzherbert.

Honesty wrestled briefly with conscience, but it was duty that decided matters.

"I think it's possible," she said. "Or maybe helped the thief. I don't have proof, but . . . now . . ." She found she didn't have a satisfactory way to finish that sentence.

"Yes, now." Mrs. Fitzherbert rubbed her brow. "Do let Miss Thorne know. I'll go check on the girls, and then you can get them ready for dinner."

Make sure the girls are staying put, Amelia translated.

"Yes, madam."

Amelia left via the door to her own room. She stood there a moment, considering what she should do. Then she hurried out into the corridor and down the servants' stairs.

Everybody who was still belowstairs seemed to be talking in whispers. Mr. Holm was in his pantry, engaged in hushed and urgent conversation with Mrs. DeLupe. The whole brotherhood of footmen was in the hall, whispering and snickering. Amelia hurried past them all, apparently unnoticed.

The corridor to the men's quarters was empty, and the door to Faller's room was unlocked. Amelia slipped inside as quickly as she could and closed the door behind her.

She looked under the bed first. His box was there, and a trunk stood at the foot of the narrow bed. Even more telling, his dressing table still had its brushes and combs, not to mention a good razor was beside the basin.

Wherever Faller had gone, he planned to return. No man would leave his razor and comb behind if he was doing a midnight flit.

At least not if it was planned.

Amelia bit her lip. She also slipped back into the corridor. It would not do to be caught in here.

She made her way back to the kitchen. There she found her luck was with her. Belinda was helping Cook assemble a tray of biscuits and tea.

"Is that for the young ladies?" she asked, all casual, as she walked in.

"'S right," said Belinda. "Her Young Highness decided she must have her tea, even with dinner almost ready."

"I expect they're bored silly after sitting all day in the drawing room and just want something to do with themselves," said Amelia. "I can take it up if you like. Miss Seymore's in a temper." Which was also a guess, but seemed likely, given her situation. "No need for you to have to take the brunt of it, and I've got to get them ready for dinner, anyway."

"Thanks, McGowan," said Belinda. "She really can be a terror that one."

Amelia smiled and took the heavy tray.

Going up a narrow stair with a tray and not spilling or rattling the contents was an art form. So was pausing at the door long enough to manage the delicate process of shifting the tray just so one could knock. It could take a while, and, if managed correctly, it tended to allow one to hear bits of any conversation happening on the other side of the door.

"What have you done, Minney?" Mary Ann demanded.

"Nothing! Nothing new. It's all fine, Mary Ann."

"It is not! Minney! Do you know where Faller's gone?"

"No, of course not. Why would I? Why are you even bothering your head about it?"

"Because he could be off on one of your errands."

"Well, he's not," she snapped, but her tone immediately grew much more conciliatory. Amelia could picture Miss Seymore taking Miss Mary Ann's hand. "Everything will be fine. I'm sure he's just late. Or with his lady friend. And why shouldn't he be?"

Movement caught Amelia's eye. A door down the hall opened, and Catie emerged with a load of linens in her arms. Amelia scratched at the door and nudged it open.

"I've brought your tea," she announced, trying to sound genuinely cheerful and not disappointed at being forced to interrupt this extremely interesting conversation.

"Thank you, McGowan," said Miss Seymore, but she kept all her attention on her sister. "You can put it here." She waved vaguely in the direction of the tea table.

Another skill one picked up in service was watching out of the corner of one's eye. Amelia set the tray down, careful not to rattle or splash, all the time watching how Mary Ann slowly wilted under her sister's determined glower.

"Is there anything else you need?" Amelia asked.

"No," said Miss Seymore.

"Miss Mary Ann?" Amelia prompted.

Mary Ann glared at her sister. "No, I suppose not."

"Well, I shall be right here." Amelia paused. "You might do well to remember that."

That caught Miss Seymore's attention. "What did you say?"

"Nothing, miss," Amelia told her. "Except that madam is worried, and you are under watch."

Miss Seymore's eyes narrowed. "By you?"

"I didn't say so, miss," replied Amelia. "But if I was you, I'd drink my tea and find where I put my patience, so madam can relax again. Miss." She bobbed a curtsy. "If there's nothing else, I'll be back in time to get you ready for dinner."

She turned and made as if to breeze out of the room, but as expected, Miss Seymore stopped her before she reached the door.

"McGowan. Wait a minute."

"Minney!" groaned Miss Mary Ann. "What are you doing?"

Miss Seymore ignored her. "Faller said you are a friend. Are you my friend?"

"I should hope so, miss."

Miss Seymore bit her lip. "Even if . . . even if I should ever need your help, and I needed you not to tell Mama?"

Amelia let her gaze slip from Miss Seymore to Miss Mary Ann. "I should not like to be involved in anything wrong, miss."

"Minney, stop it," said Mary Ann. "You're only going to get yourself into more trouble!"

"No, I'm not, because McGowan is going to help us. Aren't you, McGowan?"

"I'm sure I'm always glad to help, miss."

"There, you see?" But Miss Seymore's gaiety was forced. She also went to her dresser and pulled out her reticule. She brought out two sovereigns and laid them in Amelia's hand.

"And there's to show you I don't forget people who help me." She closed Amelia's hand around the coins.

Amelia made her curtsy and her escape.

Once in the corridor, Amelia hesitated. Then she hurried back to her room, tossed the coins onto her dressing table, and opened her trunk. She'd packed away some writing supplies when she left, and now she pulled out pen and paper and a carefully stoppered bottle of ink. She wrote furiously, trusting that Alice would be able to translate any mistakes. There was no time to be careful.

The letter finished, she made herself walk casually down to the servants' hall. No one took special note of her. Preparations for dinner were well underway, and even with Mrs. Fitzherbert dining en famille, there was still a great deal to be done.

Amelia slipped out the side door and climbed up the area stairs into the warm summer evening.

"Miss." Jim Geery, who'd greeted her when she first arrived, was on watch. He was just as saucy as he had been that other day, but sober and fairly sharp, if Amelia was any judge.

"I've a message that's got to get to Orchard Street quick as can be."

She waited for him to ask questions or demand his own sweetener for the job, but he just pocketed the note and raised his hat. "Your servant, miss."

"Thank you," she said, and she meant it. But as she turned away, Amelia froze, the hair rising on her neck. She was certain she had seen movement, that someone was watching. But Geery was already jogging across the street, without a glance behind.

Amelia made herself turn, made herself look into the shadows between the house and the mews again.

But there was no one there.

CHAPTER FORTY-FIVE

A Slender Thread

"Oh! Something dreadful has happened; I cannot read it aloud!"

Bury, Charlotte, *The Diary of a Lady-in-Waiting*

When Adam and Rosalind returned to Orchard Street, the afternoon was dimming toward evening, and Alice was waiting in the parlor, perched on the edge of her chair.

"George Dawson had been doing business with Josiah Poole for three years at least," she announced without preamble when they walked in. "How was your day?"

Rosalind and Adam stared at each other and then burst out laughing. It felt like relief. Rosalind sank down onto the settee.

"You had no trouble with Bingham?" Adam asked her.

"As if I had not been handling officious young men for much of my life," scoffed Alice. "Between myself and Mr. Tauton, the young man had no chance. Here are the extracts of the letters he'd found so far." She held out her notebook. Adam raised a brow at her. Alice's shorthand might as well be a secret code for all anyone else could read it.

"Oh, right. Well." Alice flipped through her pages. "Captain Dawson first wrote to Poole three years ago, asking for help disentangling him from some complex promises made to a consortium of moneylenders. He insists that the terms they gave him and the terms they were enforcing were entirely different, although he seems to have neglected to write the initial agreement down." She paused long enough for them all to shake their heads. "It further seems that Mr. Poole was successful, eventually, but that Captain Dawson was not the most diligent of students, because he landed in similar difficulties the next year and the one after that. And while Mr. Poole was able to get him out of trouble with these various unscrupulous parties, this only increased the amounts that Captain Dawson owed to Poole himself."

"That is certainly very bad," said Rosalind. "But it is not beyond the usual difficulties of careless aristocratic sons."

"Unless, as alluded to, his father has threatened to cut him off entirely should the moneylenders apply to him for relief." Alice turned a page of her notebook. "And, further, they threatened to take up the matter with the Duke of York, who, I am told, became a friend and patron of Dawson's after his feats at Waterloo."

And there it is. To protect his future interests, Dawson must conceal his follies, and the more he tried to hide, the more ignominious details fell into Mr. Poole's keeping.

"You did not happen to take note of his address?" asked Adam.

"What on earth do you take me for?" demanded Alice. "Of course I did." She held up a slip of paper. "Rendered into plain English."

"Thank you." Adam tucked the paper into his coat pocket. His hand hesitated, and something Rosalind could not read flitted behind his eyes. Her heart constricted with sudden apprehension, but she could not say why. "I'd best leave at once."

Rosalind suddenly wanted to urge him to stay, to have

some supper, to talk to her. But she said none of these things. She pressed both his hands and looked into his eyes, still too shy to kiss him when anyone could see, even though that someone was only Alice.

Adam smiled and kissed the backs of her hands. "I'll return as soon as I can," he said.

And he was gone, and Rosalind turned away.

"Sit down, Rosalind," said Alice. "Stop scolding yourself for whatever you think you've done wrong, and tell me everything that's happened."

Rosalind meant to say she was not scolding herself, except of course she had been. Instead, she sat down in her accustomed spot on the settee and told Alice all that had transpired at the Pooles—from the sight of the man in the scarlet coat to Letitia's accidental revelation that Mrs. Poole had access to at least some of Mr. Poole's papers, and the inclination to use them, to Judith's dismissal, and the family's concerted effort to lie about the morning Mr. Poole had died.

Then, she told Alice about the possibility that Mrs. Poole had known her husband was dead before Adam and Rosalind arrived with the news, even though it had seemed otherwise at the time.

"Shouldn't the house be watched?" said Alice. "It sounds to me as if the Pooles might decide to simply make a run for it."

Rosalind considered this. "No. I think not. Whatever the truth of the matter, the Pooles appear ready to brazen it out. Why else would Mrs. Poole be insisting on going through with Letitia's marriage? Why not make the best settlement she could and remove herself and her family to Scotland or the Continent? No. She does not think she has reason to run, at least not yet."

"And William Considen?"

"I do not think he would leave his sister. They seem intent on protecting each other."

"But this could change if they feel they are being caught in a noose."

"But not until then," said Rosalind. "What would it take for you to leave George if he were in difficulty?"

"That is a good point," agreed Alice. "So we return to the man in the scarlet coat. Why was Dawson there? Was he looking for his own papers or for the certificate? He had access to the house. He could have known from Minney that Faller could be bribed. We know he needed money. Poole could have offered to get his debts cleared if Dawson brought him the certificate. He could have gone round today to be sure that Mrs. Poole intended to honor her husband's promise."

Rosalind opened her mouth but had no time to speak. Mortimer entered, with a note in his hand. "Brought by hand," he said as he gave it to Rosalind. "A Mr. Geery. Says he comes from Tilney Street."

"That's Amelia's hand." Alice plucked the note from Mortimer's fingers. Rosalind raised her brows, and Alice looked sheepish and returned it to Rosalind.

"Thank you," said Rosalind dryly. As Mortimer retreated, Rosalind opened the letter, took a look at the hasty, wandering scrawl, and passed it back to Alice.

Alice scanned the note, her lips moving slowly and her eyes growing wide.

"What is it?"

"Tom Faller's vanished."

"What!" cried Rosalind.

Alice nodded. "Amelia says Tom Faller was sent out on an errand this afternoon and has not yet returned. She says that Mrs. Fitzherbert is sending the girls home early Friday morning, but Amelia thinks Minney is planning something. Minney gave her a sweetener to gain her help but hasn't said what she needs yet."

Rosalind let out a long, slow breath. "We must find Tom Faller."

Alice's brow furrowed. "I suppose Amelia could ask the butler if he has family he might have gone to, but what . . ."

"Judith will know where he's gone."

"Judith?" exclaimed Alice. "The Pooles' maid?"

"Yes. I strongly suspect they're married, or at least engaged."

"Did she tell you that?"

Rosalind shook her head. "She did not have to. When I asked her about the visitor in the scarlet coat, she made a particular gesture." Rosalind touched the spot over her heart. "You do something like it when you think of Amelia, and Mrs. Fitzherbert when she thinks of her husband. Judith is wearing something she keeps concealed—a ring or other token."

Employers frequently refused to hire married servants, lest family obligations interfere with their ability to perform as demanded. So, servants who were married frequently pretended not to be.

"Amelia says there's rumors that Faller had a young woman." Alice tapped a finger on her knee. "Yes. It does fit."

"And Mrs. Fitzherbert's staff wears a scarlet livery. It could well have been Mr. Faller I saw," said Rosalind. "So, tomorrow—"

"Is your at home," interrupted Alice.

Rosalind felt herself staring. "Alice, this is far more important."

"No, it isn't. Not with Countess Lieven threatening to libel you and Mrs. Fitz all over the city. You need to be right where you're supposed to be, acting as though nothing's wrong. I will go find Judith."

Rosalind was silent for a long moment.

"What is it?" asked Alice finally.

"I'm just contemplating the irony of my current situation," said Rosalind. "For all these years I have been terrified of becoming noticed, of losing my gentility and entrée into society, and now . . . now I'm looking at days of work simply updating my books and repaying calls."

"You should be pleased." Alice took up one of the few remaining sandwiches and bit into it. "And I should be jealous."

"No, you shouldn't. And you wouldn't be. You'd be worried."

"Because you are?"

"Yes. This is not establishing connection." Rosalind gazed wearily at the door. "This is notoriety, and that is much less stable."

At this, Alice simply rolled her eyes and finished her sandwich. "Rosalind, you, of all people, should know there is no such thing as a stable footing among the *haut ton*. That's why so many of them eventually run mad." She dusted the crumbs from her hands.

"Them?"

"Them," said Alice firmly. "I renounced my membership when my father died and have no regrets. But I'd take some notoriety. It would be good for sales. Do you think you can organize something for me?"

Despite everything, Rosalind laughed. "I shall put it on my list."

"Oh dear," said Alice sympathetically. "You really do look tired."

"I think I am." Rosalind passed a hand over her brow, smoothing back a stray lock of hair. "It's been rather a lot."

"Well, perhaps we will have luck. Perhaps Adam finds Captain Dawson, and he confesses all."

Perhaps, thought Rosalind. But she was not prepared to rest all her hopes there.

"Very well, Alice. Tomorrow I will entertain the fashionable world, and you will go see if Judith can be persuaded to let us know where her young man has gone."

And what he might have taken with him.

Because that was something they had not said—that the reason the certificate might still be missing was that it was still in the hands of Thomas Faller.

CHAPTER FORTY-SIX

Captain Dawson

> *". . . and all that has followed and I fear will follow, is in a great measure the consequence of his harsh and headstrong disbelief in miseries to manifest to be doubted."*

Bury, Charlotte, *The Diary of a Lady-in-Waiting*

According to the direction Alice had given him, Captain Dawson kept a set of rooms in the vicinity of St. James's. It was not an address for a man who was said to be in debt and resorting to the help of a man like Josiah Poole. But then, it *was* the address of a man who believed himself to be coming up in the world and wanted to keep up that appearance.

Night had settled in, and the young men of the neighborhood were busy making good cheer with each other. Laughter and shouts emerged from open windows. Adam kept to the wall as much as he could to avoid his fellow pedestrians (many of whom were already drunk), as well as the would-be Corinthians, in their chariots and phaetons, racing their blooded horses and egging each other on.

A few women strolled the cobbles, very obviously on their way to meet their paramours. The young men who lingered about to watch the passing scene were well dressed and sharp eyed. They plainly did not trust Adam, or each other, and sniggered as he passed them.

Adam ignored them. They, perhaps sensing that this stranger was more trouble than he was worth, left him alone.

As reported by Alice, the letters Bingham had unearthed showed that Captain Dawson was a careless man, but his choice of rooms showed that he might possibly be attempting to rein in his affairs. Despite the fashionable bachelor's neighborhood, his building was wedged into a narrow side street, with the rooms fitted into the very top and back of the house. It was a long climb up a worn, close stair to reach them. The summer's warmth was trapped in here like the heat in a dirty chimney, and Adam was sweating under his coat by the time he reached Dawson's door.

He paused, listening. Men's voices rose from inside. He couldn't hear the words, but the rhythm was unhurried and companionable.

Adam knocked. The talk inside halted. Chairs scraped. Hard-heeled shoes clacked against the floorboards. Finally, the door opened a few inches, and Adam found himself facing a short, young White man with a pleasant round face, an elaborate cravat, and a good brown coat.

"I'm looking for Captain Dawson," Adam said.

The young man looked him up and down, taking in his appearance and demeanor. "And who might you be?"

"Adam Harkness. I'm here on behalf of the coroner."

"The *what*?" A second man, who was in his shirtsleeves and waistcoat, crowded behind the first. "Hang it, Jacobs. It's not the sheriff. Let the man in."

Jacobs did not seem entirely convinced, but the second man wrenched the door out of his hand and threw it back to allow Adam to enter the room.

He seemed to have interrupted a friendly game. The cards lay abandoned on the table, along with a half-empty bottle of wine and glasses all drained to their dregs. The room around them was spare but neat—with the bed made and the furniture all in order.

Three men watched Adam warily as he entered. There was Jacobs, who had answered the door. The second fellow in shirtsleeves. A third man was still seated at the card table. He was a fair man in a plain green coat, with muddy blue eyes and a blur of stubble on his pockmarked chin. There was, Adam also noted, a scarlet coat with a captain's insignia hanging off the back of one of the chairs.

"What's the coroner to do with Dawson?" demanded Green Coat.

"I have some questions for him regarding a matter that has come before the coroner," said Adam. "And the sooner he answers, the better off he will be."

Jacobs and Shirtsleeves exchanged a worried glance. Green Coat reached for the wine bottle.

"You'll have to come back," said Shirtsleeves. "Dawson's not here."

Adam looked pointedly at the red coat draped across the back of the chair. "He's not?"

Shirtsleeves looked at him blankly. "Oh, God, you don't think . . . !" The men all burst out laughing. "No, no, no. That's mine. My name's O'Connell. Captain Bernard O'Connell, Eighth Horse. Dawson's . . ." All at once, O'Connell seemed to remember whom he was talking to, and he clapped his mouth shut.

"Better tell him," said Green Coat as he poured himself out a fresh glass. "He'll have us all rounded up or some such."

"I'd like to see him try," muttered Jacobs.

"No, I don't think you would." Green Coat drank a healthy swallow of wine. "It's hot, and he's on business, and if Dawson's been messing up his own chances again, I'm not going to let his stupidity ruin my evening."

"Good God, Norris," cried O'Connell. "I hope I never have to count on you."

"Best not," said Norris, with a shrug. "I'm a selfish bastard, and I don't like trouble. Listen . . . Mr. Harkness, did you say? Dawson's gone. Off to the West Indies to make his fortune. O'Connell here and Jacobs are taking over his rooms, and we're waiting for their things." Norris drank again. "And that's all there is to it."

"When does he sail?"

Norris shrugged. "He didn't say, but he left around nine of the clock. Said he was on his way to Dover." He glanced at the clock on the mantel. "If he caught that stage, I'm afraid he's long gone by now."

CHAPTER FORTY-SEVEN

At Home to Callers

*"I have been teased into promising to put together
some showy spectacle . . ."*

Bury, Charlotte, *The Diary of a Lady-in-Waiting*

The announcement Alice had placed in the papers was
nothing more than a double line of typeface, one of dozens
appearing that day:

> Miss Rosalind Thorne will be at home to callers
> Tuesdays and Thursdays.

It was common for a hostess to place such a notice in the
paper upon returning to town or setting up a new establishment. Rosalind never had done so on her own behalf, as it
had never been necessary. When she'd lived with her godmother, it had not been her place to make such a declaration.
When she had lived on her own, she had not had the ability
to be "at home," as society understood the event.

Now, however, she not only placed her notice but also purchased a fresh visiting book and visited a particular shop she
knew to acquire a good, although not entirely new, silver

salver. Mortimer assured her that he was more than up to the task of shepherding any and all of the quality. Alain, the young Black man who acted as page and errand runner when the house was particularly busy, wore his best coat and was practicing his French and his German, in case there should be international persons of note to conduct through the freshly polished foyer. Mrs. Napier was on hand to supervise matters, and her girls Jane and Polly had arrived to help Claire with wraps, coats, sticks, and bonnets. Mrs. Singh had procured an entire country ham for the sandwiches.

They were all needed.

The calls began at precisely eleven and continued throughout the day. Rosalind lost track of the number of cups of tea she drank and the number of dainties she nibbled as the ladies, and not a few gentlemen, trooped through her parlor.

Rosalind sat. She talked and smiled and laughed. She deflected the leading questions, the insinuating questions, and the blatantly curious questions. She kept her mind firmly and forcefully on the person in front of her. Because Alice was right. She had to be seen, and it had to be reported that she was perfectly at ease, her home was as it ought to be, her manner unaffected and natural.

Because if it was not, that would be remembered and reported on, and Lady Jersey would hear, and once she heard, so would the rest of the world, and they would all wonder what had happened and why.

Despite the stream of visitors, Rosalind was conscious of feeling unusually alone. Alice was not there, and neither was Adam. He'd sent a note to her around ten o'clock that morning.

At the posting house. I'm told a man giving his name as George Dawson did purchase a ticket for the noon stage to Dover.

Despite the evidence, I find myself doubting the situ-

ation. Mr. Norris's demeanor did not inspire great confidence in his honesty. While you're at home, I'll go speak to the Pooles. Then you and I can go to the Fitzherberts' together.

Must consider Minney Seymore in this more deeply than we thought . . .

Rosalind longed for the leisure to think this over, to consider all that she had seen and all they had learned. But the parade of visitors did not stop. As long as they came, she must sit and smile and be what she was expected to be.

The minutes crawled across her skin. It took all Rosalind's training and all her discipline to keep her head cool and her spirits up. Because what truly worried her was Alice, or rather the lack of Alice. As the day wore on and there was no word from her or George, that silence began to sink deeper into Rosalind's awareness. Surely, if the Littlefields had been able to trace Judith, Alice would be back by now. What delayed her? What had she found?

Is she all right?

But at last, four o'clock did come. Rosalind rose and bid farewell to her current visitors—a Mr. and Mrs. Treadwell—and summoned Mortimer to show them out. As soon as the parlor door closed, Rosalind sank into her chair, leaned her head back, and closed her eyes, savoring the blissful silence.

She did not intend to fall asleep, but intention did not matter. The next thing she was aware of was a brief cough and the scuff of a shoe against the carpet. Rosalind's eyes flew open.

Mortimer stood at the door, with the tray in his hand, a single card and a note lying in the center.

Rosalind felt her knees tremble. Her throat burned at the thought of making yet more conversation.

"I'm sorry," she croaked. "Whoever that is, Mortimer, you may tell them I am not at home anymore today."

"If I may, miss," said Mortimer, "I think you may wish to be at home for this person." He held out the tray. Rosalind picked up the note first.

You must, of course, see him, Miss Thorne. I would be there myself, but I am attending the queen.
Lady Jersey.

Rosalind picked up the card and read:

MR. HENRY BROUGHAM

She pressed her lips together to stifle the curses. "Yes, of course, Mortimer. Show the gentleman in."

Because not only was Mr. Henry Brougham a member of Parliament, but he was also the queen's attorney for her divorce proceedings.

CHAPTER FORTY-EIGHT

By Persons Unknown

*". . . respecting the atrocious and horrible murder
committed last evening . . ."*

Bury, Charlotte, *The Diary of a Lady-in-Waiting*

*O*ur heroine, exhausted yet determined, leaned forward
on her velvet seat, silently urging the coachman and the
horses to greater efforts as they sped forward across the
countryside. . . .

These were the words her imagination embroidered. The
truth of the matter was that Alice sat with George in a hired
cab and had to admit that they were making surprisingly
good time as they drove toward Camden Town.

That did not stop her from wishing they could go faster.

Normally, Alice loved nothing better than to be on the
hunt for news. As a schoolgirl, she had been famous for
knowing what the entire population of Mrs. Wilson's Select
Academy for Young Ladies was doing, whether they wanted
her to or not. When she was still having her season, and later
when A. E. Littlefield was the toast of the gossip columns,

she could follow the slimmest, most tangled thread of rumor to its source.

Looked at objectively, it was perhaps an odd skill, but it had served her well. And if it was not entirely proper to admit she enjoyed the challenge, well, her friends were (mostly) kind enough to overlook this flaw in her character.

Today, however, was different. Today all she could think of was that she wanted to find Judith (Faller?), and Tom Faller, and get word back to Rosalind. Even her busy writer's mind had been unable to provide a narration to lighten up the worry she saw in Rosalind's eyes when she and George had left the house that morning. She put part of that down to Adam's news that George Dawson had already fled the country. But she knew that part of it was also Rosalind's frustration at being stuck at home when she much rather would be going out herself.

Alice's first course of action, naturally, had been to apply at Mrs. Percivale's registry office. There she'd found lines of girls in their working-day best, some clutching valises of belongings, others with precious character references in their gloved hands. Mrs. Percivale herself was stout and stern and surrounded by stacks of cards and shelves of ledgers. She listened to Alice's plea to find Judith. She had a job in hand, she said, but the woman in question was sailing the next day, and a decision needed to be made quickly. Mrs. Percivale listened, and at last, she believed, or at least believed enough. She wrote out an address in Camden Town and slipped it across her desk.

Now they had left London's sprawl behind them and were passing through the ragged fringe at the edges of the city, where new manufactures were separated by slag heaps and gray ponds, a few ashy fields and stands of houses that seemed—in Alice's mind, anyway—to look nervously about them.

The ravaged landscape, victim of nothing so much as neglect, tugged at her susceptible heart, and she thought what might be accomplished by a kinder hand, a more lively heart, if these people had such a protector. . . .

"What's the matter?" George asked his sister.

Alice shook her head, clearing away her private narrations. "It's the same thing that's been the matter for the past two days. Rosalind should have said no to . . . this."

"Far too late for that," George replied complacently. "You know how she is once she's given her word."

"Yes, I do," said Alice. "But that doesn't mean I'm not allowed to worry. Aren't you worried?"

"Not yet," he said. "But give me time. I'm sure I'll get there soon enough." He peered out the window at the smoky landscape. "Right about now, I think."

Alice was used to London and its ways, but Camden Town was not somewhere she would choose to venture on her own. The houses here were low and battered; the narrow, crooked streets more mud than cobble. Women hardened by a lifetime's endless work gathered around the public pump with buckets and baskets of laundry. The cab stopped for a flock of geese and again for a flock of sheep and again for a flock of ragged, shouting children chasing a stray cat.

Clusters of men and boys idled at the corners and in the doorways. They watched the geese and the sheep and the children and their cab with the same thoughtful speculation. It reminded her of the buyers in the market, weighing up the quality of the goods in front of them.

A moment later, Alice was struck by the most unusual feeling—that she was very glad she'd decided to bring George with her.

The cab rolled to a halt, and the driver climbed down to

open the door. "Here'll have to be good enough," he told them.

"All right." George fished the fee out of his waistcoat pocket and added an extra coin. "You'll wait for us?"

While they haggled over the cost of the driver's patience, Alice noted the flock of children had left off tormenting the stray and now watched her and George warily from the other side of the street. The sight of a cab and of coins was evidently much more interesting than a cat.

Alice beckoned to one of the girls. The child hung back for a moment, but a series of sharp pokes by her cohort sent her slowly forward.

"Can you help me?" Alice asked. "I'm looking for Judith Faller." This was a guess, but it was based on what Rosalind believed, and Rosalind's beliefs were usually very sound. She held up a penny. "That's for the answer, and there's another if you'll take me to her."

The penny disappeared so fast, she barely saw the girl's hand move. The child took off at a run, with the entire gang behind her. Alice had to hike her skirts and run herself to keep up. At the sight of her ankles, the idling men whistled and cheered, which she ignored. George cursed and called her name. She ignored him, too, trusting he would eventually catch up.

The children tore down a narrow alley, out across a yard, and down another alley. Alice's imagination was constructing monastery dungeons and sinister doorways and reflecting that no one ever mentioned the *smell* of such confined spaces.

Another yard opened in front of them. The girl and her gang skidded to a ragged halt. The girl, barely out of breath, Alice noted, pointed at one particular house edging the dingy, dusty yard.

"Upstairs. In back," she said. She also held out her hand.

So, Rosalind had been right, yet again. Alice dropped the

promised penny into it. The rest of the children surged forward, hands out, voices begging. But George was ready for them. He held up his cupped hands and tossed out a shower of coppers. The children cheered and scrambled after the coins. George took Alice's arm, and they walked together to the house the girl had pointed out.

There was no bell or knocker, and when George rapped his knuckles against the unpainted wood, the door simply gave a groan and swung back for them.

Alice looked up at George. George looked down at Alice. He also took a firmer grip on the walking stick he'd brought with him.

"I'll go first," he said.

"No, I will," said Alice. "I'm less likely to scare her."

George looked skeptical at this, but he did step aside.

The stairs were as narrow and dingy as the door and creaked as loudly. It was utterly airless in the stairway and hot as an oven. Alice needed no narration from her well-honed imagination to supply the prickle of the hairs on her arms and under her bonnet.

In fact, she had to ruthlessly suppress the grim fancies trying to crowd in against rational thought. She did, however, quicken her steps.

I am not afraid. I am not alone, she told herself. *We will find the Fallers, and we will learn just what they have to do with this business. And maybe, maybe, that they have the certificate with them . . .*

The corridor was burning hot, airless, and dark as a winter's evening. Alice found herself wishing she and George had brought a lantern as well as a stick and pockets full of coins. She muttered several of her favorite curses under her breath as she felt her way forward.

As her eyes adjusted, Alice could see that the door at the end of the hallway was slightly ajar. Alice looked behind

THE MATTER OF THE SECRET BRIDE   359

them. So did George. There was no one. She listened and heard nothing.

"Something's wrong," whispered George.

Alice nodded. Despite all her determination and bravado, there was something here. It hung in the suffocating atmosphere—not so much as a scent, but as a kind of metallic taste that grated hard against the back of her throat.

Memory rose up from the depths of her bones, and she knew.

"Oh my Lord," she breathed. "Oh dear God in Heaven, George—"

Her hand was reaching out; she couldn't stop it. Fingertips touched the door, and the door drifted open just a little farther. The gray light from the single window trickled out at their feet.

Alice looked into the dingy rooms and saw the man in scarlet livery lying sprawled on the floor.

A memory overcame her in one great roaring flood, of opening the door to her father's apartments, of seeing him in his chair by the fire, the hunting rifle, and the red ruin around him.

Alice screamed. She couldn't help it. George wrapped his arms tight around her and pulled her away. She heard the door slam as he kicked it shut.

"It's all right," he whispered. "It's all right, Alice."

But it wasn't. Because she couldn't move. Because she couldn't stop the tears rolling down her cheeks, couldn't breathe properly, couldn't hold herself upright.

For the first time in her life, Alice Littlefield sagged into a dead faint.

CHAPTER FORTY-NINE

In the Queen's Defense

"The Princess of Wales speaks highly of Mrs. Fitzherbert. She always says, 'that is the Prince's true wife; she is an excellent woman.'"

Bury, Charlotte, *The Diary of a Lady-in-Waiting*

Henry Brougham was a youthful, handsome man, Rosalind reflected as the man leading the queen's counsel entered her parlor. He had a long face and a cheerful, open gaze. His dark hair swept back from a high, pale forehead. He wore his perfectly tailored coat, elaborate neckcloth, and close-cut breeches with an air of perfect comfort. His bow to her was compact and respectful.

"I am delighted to meet you, Mr. Brougham," said Rosalind as they were both seated. "Will you have some tea? Do you take milk or sugar?"

"Just a little sugar, if you please. And I am delighted to finally meet you," he replied. "My good friend Lady Jersey is full of tales of the astonishing and useful Miss Thorne."

"Complimentary, I trust," said Rosalind as she handed across the cup.

"Oh, you know Lady Jersey's style." Mr. Brougham leaned back, quite casual and relaxed. "One day she sings your praises, the next day she is appalled by some small matter, and the next it is forgotten, and everything is right as rain."

This did not comport with the Lady Jersey Rosalind knew. She could certainly be capricious, but she had a long memory, especially for small grudges. She was known to strike whole families off the visiting list for Almack's for the tiniest of slights.

This, however, was not an observation Rosalind could make to Mr. Brougham. The parliamentarian, however, did not lack for subjects of conversation. He chatted amiably about the lovely summer weather and the latest performance of Shakespeare at the King's Theatre. He added a few words of praise for Alice's novel, which were such to suggest he might have actually read at least some of it.

This very polite, very small talk lasted for exactly as long as it took Mr. Brougham to drain his teacup.

"Now, Miss Thorne, I suppose you are wondering why I have come to call on you when any truly polite gentleman would have waited at least until the morrow."

"I admit, I had wondered," she replied blandly.

"I am here, Miss Thorne, because rumors have reached Her Majesty that a certain document has gone missing. One that interests Her Majesty very much."

Rosalind felt her hands grow cold. Not trusting herself to speak, she merely arched her brows.

"May I speak plainly, Miss Thorne?" he asked.

"I would much prefer it, Mr. Brougham."

He leaned forward, resting his elbows on his knees. "Mrs. Fitzherbert's marriage certificate has left her hands, and it is in circulation. This is the reason for your visit to that lady's household."

"May I inquire as to the source of these rumors?" Had

Countess Lieven carried out her threat? Or was there another source? Someone in Mrs. Fitzherbert's orbit? Or had Mrs. Poole spoken to some old acquaintance?

Or had Ron Ranking put two and two together? But if that was the case, surely, they all would have seen it in the papers this morning.

But Mr. Brougham clearly had no intention of satisfying her curiosity. "Who knows how these things start? But the word is out now, and we must deal with the matter."

Had that word reached Mrs. Fitzherbert yet? What was she saying in response?

There was no way to know, because she was stuck here, with this man, chatting pleasantly, as she had been all day, while Adam chased down the phantom of George Dawson, and Alice was . . . Where on earth was Alice?

Rosalind pushed her fear down and returned her focus to the man in front of her.

"May I ask, Mr. Brougham, are you here on Her Majesty's behalf, or are you acting for yourself alone?"

The question clearly stung, as she had meant it to. "Everything I do is on my country's behalf, Miss Thorne," he said frostily. "We are a nation of laws, which must be obeyed even by the king. If he will not follow the law, then he will answer to it."

He meant it. Rosalind was sure of that. He was perfectly prepared to bring the king to book, to use Adam's expression. What was more, he wanted to do it. But whether that was for the sake of the laws of England or for the uplifting of Henry Brougham, Rosalind found she could not tell.

"Well, then, surely, you can ill afford to be distracted by a simple rumor at such a delicate time," she said.

Mr. Brougham leaned a little closer and beamed. Rosalind could imagine herself as a young woman becoming quite flustered by his proximity.

"Miss Thorne," he said softly. "I suspect it is not rumors but you who are attempting to distract me."

Having delivered this statement, he sat back, regarding her as if she were a particularly complex puzzle to be solved. Rosalind let him look. She did not fuss or fidget; she would not give him any opening. She could not.

"Miss Thorne, will you tell me, as a representative of Parliament who is currently engaged on a question of national import, why Mrs. Fitzherbert has asked for your help?"

Rosalind remained silent.

"You decline to answer," said Mr. Brougham. "Which is as I would expect from a lady who is much in others' confidence. Very well. If an appeal to your patriotism will not move you, let us set aside the crowns and coronets and truly consider who we are dealing with. We are dealing with a woman who has been wronged. Her marriage has been a sham from the beginning. You have heard the story of the royal wedding night?"

He did not wait for an answer. "The prince, our king, was so drunk that he had to be held up through the entire ceremony, and then when he did stagger into the bedchamber, he fell, insensible, on the hearth, where his wedded wife was obliged to leave him. She has received nothing but scorn and indifference from him while he publicly flaunts his mistresses, and now it is he who dares to make her supposed infidelities public and sue for a divorce against her. Is that right, Miss Thorne? Is that just?"

Rosalind kept her breathing even and her mouth closed. Mr. Brougham was a fascinating orator, and he clearly understood his audience. He did not shout. His voice was at all times low and intense. He spoke as if she were not just the only woman in the room but the only woman in the world, and all his hopes hung upon her next decision.

She could not afford to be hasty, and she could most certainly not afford to be fascinated. Mr. Brougham's presence was a stark reminder of how far she had strayed from her normal circles—the parlors and drawing rooms of London's hostesses, and their personal matters. Part of her wanted to shout that she did not belong here, that questions of Crown and country had nothing to do with her and never could.

But even as Mr. Brougham gathered himself for what he surely intended to be his closing argument, Rosalind heard the sound of the front door slamming open. A moment later, she heard George's urgent voice and Alice's painful gasp.

Rosalind was on her feet and racing for the parlor door. She did not excuse herself or even acknowledge there was still a visitor with her. She just ran into the foyer and saw George and Mortimer supporting a fainting Alice toward the stairs.

"Good Lord, Alice!" she cried. "George, what happened?"

"Faller is dead," said George. "And Alice found him."

CHAPTER FIFTY

In a State of Collapse

*"What a pity it is when truth is not accompanied
by any charms!"*

Bury, Charlotte, *The Diary of a Lady-in-Waiting*

It was perhaps a contradiction, but it was in times of immediate crisis that Rosalind frequently found her mind to be
sharpest.

"Get her into bed," she said to George. She turned and
found Mortimer had already summoned Laurel and they both
stood in the doorway. "We need brandy immediately," she told
them.

"Right then." Mortimer vanished into the corridor.

"I'm all right," gasped Alice as they eased her down onto
her bed. "I'm all right."

"You're not," replied Rosalind. "Laurel, bring Mrs. Napier to help, and send down to Mrs. Singh for tea and a hot
water bottle."

"At once, miss." She also vanished.

"I'm sorry," Alice croaked. "I'm sorry. I can't . . . I tried . . ."

"Shhh, sister dear," murmured George as he pulled off her

shoes. "You did everything you needed to. It's all right now. It is." He pulled the counterpane over her.

"You must think . . ."

"I think you are my best friend and twenty times as brave as anyone else I know." Rosalind laid a hand on her forehead. Despite the heat of the day, she was ice cold. "Send for whatever she needs, George. I'll be back in a moment."

George nodded, and Rosalind took herself back down to the parlor. Mr. Brougham stood in front of the fireplace. He was pretending not to read the invitations on the mantel. Rosalind felt a stab of anger at having to pull her hostess's mask on to deal with this man at this moment, with Alice upstairs, pale and shaking, and Tom Faller dead.

A second man dead. And Judith and the certificate . . . where?

Rosalind forced her features into the acceptable expression of placid calm.

"I do beg your pardon, Mr. Brougham," she said. "But a matter has arisen which I find I must attend to."

He wanted to know what it was. His curiosity thrummed through the air between them. She held his gaze, letting her demeanor inform him that she would say nothing. He would have to ask and, by asking, would reveal himself to be entirely discourteous.

It occurred to Rosalind that she could simply tell him the truth—that the certificate had been stolen and that two men connected to the theft were dead. He was not only a representative of the queen but also a representative of the government. If she told him what she knew and referred him to Sir David, her part in this could be done. She would be absolved of responsibility, and he, and others, would take over.

It is wounded pride that holds me back, that is all. I want to be the one to solve this problem.

Except, of course, that wasn't all. Whatever she said now would be repeated and enlarged upon. In a matter of days, the whole of London would know not only that the king's marriage certificate was real, but also that the king's *marriage* was real.

Mrs. Fitzherbert would be dragged into the unforgiving light of public judgment, along with her daughters. The king, the government, it would all topple. It might fall. This was not exaggeration. It was the truth.

But it was Mrs. Fitzherbert's face that was clearest in front of her mind's eye. She had asked for Rosalind's help to protect her girls, to help them walk freely into a future unencumbered by her past mistakes. That was what was at stake here.

So, Rosalind faced Mr. Brougham with her back straight and her demeanor calm. He met her gaze, and she knew he wanted to quiz her. More, he wanted to barge up the stairs and find out who had come in and what had happened. And all Rosalind had to hold him back was the strength of propriety.

It was enough. Mr. Brougham bowed. "Thank you for receiving me, Miss Thorne. I hope I may call again to continue our conversation?"

"You will find me at home Tuesdays and Thursdays."

Mr. Brougham accepted the dismissal and took his leave. Rosalind stood where she was until she heard Mortimer close the front door. Then she grabbed her hems and flew up the stairs.

Outside Alice's door, she met Mrs. Napier with a tray of tea and oatcakes. "I'll take that in. Thank you." She took the tray from the housekeeper's hands and backed through the doorway into Alice's room.

Alice was sitting up, huddled against George, who had wrapped one arm around her shoulders. She clutched the empty brandy glass in one hand and her brother's hand with the other.

Rosalind set the tray down on the bedside table. She took

the brandy glass from Alice's clenched fingers and replaced it with a cup of tea.

Then she sat on the edge of the bed. "Tell me what happened."

Alice bowed her head. It broke Rosalind's heart to see her so ashamed.

George answered for them both. "You were right," he said. "Judith is Judith Faller. Mrs. Percivale gave us an address in Camden Town. We drove out and . . ." He swallowed. His color was nearly as bad as Alice's, and Rosalind had the distinct feeling that he was able to hold on to his outward calm only because he would not break down while his sister needed him.

Rosalind poured out a second brandy and gave it to him. George sipped, and then he gulped.

"Thanks," he said. "We found . . . well, Alice found Tom Faller dead in Judith's room. We sent for Sir David right away, but Camden's not his jurisdiction, it seems, and there was a muddle, and I had to get Alice out of there."

"Does Adam know about this?" asked Rosalind.

"I don't know," said George. "I don't even know where he is. Do you?"

"At the Pooles', I think. I don't know." Frustration washed over Rosalind. "I've been trapped here all day."

George faced her, his manner grim. "Rosalind, you have to believe I wouldn't do this if it wasn't absolutely necessary. I have to get to the *Chronicle*. If I don't get this into the paper and framed right . . . Ranking may already know, Rosalind. He could have followed us today, and as soon as he finds out who Faller is, he'll play up the connection to you and Mrs. Fitzherbert. We have to try to get the story out before he does."

"Go," she told him. "I'll take care of Alice."

"Alice can take care of herself, thank you," croaked Alice. But her voice shook.

Still, the defiance was good to hear. It meant she had begun to recover.

"George, on your way, stop at the Pooles'." Rosalind gave him the direction. "Adam may still be there, but if he is not, send to the White Swan as soon as you are able. Mr. Tauton may know where to find him."

"I will." George pressed Rosalind's hands and bolted out the door.

Rosalind turned back to Alice. "Here." She handed her friend an oatcake. "You need something in you beside brandy and tea."

Alice looked like she wanted to dispute the matter, but she took note of Rosalind's set expression and evidently decided it was not worth it. She accepted the cake and nibbled. It must have tasted good, because nibbles turned to full, enthusiastic bites, and soon the cake was gone.

Rosalind handed her another.

"Thank goodness for Mrs. Singh," Alice said. "How did we manage without her all this time?"

"I have no idea," answered Rosalind. "I mean to raise her wages at the quarter day. After today, I'm sure I'll have numerous ladies attempting to lure her away from us."

Alice munched on her new cake and drank her tea. "I find I do not like the sight of blood very much."

"Few people do," replied Rosalind.

"I thought he'd been shot," she remarked. "But it seems not. It seems he was beaten."

Rosalind, who had seen the results of a man beaten to death before, felt her stomach turn over. "I'm so sorry, Alice."

They sat in silence for a moment.

"Who was that downstairs? The time for calls should have been over before we got here."

Trust Alice to have noticed, even as she was collapsed from shock.

"That," said Rosalind, "was Mr. Henry Brougham."

Alice straightened up, and just like that, she was herself again.

"Brougham! The queen's attorney! What was he doing here?"

"It seems that despite best effort, the story has escaped us. Someone has spread the rumor that Mrs. Fitzherbert's certificate is abroad in the world."

"Oh, Lord. Oh, Rosalind. Ranking . . ."

"May be the least of our worries," said Rosalind. "Lady Jersey knows."

Alice pressed her hand against her mouth. "That means everybody knows."

"Or will soon. And they know that I've been consulted by Mrs. Fitzherbert." And Countess Lieven was prepared to give them all a titillating reason why.

"Rosalind, you need to tell Mrs. Fitzherbert and, oh, Lord, Amelia . . ."

"I can't . . ."

"If you say you can't leave me, I shall be very annoyed with you." Alice scrambled out of the bed and stood perfectly steady, all her color returned to her cheeks and all the strength to her voice. "I'll stay here in case Adam, or anyone else, comes. You go."

Rosalind wanted to ask if she was sure. She wanted to insist that Alice was more important than anything else. But Alice tilted her head and glared down her nose at Rosalind. It was a gesture she had known since they'd met at school, and Rosalind's heart squeezed with a combination of pride, admiration, and fear.

She hurried back downstairs and sent Mortimer for a cab, Claire for her things, and Mrs. Napier with instructions to tell Mrs. Singh to assemble a cold collation for whoever might come to the house that evening.

Within minutes, Rosalind had climbed into a hired cab

and was speeding on her way to Mrs. Fitzherbert's, trying to formulate some kind of plan for what she would say.

Thomas Faller was dead. Josiah Poole was dead. Poole had been commissioned to acquire the certificate. Faller might well have helped, either for the sake of the payment or for the sake of his wife, who was employed in Poole's household.

But were they killed to get the certificate from them or to silence them so they could not say what had become of it? And if the certificate was not in the hands of the king and his allies, and it was not with the queen and her allies or with the papers or with the Pooles, where on earth was it? Rosalind had a sudden vision of the piece of paper sitting on a dust-heap in a dark alley while all the world surged around looking for the thing that was lying there in plain sight.

And this includes me.

CHAPTER FIFTY-ONE

Two Lies and a Truth

*"I know you dare not, you must not speak
to me."*

Bury, Charlotte, *The Diary of a Lady-in-Waiting*

When Adam reached the Pooles' house and asked for William Considen, he was not taken to the library. Instead, he was shown upstairs to the family rooms and a sunny, well-aired apartment with dark paneling and sturdy furnishings. William Considen was on his feet and gripping the edge of a round table to help hold himself upright.

"So. You've come for me now." The words fell from him, heavy and rough.

"I am here to ask if you will speak to me about your brother-in-law's murder," said Adam.

Considen gave a snort, which turned into a cough. He pressed a handkerchief against his mouth. When he pulled it away, Adam saw specks of red on the white muslin.

"Sit," said Considen curtly as he lowered himself into a round-backed chair. "What do you want to know?"

"Where he was the morning he died."

"We've told you, he wasn't home. He spent the night at the White Swan."

Adam said nothing.

"Are you calling me a liar, sir?" Considen demanded. "Are you calling my sister a liar?"

Adam said nothing.

Considen curled his fingers around his handkerchief. There was blood on his lip, Adam noted, and specks on the table. Whatever ailed him, it was squeezing him more tightly now. And yet something was missing. He was sure of it.

"Will you tell me about that morning?" Adam asked.

"No, I will not," Considen growled.

"Very well." Adam bowed. "I thank you for your time." He turned to leave.

He was almost to the door when the other man spoke. "Wait."

Adam turned.

"Sit down." Considen was wiping his hands with the kerchief now and dabbing at his mouth. "Please."

Adam did as requested.

"I don't remember what it is to be healthy, you know," Considen told him. "Not really. I've been ill for so long. But once, I was as good a man as any." He held up his hand to show Adam the scars. "I held my own in a race or a fight. Whatever was called for.

"When Melora eloped, I argued with our parents that they should forgive her and should welcome her husband. I tried to remind them his only crime was being born without family. But they refused to listen, and I thought I had done all I could. I had a future of my own to attend to. I had been hired by a manufactory in Manchester and was learning the business of wool trading. I was set to be rich. And then it all fell apart."

Adam waited.

"The manufactory failed, and I was forced to come home and stay there. Invalid. Infantilized. Stowed in a back room, my father barely able to look at me. When Melora came home, we clung together, for the sake of her broken heart and my broken life. She swore she'd find us a way out. And she did."

"Poole?"

Considen nodded. "I was part of the bargain—my bed and board, my endless doctors. Trips to Switzerland in the summer for the pure air and yet more doctors. She stayed with him and did everything he asked, and tried her best to get him received into society on a sound footing. But none of it was enough. She knows how the world works. She must have known it would fall apart eventually. Who was she, after all? A disgraced daughter of a failed family who had sold herself to a universally detested man." He shook his head. "But she kept on. She said she would not let either of us fall into poverty again."

Adam waited.

"All this is to say, yes, she lied about where Poole was that morning, and I lied to help her, and Letitia lied because . . . Well, I don't know. I choose to believe it's because she likes Melora, at least a little. Melly certainly tried to be a friend to the girl and help her be what her father wanted while holding on to some part of herself . . ." His hand tightened around the bloody kerchief again.

"But we all did it because we knew that no matter what happened, it would not look good for Melly to have a second husband dead on the doorstep."

There are better lies you could have told, thought Adam. But he remained silent. It was plain Considen was lonely as well as grieving. He wished to talk, and Adam was content to let him.

"I told Melly it would not really delay any inquiries. We

quarreled over it. She reminded me of how long she had cared for me, and begged me not to ruin all her hard work. The care of me and Letitia and the children was all she had, she said. Her only proof that the world had not beaten her."

"Will you tell me what happened that morning?"

Considen stared down at his hands for a long moment. What was missing? Adam let his gaze wander, looking for the thing out of place.

"Poole came home that night and ate a hearty supper," Considen said. "He was in an excellent mood. He even joked with me that I might this time be sent away to Switzerland for good." He snorted, then coughed.

"His sense of humor had an edge to it," Adam remarked.

"Oh, yes. And a sharp one," Considen agreed. "He quizzed Melora about the progress of the plans for Letitia's wedding. Said she must make sure everything was the absolute best. She warned him the bills were mounting, and he told her not to worry. It was all taken care of."

So she knew they were spending beyond their means, and so did he.

"I wasn't able to sit at the table any longer than that. I went . . . I was taken to bed. I slept some and then woke in the small hours, as I frequently do, and I went downstairs. I spend so much time shut up in one room." He glanced about him. "Sometimes I can no longer bear it. It was perhaps five o'clock. The dawn was just beginning. Poole bounced down the stairs, bustled out the door without sparing me a word, and was gone. We never saw him again." He dragged in a deep, ragged breath. "That, Mr. Harkness, is what happened that morning."

"Did you wake a servant to bring you downstairs?" Adam asked him.

"No. I still have that much life in me, especially after a rest."

"And how did Mrs. Poole spend the rest of her morning?"

"She and Letitia spent it closeted with a modiste, to order her wedding clothes. I was in here, for the most part, until you arrived."

"What of the maid, Judith?"

"I'm sorry?"

"Judith. The chambermaid. She was most devoted to Mr. Poole, I believe. Do you know where she was that morning?"

"You can't suspect that slip of a girl of having anything to do . . . Do you think he was . . . God! What a mind you must have!"

Considen was not the first man to make that observation. Before Adam could say as much, the door opened, and Lizzie, white faced and uncertain, appeared on the threshold.

"If you please." She bobbed her curtsy. "A gentleman downstairs for Mr. Harkness."

Considen frowned. So did Adam, but he got to his feet, and his host waved him away.

Inwardly, Adam cursed the interruption. Considen would send for his sister at once, he would tell her the whole of their conversation, and she would . . .

She would plan. She would decide. She would insist on what was to be said.

But then he looked past Lizzie, down the stairs, and into the foyer and saw who was standing there, and every other thought left his mind.

Because it was George Littlefield, looking as sick and grim as if the world had come to an end.

CHAPTER FIFTY-TWO

Capitulation

*"Want, sir, want? What's the matter with me? Sir,
I want a result."*

Bury, Charlotte, *The Diary of a Lady-in-Waiting*

The portly footman at the door took Rosalind to Mrs. Fitzherbert at once. The widow was in her private apartments, seated at her writing table by a high arching window. Several sealed letters lay beside her.

"Miss Thorne!" Mrs. Fitzherbert cried as she started to her feet. "What have you found?"

The desk from which the strongbox had been stolen waited, unused, in its corner. Rosalind felt painfully aware of its presence as she approached her hostess.

"Mrs. Fitzherbert," she said, "I am here with very bad news."

Mrs. Fitzherbert's breath grew unsteady, but she rallied herself. "What is it?"

"Your footman, Thomas Faller, is dead."

"Faller? Good Lord!" she cried. "Holm told me he had gone missing. I did not truly think . . . Was it an accident?"

These last words contained just a trace of pathetic hope, and Rosalind sympathized.

"I am sorry to say that it was not. He was found in a set of rooms in Camden Town that belongs to a Judith Faller. We believe she was his wife."

Mrs. Fitzherbert closed her eyes. Her hand moved. Rosalind was sure she meant to cross herself, but a strong habit of discretion restrained her.

"Camden Town is a very poor place, I believe," she remarked.

"I believe that is correct."

"So, it could simply have been robbery?" There was both hope and shame in the words.

"I do not believe that is true," Rosalind said. "His wife was a maid in Josiah Poole's house. She was dismissed from service today and has since vanished."

"And Mr. Poole, he is the man you suspect of being involved in the theft of my certificate?"

"Yes."

"So, he may have suborned the cooperation of my footman. Is that what you are saying?"

"Yes. And now—"

"Now they are both dead."

Mrs. Fitzherbert sat down. She moved with great care, reminding Rosalind of Mr. Considen, who could no longer trust his body to fully obey him. She picked up her letters and sorted through them as if to see that they were all still there. She laid them back down, but her gaze remained fixed on her writing table.

"And my cer-certificate?" Mrs. Fitzherbert stumbled over the word. "I fear I must sound so petty."

"There is nothing petty about your situation," said Rosalind. "I am sorry to say it has not been found."

Mrs. Fitzherbert's hand trembled where it lay on the table.

Rosalind wondered what was going on inside her—how much anger, how much fear. She wanted to offer some reassurance, but there was so little she could give.

"Mr. Harkness is interviewing the Pooles today," she said. "It may be he will uncover additional information."

Mrs. Fitzherbert took a deep breath. "I suppose that is possible, but at this point, it does not matter. I had already made up my mind to a course of action last night." She touched the letters. "And now I am very glad of it."

"Mrs. Fitzherbert—" Rosalind began.

But Mrs. Fitzherbert cut her off. "I said that I have made up my mind, Miss Thorne. Circumstances have galloped ahead, and we are left behind to manage as best we can."

Rosalind's breath froze in her throat.

"Tomorrow morning Minney and Mary Ann return to my brother's house in the country. From there, they will all remove to his new posting at the embassy in Berlin. I shall travel separately to Paris as soon as I can settle my affairs here." She straightened her shoulders. "And there I shall stay."

She was retreating to exile. She had given up.

"Mrs. Fitzherbert," Rosalind tried. "It has been only two days, and—"

"Only two days and yet two men are dead," said Mrs. Fitzherbert, interrupting. "My affairs are in the papers, and my daughter has yet again begun seeing a young man who will do nothing but take her money and break her heart, and my paper, my one protection against slander and libel, is gone. No, Miss Thorne," she said firmly, "I should have left as soon as I discovered I had been robbed. I was a fool to believe that anyone could prevent . . . well, prevent this outcome." Slowly, she climbed to her feet and rang the bell. "I admit my defeat. You have failed, and so have I. You may take your girl and go. We are all of us finished here."

The door opened, and Amelia entered. She saw Rosalind there with Mrs. Fitzherbert, and for one brief instant, her eyes lit up. She was plainly thinking that they must have achieved a victory.

Then she saw Rosalind's face clearly, and that light snuffed itself out.

Rosalind drew herself up. "I would suggest, Mrs. Fitzherbert, that you at least allow it to appear that Amelia has been called away by some emergency. Otherwise, there will surely be an even greater disruption among your staff."

Mrs. Fitzherbert gave one sharp, mirthless laugh. "Disruption among my staff, Miss Thorne, is the least of my worries. Now, you will both do me the favor of leaving at once. McGowan, I will have your things sent to you."

"I am sorry, madam," said Amelia. "I had hoped to do better. You must understand—"

"I understand," she said bitterly. "That I and my family are under threat, and that I used up all my good choices years ago. I am done with trusting the promises of others. You will do me the favor of leaving me to deal with the consequences of my actions."

Amelia looked like she wanted to protest, but all she did was bob her curtsy. "I'll go get my reticule."

"Miss Thorne will meet you downstairs," said Mrs. Fitzherbert.

It was an absolute dismissal. Rosalind had no choice but to make her own curtsy and descend the stairs. She did so slowly, as if in a dream. Her mind would not move. All her thoughts felt pressed down, as if she were filled with stones. Amelia came down the stairs behind her, with her bonnet, gloves, and reticule. Together, silently, they walked out the door.

The heat of summer enveloped them, along with all the street noises. Rosalind blinked in the sunlight. Slowly, her mind stirred. She drew a deep breath and another. She turned to see Amelia glowering back at the house and looking as if she wanted to curse or spit.

"'Scuse me, miss." A man in a battered hat and equally battered coat had stepped up to them. "Anything I can do to help?"

Amelia shook herself. "This is Jim Geery, Miss Thorne. He's all right. Find us a cab, would you, Jim? We've been pitched out."

Jim started backward but recovered and touched his hat. "Right you are, miss," he said and strode off up the street.

"Thank you, Amelia," said Rosalind.

Amelia sniffed. "You're welcome. But what brought all that on?"

"Tom Faller is dead," Rosalind said.

"What!" cried Amelia. "No! How . . . ?"

Rosalind told her.

"God in Heaven." Amelia pressed both hands against her stomach. "I knew he was up to something, but I never—" She stopped. "You said Alice found him?"

Rosalind nodded.

"Oh, no." Amelia went white. "Is she all right?"

"She'll be better when you get home to her."

Amelia nodded and swallowed hard. "What do we do now?"

Excellent question. Unfortunately, Rosalind did not have a real answer. "We hope that Mr. Harkness has been able to find out something useful."

"Well, all I have to say is, she doesn't know it yet, but she's going to regret treating you this way, and me."

"Why is that?" asked Rosalind.

Amelia looked uncomfortable. "You heard in there," she said, sounding unusually evasive. "I *tried* to tell her, but she wasn't having none of it. So, whatever comes next, it's not my fault."

"Amelia." Rosalind tried to be patient, but it was difficult. "What's happened?"

"I played chaperone and decoy for Miss Mary Ann today," said Amelia. "She wanted to sneak a message to this famous captain Dawson, who's been hanging about. Seems him and Miss Seymore are set to elope."

CHAPTER FIFTY-THREE

Checkmate

*"Who can say where discontent may end, once it
has lifted up its hydra head?"*

Bury, Charlotte, *The Diary of a Lady-in-Waiting*

Adam was down the stairs and standing beside George
without feeling himself move. "What's happened? Is
Alice—"

"She and Rosalind are fine," said George immediately.
"But Tom Faller is dead."

Adam went utterly still. "Let's go outside," he said.

George nodded. They left the house and walked down the
path, so they stood outside the area railing.

"Tell me," said Adam.

Adam listened, unmoving, indeed barely breathing, as
George told him about finding Faller beaten to death in the
rooms belonging to Judith Faller.

"I wasn't . . ." George swallowed. "I tried to look around,
but I couldn't do much. Alice, she was collapsed . . ."

Alice, Adam remembered, had been the one to find their
father's body after he killed himself. It was no wonder she

should fall into shock upon seeing the aftermath of another man's brutal death.

"It looked to me like Judith had gathered up her things and scarpered," George was telling him. "And, no, in case you were wondering, I didn't see any sign of Mrs. Fitzherbert's wayward scrap of paper."

Adam nodded and put a hand on George's shoulder. "How are you doing?"

"Badly," George confessed. "I'll be a right mess by the time I get home to Hannah, but as it stands, I've got to get to the newspaper. Ranking . . . Ranking may already have put the pieces together."

"Go on, then," Adam told him. "I'll finish here and get back to Orchard Street as quickly as I can."

George pressed Adam's shoulder briefly and strode away up the street. Adam watched until he had vanished around the corner. Then he turned and faced the house again. Adam knew that the Pooles had already spoken to each other inside. They would have coordinated their stories, probably under Mrs. Poole's direction, and she would be there to make sure no one spoke out of turn.

But all the same, he had to try. It could be instructive to watch how people chose to fight. They picked what they thought was the strongest ground and marshaled their cleverest arguments. But if you were patient, you could notice what they did not say, and map out the subjects they so carefully avoided.

And not all fronts would remain united.

Adam walked back into the house. Lizzie was in the foyer. "I'm told to bring you to the library if you should come back."

He nodded, indicating his willingness to be led.

The library, it seemed, had been chosen because it could hold all the Pooles together. Considen sat in his accustomed chair, with Mrs. Poole standing beside him. Letitia sat in a small chair in the corner, looking very much like she wished she could fade into the woodwork and never emerge again.

"I am glad to see you, Mrs. Poole," said Adam, and her expression told him she was sure that was a lie. "I need to ask if your maid Judith has returned here today."

Her brow furrowed. That was not a question she had been expecting. "No, certainly not. Why would she?"

"Because I have just received word that her husband, Tom Faller, has been killed."

"Husband?" exclaimed Mrs. Poole. "What husband? Judith had no husband."

To everyone's surprise, it was Letitia who spoke next. "Yes, she did."

Mrs. Poole turned to her stepdaughter with a look that would have given a grown man pause. "You never said so before."

"There was no reason to say anything," replied Letitia. "I didn't want to get her in trouble." She turned toward Adam. "I saw them together, and I asked her about it. At first, she tried to tell me he was her brother, but when I pressed her, she begged me not to tell you, because she would be dismissed."

"When did you last see them together?"

Letitia hesitated. Adam waited.

"Letitia?" said Mrs. Poole. "You've begun this. What more have you to say?"

Adam willed the girl to remain strong, but even as he watched, she began to wane and shrink. Letitia's gaze slipped to her stepmother, and it was clear she was looking for permission. He did not see Mrs. Poole nod, but she must have given some signal.

So. He had guessed correctly. Mrs. Poole had taken charge. There would be no more private conversations, and no more confessions to gain sympathy. What was spoken here would come from her.

Or in spite of her.

Considen remained silent, his attention fixed on the ash-filled hearth. The incongruity prickled across Adam's awareness. It was the heart of August. Why had there been such a fire in this close, still room? Was it for the comfort of the invalid?

"Was there anything else, Mr. Harkness?" prompted Mrs. Poole.

Adam drew his attention back and faced Letitia squarely. "A man in a scarlet coat was seen leaving the house yesterday."

"I already told Miss Thorne," said Mrs. Poole. "That was Captain Dawson."

"Mrs. Fitzherbert's servants wear a scarlet livery," said Adam, still looking at Letitia. "Did Thomas Faller come here? Did he speak with Judith?"

Letitia looked to her stepmother and then shook her head. Which was answer enough. He faced Mrs. Poole again.

"Does Judith have family that you know of?" asked Adam. "Or does Mr. Faller?"

"I suppose it is a failing as an employer, but I do not know and never thought to ask. Letitia?" she said pointedly. "Do you know anything about it?"

"No, I do not," she murmured.

Adam was not surprised at this answer. "Very well. I have one other question."

"Yes?" answered Mrs. Poole.

"Your husband's papers, the ones he kept here in the house. What did you do with them?"

Adam watched her eyes, waiting for her to formulate the lie. But she simply raised her chin.

"I burnt them," she said.

"You burnt them?" he echoed.

"Yes." She pointed to the heap of ash that filled the library hearth. Now that he was made aware, he could hear the soft crackle of the embers buried deep inside.

Whatever had been done here had been done recently. Within the past few hours, perhaps.

"You will forgive me, Mrs. Poole, if I ask why?" he asked. "Those papers could have been very useful to you, in much the same way they were useful to your husband." They could have allowed us to find who killed him.

"Yes, but they would have been more dangerous than useful, as demonstrated by the fact that my husband is dead, and now this Tom Faller is dead, and my life is in tatters, and you will not leave us alone."

"And were the damaging letters you used to coerce your stepdaughter's fiancé burned, as well?"

Letitia whipped around to stare at her stepmother.

"That is a private matter and none of your business," she said. "Now, Letitia. Mr. Harkness asked you a question, I believe. Did you see this Tom Faller with Judith?"

Letitia rallied. He watched the mask fall across her expression, covering over her anger and confusion in a layer of disinterest.

"Tom Faller was here," she said. "He came to see Judith, and they quarreled. I don't know about what, but she threw him out afterward. That is all I know of it."

"If this was the case then, why, Mrs. Poole, did you tell Miss Thorne that it was Captain Dawson who came here that day?"

"Spite," answered Mrs. Poole.

Adam waited.

"Captain Dawson has been here several times since my husband died," she told him. "He has coaxed, demanded, even begged to see Josiah's private papers. He has done everything but bribe the cook to get into the house. I was exhausted and angry and wanted to give him some share of the trouble he was giving me."

"You could have simply told the truth," said Adam.

"What a novel idea," replied Mrs. Poole acidly. "Especially to persons one does not know who might very well accuse one of murdering one's husband."

Adam considered this and the family arrayed in front of him. Considen had told him that Melora Poole needed to prove the world had not beaten her. Now Adam understood how tightly she clung to that need.

He also noted Considen's silence. Since they had first met him, the man had blustered. He had insisted, and he had railed. Alone with Adam, he had spoken freely, had done his best to raise sympathy and understanding for his sister and their circumstance.

Now he sat slumped and exhausted, as if something vital had been removed from him. Had Mrs. Poole said something to him in those moments when Adam was outside the house?

Considen turned his head to look at Adam, and his eyes glittered. "You have your answers, sir," he said.

"I agree," said Mrs. Poole. "We are finished here, Mr. Harkness," she said. "You will leave this house. You have no right to be here, and no warrant you can bring can compel me to allow you into my home. And I tell you, Mr. Harkness, that when I am summoned before the inquest in my husband's death, I will tell the coroner and the jury just exactly what I have told you. My husband was killed by persons unknown, and his papers are burnt." She drew herself up. "As far as I am concerned, the matter is closed."

CHAPTER FIFTY-FOUR

And Yet

*". . . there are days and times that it would be
very inconvenient to have him in society."*

Bury, Charlotte, *The Diary of a Lady-in-Waiting*

As soon as Rosalind and Amelia reached Orchard Street,
Amelia flew up the stairs. Rosalind heard her and Alice's
voices raised in an energetic duet of mutual exclamations and
recriminations. Then a door slammed, and quiet settled over
the house.

Rosalind went into the parlor and sat down in front of the
cold fireplace. The windows had been opened, but there was
no breeze, only additional heat and the occasional noise from
the street.

She tried to compose herself to patience, but her thoughts
would not settle. She needed to be doing . . . something. But
what could she do? Mrs. Fitzherbert had declared, in no uncertain terms, that their association was at an end.

Rosalind had failed her.

Rosalind had failed.

It did not matter that it had been so few days. It did not

matter that the task had been impossible from the beginning. She had promised that she would help, and she had not.

She might even have made matters worse.

At the very beginning of this business, Burrowes had tried to warn Rosalind that it was not her fellow staff members who had perpetrated the theft and betrayal of Mrs. Fitzherbert. She had tried to steer Rosalind toward the young women.

Had Burrowes known Miss Seymore was meeting George Dawson? Had she known that they planned to elope together?

Rosalind closed her eyes and tried again to calm her roiling thoughts. She was so focused that she did not hear the door open or the footsteps on the carpet. But she felt the brush of familiar warmth against her skin, and her eyes flew open.

"Adam."

He took both her hands and drew her to her feet and into his arms. They held on to each other for a very long time.

When at last they parted, Rosalind asked, "What did you learn?"

"A great deal," he said. "But nothing that gets us any closer to our answers."

They sat together, holding hands. She waited, letting him gather his thoughts.

"Faller was beaten to death, as you will have heard. The neighbors heard and saw a great deal, but no two of them agreed on what it was. I have been to Sir David, and he is not best pleased and gives me one more day before he convenes the inquest and, I suspect, reconsiders hiring me as an assistant." His sigh was harsh, and his anger at himself palpable. Rosalind pressed his hands, but he only shook his head. "George found me at the Pooles."

"Where is he now?" asked Rosalind.

"At the newspaper, trying to make sure the story of Tom

Faller's death is framed . . . less sensationally than it might otherwise be."

Rosalind nodded. "Let us hope he succeeds, but I am not sure it can be done." She caught the grim hesitation in Adam's demeanor. "What else?"

"Mrs. Poole lied to you," he said. "The man in the scarlet coat you saw . . . That was not George Dawson. It was Tom Faller."

So. "Did she give a reason for her deception?"

"She said it was because she was angry at Dawson. She says he has been pressing her for a look at her husband's papers."

"Do you believe her?"

"About that much, yes," said Adam. "We know that Dawson was under obligation to Poole. It makes sense that he might try to remove the evidence of it."

And this would explain why his was the name that came so readily to Mrs. Poole's tongue.

"Faller had an argument with Judith," Adam went on. "Or so I was told. And he ran from the house. She left sometime afterward and has not been seen since."

Rosalind thought of Judith—her red eyes and her determination, her habit of touching the particular spot beneath her collar when she thought of her husband. She thought of her loyalty to Mr. Poole, who turned every obligation into profit for himself.

She thought of the story Judith had told her, of Mr. Poole freeing "a man" she knew who was languishing in Newgate. Surely that was Tom Faller who had been imprisoned and released only because of the intercession of a man who had his wife under his thumb and who wanted only to make use of him.

What might a man in such circumstances be driven to try?

"What of the papers kept at the house?" asked Rosalind.

"Mrs. Poole says they have been burnt."

"Do you believe her?"

"I don't know," said Adam. "She was perfectly ready to lie at any moment. Her brother says there is nothing left for her but to protect her family, and that I do believe. And it is clear to me that need is driving her into darkness." He shook his head. "I did see a heap of ashes in the grate. There had been a fire there, and it had been burning within the past few hours." He paused and frowned at his own thoughts. "But I tell you, Rosalind, the whole time I had the feeling I had forgotten something or missed something or simply botched the entire business."

Rosalind pressed his hands again. Adam turned a rueful face to her. "And now have to go rouse the Fitzherbert household. Will you come with me? Mrs. Fitzherbert will need to be questioned, as will the girls. They might be more forthcoming to you."

"I'm afraid they would not," she said. "I've already been sent away from the Fitzherberts', as has Amelia."

"What happened?"

"When I heard about Tom Faller's death, I went to see her. I meant to warn her and to learn what I could. But it seems Mrs. Fitzherbert has had enough." She paused to make sure her voice did not shake. Adam noticed. Of course he noticed. "She dismissed me. She is sending her daughters back to her brother's, and she plans to quit the country for good and all."

"I find I cannot blame her."

"No. However, she may yet be in for an unpleasant surprise. Amelia says Minney Seymore plans to elope."

Adam straightened. "She saw Dawson? He is still in London?"

"I don't know the details yet. Let me go see if . . . she's able to talk."

Rosalind left Adam there and went upstairs to knock on Alice's door. "Amelia? Adam needs to speak with you."

"Yes, of course," came the answer from the other side of the door. "I will be down in just a moment."

Rosalind returned to the parlor. Adam raised his brows. She pointedly ignored him and settled herself by the windows. He joined her there and took her hand again. She held his gratefully.

Amelia and Alice both descended the stairs a few moments later, and if they were slightly flushed and ruffled, it was not enough to be worth mentioning.

"Rosalind says that Minney Seymore plans to elope?" Adam asked. "How did you find out?"

"I saw him," said Amelia. "You know Captain Dawson and Miss Seymore had met in the garden? Well, Mrs. Fitzherbert found out about it, or maybe she just guessed. Anyway, she was determined to keep the young ladies under her eye until they could be sent back to her brother's house. Well, Miss Seymore, she asked me if I could help her get a message to someone, and she gave me two sovereigns for it."

"You never told me that part," said Alice.

"It's gone into the school fund," said Amelia. "Well, it seemed to me, especially with Faller gone, I should play the part, so I agreed. It was plain they'd done this before, those two girls. They had it all worked out. Miss Mary Ann, she complained to her mama that it was too hot and she needed to take the air, and she promised to take me with her. Mrs. Fitzherbert agreed, so long as we were not gone above an hour, and so long as I did not let her out of my sight.

"Quite frankly—and you'll have to forgive me, Alice—it was like something out of a three-volume novel. We walked to the high street and went into the milliner's shop. There was an officer there, scarlet coat and gold braid and all—tall, dark haired, with bright blue eyes. Very handsome and everything you'd want your romantic hero to be. Miss Mary Ann starts into inquiring about a hat, and she drops her bag. The officer, he retrieves it, all polite. She says thank you and makes a great show of checking the bag.

"'Everything is all right,' she says, and he says, 'Seven of the clock.' Then he bows and leaves, and we go back home, and she goes back to her sister, and they close the door on me." She said this last with an air of apology. "It was only a short time after this that Miss Thorne came to tell us that Tom Faller had been killed."

"Oh my Lord!" cried Alice. "We haven't a moment to lose! Rosalind, you must send to Sanderson to ask for the loan of his carriage and his fastest horses. He may want to drive himself, and then . . ."

"We will not need Sanderson's carriage," said Rosalind.

"But surely they're planning to run for Gretna Green!" said Alice, naming the famous spot for clandestine marriages just across the Scottish border. The Scots' marriage laws did not require a license or banns published or any other of the formalities of English church law.

"If Captain Dawson needs to flee the country, he's going to need a quicker and surer exit," said Rosalind. "As soon as Miss Seymore is missed, Mrs. Fitzherbert will guess what's happened, and she will surely have them followed. It is better that they be married quickly and quietly in London and then fly to Dover together. If, that is, he means to take her with him."

"Oh," said Alice, deflated.

"You have given this some thought," remarked Adam.

Rosalind's mouth twitched. "I receive a large number of inquiries from ladies who fear their daughters plan to elope. Some of them actually go through with it. When the young ladies are recovered, I try to hear the details of the plan. It is most instructive."

"I'm certain it is," remarked Adam.

"And, as it happens, a surprising number of London clergy

will marry a couple without asking inconvenient questions or bothering too terribly about technicalities like baans," Rosalind went on. "In fact, there are two churches within a reasonable distance of Tilney Street where an eager young couple can obtain a legal enough license and undergo a ceremony for a relatively affordable sum."

Adam's hand strayed to his coat pocket.

Rosalind frowned. "Is something the matter?"

"Too much to mention just now," he said. "So. From what Amelia tells us, and from the abrupt return of the young women from the country, we can presume this elopement has been planned for some time."

"And it may be that Miss Seymore and Captain Dawson between them planned to steal the certificate to fund their escape, but matters spiraled out of control," said Rosalind.

"Poole could even have convinced them that it was their best chance," added Alice. "And they might have believed it, given the family plans to separate them."

"That's a kind thought," said Amelia. "But what if Dawson decided this was his chance to permanently end his obligations to Poole?"

"Unfortunately, that is a very real possibility," said Adam. "Dawson could have agreed to arrange the theft and then killed Poole and kept the certificate for himself."

"But then why not take the letters?" asked Rosalind. "If Dawson was in the carriage, and he stole Poole's keys so he could get to his rooms, why did he leave the incriminating letters behind?"

"But those letters weren't all that incriminating," said Alice. "I read them. It was the normal stuff of a young man's troubles, except—" She stopped.

"Except for the one that suggests he and Poole meet to discuss his situation," said Adam. "That becomes very important, although he may or may not have thought of it at the time." He paused, considering. "I have felt from the beginning that the scene at the White Swan was a distraction. If Mrs. Poole was telling the truth, and Dawson had been hectoring her, he must have believed Poole was keeping any letters he wanted at his home."

"I wonder," murmured Alice. "If Dawson had been visiting the Pooles, could it be that something he said convinced Mrs. Poole to burn the papers? Could he have threatened her? Or persuaded her somehow?"

"Perhaps he let her know that she might be blamed for Poole's death, and Faller's," suggested Rosalind. "And she took the simplest route out of the difficulty."

"It's possible," said Adam.

"But Miss Minney cannot have been involved in any of this," said Amelia. "They'd all have to have been plotting while she was still in the country."

"But they didn't need her, not for the planning," said Alice. "Dawson would have known that Faller was helping Minney. If Poole had recruited Dawson to get the certificate, Dawson could have gone straight to Faller. He might even have made it sound like the idea was really from Minney, to get Faller to go along with it."

"And Faller drove the carriage?" said Adam.

Rosalind felt the blood drain from her cheeks. Of course, the others noticed.

"What is it?" asked Adam.

"You told us the driver was fully muffled," said Rosalind softly. "Could the driver have been Minney Seymore?" It was fashionable, if slightly scandalous, for a young woman to know how to drive.

"Or could Minney Seymore have been the person inside the carriage?" returned Adam. "Sir David said the blow could have been struck by a woman."

"And," said Rosalind, "could Tom Faller have been killed because he knew and threatened to tell?"

"There's something else," said Alice.

They all turned to her.

"If the plans all failed, Minney Seymore could be brought to testify against Captain Dawson."

Rosalind realized what she meant. "But she cannot be made to testify if she is his wife."

CHAPTER FIFTY-FIVE

An Affair of the Heart

*"I was told at the same time . . . there was reason
to suppose that you were going to take the very
desperate step (pardon the expression) of marrying her . . ."*

Langdale, Charles, *Memoirs of Mrs. Fitzherbert*

The next morning the *London Chronicle* led its special
edition with:

FALLER FATALITY

*Thomas Faller, a young footman, was found
yesterday in Camden Town, seemingly the victim
of a brutal attack in the darkness. Mrs. Fitzherbert,
of Tilney Street, who was the murdered man's employer, says that he had recently left her service and
that she was astonished and saddened to hear of
his untimely death.*

The article went on to lament the prevalence of violent disorder among the poor and suggested that it was the fault of a

government who failed to protect and care for those of the working classes, whose industry undergirded London's comfort and prosperity.

It was, she thought, a valiant effort on George's part. It was also mostly invention. Still, Rosalind hoped it might have some good effect.

The *Morning Standard*, however, declared:

FITZHERBERT FOOTMAN FELLED!

Thomas Faller, a footman in service to Maria Fitzherbert, was found brutally murdered at his home in Camden Town. His wife is missing from the scene. Is this a domestic tragedy, or is it fatally connected with the great matter that has consumed the entire kingdom?

The coroner's office has declared it a matter of person or persons unknown. Perhaps they should consult the famously inquisitive Miss Rosalind Thorne, as Mrs. Fitzherbert has done. . . .

"I would like to say it is not as bad as it could have been," remarked Adam.

"So would I," said Rosalind. "But I don't think I can." Clearly, Ron Ranking's patience had deserted him.

They sat in a two-wheeled rig. Rosalind had hesitated only a little when the stable keeper disclosed the price of hiring both conveyance and horses for the day, but it was necessary. They could not trust themselves to the patience and skill of a hackney cabdriver.

They waited at a spot catty-corner from 6 Tilney Street. Adam perched on the driver's seat, with his hat pulled down against the misting gray drizzle, which threatened to coalesce into a summer fog. Rosalind found herself grateful for it, because it gave them an excuse to keep the rig's roof raised and its curtains down.

The bells had just tolled the hour of six, but the low clouds kept the morning far darker than it should have been. They had already been here for at least two long hours, circling the block every so often to keep the horses exercised, and to draw less attention to themselves as the servants and trades-people came and went in the brightening morning.

Rosalind had brought the papers to bide the time while they kept watch. Now she wondered if they were more dis-traction than was good. Her thoughts would not fix on the street but kept darting back to Orchard Street, as she won-dered if the newspapermen, with Ranking in their lead, had arrived there yet. How soon would they swarm her house? Or Mrs. Fitzherbert's?

What would Lady Jersey say when she woke and saw Rosalind's name linked to Faller's death? What would Count-ess Lieven say?

And Mrs. Levitton?

Adam's voice cut through the worries crowding in on her harried mind. "There she is."

Rosalind looked up. A cloaked figure darted out from be-hind the garden wall and hurried down the street. She had no valise or box with her, and she ran with her skirts hiked up well past her ankles, splashing heedlessly through the gather-ing puddles.

Adam touched up the horse, and they started forward at a gentle pace, following the young woman as she ran.

Miss Seymore, assuming it was her, turned one corner and another. She paused, casting anxiously about. London at first light was a busy world, regardless of the weather. The streets filled with workmen, with men and women pushing hand-carts and barrows and baskets, not to mention the carts and vans and flocks of sheep. The bawling of cattle and the distressed calls of caged geese mixed with the endless stream of human voices.

A bright green phaeton worked its way between the heavier traffic. Miss Seymore spied it and jumped up onto her toes and ran again. The driver, who was wrapped in a caped coat, drew his horses up to the walk, grasped her by both hands, and pulled her up alongside him. He touched up the horses at once, urging them into a trot, and earned the curses of those who had to throw themselves out of the way.

Rosalind clutched her hands together in her lap and concentrated on keeping her mouth closed. Adam drove cautiously. Several times she was certain they must have lost their quarry, and she came close to saying so. But then Adam turned another corner, and there they were again.

At last, the phaeton pulled up to a modest stone church. It was, Rosalind happened to know, St. Bartholomew's in the Field, although any field that might have once been there had long since been swallowed by houses and cobblestones.

Adam drove them past the church without slowing. Rosalind had to crane her neck painfully to see how Miss Seymore leapt down from her seat beside the driver and bolted inside. The rig rounded a curve in the twisting street, and Adam drew the horse to a halt.

Rosalind scrambled out of the rig and pressed his hand. They needed no words. He would meet her inside the church once the horse had been tended to.

It was extremely difficult, but Rosalind forced herself to walk at a decorous pace as she retraced the path to St. Bartholomew's.

Hurry, hurry, hurry! begged a voice inside. She silenced it ruthlessly. She did not wish to alarm the escaping couple yet.

Once she reached St. Bartholomew's, Rosalind circled around to its left. As she hoped, there were several small doors set in the length of the soot-stained stone wall.

She tested one and found it open and ducked inside.

Beyond the door waited a dim anteroom filled with barrows, buckets, baskets, and other such tools for keeping the small grounds and tiny burial yard that surrounded the church. A flight of stairs led to a dim flagstone corridor and the open sanctuary door.

Rosalind paused for a moment. She felt, rather than heard, Adam come up behind her. He reached past to ease the sanctuary door open just a bit farther, and the pair of them slid through.

No outcry was raised. All the sanctuary occupants were otherwise engaged. The priest, in his robes and surplice, had his attention trained fully on the couple who knelt at the altar with hands folded and heads bowed.

"Dearly beloved, we are gathered together here in the sight of God and this company to join together this man and this woman in holy matrimony," he intoned.

Adam cocked a brow at her; Rosalind returned his look, acknowledging the absurdity of their circumstances. There was so much at stake, and yet in this wordless moment, they agreed they should wait until the appropriate moment came to announce themselves.

Besides, Rosalind mused idly, *Alice will never forgive us if we do otherwise.*

". . . and is commended of Saint Paul to be honorable of all men: and therefore . . ."

George Dawson had worn his red coat, doubtlessly under his caped driving coat. Minney Seymore was dressed in sprigged muslin, with white ribbons and rosebuds in her curling hair. The priest, a grizzled man with unruly side-whiskers, read the service soberly but with true feeling.

It was so odd to be standing here with Adam, listening to the ceremony that she had so far refused to take part in. She stole a glance at him, trying to discern his thoughts, but for once, she could not read his face. Her heart trembled uneasily.

Fortunately, there was no more time for her self-conscious doubt to grow. The priest turned a page in his book.

"If any man can show just cause why they may not lawfully be joined together, let him speak now . . ."

Rosalind and Adam both stepped forward.

She raised her voice. "I beg your pardon, but there is such cause."

Miss Seymore and Dawson were on their feet in a flash. Dawson put a hand to his hip, as if he thought he might have to draw his cavalry saber.

Rosalind, with Adam at her side, walked up the central aisle.

"You!" cried Miss Seymore. "Mama dismissed you!"

Captain Dawson put his hand on Miss Seymore's arm. "Never mind, Minney. Reverend, this woman is a troublemaker, and this man is surely her confederate."

Adam remained unperturbed by this description of him. "My name is Adam Harkness. I am an assistant to Sir David Royce, and I am here to question Captain Dawson as regards the violent death of two persons."

"What!" shrieked Miss Seymore.

At the same time, Captain Dawson shouted, "You, sir, are a damned liar!"

"And you, sir, will remember you are in church!" barked the priest. He also slapped his book shut. "And just who might you be, young woman?" He glared at Rosalind.

"I am Miss Rosalind Thorne. I am an acquaintance of the young lady's guardian, Maria Fitzherbert."

"Hardly that," snapped Miss Seymore. "She's a fortune hunter and a publicity seeker!"

Rosalind refused to let herself be ruffled. "And even if it were not a question of Captain Dawson's actions, sir, Miss

Seymore is underaged. She cannot legally enter into a marriage without her father's permission."

"That is not true!" said Captain Dawson. "She turned twenty-five a month ago."

"And you brought her birth certificate?" inquired Rosalind.

"Miss Thorne," said Miss Seymore urgently, "leave us alone. Please. This is *not* your business."

"I'm afraid it is," said Rosalind. She turned back to the priest, who watched them all, flushed and open-mouthed in surprise. "Sir, I am sorry. This young woman has eloped from her mother's home in order to be married to this man, of whom her family does not approve. A servant in her house observed her preparations and alerted me so I could return her to her home without causing her family any further distress."

Rosalind met the priest's gaze. He had been prepared, she thought, to stand on his authority and to bluster; in short, to earn whatever fee Dawson had paid him for this morning's work. However, it was now beginning to dawn on him that there was far more to this business than a hasty marriage.

He turned on Captain Dawson.

"You should be ashamed, sir! Leading a young girl—"

"I am a grown woman, and this was my idea!" shouted Miss Seymore.

"Then shame upon you!" bellowed the priest. "And you will all leave my church at once!"

CHAPTER FIFTY-SIX

Captain Dawson's Admission

"He also confesses the crime."

Bury, Charlotte, *The Diary of a Lady-in-Waiting*

It was a very odd party that walked down the church steps, Rosalind mused—a thoroughly unhappy young couple ducking into the rain ahead of a pair of grimly bemused older people, who might be taken for parents.

Once they reached the street, Minney Seymore rounded on her and Adam.

"You are a cold, heartless *person*!" she screamed.

"I assure you I am not," said Rosalind. "I just ask you to consider what will happen when word gets out that you engaged in a clandestine marriage."

"Why should it get out?" She gestured toward the street, where their presence, let alone their argument, did not earn them more than the briefest passing glance.

"Because of who you are and who your mother is," said Rosalind. "At another time, it might not matter as much. But now she is being closely watched, and so are you."

"You're saying that to frighten her," said Captain Dawson.

"I'm saying that because the footman Thomas Faller is dead," Rosalind replied. "And his wife, who worked in Josiah Poole's household, has vanished, and the word has gone abroad that the marriage certificate is missing, and your name and troubles, Captain Dawson, have already been connected to both households."

"And you have already convinced your friends to lie for you," added Adam.

"No," said Dawson quickly. "They didn't know it was a ruse. Norris and Jacobs, they really think I am on my way to Dover." He held up his hands, as if he meant to physically push back on their words. "I promise you both, all we wanted was to make our vows before I sail for the Indies."

"But that is not all," Adam said. "And even if it was, I cannot let you sail before you answer my questions. As I told you inside, this is now a matter of murder and breach of the king's peace."

"He had nothing to do with Poole's death!" said Miss Seymore. "You cannot say that he did!"

Adam looked to Captain Dawson. The captain swallowed hard and made a decision.

"Listen, Mr. Harkness. Poole came to me. He wanted me to get him the marriage certificate. He offered to clear all my debts and even help me get married to Minney. But I told him no. I did not want . . . Minney would never have forgiven me if I did that to her mama."

"Then why would Mrs. Poole say you had come to her house after Poole was dead?" asked Adam.

"Because I had. When Minney told me about the robbery, I was sure he was the one responsible. That was when I learned he was dead. I begged Mrs. Poole for the certificate. I went back multiple times to try to convince her to give it up. She told me unless I was able to pay for what I wanted, this was none of my business."

"She demanded payment?" said Rosalind. "For the certificate? She was clear in that?"

Captain Dawson nodded.

"What of Tom Faller?" asked Rosalind quietly.

Miss Seymore's chin trembled. "I am very sorry that happened. I didn't . . . I never . . . He was a friend to me, but I don't know what happened to him."

"Do you, Captain?" asked Adam.

"No!" cried Captain Dawson. "Of course not!"

"I am afraid I will have to ask you to take your oath on it," said Adam. "And to answer several other questions regarding the matter."

"You have no . . ." he began, but his words trailed off.

"Captain Dawson," said Adam quietly, "if you love Miss Seymore, you will have a care for her reputation. The thing is done, and I will not let you go. As things stand, she can still return home quietly, while you are taken where you must go. If all is as you say, none need be the wiser for it. Or you can choose to raise the hue and cry now, and the whole story will be made public, including your name and hers."

Adam took one step closer and lowered his voice so that they all had to strain to hear. "You were under obligation to Mr. Poole. Mrs. Poole is prepared to swear that you came to her house several times since his death. Poole is known to have been involved in the theft of Mrs. Fitzherbert's marriage certificate. This is a string of facts that will not seem favorable to you, or to Miss Seymore, either in court or in the newspapers."

The last of his bravado drained from Captain Dawson's demeanor. He bowed his head.

Miss Seymore gasped. "No, George! No, you cannot let them do this to you, to us . . ."

But Captain Dawson just took her hand. "They're right. It's done. I need to answer."

"No! You do not! They have no right—" She stopped and dashed away the tears on her cheeks. "You cannot leave me," she whispered.

"I love you." Captain Dawson pulled her hand and held it close to his breast. "I swear I will come back to you. We *will* be together. Will you trust me?"

Rosalind watched them both. She noted the tenderness in Captain Dawson's manner, the gentle plea in his voice and, most of all, the hope in his warm gaze. It seemed to her that Miss Seymore wanted nothing so much as to continue to argue with him, and if that failed, she wanted to throw herself between him and these rude persons who threatened to take him away. She saw it in the set of the young woman's jaw and in her bright eyes. But Captain Dawson held her gaze and her hand, and slowly, reluctantly, she relented.

Miss Seymore nodded. Dawson kissed her gloved hand and touched her cheek. Then he turned to Adam.

"I am ready to go with you, sir."

Adam bowed. Then, deliberately, he put his back to Captain Dawson and Miss Seymore and drew Rosalind a few steps aside. She understood what he was doing. He was giving the pair a moment's privacy to say their farewells. But it was also a test to see if Dawson would take his chance to run.

"I'll take him to Bow Street," Adam said. "Stafford and Townsend need to hear whatever he has to say. So does Sir David. Will you make sure Miss Seymore gets home?"

"Of course."

He touched her hand in thanks and reassurance. "I will meet you back at Orchard Street." He turned. Captain Dawson was still with them, holding tight to Miss Seymore's hand.

There was some delay and discussion while provision was

made at the nearest stable for a man to drive Rosalind and Miss Seymore back to Tilney Street and afterward to return Captain Dawson's phaeton to his lodgings. Adam in the meantime would drive Captain Dawson to Bow Street in the hired rig.

The phaeton had barely enough room for the two of them. Miss Seymore gathered her skirts tightly against her and set her chin firmly to demonstrate that she had no intention of speaking to Rosalind.

This resolution lasted until their driver had turned the second corner.

"Why did you come after us, Miss Thorne?" she demanded. "Why could you not leave us alone?"

"Because I made a promise to help your mama," said Rosalind.

"She turned you away! She told me she would have nothing more to do with you!"

"But I still promised. Now, I ask you to consider what it will mean, Miss Seymore, if it is discovered that Mrs. Fitzherbert's daughter also entered into a secret marriage. What will be said about her?"

"But no one would have found out," she insisted. "No one would even care! Not now, with so much else going on!"

"You know that's not true," said Rosalind. "But even if the rest of the world did not care, your mama would. As it is, she is in trouble, and this will make her difficulties worse."

"Are you saying I don't care about Mama?"

"No. I believe you care deeply, but that you also wish very much to be with your sweetheart. And you have my sympathies, Miss Seymore. Truly." She hesitated. "You may not believe this, but I do know what it is to love someone you cannot openly acknowledge."

Miss Seymore stared, as if it was quite a new idea to her

that Miss Rosalind Thorne might know not only love but also its difficulties.

Perhaps it is, thought Rosalind ruefully. "And if it were only that, perhaps this morning would have gone differently. But two men are dead, Miss Seymore. This is no longer just a matter of love and broken hearts." If it ever was.

"I only wanted . . . I love him, Miss Thorne," she whispered.

"I know."

"George—Captain Dawson—he means to do right. I was the one who insisted on marrying him before he left."

"And now it is up to you what you tell your mama. She is afraid for you, Miss Seymore, and she is heartbroken."

"I know." She twisted her hands together. "The king . . . I used to sit on his knee, you know. He'd get down on the floor and play dolls with me. He was so . . . kind and funny, and we both loved him. And then . . . he turned his back on us. I never heard from him. I cried at night after he left, and she comforted me." She looked down at her hands. "She comforted me," Miss Seymore repeated.

"And now is the time for you to comfort her."

Miss Seymore turned her face away, and they drove in silence the rest of the winding way to Tilney Street.

"I suppose you are going to insist on accompanying me inside," said Miss Seymore as they rounded the corner.

"Your mama will not welcome me," replied Rosalind. "As you have pointed out, she dismissed me."

The driver halted the horse and climbed from his seat. He opened the carriage door. Miss Seymore hesitated.

"Good luck, Miss Thorne," she said. "And . . . thank you."

Rosalind nodded in acknowledgment.

Miss Seymore climbed from the carriage. The house's front door flew open, and Mrs. Fitzherbert ran up the path.

Miss Seymore walked hesitantly forward. Mother faced daughter on the flagstones for a moment. Then the two fell together into a tight embrace.

Rosalind's throat tightened. The driver closed the door and took up his seat again. As he did, Mrs. Fitzherbert lifted her head and saw Rosalind there. She nodded once. Rosalind returned the gesture.

"Drive on," she said.

CHAPTER FIFTY-SEVEN

The Means to an End

". . . to be low-spirited oneself, to have no con-solation to offer . . . is a very painful situation for anyone to be in who is her friend."

Langdale, Charles, *Memoirs of Mrs. Fitzherbert*

Rosalind paid the driver and stepped onto the path up to her front door. It was barely nine o'clock. The morning had cleared, and the sun's warmth pressed against her bonnet.

She was exhausted. Her steps dragged. She knew Alice and Amelia, and possibly George, would be inside. They would probably be at breakfast.

They would definitely be waiting to hear what had happened, and what they should all do now. Rosalind stopped and stared at her front door.

The problem was, she didn't know.

She was still stopped in the middle of the path when the door opened. Alice walked out and stood in front of her.

"Are you coming in?" she asked.

Rosalind drew a deep breath. "Yes."

"Good girl." Alice took her arm and walked her the rest of

the way to the house. When they were inside, she took Rosalind's bonnet and hung it on the peg by the door and then steered her into the parlor.

The windows were open, and the sun flooded the room. The teapot was there, along with fresh rolls, some of which had already been split and spread with butter and jam. Alice retired to the far side of the room and took up a book, which she held up in front of her face.

"What have you done with George and Amelia?" Rosalind asked as she sat down.

"They are in the dining room," said Alice to the pages of her book. "Under strict orders not to come out until sent for."

Rosalind gazed at the book that shielded Alice's face. She looked at the closed door and back at the book. Alice turned a page. Rosalind pressed her hand against her mouth to stifle her laugh. She also poured herself some tea, which she drank without even pausing to add her usual slice of lemon. She then proceeded to devour three rolls with jam.

Energy and a sense of perspective flowed back into her veins. "Thank you, Alice," she said.

Alice closed her book and went to open the door. "It's all right!" she called.

George and Amelia made a great show of crossing the foyer in a calm and decorous fashion. Alice bowed them into the room and closed the door. George took Amelia's hand and led her to a chair. He bowed; she curtsied. They both sat.

Rosalind eyed Alice, who simply shrugged and plopped down onto the stool beside the tea table. "So," she said. "What's happened?"

"Adam has taken Captain Dawson to Bow Street."

"So it was him!" cried Amelia. "Oh, poor Miss Seymore!"

"Don't tell me she was involved?" said Alice. "Good Lord, poor Mrs. Fitzherbert! And her sister . . . !"

"No," said Rosalind. "No, Dawson is not responsible for the burglary or the deaths."

"How can you be sure?" asked George.

Rosalind remembered how Miss Seymore and Captain Dawson had gazed into each other's eyes and how he had waited for Adam when he had the choice to try to run. She remembered that what robbed him of his bluster was not any threat to himself but concern for her.

She remembered also the way Minney Seymore spoke of the king and her mother and her heartbreak.

"It may be that Captain Dawson is an excellent liar," she told them. "But Minney Seymore is not."

"That's the truth," said Amelia. "Schoolgirl tricks. That was what her mother called what she got up to, and I'd have to agree."

"But Dawson could still deceive us," said Alice. "He's already tried to slip the net once."

"This is true," agreed Rosalind. "But while he may have blinded me, and perhaps Adam, as well, I do not think he will have so much success with Mr. Stafford at Bow Street."

There was a moment's silence while they all considered this.

"But there's something else," said George. "If Dawson's innocent in all this . . . What if . . . what if Stafford decides he needs a scapegoat? If Adam is to be believed, he and Townsend aren't always too particular about who gets arrested for a matter as long as someone is."

Rosalind bit her lip. George was right. It was one of the reasons Adam had left Bow Street. "Well, then, it is all the more reason for us to try to uncover the truth."

"Excellent," said Alice. "But how will you do it? Mrs. Poole is clearly ready to lie as it suits her. Mrs. Fitzherbert has thrown you out, and the newspapers have already got their claws into the whole business, and heaven knows what Lady Jersey and her friends are saying."

"Alice," murmured Amelia.

Alice had the grace to look embarrassed. "I'm sorry, Rosalind."

"No. You haven't said anything that's not true."

"So, what are we to do?"

Rosalind shook her head. She was conscious of a growing anger and shame. She had never before failed to do as she had promised. In her mind's eye, she saw the look of hurt in Mrs. Fitzherbert's eyes. The sense of failure curdled inside Rosalind, leaving her ill and deeply frustrated.

There had to be something. She could not, would not let Mrs. Fitzherbert leave London without some sort of hope. Would not let the girls be sent away with only their mama's wounded trust. Would not let herself sink into doubt and regret with the whole world watching.

Would not let herself, and Adam and Alice and all the other people in her life, her circle, her *profession*, down.

Rosalind stared at her hands in her lap.

She thought about Tom and Judith Faller.

She thought about Minney and Mary Ann.

She thought about Melora Poole and William Considen— each of them trying to protect and support the other, and how that natural urgency could lead to so many different kinds of mistakes.

She thought about George Dawson and the improbable fact that he did love Minney Seymore, about Mrs. Fitzherbert's care of her adopted daughters, about Mr. Brougham's desire for justice and power in equal measures.

She thought of something Mrs. Fitzherbert had said the very first night, as they sat calmly in her parlor, talking about the possible fall of the king. *If I tell him the marriage certificate has been stolen, it is very likely that he will panic, and in his panic, he will speak to the wrong person.*

She thought about the people who surrounded her now, and about Adam, who would return soon. This odd sort of family she had assembled across the years. She thought about the family of her birth. She thought about her father, desperate and grasping; her mother, who had let her mind be broken rather than believe his betrayal; and her sister, who had bartered herself in order to survive.

She thought about herself and how all her life she had faded into the shadows, about how she had meticulously set out to learn the ways of the world so she could walk carefully and inoffensively through it.

She thought about the Countess Lieven and her sparkling eyes, about her talking so languidly about how matters might appear to those who had only one part of the story.

And Rosalind realized that she had been so thoroughly terrified by this business and all that she did not know that she had let herself lose hold of all that she did know.

All I do know.

She lifted her head.

"I promised Mrs. Fitzherbert I would get her certificate back," she said. "I am afraid it cannot be done quietly or without fuss, as she wished, but it can be done."

"She turned you out," said Amelia. "You don't owe her anything."

"But I owe something to myself, and to everyone in this room. No, please do not say that isn't true. It is, and I will keep my word."

"You have a plan," said George.

"I should say she does," breathed Amelia. "Look at her face. Rosalind, what are you thinking?"

"I think Melora Poole has the certificate," said Rosalind. "Or, at least, she knows where it is. And I think it was someone in that house who murdered Josiah Poole and Thomas Faller."

"But how do you prove it?" said George. "From what you've said, Mrs. Poole has been lying through her teeth this whole time, and she threw Adam out of the house. Do you think she would let him or you back in?"

"I do," said Rosalind. "But first, we have to remove the danger that the certificate poses to Mrs. Fitzherbert before it's too late."

"How on earth are we going to manage that?" asked Alice.

Rosalind smiled just a little. "We're going to start a rumor."

CHAPTER FIFTY-EIGHT

Like Wildfire

"Believe me, the world will now soon be
convinced, that there not only is, but never was,
grounds for these reports, which of late have been
so malevolently circulated."

Langdale, Charles, *Memoirs of Mrs. Fitzherbert*

"Thank you for agreeing to see me so early, Mrs. Fitz-herbert."

Rosalind had been conducted to Mrs. Fitzherbert's sunny moss-green breakfast parlor by the solemn, portly footman. As soon as she entered, Mrs. Fitzherbert left her toast and tea and came to take Rosalind's hand.

"Thank you, Miss Thorne, for returning Minney to me," she said. "She explained all that you did. I fear I judged you prematurely."

"I am glad I was able to help," said Rosalind.

"Will you sit?" Mrs. Fitzherbert gestured toward the break-fast table.

"I cannot stay," said Rosalind. "I came . . ." She hesitated. "I came to say that if you were willing to trust me just once more, I may be able to finish the task you gave to me."

"How?"

Rosalind told her. Mrs. Fitzherbert listened wordlessly. When Rosalind finished, Mrs. Fitzherbert's hand strayed to her husband's miniature. Then she did the last thing Rosalind would have expected.

She laughed.

Mrs. Fitzherbert's laugh was loud and long and breathless. It turned her face pink and youthful, and for the first time, Rosalind saw the fullness of her beauty and understood how she might have captured a prince.

"Oh, my word!" Mrs. Fitzherbert dabbed at her eyes with her fingertips. "Oh, Miss Thorne. This is entirely perfect. Yes, let us put your plan into practice at once!"

Rosalind let out the breath she had been holding and reached into her reticule. "I have prepared the announcement." She handed it to Mrs. Fitzherbert. "It should go into all the major papers tomorrow."

"With pleasure." And for the first time since Rosalind had entered Mrs. Fitzherbert's house, that lady beamed openly.

Half an hour after Rosalind left Mrs. Fitzherbert's, she was shown into Lady Jersey's front parlor by a footman in canary-yellow and sky-blue livery who radiated an air of disapproval so heavy that it could have sunk a ship of the line. It was, after all, still a full hour before the time polite society decreed was set aside for morning calls.

Yet another half hour passed before Lady Jersey herself sailed into the room.

"Miss Thorne!" she cried. "You will be so good as to explain yourself this instant!"

"I do apologize, Lady Jersey," said Rosalind. "If it were not so vitally important to the queen, I would of course have waited until proper visiting hours."

"What? To the queen?" Lady Jersey exclaimed. "But what is it?"

Rosalind took a deep breath. "Ma'am, I believe there is a plan in place for some new evidence to be brought forth at her trial?"

"Yes, of course. Mr. Brougham has everything prepared. It was why he came to you. Now, if you're going to begin asking me questions about—"

"You misunderstand me," said Rosalind hastily. "I know what it is. Mr. Brougham is going to say he had found that there is evidence of the existing marriage between the king and Mrs. Fitzherbert. I must beg you to stop him from making any public pronouncements about it."

Lady Jersey's face turned thunderous. "Miss Thorne, it is not your place to—"

"It's a forgery," said Rosalind.

Lady Jersey's mouth snapped shut.

"It is thought that Maria Fitzherbert's marriage certificate is in circulation, but what is being passed about is a forgery. *That's* what she was consulting with me about. When the queen returned and the trial became definite, Mrs. Fitzherbert became afraid that something like this might happen. She thought that either well-meaning friends or some ne'er-do-wells from the newspapers or some such might spread the rumor that the marriage certificate had been found. She begged me to help her put a stop to such gossip before it began. I was too late." She dropped her gaze, indicating her intense regret. "Please. Speak with Mr. Brougham. Tell him that the paper that has been seen is a forgery."

Lady Jersey opened her mouth. She closed it again. She drew in a short, sharp breath.

"Miss Thorne, are you certain about what you say?"

Rosalind Thorne looked the most powerful woman in London straight in the eye and lied.

"I have seen the original," she said. "It is exactly where it should be." Then she reached into her reticule and pulled out a tightly folded sheaf of papers. "But I have seven copies here, all of which have been offered up for sale."

"Good Lord," breathed Lady Jersey. In the next heartbeat, she was running for the door. "Horace! The carriage! At once! I must go to the queen immediately!"

Sam Tauton plowed straight through the crowd that filled the Bow Street Police Station, with Alice Littlefield hurrying in his wake. The pair of them charged up the corridor that divided the station from the magistrate's court.

Tauton stopped them in front of a closed door and pounded his fist against it. The door opened, and Adam Harkness looked out, first at Tauton and then at Alice. Alice held up the letter Rosalind had written.

Adam met her gaze, and she grinned at him. Adam's brows rose. She held out the note, and he took it and nodded to her and closed the door.

"What is it?" Mr. Stafford asked. The chill in his voice said how very little he thought of being interrupted in the midst of taking a statement.

George Dawson was standing in front of his desk at parade rest, staring at some point on the wall and in general imitating a wooden block now that he was not being questioned directly. But Adam saw his gaze drift slowly downward and fasten on the paper in his hands.

Adam opened the note and read Rosalind's careful writing. He smiled. He could not help it.

"You seem amused, Mr. Harkness," said Mr. Stafford.

"It is a note from Miss Thorne. It seems there has been a development she thought you should be informed of, Mr. Stafford."

Mr. Stafford laid down his pen. Captain Dawson let his eyes slip sideways to Adam's face. Small beads of sweat stood out on his wide forehead.

"What might this development be?" inquired Stafford.

"The Fitzherbert marriage certificate," said Adam. "Or at least the one that is said to be in circulation. It's a forgery. One of several." He held up the note. "Miss Thorne says she has already given the news to Lady Jersey and Mr. Brougham."

Stafford sat entirely frozen for a long moment. Perhaps it was a petty sensation, but Adam was aware of a deep satisfaction in seeing Bow Street's spymaster struck entirely dumb.

Finally, Stafford nodded. "Well. I must congratulate you, and Miss Thorne. If the thing goes off, it is very well done." He closed his book and got to his feet. "I shall go inform Mr. Townsend. I am certain there are . . . persons with whom he will wish to share this excellent news." Stafford paused. "May I assume that this news will be reported in the newspapers shortly?"

"The matter is in hand even now," said Adam.

Mr. Stafford walked out the door, which shut silently behind him. Captain Dawson finally permitted himself to turn and to stare openly.

"What the hell just happened?" he asked.

"You've been reprieved, Captain," Adam told him. "And so has your fiancée. By this time tomorrow, it won't matter what's happened to the marriage certificate, because no one in the United Kingdom will believe the thing is real."

It was eleven o'clock when Mortimer let Ron Ranking into Rosalind's parlor. The newspaperman's gaze shifted from her to George Littlefield, who had his long legs stretched out to rest his heels on the hob with an air of perfect ease and comfort.

"Miss Thorne," said Mr. Ranking. "Littlefield. What's going on?"

"Thank you for coming to see me, Mr. Ranking," said Rosalind. "Will you sit?"

He did, carefully, like he thought the chair might break underneath him. "Did you have something to say about what's been in the papers?" he asked. "Because you have to allow, I gave you every chance . . ."

"Oh, no, it's not about that. Well, not directly," said Rosalind. "In fact, I wanted to thank you for your patience. I could not speak before, but now, since I have confirmation, I may give you the pertinent details."

"And exactly what details are those?"

"They're saying Mrs. Fitzherbert's marriage certificate has been found," George told him. "And that the queen means to bring it forth at her trial."

"This is not correct," said Rosalind.

Ranking raised his brows. "Ain't it, now?"

"No," repeated Rosalind. "What will be said is that the certificate is a forgery."

"Well, now." Mr. Ranking folded his arms. "That would be terribly convenient, now, wouldn't it? Save some persons a deal of embarrassment."

"I've seen five copies so far," said George. "They were being printed up by the handful to be sold off to the king's men or the queen's men or the papers," he added sourly. "Whoever'd pay."

Rosalind nodded. "Mrs. Fitzherbert was afraid something like this might happen," she said. "She engaged me to try to prevent it. I have just returned from explaining the matter to Lady Jersey, who, as you know, is a great supporter of the queen."

Ranking looked at her and then at George. A dozen calculations flickered behind his shrewd eyes. He did not believe her tale. Rosalind was not surprised. She had not expected that he would swallow the story as easily as Lady Jersey had, and she certainly was not going to hand him her sheaf of folded papers.

"So what am I doing here?" Mr. Ranking asked. "Why

would you tell me this and not leave it to your friend Mr. Little-field?" He nodded toward George.

"I pay what I owe, Mr. Ranking," said Rosalind. "You did keep your end of our bargain. I am keeping mine. And if you print this story as I have laid it out for you, tomorrow I will be able to deliver a second item."

This was the moment. If he refused to accept what she of-fered, if he instead decided that whatever she held in her hands was not worth what it might cost him to cooperate, the whole plan could collapse absolutely.

"And what would this other little item be?" Mr. Ranking inquired.

"The identity of the person who murdered both Josiah Poole and Thomas Faller."

"So, did Ranking agree?" Adam asked.

He and Rosalind sat together in the parlor. The house was empty except for them and the servants. George and Alice were at the *Chronicle*, both of them preparing pieces that would help shore up the report of the forged marriage certifi-cate.

Rosalind smiled. "He did."

"Then I hope we do not disappoint," said Adam. "Because I wouldn't like to swear we're going to be able to keep that promise."

"We know the answer lies with the Pooles," said Rosalind. "That is more than we had before."

"We may know it, but what proof is there?" He spread his hands. "And where is it?"

"The connection between the houses is Judith and Tom Faller," said Rosalind slowly. "What if Faller was the car-riage driver? We know he was frequently at the Pooles' house, because Letitia saw him. Perhaps she was not the only one who did. Perhaps Mrs. Poole or Considen offered him a sum to drive them that day. Perhaps he thought he was participating only in a robbery . . ."

"From what you say, Poole freed Faller from Newgate," said Adam. "Would he have betrayed a man who bought his freedom?"

"That sort of gratitude can chafe after a while. Poole had a hold on Faller's wife and on Faller himself. Amelia says he was someone who wanted more for himself and was trying to find a way out of service. Perhaps he was convinced if he did this one thing, it would be the way out."

"And the morning Amelia met him coming back to the Fitzherberts'?"

"He could have been planning to leave with Judith, but when he got to Poole's house, she told him about the murder. Perhaps she realized he'd played a part in Poole's death. Perhaps she broke with him, and he went after her later to try to convince her to take him back."

"But someone followed him."

"Or he surprised someone already in the room."

"It could be." Adam sighed. "But to all appearances, what evidence we might have had is now destroyed, and Mrs. Poole has determined the one course that truly can keep her family all safe. To say nothing."

"Mrs. Poole is determined to say nothing," said Rosalind. "But what of Mr. Considen? Could he be convinced—" She stopped.

Adam had gone still, his eyes unfocused and staring at something he could see only in his mind.

"My God," he breathed. Slowly, his awareness returned to the room and to her. "My God," he said again. "That's what I missed. The walking stick."

"I don't understand," said Rosalind.

"When I was at the Pooles', I knew something was wrong. Something was missing, but I couldn't see what it was. It was

Considen's walking stick. It had been burnt. She pointed right at it." He stabbed one finger toward the hearth. "She said the ashes in the grate were the remains of her husband's papers, and she pointed right at it. And it was the papers, but it was more than that. She burnt the walking stick, because that was what had been used to murder Thomas Faller."

"But which of them struck the blow?" asked Rosalind. "Was it Mrs. Poole or her brother?"

"Or both of them together?"

They faced each other for a long, silent moment.

"Mrs. Poole will not permit either of us back into her house," said Adam. "I'll need a warrant from Sir David summoning them to the inquest."

"It may come to that, but there is someone else we might ask first."

"Not Considen," said Adam. "He won't risk his neck, or hers, by talking with me again."

"No, not Considen," said Rosalind. "Letitia."

CHAPTER FIFTY-NINE

The Ties That Bind

"Poor thing! She was always looking about for some one to pour out her heart to, and never found one."

Bury, Charlotte, *The Diary of a Lady-in-Waiting*

It was Mortimer who carried the note to Letitia Poole. While he delivered it, Rosalind and Adam procured a table at the tearoom in the high street. Rosalind ordered far too much food for them. She wanted an excuse to linger.

In the end, she needed all the excuses she could contrive. She and Adam ate and drank and spoke idly of the weather and similar dull subjects. Anyone listening to them would have taken them for a long-attached pair, possibly even brother and sister, and otherwise paid them no mind.

Rosalind's nerve held until the second hour of nibbling cake and sipping tea that had gone stone cold. The room's hostess was beginning to look at them suspiciously, and Rosalind became very aware that she would not be able to drink yet another pot of tea. Adam was likewise beginning to cast a doubtful eye toward the door.

Perhaps she had been too trusting in Letitia's desire for the truth.

Perhaps Mrs. Poole had intercepted her, and she was now sitting in her room.

Perhaps they had simply been mistaken, and Letitia was also complicit in the crimes of her father and her stepmother.

But as the painted porcelain clock on the room's back shelf chimed the half hour, the door opened again, and Letitia Poole entered. She clutched a satin reticule in both hands.

Adam rose to his feet. Letitia walked to the table, stiff as a wax doll. He pulled out a chair, and she sank into it.

"I'm sorry to have been so long," she said softly. "But, well, I had to wait until my stepmother was gone."

"Thank you for agreeing to meet us," said Rosalind.

Letitia said nothing. Instead, she opened the reticule and reached inside.

And laid what had clearly once been the silver handle of a walking stick on the table. It was smeared with ash and blistered from heat.

"You were right," said Letitia. "I did not want to believe you, but you were right."

Adam claimed the handle and tucked it away in his pocket.

"I'm sorry," said Rosalind.

Letitia bowed her head. "Oddly, I find I'm rather relieved. At least I know . . . I know it was not my fault."

Rosalind drew back. "How could any of this be your fault?"

Letitia returned a small, mirthless smile. "For not being obedient enough, I suppose. If I had not protested my marriage, I could have been out of the house before . . ." She brushed at her eyes. "I am babbling."

Rosalind poured her a cup of tea. Letitia took one sip and set it down. "Perhaps we could walk a bit?"

"That is a very good idea," agreed Rosalind.

THE MATTER OF THE SECRET BRIDE 429

Adam got to his feet. "I'll settle the bill."

Rosalind and Letitia stood. She took Letitia's hand, and the younger woman did not resist but let herself be taken back out onto the street. Rosalind looped her arm through Letitia's, as if they were old friends, and together they walked away from the tearooms, moving up the high street as if nothing at all was wrong.

"What can you tell us about the morning your father died?" Rosalind asked.

"I was getting dressed," Letitia said. "I suppose it must have been about ten o'clock or so. There was a great commotion from downstairs. I looked out into the hallway to see what was the matter, and there was my stepmother, and the footman was carrying her brother up . . . He was covered in blood . . . ," she whispered. "I asked what was wrong, and Melora told me to go back into my room, that he'd had a seizure and had vomited and . . . and . . ." Letitia swallowed. "I did as I was told. I went back into my room. She came in later and told me he had had a restless night, as he did sometimes, and must have gone downstairs, because the servants had found him in the library. But, she said, it was not as bad as it might have looked at first. And I said I was glad."

"But?" prompted Rosalind.

"But what I could not understand was if he had just been in the library, why did it take until ten o'clock to find him?" She lifted her eyes to Rosalind's. "And why was he wearing his riding boots?"

As they had suspected, Mrs. Poole had left orders that neither Rosalind nor Adam should be admitted to the house under any circumstances.

"I'm sorry, miss," whispered Lizzie, who kept her eyes pointed firmly at the floor.

"I understand," said Rosalind. "If, however, you could please take this message through to Mr. Considen?" She handed over the leaf with the note penciled on it that Adam had torn from his notebook.

Lizzie bobbed her curtsy and scurried away. They waited, standing as close as they could without touching. Rosalind felt acutely aware of the front parlor waiting on the right hand, and of the scent of the candles that were still burning beside the open coffin.

It was only a few moments before Lizzie returned.

"You're to go through, sir, miss."

"Thank you, Lizzie," Rosalind said.

Adam went first. He opened the door to the library. Inside, William Considen sat in his usual chair, staring at the fireplace and the cold ashes heaped inside.

"Where's Letitia?" Mr. Considen asked.

"My footman is taking her to my house," said Rosalind. "She asked to stay for a while." Which was not entirely true, but it was not entirely false, either. "If I may ask, where are the children?"

"Gone." The word came out like a sigh. "It seems we still have some cousins who were prepared to take pity on them. But then, Melora can be very persuasive." He held up Adam's note. "Who drove the carriage?" he inquired mildly.

Adam made sure the library door was closed before he answered.

"I am assuming it was Tom Faller," he said. "But it could also have been your sister."

"Melora?" Considen laughed mirthlessly. "Yes, yes, she could have done it. I should have asked her. Perhaps this would have gone better if I'd consulted her. But that would have defeated the purpose, you see. After all, I killed Poole for her sake."

"Did you?" asked Rosalind.

"Oh, yes. Poole wanted her to use the last of our family connections to get word to the palace that he had the marriage certificate. He was sure he could sell it for thousands rather than the mere hundreds his original client offered. He said if she failed him this time, he would divorce her and disown their sons—it would have been the end of her, Miss Thorne. The last shred of pride she maintained would have been destroyed. She had already sacrificed so much . . ." The words trailed away.

"So you determined there was one thing you could do for her," said Rosalind.

"The possibility I might hang for it even seemed like a relief after all this." He gestured toward his own body. "And Poole made it easy. He was ecstatic about his own cleverness. Faller had left the doors open and told him when would be the best time. He slipped into the house, broke the box, and was out again before the noon bells ceased to toll, he said.

"But he was also in a hurry. Whoever his initial client was, they would be put off for only so long while he secured another, richer buyer. So, he was not as careful as he might have been. I saw my chance, and I took it." These last words carried with them an inexpressible weariness. "I told him I had a person who would buy the thing. I told him I would come to fetch him at the White Swan when matters were all arranged. He got into the carriage . . . We drove . . . He was crowing over his brilliance." Considen shuddered. "And I stabbed him. He was so surprised. He did not believe I had the strength, of course. I almost did not, but there was just enough left in me for that."

"How did you have strength enough to push him from the carriage?" asked Adam.

"Oh, that was easy. He simply fell out the door. Then I had my man take me back to the White Swan, and I wrecked the room there, to make it look like he was killed by someone who was looking for some paper or the other." He chuckled. "Some paper or the other.

"I was sure I had killed myself that morning," Considen went on. "I was so exhausted when I finally managed to reach home, I truly believed I might die on the spot. Melora found me here, all covered in blood. I told her I had vomited it up, and she believed me. At least I thought she did." He screwed his brow up tightly. "It can be very difficult to tell just what Melora believes.

"Regardless, after you came to say Poole had been murdered, she realized what had really happened. I told her I would turn myself in, and I would have. But she went down on her knees. She begged me not to make her watch me die in prison. All I had to do was remain quiet, she said. Poole had so many enemies, no one would ever suspect me." He gestured at his own weakened body. "As soon as Poole was in the ground, she said we would send me away to Switzerland. I would still die, and away from my home and family, but at least it would be in a bed with a view of the sky. At least I would breathe clean air.

"What could I do against her pleading?" he asked them. "I told her I would do as she asked. As I have always done, God help us both. Then we spoke to Poole's attorney and . . . well, more fool me. Us. I, she, we had thought the man actually had some money."

"He was bankrupt?" asked Rosalind.

"Not quite. Almost. That's why he was so very excited about the certificate, and willing to gamble for a bigger payment. He needed the money."

"How was it Faller came to be involved?" asked Adam.

"Ah, yes. Poor Faller." Considen shook his head. "I'd seen him and Judith together. No one pays attention to what the invalid might notice." His lips twitched into a brief smile. "I asked him to drive me and said that I'd pay him enough to take himself and her to the Americas. He agreed, but I failed to make sure of him. When he found out Poole was dead . . . he turned skittish. I tried to reassure him. But he wouldn't listen, and Judith, the little idiot, sent him away with a flea in his ear for daring to suggest she would desert her post. He ran out of the house. So, I had to make sure." He held up his pale hand. "And I did."

What was there to be said to that? What could be said to any of this? Rosalind's throat was dry as dust, and she felt as drained as if she had run a full mile. A glance at Adam told her he felt much the same.

But there was one last question, and she must ask it.

"Do you have the certificate?"

Considen reached one shaking hand into his coat pocket and brought out a leather wallet. It slipped from his fingers and dropped to the carpet.

Adam retrieved the wallet and opened it. From inside it, he pulled out a folded paper. He passed it to Rosalind.

It was a remarkably small thing, light and fragile from being opened and refolded so many times. Rosalind read the names and the dates and the formal Latin affirmations. A soft rush of breath escaped her lungs.

"Thank you," she said.

"What will become of me?" inquired Considen.

"You'll be charged," said Adam.

"Can you take me now? I do not wish to face Melora."

"If that is what you want."

"Yes. I do." But he paused. "Miss Thorne? When you . . . if you see my sister again, will you tell her I am sorry? Tell her . . . tell her I tried my best."

"You will be able to tell her yourself," said Rosalind.

He shook his head, and she saw how bloodshot his eyes were and how his lips were tinged with blue. "No, Miss Thorne. I don't think I will."

EPILOGUE

That Ends Well

*"These, indeed, gave her rights which she could
not, and would not, yield . . ."*

Bury, Charlotte, *The Diary of a Lady-in-Waiting*

The inquest in the matter of the death of Josiah Poole was held the next day at the Bow Street magistrate's court. Sir David Royce presided over a jury of twelve men, who returned a unanimous verdict of murder with malice aforethought against William Fitzwallace Considen and recommended that he be bound over for trial.

The prisoner was held at the Brown Bear public house for exactly one night. When the sheriff arrived in the morning to take him to jail, it was to discover that he had breathed his last. Sir David declared that he had succumbed to his illness at some point in the early morning.

Melora Poole buried her brother beside their parents and retreated from the public eye.

Mrs. Fitzherbert did depart for the Continent but wrote to Rosalind that she planned to return in time for the upcoming season.

The trial of Queen Caroline dragged on for two more months, with all the public rumor, spectacle, and outcry as could be brought to bear upon it by all classes of society. In the end, the king failed in his quest, and the marriage was declared to be valid and legal.

The queen declared her intent to leave England once again and this time never return.

While the world was still waiting to see if that promise would be kept, Rosalind Thorne met Letitia Poole at Gunter's Tea Shop. It was the autumn, and a gray rain drummed against the windows. Letitia had stayed three days with Rosalind during the crisis that enveloped her family but had returned to her stepmother's house after Mr. Considen's funeral.

"How have you been?" Rosalind asked her.

"I think I am becoming a ghost," said Letitia with a small smile. She had fallen back into the studied disinterest that was the acceptable tone for a young woman in polite company. "My stepmother will not even speak to me. She has agreed that my engagement can be broken, so that is something, anyway."

"I have a plan to put to you," said Rosalind. "A possibility, rather."

"Yes?"

"I have learned there is a school in Ottawa. It's an academy for the daughters of English officers who are posted in the territory. There they are instructed in the polite accomplishments and proper English manners."

Letitia frowned. "You think I should attend this school?"

"I think you should teach."

Letitia's polite mask slipped just a little, and she looked at Rosalind as if she had taken leave of her senses. "Who on earth would possibly hire me to teach?"

Rosalind laid a sealed letter down. "Your mother."

*   *   *

Still later, Rosalind returned to her darkened parlor. It was quite late, and the staff had all departed, except for Laurel, who lived in. But Laurel was in her own bed upstairs. Alice and Amelia had gone to their flat, and Rosalind was alone. She sat on the window seat, with only one lamp burning low.

She had come home to the papers filled with the latest news of the quarrels of the king and the queen. Rosalind ignored them. She had the peaceful darkness and her own thoughts to keep her company.

At last, she saw a familiar silhouette coming up the street. She smiled softly.

Adam walked up the path and, using his key, opened her door.

He came into the room, laid his hat aside, and bent to kiss her.

"How did Miss Poole receive your suggestion?" he asked as he took a place beside her on the window seat. She laid her hand over his but found her eyes would not turn away from the stillness outside.

"Very well, I think." She paused, and Adam, because it was his way, let her have her silence.

"Let us never be rich," she said eventually.

"Very well," agreed Adam.

"And power," she said. "Let us abjure that, as well."

Adam smiled. "I think I can safely promise you that."

"Good. Neither state seems to be beneficial to human rationality."

"As it happens, I agree."

"I'm tired, Adam," she said.

Adam reached out and turned her, just enough so that he could settle an arm around her shoulders. "So am I."

"I find I am sickened of this business of money and bodies, and who owns whom and what rights that confers on them, and how children may be bartered to further some end of the parents'. It is unjust, and what feels worse is it is all a colossal waste of time and effort." She frowned. "I'm babbling."

"No."

"I do love you."

"And I love you."

"I want to be with you."

"And I with you."

"I want it to be for us. Not for money, not for the sake of any children having a name. I do not want to be hidden, and I do not want you to be denied." She paused again. "Now is not the time to be talking like this."

"When is the time?"

She shook her head. "I don't know. I barely know what I'm saying. Seeing Letitia today, it brought all this summer back to me—the whole terrible business between the Pooles and the Fallers and the Fitzherberts . . ."

"It's over now. You have done what you promised, and more."

"But it will come again. It is at the heart of what I do."

Adam was silent for a moment. Then he said, "Rosalind . . . I have, well, not a proposal. I have a possibility."

She pushed herself away, just far enough so she could see his face fully.

Adam reached into his coat pocket and removed a folded paper. He placed it in her hands.

"What is this?" she asked.

"A marriage contract."

Rosalind froze.

Adam stood and crossed the room, as if he could not speak while he was beside her. "It occurred to me a while ago that it might solve . . . or at least help, or, well, perhaps it might make clearer—" He stopped. "I visited a solicitor I know. It's only a draft, and of course, you'd want to have your own man look it over, but I thought, perhaps—"

Rosalind could not stop staring at him. Her mouth opened, but no words came.

"What is it?" he asked, and for a moment, she saw fear in his wide blue eyes. "Is it too much? Are you . . . You're not offended, Rosalind, because I promise you . . . ?"

Rosalind laid the paper down and held up both her hands, begging him to stop, to wait just a moment. She jumped up and dashed into her private parlor, opened her desk, and returned.

Now it was Rosalind who placed a paper in Adam's hands.

He stared at it and then at her.

"No," he said. "You didn't."

She nodded. "Almost a year ago now. I asked my man to draft it. I thought if I could at least delineate the legal questions, it would remove some of my fears. But I couldn't bring myself to give it to you. I thought it might insult you, or that you would think I did not trust you sufficiently. I thought . . . I was afraid if love wasn't enough that we might fall apart somehow."

She gazed at him, pleading. He returned her gaze, wondering. They stayed like that for a long time, facing each other— wondering, bewildered, disbelieving.

Then believing.

Then amazed.

Adam smiled. Rosalind pressed her hand against her mouth.

In the next heartbeat, they were both laughing—a long, loud, and breathless affirmation of themselves; a wordless mutual understanding that it was not the papers and not the law that held them. It was their knowledge and need of each other, and their desire to bring this love into the everyday world. Not to try to be in some place apart—some daydream of another place and another time wreathed in a mist of "Oh, if only"—but in the world as it was.

Rosalind threw herself into Adam's arms, and he grabbed her about the waist and whirled her around. And then they were kissing each other, passionately and frantically, as if each believed the other might melt away.

"Then this is yes?" she asked.

"Yes," he answered. "And you?"

"Yes," she said immediately and without hesitation. "Yes, now and always, Adam. Yes."

AUTHOR'S NOTE

I've always used historical figures and events in Rosalind's inquiries, but this time I threw her into one of the greatest controversies of the Regency period.

King George IV did contract a morganatic marriage with a twice-widowed Catholic woman named Maria Fitzherbert. She did keep the signed and witnessed marriage license in a strongbox for the remainder of her life. She had many friends among the elite of society and was generally well regarded. Even the queen spoke of her in a complimentary fashion.

George IV did attempt to divorce his legal wife Caroline of Brunswick in a very public, acrimonious, messy, and protracted series of trials that eventually ended in failure, from his point of view.

He also really was seen riding back and forth in front of Mrs. Fitzherbert's house in Tilney Street, but he never did go inside.

Mrs. Fitzherbert did have two adopted daughters, "Minney" and Mary Ann. Minney did fall in love with a penniless but heroic cavalry officer named George Dawson. He did go off to the West Indies and did eventually return. The pair were married, much to her foster mother's dismay. But eventually, all were reconciled and maintained a long and warm relationship for the rest of Mrs. Fitzherbert's life.

For more about Mrs. Fitzherbert and her life, I recommend Valerie Irvine's biography *The King's Wife: George IV and Mrs. Fitzherbert.*

For more about Caroline of Brunswick and her battle with George IV, there's Flora Fraser's *The Unruly Queen: The Life of Queen Caroline.*